AN UNHOLY AFFAIR

EVIE ALEXANDER

First Published in Great Britain 2023 by Emlin Press

ISBN (eBook) 978-1-914473-28-9

ISBN (Print) 978-1-914473-29-6

ISBN (Audiobook) 978-1-914473-44-9

A CIP catalogue record for this book is available from the British Library.

www.emlinpress.com

To you, dear reader.
May you always have faith, even if just in yourself.

By Evie Alexander and Kelly Kay

EVIE & KELLY'S HOLIDAY DISASTERS SERIES

Cupid Calamity

Cookout Carnage

Christmas Chaos

Get Evie's books in all formats as well as special offers, early releases, and exclusive deals direct from her website:

www.eviealexanderbooks.com

EMLIN
PRESS

❧ I ❧

LONDON - ONE YEAR AGO

Eveline swirled the melting ice cubes at the bottom of her glass.

I know Estelle's hoping that if I'm in this dress and she's late, maybe someone might approach me. But I feel really uncomfortable right now, and I don't know what to do with myself.

At five-thirty on a Friday afternoon, the London bar was packed with braying and confident professionals celebrating the end of the week. Eveline had perched herself on a high stool at the far end of the bar, sitting side-on to see people as they entered. But as the minutes ticked by and her friend hadn't appeared, she'd swivelled around to face the wall of drinks. *I haven't been somewhere like this for over ten years, and back then I was always off my head...*

Estelle was Eveline's best friend and had persuaded her to take half a day off to accompany her to London for a meeting. Estelle had also bullied Eveline into wearing the kind of clothes she hadn't worn in over a decade, and to let down her long hair.

Eveline's tight red dress—borrowed from Estelle—was almost the same colour as her hair and had ridden up a few inches above her knees. She tugged it lower. *God, I feel almost naked right now. Do you think I should try that Christian dating site again? Even though it was a disaster?*

Out of the corner of her eye, she caught a couple leaning on the side of the bar next to her. The man's hand snaked around the woman's waist and caressed her bottom. Eveline kept her gaze forward, but could see their passionate kiss reflected in the mirrors on the wall in front of her. A pang of loneliness pierced her heart. No matter how much she filled her life, there was still an empty space in her chest that kept getting bigger.

I thought leaving Bexminster for Foxbrooke was a sign, but it's been nearly two years and I'm worried I'm running out of time.

Biting the inside of her cheek, she squeezed her eyes shut. *Please, God, I know you have a plan for me, but if there was ever a moment for a miracle, this might be it.*

'Hi.'

Eveline's eyes snapped open, and she jerked her head to the right. The couple had gone, and a man stood in their place. He was so close, his gaze so focused, that she didn't need to look around to know he was addressing her.

Her breath froze as her body went into meltdown. It wasn't just that he was heart-stoppingly beautiful. His soul was shining out, brighter than any sun. It wrapped itself around hers with a rush of joy, as if reuniting after millennia apart and determined never to let go ever again.

Time seemed to slow, then stop, as the universe ground to a juddering halt in recognition that this meeting was ordained beyond the stars. A flicker of something passed across the man's caramel eyes, a tiny shockwave that seemed to crack his confident expression for a millisecond.

'May I sit down?'

If the man's soul was currently hugging hers, his voice was removing her clothes. It had the deep, drugging warmth of a wood fire in winter and the skin-scorching heat of an inferno. As his question hung in the air, Eveline's nervous system whined in her ears like a siren, punctuated by the pounding beat of her heart. Sparks flashed before her as darkness encroached on the edges of her vision, marching inwards until only the bright sight of him at the centre remained.

His expression creased with concern and he reached across the small space between them.

'Are you okay?'

As his fingers made contact, the shock jump-started her breathing. Gulping air, she nodded. A tiny part of her was conscious that she was acting like a lunatic. However, most of her was lit up by his touch as flames tore up her arm.

Say something! 'I... I...' she stammered.

He smiled, and pleasure prickled across her skin.

'I'm Jasper.'

'Eveline.'

He repeated her name, as if tasting it on his tongue. She stared at his full lips and a delicious shiver ran through her.

'May I sit?' he asked.

Inbuilt politeness kicked in before rational thought. 'Yes, yes of course.'

She shifted slightly to give him space, pulling the hem of her dress lower and swallowing at the sight of his muscled thighs as they filled his black trousers. His knee was so very close to hers. She dragged her gaze up his body, past his crisp white shirt, his tanned throat, to his face.

Breathe! Breathe! Breathe!

There was a tiny flush of red on his cheekbones and his pupils seemed bigger than before.

'You're incredibly beautiful, Eveline.'

She blinked and dug her short nails into her palms, trying to process that this was actually happening. He was really talking to her.

'I—' She swallowed again. 'I haven't, erm done—I mean, er...'

He smiled. 'There's a first time for everything.'

She nodded, giving up on words altogether.

'Why don't we just chat? Get to know each other a bit?'

Yes! She nodded again.

'Can I get you another drink? What are you having?'

'Elderflower pressé with soda please.'

Jasper placed his phone and wallet down in front of him and signalled the barman. 'Elderflower pressé with soda, and whisky on the rocks.'

Eveline closed her eyes tightly and dropped her head. *Thank you, God. Thank you.*

As their drinks were made, she stretched out her clenched fingers and tried to calm her breathing.

The barman placed their glasses down and Jasper lifted his.

'What do you think we should drink to?' he asked.

The moment reminded Eveline of a line from *Groundhog Day*, one of her favourite films. It was a quote she lived by every day.

'I like to say a prayer and drink to world peace.'

His face lit up. 'Not to the groundhog?'

She tried not to squeal with excitement. 'You got the reference!'

He nodded and touched the side of his glass to hers.

'La fille que j'aimerai est comme un vin qui se bonifiera un peu chaque matin,' he said softly.

Her mouth dropped open. 'You speak French?'

'Oui,' he replied, wiggling his eyebrows.

Joyous laughter bubbled out. 'I can't believe it! I'm always quoting that film, but no-one seems to get what I'm talking about.'

Jasper put on an American accent. 'Am I right, or am I right, or am I right? Right? Right?'

Eveline chinked the side of his glass with hers. 'I think you're very right, Jasper.'

His smile faltered.

Embarrassed heat bloomed in her cheeks. *Slow down!* She cleared her throat. 'So, what does the French quote translate as? I've never looked it up.'

He took a gulp of his whisky. 'It's just a line about wine and women. Standard Gallic stuff.'

'It must be a bit more than that?'

He shrugged, staring at his glass as he swirled the ice cubes around.

'Please?'

As he glanced up, it was like the windows to his soul were open again.

'The girl I'll love is like a wine who will only get better a little every morning.'

A sudden image came to Eveline of the two of them lying entwined in her bed. Pale dawn light filtering through the curtains. Desire cracked like lightning between her legs.

For a moment, Jasper's eyes seemed to reflect her own thoughts, but then his confident smile was back on display. 'What is it about *Groundhog Day* that you like so much?' he asked.

Sipping her drink, she attempted to control her rioting heart. 'I think it's one of the most beautiful and moving films about the human condition there is,' she said, bringing her gaze back to him. 'It shows that all of us have a chance at redemption.'

An uncertain look flickered across his face. She might have missed it had she not been staring at him so intently.

'And why do *you* like it?' she asked.

He hesitated.

'You can be honest. I promise I won't judge.'

'When I saw it as a kid, I liked the idea that I could do anything I wanted to without consequence, because there was no tomorrow.'

'And now?'

He paused. 'I'm not sure. I think I watch it these days with a sense of relief. It's like remembering my childhood—which felt like living through Groundhog Day—but knowing I'm no longer there. Life has moved on and I'm not the same person I was.'

She wanted to ask more, but would she be stepping too far?

'Is it your favourite film?' he asked.

She shook her head. 'It's definitely in the top five, but number one is *The Princess Bride*.'

'Another classic.'

'Have you seen it?'

He grinned. 'Hello. My name is Inigo Montoya. You killed my father. Prepare to die!'

She laughed and inclined her head. 'As you wish.'

Another moment of unspoken intensity crackled between them.

He swallowed. 'Any other favourite movies?'

'*Galaxy Quest*.'

'Never give up! Never surrender!'

'By Grabthar's hammer... By the Suns of Worvan... You shall be avenged!' she cried.

He held his hand up and she high-fived him, the warmth from the contact sending a spark dancing down her arm.

She laughed, feeling lighter than air. 'Are we really geeky?'

'Not at all. We're just two highly cultured people who appreciate a good movie.'

'What's *your* favourite film?'

His brow furrowed, and he rubbed his jaw. It was a move that all the heroes in her favourite Polly Hart romance novels did to demonstrate their rugged masculinity. Reading the books, she hadn't understood how such a gesture could be so attractive. Now she did.

'*Star Wars.*'

'Which one?'

He flashed her a dangerous smile. 'Will my answer be a deal-breaker?'

Never. 'Well, I might have to think twice if you mention *The Phantom Menace...*'

'It's not that one.' He chuckled, lifting his glass to his mouth.

'The *Star Wars Holiday Special*?'

Jasper choked on his drink as he laughed, then put the tumbler down and started coughing.

'Do you want me to slap you on the back?'

He nodded, his eyes watering.

Eveline stood and moved closer, patting his broad shoulders.

Jasper recovered and raised his head. He was so close she could feel the movement of his breath against her lips, smell his deliciously clean scent. She could see flecks of gold in the light brown of his irises, a couple of freckles at the corner of one eye.

'Eveline,' he murmured.

How easy would it be to lean forward a couple of inches

and kiss him? Could she? She'd done far worse in the past. The thought of her past snapped her back to the present. She was standing next to a stranger in a public bar and contemplating making out. Springing back to her stool, she smoothed her hands over her dress.

'So,' she breathed. 'Not the *Holiday Special*.'

He shook his head, then turned to the barman, and held up his empty glass. 'Can I get a refill?'

More whisky was poured.

Jasper faced Eveline again with a smile. 'My favourite *Star Wars* film is *The Empire Strikes Back*. Did I pass the test?'

She grinned. 'Ten out of ten.'

He took a gulp of his drink and mimed wiping sweat from his brow. 'Phew. Well, that's movies safely out of the way. What next? Favourite colour?'

'Red.'

His gaze caressed her from head to toe. 'I agree. Favourite animal?'

Eveline was so hot and bothered that she didn't think to censor her next words. 'A pig.'

His eyebrows raised. 'O-kay... Any particular reason?'

She sipped her drink, hoping it would cool her down. It didn't. 'Well, pigs are the most incredible creatures. They're clean—'

'Like me.'

She bit back a grin. 'They eat everything.'

'Also me.'

'They're intelligent.'

He held his hand out and tilted it from side to side. 'Hmmm...'

'Their manure is great for soil fertility.'

He frowned. 'In fairness, I've never attempted to improve soil fertility.'

'And they make bacon.'

'Ah. Yes, you're right. Pigs win. Pretty much nothing can beat a bacon sarnie.'

'Do *you* have a favourite animal?'

He shrugged. 'Not sure. Cats are out as I'm allergic to them. Dogs? Dolphins?'

She laughed. 'Dolphins *are* amazing.' *And you're amazing, Jasper.*

'Tell me more about you,' he said. 'What's your favourite food?'

'I think you can probably guess.'

'Bacon sandwich?'

She nodded. 'And roast pork with crackling, and prosciutto, and sticky ribs, and ham, and sausages.'

'You're making me hungry.'

Her gaze flicked to his mouth, and she swallowed. 'What about you? What do you like to, erm, eat?'

If her cheeks had been hot before, the moment she'd spoken they started producing enough heat to smelt gold.

His eyes dropped to her lips.

'Eveline...'

Her heart was hammering so hard inside her chest she was sure he could hear it.

He reached towards her, resting his hand on the bar, the palm facing up as if in invitation.

Could she take it?

His phone lit up with a call.

She glanced at it. 'Do you—'

He shook his head, and with his free hand, turned it over so the screen was facing down.

Just do it! She placed her hand on the bar next to his. She'd prayed to God, and he'd delivered. This was meant to be. She grazed her fingertips across his.

A shock of electricity shot up her arm, and he sucked in a breath. She hesitated, thinking to withdraw, but he moved his thumb across the back of her hand. The movement was so subtle, yet so intimate. She bit her lip to stop a whimper from escaping.

Bringing her eyes up to meet his, she lost herself in the heat of his gaze. She'd never felt so alive before, so overwhelmed by desire. The only point of contact between them was their hands, but every tiny touch sent flames licking across her skin and a heavy pulse to beat between her thighs. She'd never experienced such raw and elemental sensations before, the desperate urge to consume and be consumed by him.

As if drawn by forces more powerful than her will, she slid off the stool and stood between his legs. His cheeks were flushed and his breathing matched the unevenness of her own.

'Eveline...'

Jasper's fingers were now interlaced with hers, his thumb drawing circles of fire on her palm.

His phone vibrated again on the bar beside them.

'Should—'

He shook his head.

'But it might be important?'

'I'm right where I need to be.' He reached for the phone. 'I should have turned it off when I met you.'

He picked it up, then his body went rigid as he stared at the screen.

'Is everything okay?'

He glanced between her and the phone, the colour draining from his cheeks.

Instinctively, she stepped back. Something was very, very wrong.

'Jasper?'

He looked around the bar, then froze.

She followed his gaze. Standing by the door was a beautiful woman in her late fifties, an anxious expression on her face. She had long red hair and was wearing a red dress.

Turning back to the bar, he pulled notes out of his wallet, then downed the remains of his drink, and placed the glass on the bills.

'Jasper?'

He didn't meet her eyes. 'I'm sorry,' he muttered, then strode away.

She watched him greet the woman with a huge smile, kiss her on both cheeks, then lead her out of the bar.

He didn't look back.

$\maltese$ 2 $\maltese$

LONDON - PRESENT DAY

Come on!

Jack closed his eyes, focusing on the movement of his tongue against Sylvia's clit, the pattern of her breathing as she chased a third orgasm. He projected the most lurid and depraved fantasies onto his mind, trying to persuade a particular part of his body to sit up and listen.

It wasn't enough to make her climax. She could get that for free on her own. Sylvia Lydney was paying for his cock. However, his money-making member was currently on strike and not responding to any of the urgent messages he was sending its way.

He licked faster, responding to the subtle cues he'd learnt a year ago when they'd first had sex. She was close, but he hadn't even reached the starting line. Bringing a hand to his cock, he frantically tried to rub it back to life, and allowed himself to slip into the ultimate fantasy—that of *another* red-headed woman.

But even that shot of visual Viagra didn't work. His cock was refusing to play ball.

'Jasper,' Sylvia gasped, patting his shoulder as if to get his attention.

The false name he always used with clients now turned his stomach.

He raised his head. 'You okay, Sylvia?' he asked, making sure he sounded sufficiently out of breath with arousal.

'I want to come with you inside me.'

Fuck! He vibrated the tip of his tongue against her clit. 'You sure about that?'

She laughed breathlessly. 'Yes, Jasper. There's nothing in the world as good as your cock.'

He hummed approval into her pussy, then slowly kissed his way up her body.

Eveline's legs clamped around my head as she comes on my face. Eveline screaming my name as she climaxes around my cock. Eveline begging for more. Eveline—

'Jasper? Is everything okay?'

Fuck, fuck, fuck, fuck, FUCK!

'Mmmm?' he replied, lazily circling Sylvia's nipple.

She pushed him off and sat up. 'You don't find me attractive enough?'

'No! Jesus, Sylvia, you're a stunningly beautiful woman in every way.' Kneeling in front of her, he tucked a strand of long red hair behind her ear. 'I *want* to be here. I have no idea why —' he cleared his throat, '—it's not working.'

'Has this ever happened before?'

He shook his head. Women came to him wanting to feel special and wanted. He was failing Sylvia in the way that mattered most.

'Do you have any *stimulants* you could use?'

Now he was truly impotent. He shook his head again. 'I've never needed them before.'

'Maybe it was the amount of wine we had with dinner?' she asked tentatively. 'You, er, *we* did drink rather a bit?'

Could he blame that? In the past, he'd always been able to perform completely shit-faced.

The sound of his phone vibrating in his trouser pocket broke the silence. It currently had more capability to satisfy Sylvia than he did.

'Do you need to answer that?' she asked.

'No, I'm sorry, I should have turned it off earlier.'

'It has been ringing a lot this evening.'

It has? He took her hand. 'Sylvia, this may sound a cliché, but it's not you, it's me. I don't know what's going on, but I'll refund your money.'

'No, Jasper. These things happen—'

'Not to me they don't.'

His phone kept buzzing.

'Please answer it,' she said. 'At this time of night, it might be an emergency.'

Jack stepped to the floor and pulled the phone out as it stopped buzzing, seeing around thirty missed calls from his mother and ten from his sister, Emily.

He rang his mother back, and it connected immediately.

'Jack!' she screamed in between sobs.

Adrenaline knifed him in the guts. 'What's wrong? What's happened?'

'It's your father,' she howled. 'He's dead!'

By the time he stepped off the bus at seven-thirty the next morning on Foxbrooke high street, Jack's head had gone from pounding to splitting in two. After leaving

Sylvia in the hotel room, he'd dashed back to his Soho flat to pack a bag. He'd missed the last public transport of the night, so went to Paddington station and waited to catch the first train of the morning to Bath Spa. When it arrived in Bath, he took the bus to his hometown of Foxbrooke.

He hadn't slept a wink. Was that why he felt a heartbeat away from an aneurysm? It certainly wasn't the wine from the night before. Apart from the odd foray to the UK, he lived across the channel, where people routinely put away a bottle or two a night with no ill effects.

As the bus pulled away, he paused, dreading what was to come. He hadn't been home for years. He was half expecting to find it had changed, but the old buildings seemed frozen in time. Foxbrooke was quaint and beautiful. He didn't belong here.

A wave of nausea rolled through him with unstoppable force. He made it to a drain at the side of the road before vomiting. Eyes watering, he bent over, bracing his hands on his knees as his stomach turned itself inside out.

Breathing heavily, his head dizzy, he took a bottle of water from his bag to wash out his mouth, then rinse the reddish remains of his sick down the drain. Thank god it was still early and no-one was around to see his disgrace.

Finishing the rest of the bottle, he started towards the estate where he and his sister had grown up. One side of Foxbrooke was ancient, with the high street, Manor, church and cottages. The bigger, and more modern side of Foxbrooke, extended out from the edges of the old village. The family home stood on what was called 'the new estate', even though the houses had been there for sixty years.

Was his dad really dead? Jack had spent so much of his life wishing for this outcome, but now it was here? Every cell in his body was numb. *Just get the funeral done, then fuck off back to France.*

He stopped outside the front door of his parents' house. Small, neatly clipped yew trees stood on either side of the entrance. The house was modest, and as clean on the outside as it was on the inside. His mother and father knew how to keep up appearances and attempted to force their children into doing the same. He scored his fingernails across his scalp. *Painkillers, then sleep.*

His mum opened the door. 'Jack!' She clung to him, crying.

This was new. Patricia Newton was normally as affectionate as a barbed wire fence and as emotionally available to her children as a cuckoo. In her late fifties, she was small and pretty, with a usually immaculate brown bob. Now her hair was unbrushed, and she was wearing a pair of huge black sunglasses.

'Mum? Why the shades?' he asked, rubbing her back.

She pulled away, sniffing. 'You smell dreadful. You could have at least tried to make an effort.' She smoothed her hair and adjusted the glasses. 'I had my second cataract operation yesterday.'

Jack followed her inside, immediately coming face-to-face with what he and his sister referred to as the 'ugly-mug wall'. It was every school photo they'd ever had, chronicling just how overweight, spotty, and awkwardly unattractive the two of them had been.

'I, er—'

'How *would* you have known? You never keep in touch. Neither of you do.'

In the living room, Patricia collapsed onto a chintz sofa and sobbed. Dropping his bag, Jack sat beside her and took her hand.

'I'm sorry, Mum. I'm here now. For whatever you need.'

An alarm sounded. She fumbled for her phone on a low coffee table and peered at it.

'My eye drops. You have to put them in. I can't do it on my own.'

'Of course. Where are they?'

'On the sideboard.'

Jack retrieved them and read the instructions as his mother lay her head on the back of the sofa and took off her sunglasses. He could see which eye had been operated on, as the surrounding skin was puffy and red, and the pupil was still dilated.

'I have to use them for the next six weeks and I'm not allowed to drive.'

Six weeks? His heart sank.

'You stink,' his mother continued. 'You may *live* in France, but you don't have to smell like you were born there.'

He ignored her, trying to steady the tiny bottle over her eye.

'Simon Little is coming by this morning. You have to get yourself cleaned up before he arrives. You remember Simon? Old friend of your father's from church. Lost his wife, Rosalind, three years ago.'

Jack squeezed the bottle and missed.

'No! Do it again.'

He tried.

'No!'

Third time lucky... He let out a held breath.

His mother's tears began flowing again. 'I need your father.'

Jack looked around the room for the box of tissues that was always kept inside a frilly holder. He passed it to his mother as the doorbell rang.

'That will be Simon. Can you answer it? I must brush my hair.'

Jack exited the room and rubbed his hands over his face. He remembered Simon. The man was cut from the same cloth as his dad. Both were opinionated, self-righteous, pompous arseholes.

Opening the door, he sagged with relief. It was his younger sister, Emily, with her wife, Steph, holding their two-year-old daughter, Betsy.

He opened his arms and drew the three of them in for a hug. 'Thank fuck you're here,' he muttered.

His sister pulled away first. 'Jesus, Jack, what have you been doing? You bloody reek.'

'It can't be *that* bad?' He glanced at Steph for reassurance.

She pulled a face. 'Mate, you honk.'

'Betsy-Boo?'

His niece waved her hand in front of her nose. 'Poo-ee, Dack-Dack.'

Steph snorted.

'Is it Simon?' his mother called through from inside.

They all froze.

'Hang on,' he called back.

'How is she?' his sister whispered.

'Not great. Does she know about...' He gestured towards his sister's enormous pregnant belly.

She scrunched up her face and shook her head.

'Dack-Dack,' said Betsy, pulling his cheek. 'Baby.'

Steph put her arm around Emily. 'Em, love, no matter what she says, I'm not going anywhere. Okay?'

His sister nodded. 'At least it's just her now.' She looked at Jack. 'Let's do this.'

Jack entered the living room first.

'Is it Simon?'

'No, Mum, it's Emily, Steph and Betsy.'

'But... But I only wanted—'

'Hi, Mum,' said Emily as she followed Jack in. Her voice was brittle, and he could hear the emotion behind it. 'I'm sorry—'

'You're *pregnant*? And you didn't *tell* me?'

His mother started crying again. 'This is all *her* fault. Leading you—'

'Mum!' Emily shouted. 'Stop it now, or I'll walk straight back out and never come back, so help me god.'

'Don't you take the Lord's—'

'Mum!' Jack yelled.

Betsy let out a wail and his mum shut up.

Steph bounced her daughter up and down, and Jack went to them.

'Sorry, Betsy-Boo, Dack-Dack didn't mean to shout.'

She stopped crying and reached her chubby arms towards him. 'Dack-Dack.'

Steph passed Betsy to him and he held her close, letting her mush her snotty face into his shirt.

His sister sat next to their mother and took her hands. 'Mum, we're going to get through this, okay?'

The doorbell rang.

'Simon,' their mother said, listlessly, as if all the fight had left her.

'I'll get it,' Jack said, desperate to get out of the room.

He carried Betsy to the front door and opened it.

On the other side stood Eveline.

His breathing and his heart stopped. Her mouth hung open, her eyes wide as she mirrored him. His brain froze as it rebooted, trying to calibrate this new reality. One where the woman who'd haunted his dreams for over a year was standing in front of him in Foxbrooke and wearing... *A dog collar?*

Unsure of what was going on, Betsy burrowed her head into his neck.

Eveline's gaze broke first and fell on Betsy. Her face went white.

Her eyes met his again and the pain in them pierced his heart. 'Jasper?'

Betsy raised her head. 'Dack-Dack.'

Emily came to his side and Betsy reached for her mother.

Eveline looked from his sister's bump to the three of them, as if adding the component parts to produce the answer 'family'.

'Hi,' his sister said. 'I presume you're the vicar?'

Eveline nodded, her face still drained of colour.

'And you've met Jack?'

'Jack?' Eveline replied, her voice cracking.

'Yes, my older brother. I'm Emily. We're Nigel and Patricia's kids. This is my daughter, Betsy, and my wife, Steph, is inside with Mum. I presume you heard about Dad?'

Eveline nodded and cleared her throat. 'Simon Little told me. I wanted to come and see how she was doing and convey my condolences.'

'Thank you,' Emily replied. 'I know she'll appreciate that. Come on through.'

Eveline hesitated, her eyes flicking to Jack. He stepped back.

'Don't mind him,' Emily said. 'He doesn't normally smell this bad.'

He backed further up the corridor towards the living room.

Eveline entered and glanced between their childhood photos and the two of them. Embarrassment and shame sliced at him like a knife.

Emily rolled her eyes. 'Please ignore the "ugly-mug wall". I would literally pay burglars to steal these.'

'Who is it? Is it Simon?' his mother called out.

He entered the living room, followed by his sister and Eveline.

Eveline crouched in front of his mother. 'Patricia, I am so deeply sorry for your loss.'

His mother shook. 'You...' She stabbed her finger at Eveline, who quickly stood. 'This is *your* fault.' His mother rose to her feet. '*You're* the reason he's dead. *You* killed him.' She spat at Eveline. 'Get out! Get out of my house!'

'Mum!' Jack and Emily yelled, as Eveline wiped her face.

'Patricia—' Eveline began.

'Get out!' she screamed.

Betsy started crying again and Eveline fled.

Emily thrust Betsy into Steph's arms. 'The door to the garden is at the back, through the kitchen. Take her out there.'

Steph nodded, dashing their daughter out of the room.

Jack's headache intensified with the rise in his heartbeat. Every rapid thud sent a pulse of pain to pound at the inside of his skull. His thoughts were tangled and suffocated, twisted into knots too tight to undo. Eveline was *here*? A fucking *vicar*? And his mum believed that she'd killed his dad?

Patricia was back on the sofa, wailing into her hands.

'What the hell, Mum?' Emily's face was puce.

Their mother cried even harder.

Jack sat next to her, rubbing her back and shooting a bewildered look at his sister.

'Mum!' Emily repeated. 'Dad had a heart attack. How on *earth* is that poor woman to blame?'

'She—she...' his mother hiccupped through her tears. 'The pews. She wants to get rid of the pews. It's too much.'

Jack's hand stilled. This was just the kind of petty and inconsequential thing that would tip his father over the edge.

'Pews?' Emily repeated.

Their mother nodded.

'Mum,' Jack began, trying to keep his voice level. 'You just spat in the face of Eve—Foxbrooke's *vicar*, and blamed her for Dad's death because of some wooden *seats*?'

His mother's sobs intensified.

He glanced at his sister. 'I should run after her and apologise.'

'Agreed. Mum can give her apologies later when she's calmed down.'

Their mother lifted her head. 'I've just lost my husband!'

'Mum,' his sister began, her face fierce with anger. 'We want to be here for you. But if you continue behaving like this and scaring my daughter, then Steph and I are out of that door without a second glance.' She cradled her huge bump and winced.

Jack leapt to his feet. 'Em?'

She shook her head and bent over.

He helped her to a chair. 'You okay? The baby?'

'Braxton Hicks,' she replied through gritted teeth.

'What? Is the baby coming?'

She shook her head, breathing heavily.

Jack crouched beside her, holding her hand. He wanted to help but was in freefall.

Emily's breathing returned to normal. 'It's okay. They're practice contractions. I had them with Betsy, just not as strong.'

He nodded, his jaw clenched with stress.

She leaned closer. 'We can do this, Jack. I'm alright, I promise. You run after the vicar and make amends.' She brought her mouth to his ear and whispered. 'Or we could just bury the bastard in the back garden?'

He huffed out a terse laugh. 'You sure you're okay on your own?'

'I'm fine. I've got Steph. Just go catch her up.'

He nodded and stood, glancing across at his mother, who was crying into a handkerchief.

'Go on,' his sister said quietly. 'We've got this.'

JACK DASHED OUT OF THE HOUSE AND BACK TOWARDS THE centre of Foxbrooke. Had Eveline come by car? Walked?

There was a shortcut to the high street through the recreation field, and he took it. On the far side of the large open space, he saw her striding briskly through a metal gate. He ran, his heart and head pounding, and followed her onto a side street.

'Eveline!'

She stopped, glanced back, then turned and continued on even faster.

He caught her up. 'Eveline, please. I'm sorry.'

She didn't slow her pace, her gaze fixed firmly ahead. 'What for?'

Er, everything? He ran his hands through his hair. 'My mum, me... My dad?'

Her steps faltered, and her eyes found his. 'I'm so sorry for your loss.'

He looked away. 'Don't be.'

They walked in silence onto the high street and Eveline turned towards Foxbrooke Manor and Saint Saviour's church. Words whirled through his mind, but none seemed the right ones. *Come on!*

'Look, I can explain,' he said, knowing full well he couldn't.

She stopped and faced him. Her expression was calm, but he could see the pain behind it.

'What's your real name?'

He took a big breath. 'It's—'

'Jack?'

His head jerked in the direction of the voice. Striding towards them from the direction of the Manor, her frizzy curls bouncing, was Lady Estelle Foxbrooke, one of his oldest friends.

'No fucking way! It *is* you!' She grabbed him in a bear hug. 'What are you doing here? Why didn't you tell me?' She disengaged with a frown, her nose wrinkling. 'Have you been partying all night? I've just been mucking out the stables and they smell better than you.'

'I—'

'And how do you know Eveline?' She frowned. 'Hang about, you're not "Jesuslover33" are you?' She turned to Eveline. 'I thought your date with him was tonight?'

Eveline blushed and shook her head.

'Stelle...' he began.

Estelle's brow furrowed deeper as she stared at him. 'What's going on?'

'Dad died yesterday.'

Her jaw dropped. 'What?'

'He had a heart attack.'

'But... You're here?'

'I was in London last night when I got the call.'

Estelle touched his arm. 'Oh Jack, I'm so, so sorry. Does Henry know? Finn? Connor?'

He shook his head. The emotion squeezing his chest was not for the loss of his father, but for the chasm created between himself and his closest friends by his absence.

'Do you want me to tell everyone?' Estelle asked.

He nodded.

'Oh love. I'm so fucking sorry. Who's with your mum now?'

'Em and Steph.'

'Is there anything I can do?'

He shook his head again. 'Mum's in a bit of a state. She, she, er...' He glanced at Eveline.

'We can discuss the funeral another time.' Eveline took a card from her pocket and held it out. 'The number for the rectory is there. If I'm not in, you can leave a message.'

'Do you want some company?' Estelle asked him. 'I was just coming to see Eveline, but I can—'

'No.' He held up his hands and took a step back. 'It's okay. You carry on. I need to get back, anyway.' He forced a smile. 'It's good to see you, Stelle.' He couldn't meet Eveline's eyes, so nodded in her direction, then turned and strode away as quickly as he could.

❧ 3 ❧

Eveline watched Jack's tall figure as he retreated. Any faster and he would be running.

God? I'm a little delirious right now. What's happening?

Beside her, Estelle sighed loudly. 'Poor bastard. It can't be easy losing your dad, no matter what an arsehole he was.'

'Estelle!'

Estelle linked her arm through Eveline's, pulling her towards the rectory.

'Ah, come on, Eveline. You know what he's like. He was even more opposed to your supposedly radical plans than Gram-Gram, and that's saying something.'

Gram-Gram, the Dowager Duchess of Somerset, was an eighty-year-old dragon, and Estelle's grandmother. She didn't approve of female priests, nor Eveline's attempts to make Saint Saviour's more accessible to the community.

'So, that was the Jack you've mentioned before?'

'Yep. Me, Henry, Connor, Jack and Finn were best friends growing up.'

'But... He doesn't look much like the photos in Nigel and Patricia's home.'

Estelle gave her the side eye. 'Aren't you the one always telling me not to judge a book by its cover?'

Her cheeks burned. 'No, I'm not, it just seems that Ja—him and his sister appear very different from when they were children.'

'That's one way of putting it. Have you got time for a cup of tea? I could do with a fifteen-minute bitch and whine with my bestie.'

Eveline glanced at her watch. 'Yes, I've got a meeting with one of the parish council sub-committees at eleven, so as long as you leave me enough time to get my other chores done before that, we're good.'

The rectory was a beautiful old stone building that lay to the right of the church and bordered the parkland. It provided rent-free accommodation for Foxbrooke's vicar and their family, but, as Eveline had yet to marry, she lived in the huge house on her own.

They went around the side and through the back door into the kitchen. Everything from the flagstone floor to the peeling lime-wash walls was tired and ancient. In front of the window sat a giant Butler sink that had been used to clean dishes, dogs and children before a modern bathroom was installed decades ago.

Eveline filled the kettle from the noisy copper tap and switched it on.

'So,' she began, trying to keep her tone neutral. 'What was Jack like growing up?'

Estelle was on tiptoe, pulling a battered green biscuit tin down from a high shelf. 'If you don't want to eat them, why buy them in the first place?' she grumbled.

'I buy them for other people. They're up there to dissuade me from eating them.'

Estelle lifted the lid. 'Ooh! Custard creams. Yum.'

'Don't eat them all. They're Simon's favourite and he gets a little, er, snippy, if I don't have any.'

Her friend crammed two in her mouth and crunched.

Eveline raised her eyebrows and pulled out two mugs.

'Ee's a uck uh ob oo,' Estelle said, her hand in front of her mouth to catch biscuit crumbs as they sprayed out.

'In English?'

Estelle swallowed. 'I *said*, "he's a stuck-up nob too". The only reason he's supporting you in "pew-gate" is because he wants to get in your knickers.'

'Shhh!' she hissed, glancing around. 'Simon is a friend and valued member of our congregation and community.'

Her friend shrugged. 'He still fancies you.'

Eveline shook her head and poured boiling water into the mugs. 'He's sixty-six and still mourning the death of his wife. I don't think he "fancies" anyone, least of all me.'

Estelle reached for another biscuit, but Eveline whipped the tin away.

'Tell me about Jack.'

'What's it worth?'

She looked down. 'There's only one custard cream left.'

Estelle leaned back in her chair, crossed her arms, and raised an eyebrow.

'You can have it after you've told me about Jack,' Eveline said firmly.

'Can I have a Bourbon to keep me going?'

She handed one over.

'Thank you, lovely friend. You're definitely going to heaven.'

Eveline rolled her eyes, took a pint of milk from the fridge and put it on the table. 'Come on, then.'

'Okay, Jack Newton, the abridged version. I've known him since I was four. Back then, he was shy, sweet, kind, and just lovely. He struggled academically but really loved art.' Estelle stared at her mug and frowned. 'I don't think he'll mind me telling you any of this, but it's not very nice.'

Her heart rate spiked. 'You don't have to tell me. And I don't want you breaking his confidence.'

Estelle's face had lost its usual sparkle as she held Eveline's gaze. 'You know how Henry, Connor and I had a shit time of it growing up because of our crazy-ass parents?'

She nodded. The Duke of Somerset was a committed naturist, hosted sex parties, and had two wives as well as six children.

'Well, Jack did too. His parents should have lived a hundred years ago. We used to call them "Victorian Mum" and "Victorian Dad" behind their backs. We didn't know at the time just how bad it was, but Nigel used to hit Jack. Patricia would make him wear trousers instead of shorts, and long shirts in the summer to hide the bruises.'

Tears pricked Eveline's eyes. 'That's awful,' she whispered.

Estelle shrugged. 'Like I said, we didn't know until it was over. But we knew how much his dad hated Jack being into art. He made him stop by the time we left Foxbrooke Primary and used to accuse him of being a—' She shook her head. 'He was disgustingly homophobic.'

'Jack's gay?'

'No, I'm pretty sure he's not. He never had a girlfriend when we were in secondary school. But then neither did Finn, Connor or Henry.'

'What happened when Emily came out?'

'Jack's sister?' Estelle huffed. 'She didn't. Watching what Jack went through, she kept quiet, went to uni in York, then stayed up there. I think the first inkling her parents had that she was gay was when they received an invitation to her and Steph's wedding.'

Eveline pressed her hand to her heart. 'What happened?'

'They didn't go.'

'Oh no.'

'Honestly, I'm sure everyone had a far nicer time without them there. And after the ceremony, Emily changed her surname to Steph's.'

Eveline wiped her eyes. She understood people's cruelty came from their own pain, but she could still never fathom how a parent could treat their own child so terribly.

Estelle reached across the table and took her hand. 'It's okay. It's in the past now.'

Eveline sniffed and pulled a handkerchief out of her sleeve. 'What did Jack do after he left school?'

'He went travelling and never came back. He started in Australia and ended up in France. I think he's been back to Foxbrooke maybe twice in the last twelve years.'

'What does he do for work?'

Her friend shrugged. 'Henry says he's some kind of party-planner for the über rich. I wish he would stick around for a bit. I could do with a hand organising the Manor's Winter Ball.'

'You don't think he will?'

'What? Help?'

'Stick around?'

'Fuck no, his life is in the glamorous south of France, not the backwaters of Somerset. As soon as Nigel's in the ground, he'll be out of here.'

God, is that really your plan?

'Okay, give it up,' Estelle said.

'What?'

'My custard cream.'

Flustered, Eveline handed it over.

'Thank you, my friend.' Estelle nibbled the edges of the biscuit to expose the cream layer in between. 'So... Excited about tonight?'

'Tonight?'

Estelle gave her a cheeky grin. 'Isn't "Jesuslover33" going to show you heaven?'

Eveline held her palms to her cheeks, trying to cool them down. 'We're going for dinner. That's all.'

'Do you even know what he looks like?'

'Yes, of course I do. Leslie is—'

'Leslie?'

She gripped her mug. *This* was why she hadn't given Estelle this particular bit of information. She knew *exactly* what her friend's response would be.

'Yes. Leslie seems a lovely gentleman, and I am very much, er...' She couldn't lie. She wasn't excited about meeting him anymore.

Estelle leaned back in her chair and tapped the edge of her custard cream on the table. 'Cancel.'

'I can't. It's tonight. That would be very rude. And besides, he might be, you know...'

'The one?'

She nodded.

Estelle grabbed a book that Eveline had hidden under a Christian newspaper. It was one of her favourite romance novels by the bestselling author Polly Hart.

'Hey!'

Estelle held up her hand as she read the title. '"*Christmas Sparkles and Homely Hedgehogs at the Tiny Village School on Bluebell Bay*".' She made loud retching noises.

'Oi! I love those books.'

Estelle flicked through. 'Aha! Now, I wonder why you've turned down the corner of this page. Could it be, perchance, a description of a fictional Leslie?'

'Estelle, you know my love for you is infinite, but I am considering denying you further access to custard creams.'

Estelle took another nibble of the biscuit in her hand and read out loud. '*So here I am, in an absolute pickle. I'm stuck in a snowdrift with my vintage bicycle, Bluebell. Poor Bluey has a puncture and I don't know how I'm ever going to get my hand-crocheted tea cosies to the village hall for the hedgehog charity auction!*'

Eveline turned her back on her friend and started washing dishes as loudly as she could.

'*But I hear a car. I stand in the road, waving my brightly coloured scarf as a sleek and very expensive-looking car pulls up. Who could this be? I wonder. The door opens, and a man steps out. He's wearing polished brown brogues, quite unsuitable for the middle of a Cornish winter, I must say, and olive-green corduroy trousers. Oh my golly gosh, I think, as my gaze peruses the cosy argyle sweater he's wearing under his Barbour jacket. But my heart skips a beat as I behold his ruggedly handsome face. "Hullo," he says. "I'm Wolf Redwood. May I be of assistance?"*'

Estelle slammed the book on the table. 'Fuck my life, Eveline. Is this really what you're hoping Leslie is like?'

Eveline stared out of the window at the yew hedge that lay a few feet away. As Estelle had been reading, all she could picture was Jack in the London bar. The way his voice made her shiver, and how his touch made her come alive.

'Eveline? You in the kitchen?' A man's voice called through from inside the front door.

'What the fuck?' Estelle hissed. 'Try knocking, arsehole. Seriously, Eveline, he doesn't fucking live here—'

'Simon!' Eveline cried, wiping her hands on a tea towel as an older man entered the room.

'Hi Simon,' said Estelle. 'We didn't hear you knock.'

His lips thinned. 'Lady Foxbrooke.'

Eveline's stomach knotted as Estelle flinched. Her friend hated people using her title.

Simon turned to her. 'I thought I'd pop by and see how it went with Patricia this morning?'

Eveline pulled a face. 'Not very well, I'm afraid.'

'Well, it was to be expected.'

She bristled. Patricia's behaviour earlier was most definitely *not* to be expected.

'But no need to worry, dear. I'm here to offer my assistance as always.' He sat at the table. 'Has the kettle just boiled?'

'Yes,' she replied, moving on auto-pilot to make him a cup of tea.

'Jolly good.' He reached for the biscuit tin and peered inside. 'Where are my custard creams?'

Eveline looked over her shoulder to see Estelle holding up the nibbled remains of the last one.

'I'm afraid this is all that's left,' Estelle said. 'Want to finish it? I've saved the best bit till last.'

Simon stared at her as if she'd just offered him a sheet of second-hand toilet roll.

'No, thank you, *dear*.'

The kettle came up to the boil at the same time as Estelle. Eveline took her friend's arm and hauled her up.

'Estelle was just leaving.' She tossed her friend a pleading look.

'Humph,' said Simon.

'Yes, I was,' Estelle agreed. 'Good luck tonight, Eveline.'

'Eh?' Simon interjected.

'Eveline's going on a thrilling date later,' Estelle said. 'A chap called Wolf Redwood she met on some Christian website. I've seen a photo. He's mid-thirties, plays squash three times a week and is incredibly rugged and handsome. He's a hedge fund manager and has a Labrador called Bunty.'

If Simon had appeared displeased at the lack of custard creams, this piece of information looked like it might send him into apoplexy.

Estelle gave her an over-exaggerated wink. 'Don't do anything I wouldn't do, you saucepot!'

'Estelle!'

Her friend popped the remains of the custard cream in her mouth and waggled her fingers. 'I'll see myself out.'

                            ❧ 4 ❧

Jack stood outside the front door of his family home,
summoning the strength to knock. The only reason he
wasn't on a bus back to Bath right now was the love he
had for his sister and her family.

The intense nausea from earlier had returned. He'd been
over twenty-four hours without sleep and over twelve without
food. Throw in his dad's death, his mother's meltdown, and
discovering Eveline was here in Foxbrooke and he was unravel-
ling too fast to control.

His sister opened the front door. 'I saw you through the
window. Come in.'

'How is she?'

'Upstairs, with Steph and Betsy.' She smiled at the look of
confusion on his face. 'Let's go into the kitchen and have a cup
of tea. Kettle's just boiled.'

He followed her through and sat at the dining table in the
same place he'd always done. His fingertips ran along the faint
indentations underneath, lines he'd scored in the wood with

the point of a pair of scissors. One tiny rebellion. A little 'fuck you' to his parents, right under their noses.

Emily put a mug of tea in front of him and a glass of water.

'Drink the water first. You smell hungover.'

He sipped it slowly, worried he might immediately throw it back up again.

'Betsy needed her nap,' his sister continued. 'And Mum had a fit of remorse and wanted to help put her down. She lay on the bed next to her and pretended to fall asleep, which Betsy copied. They're both sparko now.'

A shocked laugh escaped him. 'What the fuck?'

His sister grinned back. 'I know, right? Mental. Anyway, Steph's sitting up there with them just in case Mum wakes first, or rolls onto Betsy.' She tapped the side of his water glass. 'Keep going.'

'Yes, Mum.'

She smiled. 'Did you catch the vicar up?'

He nodded and pulled out the card that Eveline had given him. 'She said we could discuss the funeral another time.'

Silence hung between them.

'Jack—'

'I know you can't stay. I'll sort everything out.'

'But your work?'

'I'm due some time off, anyway. It's not a problem.'

'I'm so sorry, it's just we're so far away, and with Steph's work, and Betsy, and me being about to pop, I don't know how we can do it.'

He reached across and squeezed his sister's hand. 'It's fine. I don't want you here, anyway.'

She raised an eyebrow.

'You know what I mean. There's no way I'm having you near this toxic cesspool.'

Her eyes filled with tears. 'Thank you. You've always looked after me.'

'It was never enough.'

'It was. I got off lightly and you know it.'

He stared at their clasped hands. He couldn't believe their father was actually gone.

'Are you okay?' she asked. 'How are you feeling? About Dad?'

He released her hands and rubbed his forehead. 'Honestly? I thought I would feel relief or even happiness, but I don't. I'm angry that I never got to say to his face everything that's been running around my head for years.'

His sister nodded. 'Most people regret not telling someone who's passed just how much they loved them. But I regret not telling him what an evil bastard he was. You know, he never even came to see Betsy? Mum did, but he didn't.' She shook her head. 'He was such a fucking arsehole. And the worst part? I know I'm going to be really, really sad about this. It's going to stir up all the shit from our childhood again, just when I thought I'd got over it.'

A lump filled Jack's throat, and he nodded.

'Before I forget,' Emily continued, 'I rang Foxbrooke Surgery and told them Mum wasn't coping. A locum is going to come by later and hopefully give her something to take the edge off. Or at least make her think twice before assaulting the vicar.' His sister sighed. 'That poor woman. She seemed so nice.'

'She is. I mean, she seems very nice.'

Emily glanced at her watch. 'Look, if we're going to leave you here on your own, then you need to get some rest. Go take a shower and get some sleep.'

He yawned as a wave of tiredness hit. 'You sure?'

'Yes, of course. You stink and look like you haven't slept for a month. I'll deal with the doctor when they come.'

IT WAS LATE AFTERNOON BY THE TIME JACK WOKE. HE LAY in his childhood bed and stared up at the ceiling. He'd hoped to see faint marks from where he'd once stuck glow-in-the-dark stars. But the room had been repainted and every trace of him and his childhood had gone.

He listened for noises from downstairs, but the house was silent. His sister must have already left. Sitting up in bed, he scrolled through his phone, dealing with work first. He refunded Sylvia her money. Had that really only been last night? *What a shitshow.*

Thoughts of Eveline shimmered at the edges of his mind, but he ignored them. He sent emails, putting off his regular clients back in France, then messaged the only friend he had who actually knew how he earned money. Cyrille Blanchett was a flamboyant party planner in his forties and adored Jack and the intrigue of his job.

> Jack: Have to stay in the UK for a bit. Dad died yesterday.

> Cyrille: Putain! You okay?

> Jack: Yeah. Can't talk. I'll ring soon.

> Cyrille: I'm here for you. Bisous à ma petite putain.

Kisses to my little whore. Jack rolled his eyes and smiled. Cyrille may take the piss, but he never judged. Jack took a breath and opened the messages that seemed the most difficult to answer.

. . .

Estelle: I've told the boys. If there is anything we can do to help, you only have to ask. Promise? You can stay with me in the livery if you don't want to be near your mum, or at the Manor as there's always tons of rooms empty. Let me know, okay?

Henry: Estelle just rang with the news about your dad. I'm so sorry. Can I do anything? Do you want some company?

Connor: I just found out from Estelle that your dad has passed on. This must be really difficult for you in so many ways. How's your mum doing? Your sister? Let me know if there is anything I can do. I know it's early days, but I'll pick up a leaflet about bereavement counselling from work. I get off shift at six if you want to meet up? Henry and Finn should be free as well. Big hugs, Connor.

Connor: Seriously, Jack, anything you need at all, please don't hesitate to ask.

Finn: Mate, I just heard about your dad from Stelle. Want to get shitfaced?

JACK CREATED A GROUP CHAT WITH ALL OF THEM AND SENT A message.

Jack: Hey all. Thanks for the messages. You up for the pub later? I need to make sure Mum's okay first. Horse and Hounds at eight?

Finn: See you there.

Henry: Me too.

Connor: Me three.

Estelle: Me four xxx

❧

EVELINE SMILED ACROSS THE SMALL TABLE AT LESLIE. 'WELL, isn't this nice?'

They were seated by the window of *The Colour Palate*, a restaurant on Foxbrooke high street owned by local chef Leia Perry. She ran it with her boyfriend, and the food was not only local, but out of this world.

'Indeed,' Leslie replied.

Eveline indicated the menu in his hand. 'Have you seen anything you like?'

He scrunched up his nose and his glasses rode higher on his face. This was the fifth time he'd done this in the last twenty minutes, and Eveline chastised herself for having counted every one.

On paper, and in person, there was absolutely nothing wrong with Leslie Porter. At thirty-five, he was the same age as her, with a pleasant face, average build and height, and all his own hair. He'd been polite and well-mannered since meeting her at the rectory, and she felt safe in his company. Of all the men she'd met through the Christian dating website, he was the most promising by far.

'The prosciutto is hand cured and apparently the pork belly is melt-in-the-mouth,' she said.

His glasses rode up his scrunched nose for the sixth time. 'I don't eat pork. It's unclean meat.'

Eveline froze, glad she had yet to mention the two pigs currently rooting around the rectory garden, the sides of meat in the curing room she'd created upstairs, and the chest freezer full of sausages.

'Jesus didn't eat pork and I like to lead my life by his example,' Leslie continued. 'I think I'll have the vegetable soup to start, then the fish. What about you?'

The chance for a husband and children is more important than bacon. She swallowed. 'Sounds lovely. I'll have the same.'

After Leia took their order, Leslie leaned forward.

'So, Eveline, in our online exchanges, you haven't told me anything about your family.'

Breathe. You've got nothing to be ashamed about. 'My father, Peter, is in the motor trade. He lives in Kent. My mother is called Diana and lives in Germany with my stepfather and half-sisters.'

Leslie's glasses rose a centimetre. 'Your parents are *divorced*?'

Eveline pasted on a brittle smile. 'Yes. When I was ten.'

'Oh.'

Is something I had no control over going to be a deal-breaker, Leslie?

He cleared his throat and arranged his features into a smile that looked even less convincing than hers felt.

'Germany?'

'Yes, my stepfather, Hugh, is in the army, so when he married my mum, I went to boarding school in England. My sisters are a lot younger than me. Abigail is twenty-two and studying to be a lawyer in The Hague, and Eleanor is twenty and studying medicine in Munich.'

'Do you see much of them?'

Eveline hesitated. 'Not as much as I'd like, unfortunately. We all have busy lives.'

'And your father?'

'He also works a lot, and it's a four-hour drive to Margate, so we don't get to see each other that often.'

He wrinkled his nose again. 'That's a shame. Family is very important.'

She nodded. 'Yes. I would love to have my own one day.'

Leslie cleared his throat. 'I'm glad we're both on the same page. And this is why I'm glad to have found someone like you.' His cheeks coloured. 'Someone who understands the importance of saving oneself for the sanctity of the marital bed.'

Oh no. Her personal sex ship, the HMS *Virginity*, had sailed a long time ago. Eveline may not have slept with anyone in over a decade, but before she found God, she and her friends dipped into pretty much any port that took their fancy.

Leia arrived with their soup, which saved her from replying. When the bowl was placed in front of him, Leslie sniffed and waved his hand above it, wafting the scent into his scrunched-up nose.

Nine...

Eveline glanced over his shoulder out of the window, already visualising leaving. Despite the darkness of the October night, the high street was lit up from streetlamps, and the glow from the flats above the shops. In the distance, walking towards the restaurant on the other side of the road, was a figure. She couldn't yet make out their features, but her heart and hormones recognised who it was.

Jack...

As he got closer, he glanced toward the restaurant, and their eyes met. His pace slowed as her pulse rocketed. She felt locked inside his gaze as a million messages darted between them.

'Eveline?'

She started at the sound of her name, and Jack's attention

flicked to Leslie. He dipped his head towards the pavement and strode on.

'Ye-es?' she stammered, bringing her awareness back to the man in front of her.

Leslie wrinkled his nose again and his glasses lifted.

Ten...

'I thought we could discuss a roadmap for the progression of our relationship?'

⚜

JACK DUCKED HIS HEAD TO ENTER THE SNUG IN THE HORSE and Hounds pub. The ceiling was low, with blackened and bowing Tudor timbers waiting to bring anyone over six feet down to size. It was the most inappropriate part of the pub for him and his equally tall friends to meet, but it had an open fire and was private.

His heart tugged in his chest at the sight of Henry, Connor and Finn, who'd commandeered a sofa and chairs around the fire. They stood, slightly hunched to avoid cracking their heads on the low beams, and embraced him. There was already a pint of beer and a double shot of whisky in a glass waiting for him.

'We weren't sure what you wanted to drink first,' said Finn. 'Or whether it's only wine now that you're basically a frog.'

Jack necked the whisky. The burn was a welcome balm. 'Wine's for food. This is for friends.' He reached for the beer and glugged half of it. 'Thanks. I needed this.'

'Estelle's running late,' said Henry, her twin and heir to the Foxbrooke estate.

'No Libby?' Jack asked him. 'I was looking forward to meeting her in person.'

Henry's face lit up at the mention of his girlfriend. 'She

wanted to give us a chance to catch up first without having to stop and explain all our inside jokes.'

'We have jokes?' Connor asked. He was a nurse, and Henry and Estelle's stepbrother.

Finn snorted. 'The four of us are about as funny as a hole in the head. Stelle's amusing, but mainly when she's bawling someone out or farting inappropriately.'

'Libby says I'm naturally funny,' Henry said proudly.

Jack gaped at him. Out of all of them, Henry had been the shyest and most reserved. Now it appeared he'd been saving his smiles for the moment he fell in love.

'Wow,' was all he could manage.

'Yep,' said Finn. 'Welcome to Henry Foxbrooke version two-point-zero.'

Jack finished his pint. 'I'm getting another round in. Who wants what?'

Connor stood. 'It's my shout. Same again?'

He nodded. 'Cheers.'

As Connor left, Henry leaned forward. 'How's your mum doing?'

Jack's guts twisted. He needed more alcohol to dull the pain of the day.

'Deranged. She spat in the vicar's face.'

Finn choked on his beer. 'What the fuck?'

'Mum accused her of killing Dad.'

'How?' Henry asked, his mouth hanging open.

'Apparently she wants to get rid of the pews and that was enough to give Dad a heart attack.'

'Fucking hell,' Finn muttered. 'Poor Eveline.'

A hot spike of jealousy stabbed Jack in the stomach and he forced his voice to stay level. 'How well do you know her?'

Finn shrugged. 'A bit? We've chatted about me buying the pews and repurposing them if she's given the go ahead to get rid of them. Stelle's closer to Eveline than anyone. She keeps trying to set me up with her.'

Adrenaline roared through Jack's body as his fight to the death reflex kicked in.

'*You?*'

'Don't sound so sceptical. I'm not that bad.' Finn rubbed his scruffy beard. 'But it's never going to happen. She may be the nicest person in Foxbrooke, but she's not my type and I'm not hers, either.'

Jack thought of the insipid man Eveline was currently having dinner with. 'Does she have a boyfriend?'

Finn shrugged. 'Don't think so. Stelle says she's desperate for marriage and kids. But can you imagine being married to a vicar?'

Jack could not. Eveline was a woman of God and he belonged in hell.

'Why?' Finn asked. 'Do you like her?'

He forced his head to shake. 'Nah. And anyway, what's the point? I'm leaving as soon as I can.'

Connor returned with a tray of beers and another double whisky.

Jack took the tumbler straight from the tray and downed it.

'Going to be that kind of night, is it?' Finn asked.

He nodded. 'I need to get wasted.'

✿ 5 ✿

Jack dreamt he was in a windowless and grey hospital room. The only furniture was a bed containing his father hooked up to an array of beeping machines. Jack had to be there with him, but wanted out.

His father opened his eyes, and the beeping intensified. Now, skin-crawling terror replaced the low-level panic. His dad wasn't dead after all.

Jack glanced around. No door.

His father rose from the bed, his eyes pitiless black holes. A heavy, inescapable inevitability cloaked his movements. Feet hitting the floor, he stepped forward.

Jack backed up against the wall, his hands running along the paintwork in a fruitless search for a way out. He felt something under his fingertips—the faint indentations from lines scored with the point of a pair of scissors.

He knows.

The beeping reached an ear-splitting volume, tearing Jack from the nightmare. He cried out, sweating and gasping for breath. The beeping continued.

46

Throwing back the tangled covers, he grabbed his phone and silenced the alarm. *Fuck!* He'd set reminders for when to put his mother's eye drops in and had overslept.

Leaping out of bed, his head lanced with pain from the sudden change in pressure, and his stomach cramped. *You drank too much last night, you dick.* He didn't have time to put clothes on, so ran out of the room in his boxer shorts. Thundering down the stairs towards the living room, he yelled to his mum that he was coming.

Jack threw open the living room door and stopped dead.

His mother was sitting on the sofa, her head resting against the back as Simon leant over her, administering the drops. But that wasn't the worst part of the tableau.

Perched on a sofa, directly facing the door he'd just rushed through, was Eveline.

Colour rose in her cheeks and her mouth opened as she stared at him. It seemed she was as unable to look away as he was. Her nostrils flared and her eyes dilated. Her tongue darted out to wet her lower lip and his cock twitched.

Now, you decide to work?

A loud harumphing from Simon broke the spell.

'Ah, the prodigal son. So glad you could make it.'

Jack's gaze passed by him on its way to his mother.

'Mum, I'm sorry I overslept. Give me five minutes to get dressed.'

He didn't wait for a reply, but bounded back up the stairs and into the bathroom.

Standing under a cold shower, the part of his body that had let him down so spectacularly two nights ago was now reporting for duty with head-bobbing enthusiasm. *Seriously?* He'd thought he needed to see a doctor, but it was clear the issue was psychological, not physiological.

Scrubbing shampoo into his hair, panic gripped him. Could

he ever get it up for another woman again? Without his cock, he couldn't do his job. And without his job, he had nothing. After flunking his A-levels, he'd left education behind. He'd done no further courses, learnt no skills, had no career.

Fuck! He rinsed the suds from his body. He was clean, but in no fit state to exit the shower. He stared at his cock. No way could he touch himself, thinking about the untouchable woman downstairs.

Really? So who's been in every fucking fantasy of yours for the last year, then?

Resting his head against the tiled wall, he closed his eyes. He couldn't get away with a lie that big, even to himself.

As an escort, his cock may have been the star of the show, but his mind made everything happen. Before meeting Eveline, he'd never had an issue finding the women he was with attractive. If he needed a little help, his brain stepped in with erotic images to jumpstart the process and keep it going.

But since meeting Eveline, everything had changed. No matter how he tried to force himself to think of another woman, his thoughts recoiled immediately, springing back to ones of her. And now, with his clients, he was closing his eyes more and giving even more oral. Doing anything to trick his body into believing he was with the redheaded woman he'd met one night in a bar.

Seconds ticked by, but his cock was still as hard as steel. He reached down. The burst of pleasure as he ran his hand over his length made his eyes flicker. He forced them to stay open, focusing on the lines of grout between the tiles. He couldn't think of Eveline. This was a practical solution to a socially unacceptable problem—a physical release, not enjoyment. He needed to get it done, and fast.

He tugged, his muscles tensing and his breath ragged, as sharp jolts of almost painful sensation shocked through him.

The tiles, the tiles. Think about the tiles. But as he stroked faster, no matter how hard he stared at the shower wall, images of Eveline flooded in.

He gave in, sucking in a last, desperate breath before being dragged into an ocean of her, so deep it consumed him. His orgasm shot up his spine and he clenched his jaw to stop a roar from escaping. Waves of fierce pleasure crashed through him, so powerful his whole body shook.

Gasping, he rested his forehead on the cool wall, his hand still tugging his cock as it spilled his shame on the tiles. He was a weak and worthless piece of shit compared to the incredible woman he'd just debased in his mind. Could he hide up here? No. He had to deal with her. And his mum needed him. Once the funeral was over, he could run away.

AT THE SOUND OF FOOTSTEPS ON THE STAIRS, EVELINE pressed her legs together and sat a little straighter on the edge of her chair. She'd spent the last ten minutes nodding and smiling, whilst snapshots of a near-naked Jack flashed through her mind.

After he'd left the room, both Simon and Patricia had taken her flushed face as a sign of innocent embarrassment. Patricia had apologised on behalf of her son, and Simon had made a series of disapproving noises. Luckily, neither of them interpreted her flustered response to him as arousal.

But now, as Jack entered the room, heat once more scorched across her cheeks and her heart raced in her chest. She kept her eyes on the beige carpet, swallowing as his tanned, bare feet came into her peripheral vision.

'Where's Simon?' he asked.

'I told him that you would handle things from here,' his mother replied. 'You're now the man of the family.'

Eveline glanced up. A muscle was twitching in Jack's jaw.

'I'm sorry, Mum, for oversleeping.' His caramel eyes found hers. 'And to you, Eveline for barging in like, er...'

Lost for words and light-headed as the more undisciplined part of her brain mentally undressed him, she managed a nod.

An awkward silence descended on the room. His mother's jaw was wobbling again. This was the point she needed to stop thinking about naked Jack, step up and do her job.

'Patricia, do you know if Nigel had planned what he might want at his funeral?'

Shaking her head, Patricia stared at her hands twisting on her lap. Jack sat next to her and rubbed her back.

'Have you had any thoughts about what you might like? Any particular readings or hymns?' Eveline continued. 'And do you have a preferred date for the service?'

Patricia shook her head again, and a tear tracked down her cheek.

'Well, we've got time. You don't have to make any decisions at the moment, and I can come back as often as you need. Has the medical certificate been issued so you can register his death?'

She crumpled into Jack's chest. 'I... I can't do this.'

Jack held her carefully, but his face was grim. 'It's okay. Like Eveline said, we don't have to do anything right now.'

The sound of her name on his lips sent a tremor through her. *Be professional!*

'No, you don't understand,' Patricia continued. 'I don't want to do *any* of it.'

Eveline caught Jack's eye. His expression was one of someone stoically facing a firing squad.

'Mum, even if you don't know what Dad might have specifically wanted. Wouldn't you like to choose what we, er, how it goes?'

His mother shook her head. 'It's not my place to speak for Nigel.'

Eveline tensed. She was used to seeing Jack's parents in public but had no idea that their relationship was so unbalanced. Had Patricia relied on him that much? Estelle's words about Jack's childhood stabbed at her heart. *God, what is the best way forward here?*

'Patricia, would you like to pray with me?'

She shook her head and stood, staring at her navy slip-on shoes. 'I'm tired. I'm going to take a pill from the doctor and go to sleep.'

Panic flashed through Eveline like lightning, tearing a hole in her memories and releasing ones she thought she'd laid to rest.

She sprang to her feet. 'Can—'

'Where did you put the packet?' Patricia asked, her head turning listlessly to glance around the room.

'In the medicine box,' Jack replied. 'Do you want me to bring you one up?'

She nodded and started towards the door.

'Patricia,' Eveline began.

She wiped the corners of her eyes. 'Jack will take over from here. I don't want to deal with any of it.'

They both left and Eveline's knees wobbled. She gripped the side of the chair.

God, that was a bit of a shock.

Taking a slow breath in through her nose, she pursed her lips and exhaled it for as long as she could. She repeated the cycle until the pounding in her head lessened.

I'll be alright. It just took me by surprise, that's all. What happened with Gracie seems like a lifetime ago, but then suddenly I'm right there again, as if it was yesterday.

At the sound of the door, her gaze snapped to meet Jack's as he entered the room. They spoke at once.

'Is she—'

'Are you—'

'—okay?' they said in unison, then both nodded.

Putting her notebook in her bag, she stood.

His eyes widened. 'You're going?'

Her heart raced. 'Yes, I have a long list of things to do this morning.'

'But—' He ran his hands through his damp hair. 'I don't know what the fuc—what the hell—' He huffed. 'I don't know what to do in this situation.'

She tried not to smile at his attempt not to swear. Most people didn't realise she saw the worst of people every day, as well as the best. Not much shocked or offended her anymore.

'There are lots of resources online,' she began, trying to keep her voice steady as she focused on closing her bag as slowly as possible.

'Could you—I mean, er... Would you mind...?'

Look at him! He's just a man! She dragged her gaze up his body to his face. Her lips parted, but only air came out. *Oh, but what a man...* The effect he'd had on her in the bar seemed to have multiplied over the past twelve months. Now she was aroused beyond belief and struck dumb as well.

His brow furrowed, his eyes pinched as if in pain. 'Eveline... I know it's a lot to ask, but would you be willing to help me? Help guide me through what I need to do?'

His plea lodged deep in her heart. Not being a priority to her family growing up meant helping others gave her life meaning and value. She would never say no to anyone. And right now, Jack seemed as lost as she'd been, many years ago.

She nodded. 'Yes, I will.'

He sagged with relief. 'I can't thank you enough.'

She held her bag to her chest like a life preserver. She needed to get outside into the fresh air, but in order to do this, she had to walk past him to the door. *Do not look to your right. You CANNOT climb out of the window!*

'When?' he asked.

'What?'

'Can you help? Are you free now?'

She stared blankly at him, whilst her brain displayed her diary for the day and her body attempted to tear it into pieces.

'Um, I have quite a lot on.'

'Can I walk with you back to the rectory, then? Maybe ask you a few questions on the way?'

Yes! She nodded. 'It would be a sensible use of that, er, interlude in my day.' *Interlude? Seriously, Eveline?*

His face broke into a dazzling smile. 'Interlude. I don't think I've ever used that word before.'

She needed to get out of the house before she combusted. 'Well,' she replied primly. 'There's a first time for everything.'

She froze as the smile stuck on his face. Memories of when he'd said those words to her a year ago crackled between them.

His gaze darkened, and a flush swept across his cheekbones.

She clutched her bag tighter against her chest.

He broke first. 'Give me a moment to grab a pair of socks,' he said, backing out of the room.

❦ 6 ❦

The October air was cold, but Jack welcomed it. Having Eveline so close kindled a fire inside him that burned brighter each moment he was with her. He needed to get his body and mind to chill the fuck out. *Now*.

She's a vicar. Nothing is going to happen. Nothing is EVER going to happen.

Eveline walked fast, and Jack matched his pace to hers. Since leaving the house, neither of them had spoken a word.

Come on! He cleared his throat. 'So you and Estelle are pretty close?'

'Yes, after I arrived in Foxbrooke, she turned up at the rectory with a tupperware of Chelsea buns and told me we were going to be friends.'

He smiled. 'Sounds like Estelle. I take it she didn't give you a choice in the matter?'

'Not in the slightest, but I really didn't mind. She's the most loyal and caring person I think I've ever met.'

'In a slightly scary, and extremely sweary way?'

Eveline glanced at him and grinned. The sight stabbed him in the heart and the groin.

'Estelle says God sent her to me as a test.'

'A test?'

'To see how much I can take.'

'Does it bother you when she swears?'

'Not in the slightest.' She paused. 'I'm saying this because you know her so well. God didn't send Estelle to me. He sent *me* to Estelle.'

Huh? 'Why?'

'To show her she can be loved unconditionally by someone who's not family. Sometimes I know she baits me on purpose to see if I'll push her away. It's like some sort of negative self-fulfilling prophecy of hers. But I never will.'

'I'm not a Foxbrooke, and I lo—like her.'

'You've known her all your life. You *are* family to her.'

'So, you think God wanted you and Estelle to meet and be friends?'

'Yes.'

'Do you think God has a plan for all of us?'

'I know he does.'

Jack's mind went back to the bar, and the mistake he made by approaching Eveline. The way her hand felt in his. The way his soul seemed to recognise hers, as if finally finding its way home.

He shook himself. 'I don't believe in God.'

'That's alright.' She smiled at him as if nothing he could ever say or do would dent her worldview. 'God still believes in you.'

Jack forced his gaze from the sunshine of Eveline's face to the grey clouds on the horizon. Where the fuck was God when his dad was battering him? And if God, fate, or the universe really *did* have a grand plan for Jack Newton, what on earth was Eveline's part in it? Was she some kind of test for him to fail?

I need a drink.

'Jack?' Her voice was tentative.

'Hmm?' He kept his attention on the road as they turned onto the high street.

'God can never guarantee a life free of pain and suffering. But he loves you.'

Jack resisted the urge to shake his head. *Great. Just great. I grew up hating myself. My parents didn't even seem to like me, but hey! No worries! Some nebulous being on a fluffy fucking cloud has got my back.*

They'd nearly reached the rectory, and he still hadn't asked her a single question about arrangements for his dad. He rubbed his forehead, needing a shot of whisky to take the headache away.

'You got any spare communion wine knocking about?' he asked.

'At home? Would you like some?'

He forced what he hoped was a charming smile. 'Best hangover cure is always hair of the dog.'

'I don't have any alcohol in the house, but I can offer you a couple of paracetamol. Would that do?' Her gaze was searching. It made him want to hide.

'Yeah sure, unless you've got meths under the sink?'

Her face went white.

'It's a joke!' *Rein it in. You're talking to a vicar, not Finn.* 'Sorry, ignore me. I was just being a dickhead.' He sighed. 'Look, I haven't asked you anything about the funeral. Could I help with your chores? Maybe ask my questions at the same time?'

He watched the blush of pink across her cheeks as she hesitated. She was sweeter than summer strawberries and, despite how hungover he felt, he wanted to eat her up. Their connection back in London had been the most intense experience of his life. And now, even knowing she was completely untouchable, it kept hitting him again and again.

'I, er, suppose so,' she said. 'Are you okay with pigs and vacuuming?'

'Together?'

She grinned. 'I'd like to see you try.'

He stood a little straighter. No matter what she asked of him, he was determined to be the best at it.

'Whatever you need, I'm your man.'

She stumbled on the cobbled path at the side of the rectory, and he grabbed her around the waist to stop her falling to the ground. For a split second, he felt the rise and fall of her chest against his arm, then let go and stepped back.

'Sorry—'

'No, I'm sorry,' she interrupted. 'I'm such a clumsy clot. Come into the kitchen.'

The back door was wooden and warped, with peeling paint. Eveline shoved it with her shoulder and it opened with a squeak of protest.

'Don't you lock it?'

'Only at night.' She led the way into the kitchen, put her bag on the table and swept a book under a newspaper. 'There's no point, really. I don't have anything worth stealing and some of my parishioners like to know they can drop by whenever they like.'

Jack didn't want to imagine what might happen if his clients knew where he lived. He was at one end of the privacy scale and Eveline at the other.

'Do you have a list of what you need to do?' he asked as she dashed around the room, piling up crockery and paper.

'Kind of. I'm sorry about the mess. I work quite a lot and don't have anyone to help with the domestic side of things.'

Jack could tell how embarrassed she was. 'Eveline.'

She froze at the sound of her name.

'Please let me help.'

Turning to face him, her face was etched with insecurity. He wanted to draw her into his arms and kiss away every line of worry.

'I want to help. I'll do anything you want.'

Her cheeks coloured to match her hair.

Jack tried to lighten the mood before his thickening cock became too obvious. 'Washing pigs, vacuuming their sty, cooking a ten-course meal for the Bishop, or writing next Sunday's sermon. Whatever you need.'

'Really?'

'Well, come to think of it, scrub the sermon idea unless I can get AI to do it.'

Her smile was hesitant. 'I'm not used to people offering to help. It's usually the other way around.'

I bet. 'Well, I was almost on my hands and knees in front of you earlier, begging you to—' *Shut up!* Vivid fantasies flashed through his mind and he willed his gaze not to drop to her skirt.

Eveline turned her back and fished her notebook out of her bag.

'There's a meeting in the church in a couple of hours that I need to set up for,' she began, her voice a breathy blur. 'And before that, I have to feed the pigs, pick the last of the flowers and arrange them in the church. Then do the dishes, vacuum downstairs, make a cake and answer emails. Also, I need to write to the Bishop, ring Foxbrooke Haven to discuss a project, and see if I can work out what's going on with the boiler.'

Holy shit. 'And does your to-do list ever get done?'

She gave him a rueful smile over her shoulder and shook

her head. 'It may only be me living here, but it's like Piccadilly Circus sometimes. People don't bother removing their shoes, so it gets dirty really easily.'

He went to take his off, and she shook her head.

'I'd rather you didn't, I don't know what people's feet have tracked in. Luckily, it's either flagstones or floorboards in most of the downstairs.' She chewed her lip, and he swallowed. 'If I show you the vacuum cleaner, could you start with that? I can dash and do the pigs and the flowers.'

Jack opened his arms. 'Your wish is my command.'

TEN MINUTES LATER, JACK CONSIDERED SENDING A VIDEO OF himself cleaning a threadbare rug to Cyrille. His French friend considered himself to be the ultimate arbiter of taste, and Eveline's vacuum cleaner would horrify him. It was a beige monstrosity, older and heavier than Finn, louder than Estelle, and only effective if run back and forward over the same spot several times. *What a piece of shit*. Jack knew how to clean, but why bother when you could pay someone else to do it?

Last week he'd been lounging on the balcony of his immaculate Monaco flat, a glass of Châteauneuf-du-Pape in his hand. Now, stripped down to a tight undershirt, he was breaking a sweat trying to clean a house where the layers of grime went back to the Georgian era.

The living room contained moth-eaten sofas, a couple of tatty armchairs, faded curtains, and scratched wooden furniture. On the walls hung cracked and dismal oil paintings of previous vicars. The rectory seemed frozen in time—the house of an old man from the nineteen-hundreds, not a beautiful young woman in the twenty-first century. Did vicars make *any* money? Whatever Eveline did earn, she didn't spend it in IKEA.

Over the roar of the vacuum, he heard a shout. He flicked it off and turned. Eveline was in the doorway, an enormous bunch of flowers in her arms.

'Beautiful,' he said without thinking.

She stared down. 'I agree. I plant throughout the year, so I've got flowers most months.'

'What are they?'

'The pink ones are nerines and sedums. These are dahlias, and these are chrysanthemums. And some pretty grasses.'

'Do you want me to put them in water for you?'

'Oh no, thank you. These are for the church. It's much cheaper for me to grow them than to buy them from the florist.'

'You don't save any for you?'

She stared blankly at him. 'Me?'

Fuck my life. 'Yes, *you*.'

'Why?'

'Because they're lovely to look at?' *Like you*.

She smiled. 'But I can see them in the garden and the church any time I like. Are you alright to keep going a bit whilst I pop these over the road?'

'As you wish.'

She blinked at the line from *The Princess Bride* and scurried out of the room.

JACK FINISHED VACUUMING AND WIPED HIS BROW. HE'D done his best, but his efforts had failed to transform the rectory into a place he wanted to spend any time in—unless Eveline was there.

Moving through the ground floor, he collected piles of dirty crockery and took them to the kitchen. By the amount, he wondered if Eveline also operated a café. As he lifted a chipped plate from the kitchen table, it knocked into a paper which slid off the book she'd hidden earlier. He read the back.

In the tiny picturesque village of Bluebell Bay, schoolteacher Daisy Spring is preparing for the most magical time of the year – Christmas. Her spare time is filled with rescuing hedgehogs, but her heart is set on one thing: saving an ancient wood from being transformed into a shopping centre by property developer Wolf Redwood. Wolf, however, is a scrooge who despises Christmas and is determined to bulldoze the wood, including the hedgehog sanctuary.

When Daisy sets out to convince Wolf to change his mind, she never expects to fall for him. But as the festive season approaches, the magic of Christmas begins to work its spell, and soon Daisy and Wolf find themselves drawn to each other, and to the wonder and joy of the season. 'Christmas Sparkles and Homely Hedgehogs at the Tiny Village School on Bluebell Bay' is a heartwarming love story that will have you believing in the magic of Christmas and the power of love.

Inside the flyleaf were Eveline's initials. So, this was the sort of book she liked to read? Jack puffed out his cheeks. Further proof that her happy ending did not lie with someone like him. He replaced it carefully under the newspaper and looked for the dishwasher.

There wasn't one.

Running his hands through his hair, he bit back a growl of frustration. Was this his life? *No, dickhead, it's Eveline's. Now get on and help her.*

He went to the huge and archaic sink in front of the window and wrenched open the copper tap. It made an ominous shriek before a thin trickle of water dribbled out into a stained plastic bowl.

Jesus Christ, this place is a dump. His mind returned to his chic apartment in Monaco overlooking the sparkling sea. But this time Eveline was there, standing on the balcony with the warm breeze catching the ends of her hair. Closing his eyes, he imagined standing behind her, running his fingers down the outside of her arms. Kissing her neck and making her shiver.

The rectory phone rang, jolting him back to a house in Somerset that was more museum than home. The noise was offensively loud, but before he could get to it, there was a beep and an answer phone message sounded.

'Hello, you've reached the rectory and Eveline Shaw. I'm not in right now, so please leave a message after the tone with your name and number and I'll call you back as soon as I can.'

The machine squealed, and the caller hung up.

Jack started on the dishes, staring blankly through the grimy window to a small area of lawn bordered by a yew hedge. In the middle was a rotary washing line, and to one side was a stand holding bird feeders. Birds fought and chattered as they pecked at the seeds and fat balls, oblivious to him.

'Oh my goodness, thank you so much!' Eveline entered the kitchen, her eyes flicking to the paper, which was hiding her book. She pulled a face. 'I can't help but feel incredibly guilty about you doing all of this.'

Seriously? He smiled. 'Please don't. It's the least I can do. And anyway,' he nodded towards the birds, 'I'm watching a nature documentary. It's very relaxing.'

The tension left her face. 'They're pretty feisty. I've added as many feeders as the stand can hold, but they'll still fight each other, even though there's plenty to go around.'

Like most humans... He glanced at the clock on the wall. 'We've still got time to do more of your list. If you give me a recipe and show me where the ingredients are, I can make a cake. I think it's safer that I bake than answer your emails and write to the Bishop.'

Eveline laughed. 'True, but you're taking the credit for it.'

'Are you saying that in case I burn it?'

'Definitely. I have a reputation that I do not intend to

tarnish.'

Jack's hands froze in the soapy water. His dirty little secret wouldn't just tarnish her reputation if it got out, it would destroy it.

As he finished the dishes, Eveline bustled around the kitchen, putting everything he needed on the worktop.

'I want to make a Victoria sponge for a meeting with the Parish Council. They're always more amenable to my radical plans if they're eating homemade cake.'

'Radical plans?'

'Oh yes, haven't you heard? I'm absolutely scandalous.'

You wanna bet? 'Really? What are you trying to get past them?'

'I want to include vegetables in some of the town's flower beds as a project with children from Foxbrooke Primary School. They could pick and eat them next summer when they're grown.'

'That's radical?'

'Oh yes.' She sighed. 'Trying to get anything done differently around here can be rather challenging.'

Of course. All the older, small-minded people like his father. People with nothing better to do with their time than ensure the world existed exactly as it did in the eighteen-fifties.

'Eveline. I've been meaning to ask. Has my mother apologised for assaulting you yesterday?'

'It wasn't really an assault. But yes, she has. This morning before you, er, appeared.'

'Half-naked?'

Jack had made it his job to read women's bodies, but Eveline's emotions were telegraphed so loudly even a child could work out the gist of what she was thinking. Her face flushed, and she turned for the door.

'I'm just going to get my laptop so I can work here with you.'

Jack gazed at her shapely form as she departed, then hung his head and stared at the soap suds.

Don't flirt. Don't lead her on. Keep it in your pants.

It was one thing to tell himself that, but his dick hadn't received the memo. It was currently behaving like an eager-to-please puppy, desperate to play.

Eveline returned with a laptop that was almost as large as a briefcase, sat at the table, and lifted the lid.

'I've got an Aga, so you don't need to preheat the oven.' She eyed him as he measured the flour. 'Have you done much baking before?'

'Not for years, but I used to do a lot as a kid. Well, I did it when my dad was out of the house. He didn't approve of boys baking.'

There were lots of things his father didn't approve of him doing: crying, showing emotion, art, cooking, dancing. All were signs that Jack was veering dangerously off a masculine path.

Eveline cleared her throat. 'Estelle told me Nigel was physically abusive to you.'

He stilled. Hot anger scratched at the inside of his skin. He never got the chance to fight back, to tell his father to his face just what he thought of him.

'I'm not saying that to start a conversation about it,' she continued. 'I know how painful it can be to talk about difficult memories and experiences. It just felt disingenuous not to mention that Estelle had told me.'

Jack nodded, continuing to measure out ingredients.

After a few seconds of silence, he heard her tapping on the keyboard.

Eveline's fingers flew across the keys, but her mind whirled faster. Her life was always busy, but even when things weren't going her way, she generally had a handle on the situation. Now, her thoughts were scattered like snow in a globe and she was waiting for everything to settle.

Each time she thought she had control of her reaction to Jack, one smile, one considered gesture, would shake her up all over again. Her parishioners weren't thoughtless people, but they expected far more from her than her elderly—and male—predecessor. The women of the parish had cooked and cleaned for him for free. However, they hadn't extended the same favours to her when she took on the post. It was simply unconscious bias. They assumed, as a woman, she already knew how to do everything and therefore didn't need any help.

But working sixty or more hours a week and without a partner to help shoulder the burden, keeping up the house and garden was an impossible task. She sneaked a glance at Jack as he carefully smoothed the top of each sponge layer. He was painfully handsome. Just the sight of him did funny things to her insides, and when he showed kindness, her heart melted.

He surveyed the ancient Aga stove, one hand on his jaw. 'Which oven should I use?'

She stood. 'The top one, but be careful with the handle, as it can get hot. Have you ever cooked with an Aga before?'

He shook his head. 'I can't remember the last time I used *any* oven.'

'Do you eat mostly salad in France?'

Opening the door, he slotted the tins inside. 'No, I always eat out.'

'What, every *day*?'

He shrugged, picking at the chipped enamel of the ancient stove with his fingernail. 'I guess I don't like washing up.'

She set the timer for the cake. 'Well, you've managed to overcome your aversion this morning.'

He lifted the wooden spoon and silicone spatula, covered in cake batter.

'There are always more creative ways to clean up,' he said, holding them out to her with a smile.

'What, er... Do you want me to do with them?' she asked, knowing full well what his unsaid question really was.

'When you bake, what do you do with these before you take them to the sink?'

The answer suddenly felt far too indecent to vocalise. There was no way she was going to say the word 'lick'. She swallowed and shrugged, her heart thumping in her chest.

'Don't you want to taste it?'

I really want to taste you.

'In case I've mixed up sugar and salt and poisoned the parish council?'

His words and his expression may have been bland, but Eveline felt as if she'd just drunk a bottle of Tabasco.

She fluttered her hand at the utensils. 'It's the cook's prerogative to, erm, pre-clean them.'

'Pre-clean?'

She nodded.

He passed the wooden spoon to her. 'One each.'

She took it. This was a moment which Estelle would have handled with aplomb. Her friend would have licked the spoon with such sexiness that whoever was watching would be reduced to a puddle.

She, however, was not Estelle. Spinning around with the pretext of looking at her notebook, she stuck the whole spoon in her mouth, sucking the batter off. The combination of butter and sugar made her want to moan.

'Very good,' she said, keeping her gaze averted as she took it to the sink.

'Bloody hell—I mean, that's delicious,' Jack said behind her. 'Makes me remember I haven't had breakfast yet.'

She turned. 'Oh, sorry. I didn't think.'

'It's not your fault I overslept.'

'Yes, but I should have noticed.' Taking the spatula from him, she put it in the sink. 'Please, let me get you something.'

'I'm fine. Really.'

But *she* wasn't. Jack had been so kind and helpful, and she wanted to do something for him. *You just want to show off...* Ignoring her thoughts, Eveline took a blue and white striped pinny from the back of the door and tied it over her dress.

'Bacon sandwich?'

He paused. 'Your favourite food.'

He remembered. She nodded. 'I know it's immodest to say so, but they really are the best.'

His hand covered his flat stomach as it gurgled. 'Excuse me.'

She grinned. 'I think your tummy just accepted my offer.'

'Are you *sure* you have time?'

'Yes, thanks to you, I do. Please sit and I'll make it for you.'

He ignored her and took the dirty mixing bowl to the sink. 'I'll deal with these first. Have you got any more washing-up liquid?'

Huh? Confused, she glanced at the empty bottle. It had been nearly full an hour ago.

'You used *all* of it?'

'Yeah… I wanted to do a good job, and the water didn't seem hot enough.'

'Oh, yes. The boiler's on the blink again.' She went to the draining rack. The pile of crockery was glistening with soap. 'Jack… Did you rinse these?'

'Did I need to?'

She lifted a china cup. 'Oh dear.'

He sighed. 'I'll redo them.'

Biting her tongue, she removed the metal pan scourer from the back of the sink, taking it to the other side of the kitchen.

'Don't I need that?' he asked.

Embarrassed heat moved across her face. 'It's best not to use that with the crockery.'

'Why not?'

'Um, well, unfortunately you've removed most of the pattern.'

'What?' He picked up a cup. 'Fuck! Eveline, I'll replace them.'

'It's okay, honestly. If you're not used to washing up, then you weren't to know.'

'Where did you get them from?'

Opening a cupboard, she brought out an unopened bottle of dish soap. 'They came with the house.'

He huffed. 'So, they're antique.'

'They're *old*. They're too chipped to be of any real value, I'm sure.'

'I'll make this right.'

'It's fine. If you could just rinse what you washed earlier and use the soft cloth from now on, then we're all good.'

Jack hung his head. 'So, I've wasted a bottle of washing-up liquid, failed to rinse anything, ruined your antique crockery, and now you're making me a bacon sandwich? That hardly seems fair.'

'Would it make you feel better if I also made one for myself?'

'Yes.'

Her heart pitter-pattered in her chest. 'As you wish.'

EVELINE WATCHED IN ANTICIPATION, HER MOUTH WATERING as Jack took his first bite.

God, I know I'm overflowing with pride right now, and I have to admit it, also quite a lot of lust, with a side-order of gluttony. But making this for Jack has made me so very happy.

His eyes fluttered closed, and he made a noise of appreciation that caused her thighs to squeeze together.

Thank you, God.

Jack chewed with such a look of dreamy satisfaction on his face that Eveline wished her phone was to hand so she could take a picture. He swallowed and opened his eyes. If she didn't already know that he wasn't a believer, she would have thought he'd just found God.

'This is indeed the best bacon sandwich in the world. Thank you.'

She couldn't stop her smile from spreading across her face, even if she tried. 'You like it?'

'It is...' He paused. 'Inconceivable.'

Eveline pressed her lips together to stop a squeal from escaping at yet another *Princess Bride* quote.

'Well, I've used the best quality components, perfect timing, and a secret ingredient.'

'Is the bacon yours?'

'Yes. You're eating Priscilla.'

He didn't immediately reply, and she ran her words back through an innuendo filter. *Oh no…*

'Priscilla?'

'I name all my pigs. I like to thank them before I, er, eat them,' she replied, her face heating.

'Ah. Well, she is very…'

'The bread is made by Henry's girlfriend, Libby,' she interrupted. 'It's sourdough. And the butter comes from Jersey cows and is biodynamic.'

He cleared his throat. 'And what's the secret ingredient?'

Love. For the umpteenth time that day, Eveline felt the heat rising in her face. She tried to do everything in her life with love, but to articulate that word in relation to Jack seemed too raw and intimate.

'I put my good intentions into it.'

He nodded. 'Well, it worked. This is truly the ultimate meal.' He gestured to her plate. 'Are you going to eat yours?'

Her stomach was filled with butterflies caught in a cyclone, but she still managed a bite. Had she ever felt such happiness, excitement, and nerves all at the same time? In all her prayers asking for a Wolf Redwood-style hero, none of her imaginings had conjured up a man like Jack. It wasn't just how attractive he was, or the way their souls already seemed to know each other. It was how interesting he was to her. He'd changed his life so completely from when he was an abused child. Now he spoke another language, lived abroad, and had a super glamorous job planning parties for the jet set.

Jack finished his sandwich and took a gulp of tea.

'Eveline...'

Her heart rate rose. 'Hmm?'

His hands reached towards hers, then sharply withdrew to his lap.

'I want to apologise for my behaviour in London a year ago.'

Oh...

He sat up straighter, his expression serious. 'I was meeting a woman for the first time, and thought you were her.'

She'd guessed as much, but didn't know how to reply.

'I can't really explain why I called myself Jasper.' His gaze slid away to the floor. 'Sometimes I hide behind that name.'

Eveline thought of what she knew about his childhood. How unhappy he must have been. How he must have wished he was somewhere and someone else.

'It's okay,' she replied. 'I understand.'

He huffed out a bitter laugh and shook his head.

'No, Jack, I do. I know how it feels to wish you were a different person.'

His eyes found hers. For a second, he looked so anguished it was like a spear to her heart. Then he hid the emotion away.

'How did your date go?' she asked, trying to appear cool.

He picked up his mug and stared into it. 'As expected.'

'Is she your... Your girlfriend now?'

He huffed out another empty laugh. 'No. I don't have a girlfriend.'

She swallowed and bit the inside of her cheek to keep her excitement at bay. *He doesn't have a girlfriend!* But what should she do now? How should she act? *God, what's the right way forward? What should I say?*

She jumped at the bang of the front door and Jack looked up.

'Something smells good!' Simon called through. 'You must have known I'd drop by.'

Jack's brow furrowed. 'He doesn't knock?'

Eveline pulled a face and lifted a shoulder in a half shrug. 'Most people don't.'

'And is the kettle on?' Simon's voice was getting louder.

She stood as Simon entered. Jack stayed seated, lounging back in his chair.

Simon's cheeriness disappeared, to be replaced with confusion.

'Hi Simon,' said Jack.

'What are *you* doing here?' Simon asked, his gaze travelling to the mugs of tea and crumb-covered plates on the table.

'Jack and I were about to discuss funeral arrangements for Nigel,' Eveline said, trying to appear at ease when she was anything but.

Simon ignored her, his attention still on Jack. 'Why aren't you with Patricia? She can't be left on her own.'

Jack's body language was relaxed and open, but it seemed to Eveline that he had the readiness of a tiger preparing to pounce.

'My mother,' he replied, his tone placid. 'Is sleeping. She's asked me to deal with everything, so I am.'

'Humph.' Simon turned to her. 'Could you rustle me up a bacon sandwich, dear? I'm rather peckish.'

'I—' she began.

'No, she can't,' Jack interrupted. 'I'm afraid I've eaten the last of the bread, and Priscilla.'

Eveline fled to the kettle. 'Can I make you a cup of tea, Simon?'

The timer for the cake went off.

'What's in the oven?' he asked.

Opening the door, she transferred the cakes to cooling

racks. 'It's for the Parish Council meeting,' she replied, glancing at Simon over her shoulder. 'But I've got biscuits you can have.'

Simon leaned into Jack's personal space and reached for the tin. 'Have you replaced the custard creams that Lady Foxbrooke took?'

Irritation flared inside her. If Simon liked them so much, then why on earth didn't he bring a packet with him? She glanced at Jack. A muscle was twitching in his jaw.

'Unfortunately, not yet. I might have time after Evensong, although I'd planned to visit Foxbrooke Haven.'

'You can drop by the Co-op on the way,' he replied, selecting a biscuit. 'Kill two birds with one stone. I'll accompany you and pay Mother a visit.' He hung his Barbour jacket over the back of the chair in between hers and Jack's, and sat, his corduroy-clad legs spread. 'How did your "exciting date" go last night?' he continued, his eyes flicking to Jack's as if wanting a reaction.

Eveline tensed, her fingers gripping the kettle handle as water dribbled in from the tap. She'd forgotten all about Leslie. Stalling, she set the kettle down and switched it on, keeping her back to the table and popping a fresh tea bag in a mug.

'It was very pleasant, thank you.'

There was another 'humph' from Simon behind her. 'Are you going to be seeing him again?'

No. She squeezed her eyes tightly shut. She couldn't lie, but equally, she didn't want to tell Simon how disappointing it was. Or somehow reveal that she was thinking about Jack almost the whole time.

The kettle came to the boil, and she filled Simon's mug.

'I'm sure that I'll see him again at Christian events in the future,' she managed. 'But as friends.'

'Good,' said Simon emphatically. 'He wasn't right for you.'

And how would you know? She added milk to the mug.

'And *Leslie?*' he continued. 'What a ridiculous name for a man.'

Eveline turned with a jerk, tea spilling over her hand. 'How do you know his name?'

Simon gave a stiff shrug. 'I bumped into him at the end of the night and we had a little chat.'

'*Bumped* into him?' Jack asked, his expression scathing.

Simon ignored him.

Placing his drink on the table, Eveline went to the sink to rinse her hand. 'Simon?'

He sighed loudly. 'I'm just looking out for you, dear. I have your best interests at heart.'

She took a breath. 'Si—'

The juddering squeak of the back door opening interrupted her.

'Only me,' a voice called out before a woman in her mid-seventies entered the room. 'Is that cake? Oh, hello Simon.' She smiled at Jack and extended her arm. 'Beryl Pope. I'm one of Eveline's flock. Who are you?'

Jack stood and took her hand, a polite smile on his face. 'Jack Newton.'

Beryl frowned. Eveline could almost hear the cogs whirring.

'Beryl—' she began.

'Nigel's boy!' she cried, her eyebrows lifting before crashing back down. 'Oh, my dear child, I'm so terribly sorry for your loss. How is your mother doing? I'd like to visit, but I don't want to overstep.'

'She's not great,' he replied. 'I'm sure she would appreciate the company.'

Beryl nodded. 'I'll visit later. Would you like a cup of tea?' She gave his hand a squeeze in both of hers, then dropped it and bustled past Eveline to the kettle. 'Looks like it's just boiled. Oh, look at that cake. Is that for the Parish Council meeting? Do you think they'd notice if a slice was missing?'

Eveline bit back a scream. 'Beryl, Simon, I was in the middle of discussing Nigel's funeral arrangements with Jack.'

'But don't you need to set up for your "special" meeting in ten minutes?' Beryl asked.

Oh, for goodness sake! Her use of actual air quotes just drew even more attention to it.

'Can I help?' Jack asked.

'Well—' Eveline began.

'Don't you have to assist your mother with her eyedrops?' Simon interrupted.

'Oh, yes, her second cataract op,' said Beryl. 'How did it go? How many weeks before she's allowed to drive?'

Jack glanced at the clock. He looked stressed to the point of snapping. 'I—I need to go.'

Eveline stepped forward and touched his arm. 'I'll see you out.'

He followed her into the corridor and she shut the kitchen door behind them.

'I'm so sorry,' she whispered. 'We didn't get a chance to talk about anything to do with the funeral.'

He shrugged, his face tired and strained. 'Can I come back when you next have a moment?'

'Yes, of course.' She bit her lip as she mentally scanned through her overly full diary. 'Can I text you?'

They reached the front door, and he passed her his phone. 'If you put your number in, I'll send you a message so you've got my contact details.'

She put hers in and handed it back.

He tapped on the screen, then put it in his back pocket. 'Done.'

They stared at each other in the silence of the dark hallway.

'Thank you—' she began.

He stepped back and opened the door, breaking the moment.

'I'll see you soon.' He gave her a brief nod, then left.

❈ 8 ❈

Jack: This is my number.

Eveline: Thank you for everything you did to help today and sorry about the interruptions. I'll look at my diary as soon as I can and let you know the next time I'm free.

Jack: No worries. And thank you.

Eveline: I know it's late, so I hope this doesn't disturb you. Tomorrow is a bit of a busy day, but I'm free between six and seven-thirty in the morning. Does that work?

Eveline: Sorry, it is a little early for most people. I keep forgetting as I've usually been up an hour or so by then.

Jack: Just got message been pub with Finn. Lock-in. Half two now sorry. Need sleep. Sorry.

Eveline: I'm sending this after matins (morning service) as I didn't want to reply earlier and wake you up. I hope you had a lovely time with Finn and a restful sleep. Tomorrow I am free: 06:00-07:30, 11:00-12:30, 15:00-16:00. Do any of those times suit?

Jack: Good morning and sorry for my text last night. I'm afraid I don't remember sending it. I have an appointment with the undertakers tomorrow at eleven, and Mum wants me to take her food shopping in the afternoon. What's your diary looking like for the day after tomorrow?

Eveline: I must apologise that I'm not giving you many options. Especially as I promised to help. I'm in Wells at the moment, waiting to see the Bishop. I've got a few minutes, so I'll send you some useful links regarding the legalities of registering a death and what else you might need to think about.

Jack: It's okay, I've manned up and am Googling. I should have done that in the first place and not hassled you to hold my hand through this.

Eveline: It's my job and I like helping people.

Jack: I don't want to be yet another person taking advantage of your good nature.

Eveline: You're not. I promise. How's your mum doing?

Jack: Not great. She stays in bed most of the time. I don't think she knows what to do with herself.

Eveline: That's understandable. I hope I'm not overstepping by saying this, but your father did seem to take the lead in their relationship.

Jack: Say what you like. He was a terrible human.

Eveline: Got to go. Will msg ltr.

Jack held his breath to stop his hand shaking as he positioned the tiny bottle over his mum's eye. After Henry and Connor had left the pub last night, he'd carried on drinking with Finn, intent on obliterating all thoughts of Eveline from his mind.

'What are you doing?' his mother snapped.

Fucked if I know. 'Sorry, Mum, I'm feeling a bit worse-for-wear.'

'Are you going to go out drinking every night?'

If only. 'No, I just haven't seen my friends for a long time.'

'And whose fault is that?'

He didn't reply, but squeezed the bottle, sending a drop splashing onto her eyeball. *Thank you, God.* Repressing a sudden smile at the irony of his thoughts, he moved to her other eye. *You can do this.* The drop hit its mark, and he resisted the urge to fist pump.

His phone buzzed with a call from his jeans pocket, and he pulled it out.

Eveline Shaw.

Jack stared at the screen. He was desperate to talk to her, but to put one foot on that irresistible path would send at least one of them to a living hell.

'Who is it?'

'The vicar.'

'Well, answer it then. Don't be rude.'

He hesitated.

His mother took the phone from him, accepting the call. 'Eveline, it's Patricia.'

Jack couldn't hear what Eveline was saying, but his mother was nodding, her eyes filling with tears.

'Thank you. Yes, it has been very hard,' she said, the snippiness leaving her voice.

He passed her a box of tissues and left the room.

Eveline: I'm sorry I missed you earlier when I rang from the car, but it was good to speak to your mum. The day after tomorrow I have moved some appointments around and am free 13:00-16:00.

Jack: You're not free 06:00-07:30 anymore?

Eveline: I presumed that time was too early. Would you like to come then?

Jack: One will be fine. You don't want to see what I look like at six in the morning.

Eveline: As you wish.

JACK'S THUMBS ITCHED TO REPLY. BY USING THE LINE FROM the *Princess Bride*, Eveline was, in her own sweet way, flirting with him. It would be so easy to reciprocate. When they'd met a year ago, his attraction to her had been instant and powerful enough to have haunted and taunted him ever since. But he couldn't. She didn't belong with anyone like him, and he sure as shit didn't belong in Foxbrooke.

He sat at the kitchen table with a notebook where he'd carefully written down everything he had to do. He'd struggled at school and felt like it always took him twice as long to do anything as everyone else. The slower pace of writing helped order things in his mind, and using block capitals made the scrawl of his handwriting more legible.

'Jack?' His mother was calling from upstairs.

He found her in his father's bedroom, sitting on the side of the neatly made bed. As far back as he could remember, his parents had never shared a bedroom. His dad said it was to protect his mum from his snoring, but Jack had never heard him.

'I found your father's will.' She held out a cardboard folder. 'Can you deal with it?'

'Sure. Is it complicated?' He took it from her. 'I just presumed everything would go to you?'

She nodded. 'Mostly, but there is something you need to speak to Eveline about.'

'Eveline?'

'It's a bequest for the church. When are you next seeing her?'

'The day after tomorrow.'

'Okay.'

He turned for the door.

'Jack?'

'Yes?'

'How long are you staying for?'

Panic prickled inside him. 'I don't know. I'll stay for as long as you can't drive and need to put the eyedrops in. Why?'

His mother was staring into the middle distance, her hands folded in her lap.

'What am I going to do now your father's gone?'

⁂

Eveline: I know you're due here at one today, but I wondered if you might be able to come over a little earlier?

Jack: Yes, of course. Is everything okay?

Eveline: Absolutely fine, I could just use a little help to move some furniture in the church. I'm sorry to have to ask.

Jack: I'll be there in fifteen.

IT WAS ANOTHER GREY AND CHILLY DAY, BUT THE CLOUDS were high and there was little chance of rain. Jack left his jacket behind and strode briskly away from the house. It had been three days since he'd seen Eveline and his legs wanted to run towards her. No matter how he attempted to deny or rationalise his feelings, he was buzzing at the thought of seeing her.

His footsteps slowed as he approached Saint Saviour's church. The previous vicar had the appearance and charm of a tombstone, and had been there since the dark ages. Despite being thin and of average height, he loomed like a thundercloud, as if perpetually waiting for an excuse to unleash God's wrath. As kids, Jack and his sister had been terrified of him.

Entering the church, Jack spotted Eveline's bright red hair, and it banished the stormy memories. She glanced up and her smile brought out sunshine in his heart.

Then he noticed the sling.

He strode up the aisle towards her. 'What happened?'

She looked at her arm, as if surprised to see bandages.

'Oh, this?'

What the fuck? 'Yes, *that*. Are you okay?'

There were dark circles under her eyes and she was paler than he remembered.

'Yes, yes, I'm absolutely fine.' She smiled. 'It's just an inconvenience, that's all.'

Eveline appeared to be in the process of moving chairs into the small space between the altar and pews.

'What happened?' he repeated.

'The silly pigs got out again. They're clever and boisterous, and now they're also big and strong.' She rolled her eyes. 'Anyway, when I was getting them back into their pen, I fell. Honestly, the sling is overkill, but the doctor in A&E insisted I wear it for a week or so. It's just a few cuts and bruises and a minor separation of my AC joint.'

'*What?*'

'There's really no reason to look so horrified. Honestly. It's just a light sprain and a few little stitches.'

She grabbed the back of a chair with one hand and began dragging it across the floor.

'Eveline!' Jack rushed forward, taking it from her. 'Jesus Christ!' *Fuck!* 'I mean, holy—' He broke off and gritted his teeth to stop further expletives spewing forth.

She touched his arm. 'I'm fine. I promise.'

He took a ragged breath as he stared at her. 'Eveline.'

She withdrew her hand. 'Ye-es?'

'Please tell me what to do with these chairs and sit down. You look... Are you tired?'

Something in her upbeat expression faltered, like a glitch in her perfect matrix. She glanced around as if about to impart a great secret that she didn't want anyone else to hear.

'I am a little, er, less chipper than normal.'

His heart cracked. *Chipper?* Did she *ever* put herself first?

He sighed. 'Please order me about from a seated position. I currently have one hundred per cent more functioning arms than you.'

Eveline hesitated, then sat on the first pew, looking uncomfortable, as if she shouldn't be there.

'Right, I take it these should be in some sort of circle?'

'Yes. Making it work is tricky, but the hall isn't suitable as the roof is leaking too much.'

Jack pulled chairs from a pile. 'Is this for the Parish Council?'

'No, it's our regular AA meeting.'

'And you always set it up?'

'Usually, yes, if Kieran can't get here in time.'

'And afterwards?'

'They put everything back.'

Jack assessed the space between the rows of pews and the stone altar.

'It's not that big.'

Eveline screwed up her nose. 'I know. That's why I've been trying to get rid of these.' She indicated the pews. 'If we could replace them with chairs, then we could do so much more with the space.'

'But...?'

'People are very attached to them.' She gave him a rueful smile. 'Some of the most vociferous opposition has come from people in the community who don't even attend church. They may want them to stay, but unless I can find more ways to bring in people and money, this place is going to be luxury flats or a London banker's second home within ten years.'

Jack took in the large interior, filled with rows of dark wood pews. He remembered how uncomfortable they were, and how imprisoned he felt when stuck in the middle. As a child, the church had a dwindling population. Nowadays, even with the most heavily attended wedding, he couldn't imagine all of the pews being filled.

'The ridiculous thing is,' Eveline continued, 'is that when this church was built, it didn't even *have* seats. People were expected to stand.' She gestured to the stone recesses that ran along the side walls. 'If you were elderly or infirm, then you sat there.'

'Do you need funds to buy new chairs?'

'Yes, but not a huge amount. Finn said he would buy the pews from me and re-sell them.'

'Did you know my dad left a bequest in his will to the church?'

She shook her head.

'It's only a few grand, but mum said I should decide with you what to spend it on. I want to spend it on getting rid of these.'

'Jack, we can't.'

'Why not?'

'Your father was fairly vocal in his opposition to my idea.'

'So?'

She gave him a look. 'I can't take his money and spend it on something he was vio—*extremely* opposed to. And besides, it's not as simple as that. I need the approval of the Bishop, English Heritage, and my parishioners.'

'And how's that going?'

'The Bishop is onside, and Simon is helping me canvas support from the congregation. Unfortunately, the Dowager Duchess is against my plans and has a great deal of weight in the community.'

'Can't Stelle talk her around?'

'Estelle's grandmother is ten times fiercer than her, so unfortunately no. Although if English Heritage approves the plans, then that will swing it, no matter how many locals disagree. I've got a meeting with them in a couple of weeks.'

Jack looked up as the main door to the church opened, and a man in his thirties entered. Dressed in jeans and a leather jacket, one ear had multiple piercings, and a tattoo extended up the side of his neck. He was good-looking, but his face had the lines of a man who'd partied hard in the past.

Who the fuck is this?

Eveline stood as he approached and held out her good arm. 'Kieran!'

'Hey, sweetheart, what happened to your arm?' he said, carefully hugging her.

The sight of another man being so physically familiar with Eveline unleashed a raging, green-eyed monster that Jack didn't know he had. As it clawed its way up into his chest, he tried to relax his stance.

'Oh, 'tis but a scratch,' she said to Kieran.

'A mere flesh wound?'

And now they're quoting The Holy Grail? Kieran had just pushed Simon to second place on Jack's shit list. *Get a grip!*

Eveline laughed. 'Kieran, this is Jack. He, er...' Her smile disappeared. 'I'm helping him with arrangements for his father's funeral.'

Kieran's face fell, and he extended his hand. 'Mate, I'm sorry.'

Jack shook it.

'And Jack, this is Kieran, a good friend who runs the AA meetings here.'

Jack nodded, not knowing what to say without it coming out as a feral growl. He'd never been possessive over a woman before, and Eveline was as far away from being *his* woman as Mother Teresa. *You're losing your mind.*

'Well, it's all set up now, so we'll leave you to it?' Eveline said to Kieran.

'Yeah, sure,' he replied. 'I'll make sure we put everything away after so you don't have to.'

'Thank you.'

Jack was itching to leave, feeling seconds away from shapeshifting into a bear and carrying Eveline back to his den. He had an overwhelming urge to protect and look after her.

She glanced at his face and blinked, as if seeing the battle raging inside.

'Okay then,' she said brightly. 'Let's go back to the rectory for a cup of tea.'

‰ *9* ‰

'**G**od, Eveline, don't do that!'
She was moving towards the stubborn back door of the rectory as if to shoulder it open.

Her forehead furrowed as she glanced at him. 'But this is my good side.'

Jack held a hand to his head to stop his internal volcano from venting. 'Eveline. The action still involves the rest of your body. Please, let me.'

She stepped back, a little smile on her face.

He depressed the handle and pushed.

It didn't budge.

'Is it locked?'

Despite how tired she seemed, her smile was cheeky. 'No...'

He gave it a hard shove. Nothing. How knackered *was* this thing?

'Apart from brute force, am I missing a trick?'

She nodded. 'You have to kick the bottom corner with your foot at the same time. To be fair, it's not usually this bad.

We've just had a lot of rain over the last couple of days and easterly winds, so it's swelled more than normal.'

Jack glanced at the bottom edge, where a patch of paint was missing. Eveline was going to open this despite one arm being completely immobile?

Frustration formed into a point of fury. Throwing his shoulder at the door, he gave it a boot. It flew open, crashing against the inside wall. The force caused a picture to jump off its hook to the floor with a smash.

'Fuck's sake!' He sighed. 'Eveline, I'm sorry. Stay there. I'll pick up the glass.'

'I can help,' she said, moving up behind him.

Turning, he straightened, blocking her path. She stared at him, her eyes wide, her pupils dilating, colour filling her pale cheeks. She was so close he could feel her breath on his lips. Desire roared through him, with panicked helplessness following on behind. He didn't want to feel this way about her. It wasn't just an overwhelming physical attraction. It was a primal need to take care of her and return some of the love she spilled out to everyone with no apparent thought of herself.

Her gaze flicked to his lips. 'Jack...'

Fuck! She wanted to kiss him as much as he wanted to kiss her. He dug his nails into his palms, summoning every last whisper of self-control and praying she wouldn't have the courage to make the first move.

Stepping back, he hardened his expression. 'You've already been to A&E once today. I don't want to be the cause of a second visit. Please, let me do this.'

'Oh, yes, sorry,' she stammered breathlessly. 'I'm not trying to be difficult. I'm, er...'

Fuck! Don't be an arsehole.

'Eveline, it's not you. You're per—it's not you, okay?' He ran his hand through his hair. 'I'm sorry. For smashing your picture and for being a twa—tool. You're far too nice for your own good and I don't want to see you hurt.' *Most of all by me...*

She nodded.

He turned away before he reached for her and crouched to pick up the glass. Jesus stared out at him from the frame, his hand raised as if to bless whoever looked upon him, his gaze filled with compassion.

Jack shook his head. *Don't look at me, mate. I'm beyond saving.*

ONCE HE'D PICKED UP THE SHARDS OF GLASS, EVELINE handed him a newspaper, and he wrapped the pieces carefully before putting everything in the bin. The kitchen was a mess, piled high with unwashed dishes.

'I'm so sorry about this,' she fretted. 'Quite a few people have popped by over the last couple of days and I haven't had a chance to clear up properly.'

Jack rolled up his sleeves and went to the sink, running his finger under the tap as he waited for the water to warm up. Had none of these people she'd entertained seen her arm and offered to help?

'Oh no, that won't work,' she said. 'The boiler's gone. I've been using the kettle if I want hot water.'

He turned off the tap, feeling like his head was about to explode. 'Since when?'

'Yesterday?'

'You haven't had any hot water since yesterday?'

'No, but the shower upstairs is electric, so I can still wash.'

'Heating?'

She shook her head. 'The Aga runs on oil, so the kitchen is warm enough. At night I have a hot water bottle.'

He gripped the edge of the cracked porcelain sink and hung his head as the birds chattered noisily outside. In his mind, he remembered his Monaco apartment with the white leather sofas and paintings he'd done from his balcony. Everything was beautiful there. And everything worked. He imagined opening the bathroom door. Inside, Eveline was lounging in a hot bubble bath and holding a glass of champagne, her vibrant hair piled up on the top of her head. She lifted a hand and blew him a bubbly kiss.

'Jack?'

He straightened, turning to face her. She was so beautiful it made his chest hurt.

'Have you rung a plumber?' he asked.

'Yes, but they can't come until Monday.'

'Monday? What about twenty-four-hour call out?'

Her gaze fell away. 'It's too expensive.'

He pulled out his phone.

'What are you doing?'

'Getting you a plumber.'

'But I can't afford one.'

'I'm paying.'

Her hand fluttered to her chest and her eyes widened. 'You can't do that!'

'Why not?'

'Because, er...' She glanced around the room as if hoping to land on the perfect excuse.

'Eveline, when was the last time someone did something for you that made your life better?'

Her mouth opened and closed, but no sound came out.

There was a loud banging on the back door.

'Are you in?' Estelle yelled from outside. 'It's me, your BFF.'

Jack strode out of the kitchen before Eveline and yanked open the back door.

'Hey Jack!' Estelle said, before pausing at his expression. 'What the fuck's happened now? Is Eveline okay?'

'Yeah, she's dandy. Just a fucked-up arm, no hot water or heating, and no help from any of the leeching wankers who seem to use this place as a free café.'

Estelle held up her hands. 'Woah! And am I one of these "leeching wankers"?'

He deflated. 'Sorry, Stelle. No, not you.'

She looked over his shoulder at Eveline. 'What have you done? Why didn't you ring me?'

'I didn't want you to worry.'

Estelle pushed past him. 'And your boiler's gone? Did you ring Finn?'

Eveline shook her head. 'I didn't want to disturb his weekend.'

'What the fuck? Look, come and stay with me in the livery. Or if you need to be close to the church, stay at the Manor. As long as you don't count my family, everything's functional there.'

Eveline went back towards the kitchen. 'I'll be fine here.'

'See?' Jack said to Estelle as they followed her.

Entering the room, he watched Estelle take in the dirty mugs and plates. He caught her eye and mouthed *'leaching wankers'* at her.

She rolled her eyes in return and turned to Eveline. 'Love, please sit down. Jack's got his sleeves rolled up, which means he's either going to fight or do the dishes. He's not going to try to punch me 'cos he knows I'd deck him, so let him wash up and you can tell me what you've done to your arm.'

Estelle sat Eveline down, and Jack put the kettle on. As soon as it had boiled, he started carefully dealing with the piles of dishes and listened to the two women chatting. He grinned as Estelle sounded off. She was indignant that Eveline hadn't called her, and more vocally pissy than he'd been about the lack of support she'd got from her congregation.

'I take it my parents don't yet know?' Estelle asked.

Jack looked over his shoulder to see Eveline shaking her head.

'Thought not. You know they'd be over here like a shot trying to help.'

'Please Estelle, I'll be fine.'

Jack could see Eveline's lower lip beginning to wobble. *Oh fuck*.

Estelle leapt out of her chair and carefully hugged her.

'I'm sorry, sweetheart. Are we haranguing you? It's only because we love you. Well, I love you. I can't speak for Jack. He's only known you a few days. But hey! Love at first sight and all that?'

Eveline's gaze flicked to his, and he turned with a jolt back to the dishes, his heart hammering. *Love?* He wasn't going to go there.

'Oh, don't blush, you big ninny,' said Estelle. 'It's only Jack. Anyway, as soon as we're done here, I'm going to ring Finn and get him to come and look at your boiler. And I won't hear another word about it. Okay?'

Silence.

'Excellent', Estelle continued. 'Now, I came here to have a bitch and whine with my bestie, but now Jack's here. I can kill two birds with one stone.'

Huh? He turned and raised an eyebrow.

'I need your help,' Estelle said to him.

'*My* help? Doing what?'

'How long do you have to keep putting those eye drops in for your mum?'

'Another two to four weeks? Why?'

'Well, that'll take us up to the Manor's Winter Ball. I wanted to ask if you could take over the organisation of it.'

'*Me?*'

'Yeah, I'm up to my ears in this funding application for the music and arts festival I'm trying to put on next summer. There's a big events company interested in footing the bill, but they need so much information before they commit. I can't deal with that *and* finish organising the Ball.'

'What about Henry?'

'He's snowed under with the über boring shit of estate admin and stopping Dad from fucking everything up again. Plus, he's not exactly Mr Party-Pants.'

'And I *am*?'

'Duh, doofus! It's your actual *job*. I take it you're not doing much party planning at the moment for the Côte d'Azur elite?'

Jack shook his head, ice-cold panic running through his veins.

Estelle held up her hands. 'Well then, win-win. You get to help your best friend out and have something to do other than being at the beck and call of "Victorian Mum".'

'Estelle,' Eveline said. 'Patricia's just lost her husband.'

Estelle pulled a face. 'Soz, Jack.'

How could he get out of this? He didn't have the first clue how to organise a party. Could he ask Cyrille?

'I'd love to,' he began. 'But I need a quiet space to work and I won't get that at Mum's.'

'You can work here,' said Eveline, quickly. 'There are plenty of rooms in the rectory that never get used. And I have wi-fi.'

He stared at her, his brain stuttering to a halt.

'There we go,' said Estelle. 'Problem solved. And Brucie-bonus, you can keep an eye on all the uninvited freeloaders who barge in here without knocking.'

'Estelle!' Eveline cried.

'Oh, come on. It's fucking rude, and you know it.'

Jack stared at the dark circles under Eveline's eyes, the sling around her arm. He thought about everything the rectory needed doing to it. Simple jobs that just required someone with time or money to get them done. But could he be around Eveline and resist the magnetic pull between them?

He ignored his own question. 'Okay.'

Eveline's cheeks pinked and her mouth opened.

'Okay, what?' Estelle asked.

He swallowed, his heart pounding against his ribs. 'I'll work from here. And organise the Winter Ball.'

Jack glanced at his watch, straightened his jacket, and knocked. It was a quarter to nine on Monday morning and he felt like a salesman making his first ever call.

Eveline opened the front door of the rectory with a smile. 'Good morning, Jack. How are you doing?'

Outside the radiance of her face, his peripheral vision picked up the black and white of her clerical top and dog collar. *See that? Vicar, remember?*

'Fine, thanks. How's your arm?'

Her smile flickered, then reappeared, shining brighter than ever. 'Can't complain. Come in out of the cold. The weather's really turned.'

Jack followed her down the hall, her hair lighting up the dark space as she chattered.

'Finn got the boiler going yesterday, so I've managed to get the chill out of the drawing room for you. You know, you don't need to knock or come in the front. Feel free to come and go as you please.'

She pushed open a wooden door and let him into another

fusty room. The lined wallpaper was peeling, and the furniture was old and tired. A wooden desk sat under the window and a bunch of flowers stood on top.

'Is it okay?' she asked.

Jack's chest felt too tight to breathe. Eveline would never pick flowers for herself, but she'd done it for him. And judging by the divots in the rug, the desk used to stand in a different place.

He glanced at her arm and she blushed.

'I asked Finn to move it,' she said quickly. 'I promise I've been careful.'

He cleared his throat. 'Thank you.'

'This is the wi-fi password,' she said, passing him a piece of paper. 'I've got to dash to Foxbrooke Primary School for morning assembly, but I'll be back around half-ten. Help yourself to anything you need.'

He nodded.

'Okay then, see you later.' She backed out of the room, stroking her palms over the sides of her skirt as if to make sure it was in the right place.

As the sound of the front door shutting echoed down the corridor, Jack let out a breath and slumped into the nearest armchair. *Now what?*

He'd messaged Cyrille asking to chat, but his French friend hadn't got back to him. Even though it was still early, he rang his number.

'Putain! I just got in!'

Jack smiled. 'Partying hard on a Sunday night, were you?'

'You know me. Sleep is for babies or the dead. You good?'

'I need a bit of advice.'

'From moi? About what, my petit putain?'

Jack rubbed his hand over his face. 'My friends think my job is, 'er, what you do. They want me to help organise a big party and I've only got three weeks to do it.'

Cyrille hooted with laughter. 'You are a funny man, Jack. Very funny. Where?'

'Foxbrooke Manor.'

'Ooh la la... Can I come?'

'Would you behave?'

'I'm offended you would even ask such a thing. Of course I would not.'

Jack grinned. 'Then I'm afraid to say it's a big fat "non".'

'Pah! English pig dog! Your mother was a hamster and your father smelt of elderberries!'

He snorted. 'Once again, I regret showing you *The Holy Grail.*'

Cyrille giggled. 'I fart in your general direction!'

Jack rolled his eyes. 'Yes, yes, are you going to help me or not?'

There was a theatrical sigh on the other end of the line. 'Only because I have a soft spot for you, mon petit putain.'

J ACK SCRAWLED NOTES AS C YRILLE TALKED, THEN LET HIS friend go when there were more yawns than words coming down the line. Putting down his pad and pen, he went to the kitchen. Even though Eveline had said there was no alcohol in the house, he still searched the cupboards. He needed something to take the edge off after Cyrille's crash course in party-planning.

Coming up empty, Jack checked the time—not long before Eveline was due back. He did the dishes, careful to do a good job, then took a couple of rashers of bacon from the fridge. When was the last time anyone had cooked for her?

The smell of sizzling bacon was percolating through the air

and making his stomach growl when the front door banged open. He smiled to himself. *Perfect timing.*

'Only me!' Simon called out. 'Looks like I've timed this perfectly. Ha ha ha!'

Jack tightened his grip on the spatula and eyed the bread knife with longing.

'Can't believe I missed out last week,' Simon continued, his voice coming closer. 'Well, that won't be happening again any time soon—' He stopped dead as he entered the kitchen. 'What on earth are *you* doing here?'

'I'm working out of the drawing room for a few weeks,' Jack replied, carefully turning the rashers of bacon.

'Then you're going back to France?'

His hand stilled, then he nodded.

'Well, you can't just help yourself to the vicar's food like that.'

'I'm not. I'm making it for Eveline.' Jack started buttering two pieces of bread. 'I thought it might be a helpful thing to do.'

'What do you mean?'

'With her injury?'

'Oh—oh yes. Of course.'

'And also, because it seems all she does is look after other people. I wondered when was the last time that someone had looked after *her*.'

Simon's red cheeks inflated and his eyeballs protruded until he resembled an annoyed pufferfish. Was this how Jack's father had gone? In a fit of self-righteous indignation?

'Now, steady on, boy,' Simon began.

Boy?

'I'm back!' Eveline called. 'Something smells delicious. I'm so glad you helped yourself.'

Jack continued to stare at Simon, throwing back the

daggers that were coming his way and adding some of his own for the return journey.

'I hope you got on okay with the wi-fi. It can be—oh...' Entering the kitchen, Eveline glanced between him and Simon.

Jack smiled. 'I was making this for you, not me. Are you hungry?'

She swallowed, her unbandaged hand moving reflexively to her stomach, then away. 'Er...' She looked at Simon.

No way are you eating this, you fucker. Jack stared at Simon, willing him to do the right thing.

Simon moved to the kettle. 'Why don't you sit down and eat?' he said to her. 'How about I make you a cup of tea?'

Eveline's eyes widened. Jack pulled out a chair, and she sat on the edge, her back straight, as if tensed to leap up at any moment. He finished making the sandwich and placed it in front of her.

By the sink, Simon was struggling to turn on the tap.

Jack wandered over. 'First time?' he asked, wrenching it open. 'It is a bit old and stiff.'

'Shouldn't you be with Patricia?' Simon replied, hovering near boiling point.

Jack glanced at the clock, then addressed Eveline. 'Mum's due her eyedrops in twenty minutes so I'm going to pop home now. I can come back later.'

She nodded. The sandwich was in her hand, but she'd yet to take a bite.

'Aren't you going to try it?'

Blushing, she took a mouthful. Fierce pride rushed through him as her eyelids briefly closed. She gave him a thumbs up as she chewed, then swallowed and smiled.

'Thank you, Jack. This is perfect. You can make me one of these again.'

He grinned back. 'As you wish.'

An intimate moment of silence stretched between them before he broke it. He gave Simon a terse nod and left.

BACK HOME, HIS MOTHER WAS IN BED. JACK HAD MOVED THE TV to her room, and she appeared to be using it as visual sedation. She'd started with daytime shows about antiques, but had regressed to the other end of the age spectrum and was currently watching CBeebies.

'Children's television wasn't like this when you were young,' she said, her voice empty.

Jack didn't know what to say, so stood by the bed, watching it with her for a few minutes. The screen was filled with colour, joy, and love. Three things that had been in short supply when he and his sister were growing up.

'Do you think Betsy watches this?' she asked.

Jack knew she did but didn't want to rub salt in the wound by telling his mother about all the times he'd flown to the UK only to visit his sister.

'Probably? Why don't you give them a ring and ask?'

Patricia stared at the house phone by her bed, then at the door, as if expecting her husband to come through it and tell her not to call them. She changed the channel to a rerun of a detective show from the seventies. 'Are you going back to the rectory?'

'I was planning to. If you're okay with that?'

She nodded. 'Will you do the eulogy?'

Jack's heart sank. He'd expected this, but it was still the last thing he wanted to do at the funeral. He'd much rather hide at the back, get wasted, then piss over his father's grave. That, or simply not show up at all.

'Yes. Is there anything you want me to say? I don't know much about Dad's childhood.'

She shrugged and changed the channel again, landing on a cookery show.

'Not now.'

He hesitated, wanting to leave, but not sure if he should.

'I'm fine, Jack.' She sighed. 'You can go.'

OUTSIDE THE RECTORY, JACK INSPECTED THE BACK DOOR. IT was clear how much it had swelled in the wet weather. He took a few photos and sent them to Finn.

Jack: Could you replace this door? It's at the rectory and is almost impossible to open and close now.

Finn: Yeah, I saw it yesterday. Eveline said she couldn't afford it.

Jack: I'm going to pay.

Finn: Er…

Jack: Can you do it, or not?

Finn: Course I can. Is she okay with you doing that?

Jack: It can be instead of paying rent for the room I'm using as an office.

Finn: Let me know when she agrees and I'll come and measure up.

Jack: Will do. You don't need to give me mates rates, but if she asks, say you did.

Finn: You want me to fleece you, then lie to a vicar?

Jack: Or you could actually give me mates rates.

Finn: Nah. First option is more fun.

Jack went to the front of the house and knocked on the door. Eveline opened it, an apron over her clothes.

'You don't have to knock,' she said. Her hair was tied back in a bun, and there was a smudge of blue paint across one cheek.

'It's your house, not a one-stop shop or day-care centre.'

'It does feel like that a lot of the time.'

'And that's why I knock.'

'Thank you, Jack. Come on through. Is your mum okay?'

A terse sigh escaped him. 'She's depressed.'

Eveline paused, her face creased with concern. 'That's understandable. I must find time to visit in the next couple of days. Have you spoken to her about the service?'

He cleared his throat. 'She asked if I could do the eulogy.'

'How do you feel about that?'

'I'm sure you can imagine.'

Her hand raised towards his arm, then she dropped it.

'I don't know the first thing about him,' he said. 'Nothing about his childhood, or before they had me.'

'Are there any old photos? It would be lovely to have a display of them at the funeral.'

'Thanks, I'll ask mum later.' He gazed at her cheek. 'What are you painting?'

'Oh dear, do I have some on me?' Turning to a picture on the wall, she squinted at herself in the glass.

'Just a little.'

She shrugged. 'I'll deal with it later. At the moment, I'm doing a self-portrait.'

Jack tried to hide his shock. He couldn't imagine Eveline having the time, nor putting attention onto herself.

'I'm learning to paint,' she continued. 'And I have to be able to do faces, so I'm practising on the one I have available to me at any time.'

'You could always paint from a photo?'

Her nose wrinkled. 'Yes, I could. Although it feels a little unkind.'

'Unkind?'

'Yes. So far, my paintings are a little, er, *offensive* to the eye.'

'You could choose someone who's dead? I don't think they'd mind.'

'But I would. I'd still feel I was mocking them in some way.'

Jack shook his head as he smiled. 'Why do you need to do faces?'

Hers fell. 'I got carried away and suggested a project for Foxbrooke Haven, the assisted living facility in the village.'

'The old folks' home?'

Eveline winced. 'I'm not sure we should use that term, even though most of the residents do.'

'And your project?'

She brightened. 'I want to do a mural of everyone there and their memories of Foxbrooke.'

'That sounds, erm, *ambitious*?'

'Unfortunately, yes. I'd hoped to involve the art department at Foxbrooke Secondary, but it hasn't happened yet. The residents are very keen on the project, but aren't particularly artistic. So I'm learning how to paint so I can take the lead.'

'Because you've got so much free time on your hands.'

She blushed. 'I said I would do it, so I will. Only it's far more challenging than I anticipated.'

'How are you learning?'

'YouTube tutorials.'

'May I see?'

She hesitated, then huffed out a short laugh. 'Of course. But please don't say it's good, as I know it's not.'

Eveline led him into the living room, where a large piece of paper had been sellotaped to the wall next to a mirror. Her laptop lay open to one side, next to a dining plate covered in blobs of paint.

Jack stared at the painting, trying to compose his expression as well as his thoughts. He wondered if—with a little more coordination—Betsy could have produced a more flattering portrait of Eveline. The eyes were too close together, and the nose was off to one side. Her lips appeared as if she'd been too enthusiastic with fillers, and she'd failed to give herself enough of a forehead.

'Um... It's got late Picasso influences,' he finally managed.

She snorted, then burst into peals of laughter. 'I told you it was bad.'

'The greatest of artists didn't start off good. It's all about practice.'

'You're too kind, but unfortunately, I don't have a lifetime. I promised them a mural by Christmas.'

'*Christmas?* Seriously?'

Her smile faded, and she nodded.

'Okay, the thing to remember is that faces are based, more-or-less, on symmetry. If you get the basics in place, then you can start to add detail. Have you got paper and a pencil?'

She picked up a sketch pad from a table, along with a pencil, and handed them to him.

'Can I show you what I mean?' he asked.

'Yes, please.'

Eveline stood beside him and he bit the inside of his cheek to counter the thrum of awareness running through his body.

'Okay, so I'm going to draw an oval, which is the basic face shape.' He ran the pencil across the page in confident movements. 'Now, we bisect the oval vertically and horizontally. We always think the eyes are further up in the head, but they're actually about halfway down.'

She moved closer. 'Oh, I see.'

Warmth emanated from her, as if she was touching him. Blood roared through his veins, heading south at the speed of sound.

He stepped back. 'Look, why don't you sit down, and I'll do a quick sketch of you. It won't take long, and then you can see how it all fits together.'

Glancing around, she seemed unsure. 'Where should I sit?'

He brought a chair to the window. 'Natural light and facing north. This is perfect.'

She carefully sat. 'What do you want me to do?'

'Nothing. Just get comfortable.' He smiled. 'You can look at me, or over my shoulder. Wherever feels right.'

She gazed straight at him and his heart jumped in his chest.

Focus! Turning the page, he took a breath. His father may have beaten art out of him by the time he finished primary school, but when he left Foxbrooke Secondary and the UK, he started again. Art didn't turn out to be his job, but it was his refuge.

As the pencil skated across the page, Jack let his eyes, hand and brain work as one. He could lose himself for hours when he sketched or painted, but now, drawing Eveline, he reached a new plane of awareness. It was as if everything that had gone before was simply preparation for this moment, when his talent could do justice to the beauty of the woman before him.

His heart thudded rhythmically in his chest, beating out time as his hand danced over the paper. *Don't think about how long it might take, or what she might think of it. Just keep going.*

The phone rang loudly, and he jumped, the pencil skittering.

Eveline looked as shocked as he felt, blinking rapidly, then went to answer it.

'Hello, this is the rectory. Eveline Shaw speaking.'

Jack turned to the table, finding a rubber and carefully removing the scrawl he'd just made, as Eveline spoke to one of her parishioners about the Remembrance Service from the day before.

She finished the call. 'Jack, I'm so sorry, I didn't realise the time. I have to go to another meeting.'

'That's fine, no worries. I got a bit carried away. Sorry.'

'Don't apologise. It was very ...' Her cheeks pinked. 'Can I see it?'

His face heating, he passed her the sketch pad.

Her eyes widened and her mouth dropped open. 'Oh, Jack!'

Thrusting his hands in his pockets, he shrugged like an embarrassed schoolboy being praised in front of his friends.

'It's beautiful!'

'*You're* beautiful,' he mumbled. 'I just drew what I saw.'

Her nose wrinkled at the compliment. 'But you're gifted! I've never seen anything this amazing before!'

'You've seen a mirror, haven't you?'

'Fiddlesticks. You're incredibly talented.'

'*Fiddlesticks?*' He grinned, attempting to deflect her praise. 'Who even *says* that?'

She drew herself up. '*I* do.'

They stared at each other. The mood shifted. He stepped back.

'Jack?'

'Hmm?'

'Do you think you might be able to help us out with the mural over the next few weeks? I know it's a lot to ask with everything else you've got to do, so please say no if you don't have time.'

He paused. 'I'll do it under one condition.'

She gazed nervously at him. 'What?'

'You let me buy you a new back door.'

❧ 11 ❧

'Can you please explain to me again how a condition of you helping me is that you help me some more?' Eveline asked Jack as they walked briskly through the town towards Foxbrooke Haven the next day.

A biting wind whipped around them.

'And are you sure you're not cold?' She peered at him. Even with the tan, he looked pale. 'Do you want to wear my bobble hat? I really don't need it. I've got plenty of layers on.'

Jack smiled. 'Which question do you want me to answer first?'

'Do you want my hat?'

He shook his head. 'I'm good, thanks.'

His shoulders were hunched, and his hands buried inside his jacket pockets.

'You look like you're freezing.'

He gave a shiver. 'I'm used to the south of France. Is it much further?'

Stopping, she unwound her long red scarf and held it out. 'Please, Jack. The collar of my coat comes up to my chin.'

His gaze flicked to the scarf, but he still shook his head.

'Well, I'm afraid it is a condition of us going any further that you wear it.'

He gave her a look. 'I thought *I* was the one with all the conditions?'

She grinned. 'You are, and obstinacy and hypothermia are two of them.'

Before he could reply, she wound the scarf around the back of his head with her unbandaged hand. Suddenly, he was close. *Very* close. She stared at the flecks of gold in his irises, surrounding the fathomless black of his pupils.

Breaking her gaze, he moved away, then gestured up the street. 'This way?'

Flustered, she nodded and set off, noticing he'd increased the distance between them.

God, you've sent Jack to me twice now, and the connection we have is beyond anything I could ever have dreamt possible. He told me he doesn't have a girlfriend, and I believe him. So why does he keep withdrawing? I really don't think I'm being arrogant or immodest to say he likes me. What am I doing wrong?

It might have been helpful to have had this conversation with Estelle. However, Estelle was one of Jack's oldest friends, and Eveline didn't feel comfortable bringing up this subject. The previous year, when Estelle had finally turned up at the bar, Eveline didn't tell her about the mysterious Jasper. Now she was glad she hadn't. It would have been even more awkward for Jack if his friends knew he'd given her a false name and mistaken her for another woman.

FOXBROOKE HAVEN LAY ON THE OUTSIDE OF THE VILLAGE, set back from the road in a couple of acres of gardens. The main building had been built in the eighteen-hundreds for a wealthy family in the wool trade. It housed the communal areas and the residents who needed the most care.

Dotted around the property were more modern buildings, containing self-contained flats for those with more independence.

'Simon's mother, Gladys, lives in the main house,' Eveline told him as they approached. 'We'll pop to the office first so I can introduce you to Erica. She's the manager.'

She entered the code for the building and led Jack inside, unbuttoning her coat as the hot and stuffy air hit her.

Jack unwound her scarf from his neck. 'Now, this is a temperature I can get behind.'

'More like the south of France?'

He scrunched his nose. 'If you remove the smell of bleach and boiled cabbage.'

'You get used to it. Erica's office is this way.'

After Eveline knocked on a door further down the corridor, a smiling woman in her fifties opened it and ushered them into a room.

'Ooh, and who might this handsome stranger be?' She gave Jack a blatant once over and extended her arm. 'Erica Conway. Are you looking to move in? You're a bit young, but I know our staff won't mind. In fact, they'll be queuing up to offer you a bed bath.'

'Erica!'

Jack laughed and shook Erica's hand. 'I'm Jack, a friend of Eveline's. She's roped me into helping with the mural.'

'Are you an artist?'

'Well, not—'

'Yes, he is,' Eveline interrupted. 'He's incredible.'

'Alrighty then,' said Erica. 'I'll take you through to the lounge and show you where it's going to be.'

The social hub of Foxbrooke Haven consisted of three

rooms that had been knocked through into a much larger one. The lounge overlooked the garden, and one end wall had been cleared of pictures and painted white.

'This is our blank canvas,' Erica said. 'We've been given paints and brushes by a local company but didn't want to start without a plan or direction from someone who knew what they were doing.'

'Acrylics?' Jack asked.

Erica looked blankly at him.

'The paints,' he added.

'They're in tubes. That's as far as my knowledge goes.'

'Eveline told me the plan was to paint the residents and staff, and some of their memories of Foxbrooke?'

'Yes, although...' She lowered her voice slightly. 'Not *everyone* is keen.' Erica's gaze flicked to a chair halfway down the room, where Gladys Little was sitting. She was clutching a magazine in her arthritic hands and watching them as if they were about to steal the family silver. Eveline smiled at her and waved, determined to treat even the most challenging people with compassion.

'Is that Simon Little's mother?' Jack asked Erica.

Her eyes widened. 'Yes! It is, do you know her?'

The corners of his mouth twitched. 'No, but I know Simon, and there's a strong family resemblance.'

Erica's eyes were sparkling. 'Hmm,' she said, non-committally. 'So then, Jack, what's your plan for this and how can we help? It would be amazing if we could get it done by Christmas.'

Nodding, he stood back a couple of feet, taking in the space.

'The first thing is for me to meet everyone who wants to be involved,' he said. 'Once I know how many faces we're dealing with, and what landmarks or events they want in the picture, I can sketch a scale drawing for your approval.'

He's so amazing! Thank you, God!

'Once that's been signed off, I'll transfer the sketch to the wall,' Jack continued. 'Big areas can be blocked out with base colours, such as the sky, buildings, clothes and so on. After that, I can outline everything. That way, people can paint-by-numbers if they don't feel confident or go to town if they do.'

Erica appeared to be champing at the bit to grapple Jack into a thank you hug. Instead, she threw her arms around Eveline, squeezing tightly.

'This is so exciting! Thank you, Jack!'

He smiled at her. 'I haven't done anything yet.'

'Oh, but I know it will be fabulous. You've got the hands of an artist.'

'I do?'

Erica let go of Eveline to take Jack's hands. Jealousy stabbed at Eveline's stomach.

'Yes,' Erica continued, running her fingers over his skin as if she were a palm reader, getting a feel for his future. 'I bet you can do incredible things with these.'

His cheeks flushed. 'Er...'

Erica glanced up and cackled. 'I didn't mean like that.' She turned to Eveline and winked. 'Although...'

Feeling far too hot, Eveline pulled Erica away from Jack. 'Behave!'

Erica playfully slapped her arm and did a terrible *Austin Powers* impression. 'Oh behave!'

'Yeah, baby!' Jack replied with a grin.

Erica snorted with laughter and high fived him.

A loud throat clearing drew their attention. Gladys was staring daggers and shaking her magazine at them.

'This is supposed to be a quiet time,' she rasped.

'Sorry, Gladys,' said Erica. 'We'll keep it down. But don't forget the tea dance is in a bit.'

Gladys gave a loud harrumph and peered back at the papers in her hand.

'Right-o,' whispered Erica. 'I'm going to round up the residents who've expressed an interest in the mural and put the word out that we've got a handsome young artist in to help us. That should swell the numbers.'

Eveline rolled her eyes.

'Oh, come on, Eveline,' Erica said, squeezing her arm. 'You know men are in very short supply around here, especially ones under seventy.' She turned to Jack. 'And if you think I'm a flirt, wait till some of our more feisty ladies get a load of you...'

As the room filled up and Erica introduced more people to Jack, Eveline hung back, watching him. She knew it took a certain skill to draw people out, and Jack seemed to possess it in spades. He was a natural with the women, maintaining eye contact, listening attentively, and encouraging them to share their stories. Soon he was surrounded, but appeared to take it in his stride.

A handsome older man entered the room and stood just inside the door, his hand resting on a cane. Eveline hadn't seen him before. A new arrival?

Approaching, she held out her hand. 'Hello, I'm Eveline Shaw, the vicar at Saint Saviour's.'

The man transferred the cane to his other hand so he could shake hers. 'Robert Lang. I arrived a few weeks ago.'

'Oh, I haven't seen you around. Are you settling in okay?'

He gave her a smile. 'Everyone is very friendly. I'm just not used to this kind of *environment*.'

There was a cackle from the women clustered around Jack.

'The noise, or the amount of people?' Eveline asked.

Robert's cheeks flushed. 'Well, I haven't spent a lot of time around women. I'm not really sure how to talk to them.'

She tried to hide her surprise. 'You're talking quite successfully to me?'

His smile broadened. 'Ah, but you're a *vicar*. I'm safe with you.'

Is this why Jack keeps pulling back?

'The ladies here aren't scary, I promise.'

As if on cue, one of the women leaned back in her chair, striking a pose. 'Paint me like one of your French girls, Jack!' she cried, setting off shrieks of laughter from the other women.

Robert glanced at Eveline and raised an eyebrow.

She swallowed her smile. 'So, if you don't mind me asking, how come you haven't spent much time around women?'

He shrugged. 'I studied chemical engineering at university and there were only a couple of women on our course. They were in hot demand, and I'd come from an all-boys boarding school, so wasn't terribly confident.' His gaze travelled to Jack, and hers followed. 'Unlike him.' Robert smiled. 'He's naturally charming.'

Eveline nodded, remembering London, and when Jack had turned that charm up a few notches. A rush of pleasure fizzed through her, and she took a sharp breath.

'Anyway,' Robert continued. 'After university, I went to work on the installation of big chemical plants all over the world. They were always in pretty remote areas and the construction staff were men. Occasionally we might have a lady on site, but they kept themselves to themselves.'

Eveline watched Robert staring at Jack and his adoring

crowd. The older man seemed wistful, as if contemplating a road he'd never travelled.

'So, you decided to retire here?'

Robert nodded, his gaze falling to Shirley, one of the loudest residents at Foxbrooke Haven. 'I put off retirement for as long as I could, but when I injured my leg in an industrial accident, I had to go. I grew up nearby and thought this place might be a pleasant place to live.'

'And have you got to know any of the ladies? They're really very nice.'

'I'm afraid I'm quite shy.' He let out a small sigh. 'It's not so much that I've lost my touch. Rather, I never had one in the first place.'

'Do you want me to introduce you to some of them?'

Shirley turned her head and smiled over at them.

Robert took a step back. 'Not right now,' he said quickly. 'The thought makes me feel a little panicked, to be honest.'

'That's okay, I understand,' Eveline replied. 'I remember the first time I had to deliver a sermon. There were only four people in the congregation, and two of them were praying so hard they were snoring.'

Robert laughed, his whole face lighting up.

'I was so nervous my hands were shaking,' she continued.

'Did you need a fortifying nip of the communion wine?'

'That might have worked, but I gave up drinking a few years before. So I just asked God for strength and got on with it. The first time is always the most difficult, but now I think I could deliver a sermon in my sleep.'

'Okay, ladies and gentlemen,' Erica called out. 'It's time to dust off your dancing shoes and get ready to rumba. Shirley, Doris, Ada and Enid, please allow Jack to leave Foxbrooke Haven unmolested, or... you might persuade him to stay for a waltz?'

'I call first dibs!' Shirley cried, pulling Jack to his feet.

Eveline caught his eye, and he smiled at her. It was so unrestrained and free that her hand flew to her chest as if to stop her heart from flying out. It was like the first time they met and her soul recognised his. He smiled at her as if there was nothing and nobody between them, and they were one being in two separate bodies.

Erica started the music. 'Come on, everyone, pair up. Robert! Fancy a turn around the room?'

He shook his head, holding his cane up as if it excused him.

'You could always dance with me if you like?' Eveline said.

'I wouldn't know where to start. Actually, I'm feeling a little tired. I think I'll head back to my flat for a rest. Lovely to meet you, Eveline.'

'And you too, Robert.'

She watched him go. *Please God, I'm asking if you could give Robert a little more confidence. He seems like such a lovely man, and I think he could be so happy here.*

Turning back to the room, Eveline smiled as she watched Jack and Shirley dance. He'd clearly had lessons at some point as he matched Shirley step for step. When the number finished, Shirley was elbowed out of the way by another woman who stepped with enthusiasm into Jack's arms.

Eveline edged around the room to where Erica stood.

'Where *did* you find him?' Erica asked. 'And can we keep him?'

She laughed. 'He grew up here, but now lives in the south of France.'

'Explains the tan. Is he here on holiday?'

'No. His father died last week, so he's sorting out the funeral, then staying a few more weeks to support his mother and help organise the Manor's Winter Ball.'

'I'm sorry to hear that. Are you sure he's got time to help us out?'

'I think so. He's very good, so he'll be far quicker than you or I.'

'Well, I appreciate you finding him for us.'

The two women lapsed into silence as they watched the couples dancing. Jack was the only man, and every few minutes when the songs changed, a different woman grabbed him.

When he'd danced with every lady present, Shirley took his hand, but this time dragged him over to where she and Erica were standing.

'Eveline, you need to dance with Jack,' she said.

'Me?'

'Oh yes,' agreed Erica. 'Good idea, Shirley.'

Eveline caught Jack's eye. He looked wary.

She lifted the arm that was in a sling. 'I can't.'

'You've still got both feet,' Shirley replied. She turned to Jack. 'You'll dance with Eveline, won't you?'

He hesitated, then nodded. 'It would be my pleasure.'

The way he said "pleasure" sent a shiver running through her. Was it safe to dance with him? *What's the worst that can happen? You drool?*

He bowed deeply and held out his hand. 'Eveline, may I have this dance?'

She swallowed.

'Yes, she will,' Erica said, pushing her towards him. She pressed the remote for the stereo system. 'Let me just find something a little slower.'

Eveline placed her hand in Jack's and he drew it forward and placed it on his shoulder, then carefully held her, making sure he wasn't touching her injured arm.

'Okay?' he asked.

She nodded, memories from the bar in London flooding

through her. A slow melody played, and he moved them into the room.

'I don't know any steps,' she whispered.

'You don't need to,' he murmured. 'Just listen and feel.'

Holding his gaze, Eveline let herself slip into a world where there were just the two of them, getting closer and closer until they merged into one. She wasn't aware of the music, nor the other couples swaying next to them. All she felt was the fire of Jack's touch and her own deep longing to join her body with his.

How would it feel to kiss him? As if reading her mind, his eyes flicked to her mouth. She sucked in a breath, then ran the tip of her tongue across her lips. His own were parted, his breath coming quicker, as his hands tensed around her waist.

There was a desperate ache of desire between her legs, an urge to feel his body pressed hard against hers. The flecks of gold in his irises seemed to shine even brighter, as his gaze grew darker and more heated. *Please... Please...*

A loud throat-clearing made her jump. Eveline turned to see Gladys staring at them with gimlet eyes, her face pinched as though she'd been sucking a lemon dipped in battery acid.

A jolt of guilt and hurt shot through her, followed by a quick appraisal of her actions since arriving at Foxbrooke Haven. *Had* she been inappropriate with Jack?

She glanced at him. For a nanosecond, she could see the tension in his jaw. Then it relaxed, and he smiled. He raised an eyebrow and a nervous thrill ran through her. Before she could ask what he was thinking, he whirled her into the centre of the room. Holding her tightly, he dipped her, his lips so close to hers that his face became blurry.

Then, before she could take a breath, she was righted, and Jack stepped back, giving another bow as people clapped and cheered.

Eveline acknowledged everyone with a brief nod, then dashed to Erica, her cheeks on fire.

'So, shall I leave Jack to sort out the mural?'

Erica grinned and leaned closer. 'I don't think the mural is the only thing he's going to be sorting out between now and Christmas...'

❧ 12 ❧

Eveline wound her scarf around Jack's neck as they left Foxbrooke Haven. The soft fabric caressed his skin, and he imagined her fingers doing the same. Despite how many times he lectured himself to stay away from her, his body overruled his mind. Now, his fingers twitched, desperate to bridge the gap between them and take her hand.

When was the last time he'd held a woman's hand in public? Ten years ago? *Fuck*. Was it really that long? Since then, sex had been contractual, and neither his clients, nor him, wanted to be seen touching each other intimately in public. Behind closed doors, however, it was a different matter...

But now, breathing in Eveline's scent from the scarf, he wanted to hold her hand. To discover everything about her, then kiss her until he forgot who he was and what his life had become.

'Tell me about your family,' he began. 'Where were you brought up? Do you have any siblings?'

She hesitated. 'I was born in Shropshire. My father, Peter, is in the motor trade and lives in Kent. My mother, Diana, lives in Germany with her second husband, Hugh, who's in the army. I have two half-sisters. Eleanor is twenty and studying medicine in Munich. Abigail is twenty-two and studying to be a lawyer in The Hague.'

Eveline's words were stilted, as if this was a script she was used to presenting. Jack tried to fit this new information into his picture of her. He didn't know how old she was, but it must have been a disruption to have a stepfather and two younger siblings arrive when you were old enough to remember it.

'I'm thirty-five,' she said, as if her age was a distasteful piece of information she needed to divulge before he enquired.

Five years older than me. A woman's age didn't bother him. All his clients were older than him, and most by at least two decades.

'Did you grow up in the UK or Germany?'

'Mainly in the UK. I was eleven when Hugh married my mum and it was easier for me to go to boarding school. The holidays were split between them in Germany, my father in Kent, and one set of grandparents in Shropshire.'

Despite Eveline's smile, her tone was becoming increasingly brittle. Jack's own childhood had been awful, but at least he had the continuity of people and place. He tried to imagine how hard it must have been being shunted from pillar to post like a parcel that nobody really wanted. Maybe he was wrong? Maybe she *had* been happy?

'Do you see them much? Your parents and sisters?'

Another pause. Another smile that looked stapled into place.

'Not that often, unfortunately. We all have very busy lives.'

Jack wanted to ask so much more. To unpick the façade and see inside Eveline's heart. For her to share her truth, no matter how hard it was. He wanted to hold her, comfort her, protect her, lov—. He jammed his hands deeper into his pockets. *Stop it.*

'Have you had a chance to look for old photos of your father?' she asked, seemingly as keen to change the subject as he was.

His stomach cramped, twisting into the form that defined his childhood. The funeral was on Sunday.

'Not yet.'

'I'm afraid I'm really busy the rest of the afternoon and evening,' she said. 'But we can go through everything tomorrow if you're free?'

A wave of exhaustion broke over him, battering him to the bones. It wasn't just physical tiredness, but the numbing emotional weariness from his past catching up with him and forcing him to look it in the eye. He wanted to drink until he lost himself in sleep so deep, even the nightmares couldn't find him.

'Jack?'

He rubbed his hand over his face. 'Yeah, sorry. That's fine. Thank you. I'll look in the loft later.'

'Eveline!'

A man was waving at her from across the high street. An *extremely* good-looking man. Jack's inner alpha pricked up its ears.

'Isaac!'

The man crossed the road and carefully hugged her. 'Are we still good for tonight?'

She looked genuinely happy to see him. 'Absolutely. I've been so looking forward to spending some quiet time with you.'

'Quiet' time? What the fuck?

Isaac held out his hand. 'Hi, I'm Isaac.'

And? Boyfriend? Friend? Foe? He shook it. 'Jack.'

'Are you a friend of Eveline? I haven't seen you around.'

Unlike Simon, or beta-man Leslie, Isaac was objectively handsome, with green eyes, tousled curly brown hair, and a dusting of stubble on his tanned jaw. To add insult to injury, he also seemed nice. *Back down. Eveline's not your girlfriend and you don't even want her as your girlfriend.*

'I, er...' What *was* he to her?

'Yes, Jack's a friend,' Eveline jumped in.

Hear that? Friend. Spelled 'don't-touch-her-and-by-the-way-she's-the-fucking-vicar.'

'Jack's in Foxbrooke for a few weeks helping me with the mural project at Foxbrooke Haven, and Estelle with the Winter Ball,' she continued. 'His father passed away last week, and the funeral is this Sunday.'

Isaac's smile left his face. 'I'm sorry to hear that.'

Jack nodded. An awkward silence descended. He needed to get away.

'I need to head back to do Mum's eye drops,' he said to Eveline. 'Will you text me when you're free tomorrow to go over the funeral preparations?'

'Yes, of course.'

'Thanks.' Jack nodded at Isaac and hurried away.

'FUCK'S SAKE!'

Jack rubbed his head for the third time after smacking it on one of the low beams in the cramped loft.

Being here was like being locked in the past. Dusty memories he'd tried to forget were waiting to be rediscovered. His mum said there was a box of old photos belonging to his father somewhere, but she wasn't interested in helping find it. So Jack went through each box in turn, bringing the past back to life until he couldn't bear it anymore.

He found Christmas decorations, remembering ones he'd made for the tree at school. His mother was always appreciative, but by the following year, each one had disappeared. There was nothing personal left in the box. No photos stuck inside plastic baubles, or baby handprints pressed into modelling clay.

Stupidly, he'd hoped there would be something up here from him and his sister's childhood. Something to make him believe his parents cared for them in the way he'd always dreamed they would. But there was nothing but the same old tired shit people stashed in their attics.

He opened another box filled with crockery. Wasn't this the stuff they'd got from his grandmother's house after she died? Most of the pieces were wrapped in newspaper, but a glimpse of dusty cream paper snagged an almost-forgotten memory. He lifted out a cup wrapped in sugar paper, the kind that was ubiquitous at Foxbrooke Primary school. On the paper was a stick-figure painting of him, his sister and a dog under a rainbow. The words *Jack Newton, age 6* had been written by a teacher underneath.

A sharp pain pierced his chest, and he took a shaky breath. Jack saw himself as a little boy, filled with excitement about what he'd created. Only to have it dismissed and used for packing up cups and saucers that were never used. The sight broke his heart. If only he could go back in time and hug that little boy. Tell him everything was going to be okay. Tell him that he was loved.

Jack replaced the cup and resealed the box. Why did his parents even *have* kids? Were they just doing what was expected of them? He looked around the attic space as if it were an Escape Room, holding clues as to why his childhood had been the way it was. Maybe if he could work that out, he would finally be free.

. . .

'I FOUND THIS.' JACK HELD A SHOEBOX OUT TO HIS MOTHER. 'It's got old photos inside.'

Patricia was sitting in bed again, staring at the television.

'Do you want to look through them?' he continued.

'Why has CBeebies stopped? Don't these channels run twenty-four-seven?'

CBeebies? Jack bit his tongue. 'I think it's because it's past seven, and pre-schoolers are usually asleep by then.'

'Oh.' His mother lifted the remote and changed the channel.

'Do you want to go through any of these photos?'

Shaking her head, she continued to channel-hop.

He gazed at the box in his hand. Should he bury it? Burn it?

'Okay,' he said. 'I'll be downstairs if you need me.'

She nodded, but didn't look up.

DOWNSTAIRS, JACK PUT THE BOX ON THE KITCHEN TABLE and went to find a drink. When he'd arrived the previous week, he'd discovered two bottles of wine and half a litre of whisky in a cupboard.

They hadn't lasted long.

He'd planned to stock up with booze that afternoon, but after meeting Isaac, he'd gone straight home.

After a thorough search, Jack finally found a bottle of sloe gin under the stairs that had been an unwanted gift his parents received when he was still a kid. He took it to the kitchen and poured a slug into a water glass.

Knocking it back, the burn was soothing. He'd already flicked through the photos when he'd been up in the loft so knew they were of his father, taken before he'd married his mother. But now he had to go through them again, and work out which ones they would use to celebrate his dad's life at the funeral.

Jack put the bottle of gin to his lips. There seemed little point in using a glass right now.

❧

EVELINE OPENED THE FRONT DOOR OF THE RECTORY THE following morning, and a prickle of panic ran across her skin. Jack may have been smiling, but it was a poor mask for the emptiness she saw underneath. A faint smell of alcohol hung about him, and her unease grew.

'Morning!' she said with forced cheeriness. 'I was just about to feed Pinky and Perky. Want to join me?'

He raised an eyebrow. '*That's* what you called your pigs?'

'These ones, yes. The last two were Priscilla and Hamlet.'

His smile strengthened into something that looked real, sending a surge of pleasure straight to her heart.

He held out a shoebox. 'I found this in the attic. Photos of my dad from years ago. I've flicked through them but can't face a closer look. Would you mind helping in a bit?'

'Not at all. It would be my pleasure. Come in.'

'How's the arm?'

'Oh, fine. I've only got the sling and bandages on to please the doctor. It should be off by next week.'

Jack followed her through the house, and Eveline passed him a pair of wellies. 'These should fit.'

He gazed at them. 'Whose are these?'

'No-one's and everyone's. They're for whenever a man needs to borrow a pair.'

'Do they get used often?'

She glanced at him. He seemed... stressed? Unhappy? Was

he thinking of Simon? Kieran? *Isaac?* How could she tell him she didn't have a boyfriend without it seeming so obvious? Surely, what she'd said to him and Simon about her date with Leslie had been clear enough?

'No,' she eventually replied. 'Most people find the pigs too dirty and smelly. The last person who used them was Jonathan.'

Jack's eyebrows raised, then he quickly lowered them, his face returning to a bland mask.

'Palmer. He's the Bishop of Bath and Wells.'

His features softened slightly.

God, I know you sent Jack to me, but was it so I could help him?

He took off his shoes and put on the wellies. 'Right. Introduce me to a bacon sandwich in training.'

Eveline smiled and led the way around the back of the rectory, through the small, hedge-lined patch of lawn with the bird feeders, and into the main garden.

Jack whistled. 'It's huge.'

'Yes. It was supposed to provide the Vicar and his family with food year around, and also have ornamental areas for entertaining. My predecessor let brambles take over most of it, and it took a while to clear. But pigs are great for that.'

'Are they good with power tools?'

She laughed. 'They're good with roots. I cut the brambles down to the ground and burnt them. The pigs made sure they never came back.'

Jack was gazing over the far wall of the garden, to where Foxbrooke Manor's parkland lay, with the Dowager House in direct line of sight.

'You burnt them? I bet Estelle's granny was over the moon about that.'

'That was definitely my first black mark. I think she fantasised about sticking me on top of the pyre.'

He smiled. 'And what was the second thing you did to piss her off?'

'Oh, one hundred per cent it was the pigs. Then AA meetings, then Sausage Saturday, then—'

'Sausage Saturday?'

'Once a month, I make sausage rolls and hot dogs and feed anyone who shows up at the church. If people can afford it, they make a donation and the money goes to the local food bank. If not, then everything's free.'

Jack was staring at her, a complex mix of emotions on his face—amusement, what looked like awe, but also pain.

'But what really tipped her over the edge were the pews.' Eveline continued with a smile. 'I got the front row removed last year and haven't heard the end of it.'

'How did you manage that?'

'They were so close to the altar that there was a really tight turning space for coffins. Unfortunately, we had an incident...'

His eyes lit up. 'An *incident*?'

She felt the first blush of the day filling her cheeks and strode towards the small shed which housed the pig feed.

'Oh, come on, now,' he said, following her. 'You can't say there was an "incident" and not tell me what it was.'

Opening the door, she handed him a bucket. 'Can you please fill this to the black mark with pellets from that metal bin?'

He took it. 'Sure. Will you tell me what happened if I do?'

'Maybe.'

He filled the bucket, then carried it to the pigpen, where Pinky and Perky were squealing with excitement at the prospect of food.

'Please spread it out in their trough.'

Leaning over the fence, he poured it in, then frowned.

'Who's been doing this for you whilst your arm's been out of action?'

Eveline didn't know how to reply, so deflected. 'The funeral was for a gentleman who was six foot six, and the coffin was the best part of seven feet long.'

Jack held the empty bucket up, pointed at it, and gave her a look.

'Do you want to hear the rest of the story?' she asked.

'On one condition.'

She bit the inside of her cheek, trying to keep the smile off her face. '*Another* condition?'

'Yes. They're like buses. You wait ages for one, then three come along all at once.'

'And what is *this* one?'

'Tell me what the pigs eat and when, and I'll do it until I see a note from the doctor clearing you for manual labour.'

'You don't have time—'

'Yes, I do. It's important.'

Reflexively, she touched her bandaged arm. It *had* been difficult to handle the pigs. He stared pointedly at the sling. She dropped her hand.

'Thank you, Jack. That would be a great help.'

His shoulders relaxed. 'Okay, so we've got a giant coffin and a narrow turning circle. What happened next?'

He looked like a cheeky schoolboy, his eyes sparkling with barely contained mirth.

She glanced around the empty garden and lowered her voice, just in case. 'Well, they got stuck halfway around. They tried lifting the coffin over their heads, but weren't strong enough. The lead pallbearer tripped on the front pew and dropped his corner, then the man behind him went down as well. Unfortunately, the lid wasn't secured and it... It fell into the front pew along with the flowers, injuring four of the mourners...'

Jack's face contorted as he tried to hold in his laughter.

'But that wasn't the worst part. The, er, deceased, also fell out of the coffin. Jack! You can't laugh!'

But there was nothing she could do or say to stop him. He dropped the bucket and held his sides, his face scrunched up as he howled with laughter.

'Jack!'

He shook his head and held his hand out, as if asking for a moment to compose himself. He seemed to get his breath back, then caught her eye and set off laughing even harder.

Grabbing the bucket, she took it back to the feed bin, allowing a smile to escape when her back was turned. Her heart filled to see him happy again.

'Sorry, sorry, Eveline,' he managed as he caught her up. 'Here, let me do this.' He wiped the tears from his eyes and hung the bucket on a hook. 'Okay, you might as well start my first lesson. Apart from this dry food, what else do pigs eat?'

¶ 13 ¶

'T hey'll eat literally *anything*?' Jack asked Eveline as they re-entered the rectory and made their way to the kitchen. 'Even us?'

'Oh yes. There have been several documented cases of pigs eating humans,' she replied, moving towards the kettle.

'Here, let me do that.' He took it from her and went to the sink. 'What, like in a mafia-murdery kind of way?'

She shuddered. 'I haven't researched that, but I'm sure it's possible. Humans can do terrible things, and pigs are very strong.' Opening the fridge, she pulled out a pack of bacon. 'Plus, they'd be incredibly good at eating the evidence.'

He gazed at what she was holding with a hopeful expression.

'Are you good at eating evidence, Jack?'

'Hmm?'

'Well, there's been a report that contraband charcuterie has been spotted in the rectory, and the food police are on their way. Want to help me destroy any evidence?'

His face lit up. 'It would be my pleasure.'

She reached for her cast iron pan, but he got there before her and held it in the air.

'On one condition,' he said.

She rolled her eyes. 'You make the sarnies?'

He grinned. 'You're getting this whole "condition" thing very well.'

She smiled, then glanced around the kitchen for a job to do.

'You could catch up on your messages?' he suggested. 'Or look through the photos I brought if you're really desperate.'

'Good idea.' She sat at the table with the box and lifted the lid, pleased to be making herself useful.

As Eveline looked through the photos, she listened to the sounds of sizzling bacon, the kettle coming to the boil, the birds chattering away outside, and Jack as he moved around the kitchen. She was struck by how at ease she felt, how utterly content she was in the moment. Glancing up, she caught his eye. They smiled in synchronicity.

Her gaze flicked to his mouth, and suddenly the look in his eyes wasn't so placid. He turned back to the Aga as heat rushed through her.

'So, how do you know about pigs eating humans?' he asked.

Well, that's one way to break the mood. She fanned her flushed cheeks. 'There are documented cases of farmers suffering heart attacks whilst in the pen and then being eaten.'

'Wow.' He cut slices of Libby's sourdough bread, then buttered it. 'I've been thinking.'

'Yes?'

'Mum doesn't want to have anything to do with Dad's funeral, and neither do I. Emily lives up north and needs to rest as she's about to pop. So... I've had an idea.'

She gasped. 'Jack! No!'

He finished the sandwiches and put them on the table. 'Ah,

come on now. It makes perfect sense. It's the circle of life. Milk, no sugar, right?'

'What?'

He went to the fridge. 'In your tea?'

'Er, yes. Thank you.'

'So, how about it? In Tibet, they have sky burials where vultures eat corpses. I propose we give Dad to Pinky and Perky. Same same, but different.'

'Jack!'

He placed her mug of tea down and grinned. 'You're no fun.'

She shook her head, the corners of her mouth twitching. 'And you're a rascal.'

He wiggled his eyebrows. 'That I am.'

His expression suddenly froze, as if he'd just been caught with his hand in the biscuit tin. He inclined his head at the box of photos. 'Any good?'

'Yes, lovely. But they're mainly of your father with one of his friends. There aren't any with Patricia, or you and Emily. Could you possibly bring some from home?'

Jack paused. 'I'll ask Mum. But—' He cleared his throat. 'I don't want any of me from when we were kids, and I expect Emily feels the same.'

Eveline remembered what his sister had referred to as the 'ugly-mug wall'. The school photos where the two of them were overweight and spotty, with forced smiles that didn't disguise the unhappiness behind them.

'We can make the board with only photos of your father? It's your choice.'

'Thanks. I don't want to remember my childhood any more than I have to. Those photos can stay with Mum, and when she's gone, they'll go to landfill.'

'Adolescence can be a really hard time.'

He nodded. 'My life started properly when I finished school.'

She put her sandwich down. 'What happened?'

'I failed my A-levels, so I had to defer my place at uni.' He rubbed his hand over his forehead. 'It's such a load of bullsh— crap, this idea that university should be for everyone. I barely got enough GCSEs to go onto A-levels anyway, and had no interest in doing STEM subjects like Dad wanted me to. So, at the end of the summer when the results came out, I packed a bag and fucke—went off to Australia.'

'Jack, it's okay for you to swear. I really don't mind.'

'*I* mind. I'm trying to be a better person around you.'

'You don't need to. Really. You're perfect just the way you are.'

He huffed out a harsh laugh. 'No, I'm really not.'

'Jack—'

'Anyway, *Australia*,' he said, pinning her with a look which said the subject of how imperfect he thought he was, was now closed for debate. 'I started working on a farm, and four months later had lost my excess fat and gained muscle and a tan. When I moved to a different ranch, nobody there knew I'd looked any different. On my first night, a Canadian girl called Daisy dragged me back to her room and, er...'—he glanced down—'...jumped me.'

Eveline's mouth ran dry as she imagined doing exactly the same.

'That must have been...'

His gaze was still glued to the table, but a smile played on his lips. 'It was like being reborn.'

A sensuous silence stretched between them as Jack seemed lost in his memories and Eveline fell into her fantasies.

He cleared his throat and raised his head, his expression

neutral. 'That year I shed the skin of my childhood and started exploring who I actually wanted to be as an adult.'

'A party planner?'

A brief look of shock crossed his face, and the colour heightened in his cheeks. 'Er... That came later.' He took a gulp of tea. 'Did you have a "road-to-Damascus" moment, or did you always want to be a vicar?'

Eveline stared into her mug. *God, should I tell him everything? Is this how I help him? And anyway, if we are meant to be together, we shouldn't have secrets from each other. Should we?*

'You don't have to tell me if you don't want to.'

She glanced up. 'Oh, sorry, it's fine. I don't mind telling you. I was... I was just talking to God.'

His eyes widened a fraction. 'Do you do that a lot?'

'All the time. I'm either chatting or praying to him.'

'And does he ever talk back?'

'Not in the traditional sense.' She smiled. 'I usually feel his response. Or something happens when I pray.' *Like you turning up at a bar in London.*

'God working in mysterious ways?'

'Exactly. But the first time he ever spoke to me, it was utterly life changing.'

Jack leaned forward. 'What happened?'

'It requires a bit of backstory, if you don't mind listening to it?'

He quickly shook his head. 'Not at all.'

Eveline cast her mind back to her late teens and twenties— a life that was so very different from the one she lived now. Back then, she'd been a social butterfly. Now she looked back at that period as if she was still in a cocoon, being formed to fly for real in the life she was now living.

'I didn't go to university either. I was quite unhappy growing up and wanted freedom and the chance to be an adult, rather than staying in education. With hindsight, I know I was lost in so many ways. But at the time, it felt like I was finally building a life for myself. I got a fast-paced job in recruitment and absolutely loved it. I had a company car, fancy clothes, and a social life.'

Eveline smiled as she remembered those days. Despite what happened later, she had happy memories as well as sad ones.

Jack was still as he listened and she was reminded of the previous day when he'd been at the centre of a gaggle of grey heads. He'd been such an active listener. Someone who actually allowed another person to speak, without simply waiting for the opportunity to interrupt them.

'One of my colleagues was my best friend. Her name was Gracie, and she was a year older than me. The hours were long, but it was a sociable job, with lots of bar lunches and late nights with clients. We bounced between the office, bars and nightclubs, working and partying as if we were invincible and life was for living.'

The pain in her chest when talking about Gracie was powerful, despite how long ago it was. The grief she dealt with internally always became more acute when vocalised, as if it polished up the memories and brought them into the light.

'Gracie and I encouraged each other and never wanted to be the first one to call it a night. It was as if we were afraid to stop and question anything we were doing in case the wheels came off the party bus and we crashed and burned.'

She gazed at him, willing him to understand that she could see in him the same suffering she'd ignored until it was too late.

'I was so caught up in this crazy life I'd created, I never noticed the signs that Gracie was struggling. She was drinking as much as I was, so nothing seemed different. Of course, looking back, it was clear she was on the edge, but I didn't see it in time.'

She took a deep breath, determined to get through this without tears. 'One Saturday night, Gracie had been messaging me non-stop, wanting to meet up. But I was with a boyfriend and didn't get back to her until Sunday. When she didn't return my calls, I went to her flat and found her.'

Eveline tried to swallow back the memories, but they filled her throat. Jack reached across the table and took her hand in both of his.

She sniffed. 'I'm okay. It's just I haven't talked about this for many years now.'

'I'm here.'

She smiled at him, her tears making light sparkle around him like a halo. 'Thank you.'

His warm grip assured her she could tell him anything and he wouldn't judge or criticise.

'I'll never know if Gracie meant to take her own life, or if it was an accident. But I felt entirely to blame. I fell into a deep depression and drank even more heavily. I became scared of everything until one day I couldn't even leave my flat. Lying in bed, staring up at the ceiling, I asked myself if this was my life now? And would I be better off not here at all?'

His hands tightened ever so slightly around hers.

'In that moment, God came to me and I was filled with overwhelming love. He gave me the knowledge that I was loved beyond all comprehension and that I was not alone. This life was only the start, and Jesus had come down to earth to help us understand this truth. The experience lasted for hours. And when it faded, God stayed in my heart.'

'What did you do then?' he asked, his voice soft.

'I had a shower, left the flat and went into the first church I found. I'd asked God to show me what I should do, and he delivered with perfect timing. An AA meeting was about to start, so I joined it and started the twelve-step programme.'

'So... You're...'

'I'm an alcoholic.' *And I'm worried you are too*. 'I haven't had a drink in thirteen years, but I don't want to use the word "was" because there's still the possibility I could lapse.'

Jack pulled his hands away from hers. 'But you only drank for a—what? Three, four years *max*?'

Eveline nodded.

'Have you ever felt the urge to drink after that moment?'

'No.'

He held his hands out, palms up, as if presenting a self-evident truth. 'You partied hard, but that doesn't qualify you as an alcoholic. And look at you now. You're a vicar. You're literally perfect.'

Eveline knew that behind his belligerence, Jack was afraid. Getting into an argument about what constituted alcohol abuse wasn't going to help him, so she took a different approach.

'I'm far from perfect, Jack.'

He ran his hands through his hair. 'Didn't you just say, not ten minutes ago, that *I* was perfect?'

'Yes, I did. I believe we are all perfect in God's eyes, but that's not the same perfect that you mean.'

He raised his head to the ceiling and let out a strangled cry of frustration, then closed his eyes and exhaled a long breath.

'Eveline, I'm sorry.' He looked at her. 'I'm being a twat, and I apologise unreservedly.' He pinched the bridge of his nose. 'Dad dying, coming back to Foxbrooke, seeing y—' He dropped his hand to the table. 'I'm sorry.'

She tentatively touched his arm. 'I understand. These times are unbelievably stressful. It won't go away after the funeral, but it will get easier. Do you want to go through everything now? Would that help?'

He nodded.

After Jack left, Eveline thought about how different her family was to his. Her upbringing hadn't been ideal, but she knew she was loved.

God, I know I keep saying this, but I must make more of an effort to keep in touch. Especially considering how busy they are.

Taking out her phone, she rang her mother in Germany.

'Eveline, darling! How lovely to hear from you! How are you?'

'Hey, Mum! Yeah, I'm doing great. Still battling to get rid of the pews, but I've found someone to help with the mural for Foxbrooke Haven.'

'Mural? In the church?'

'No, it's at the assisted living home at the edge of the village.'

'An old people's home? Why are you getting involved with something like that? I don't remember you being particularly arty as a child.'

'It's a project for the residents to get involved in and to talk about events they remember over the years.'

'Oh. Well, that sounds very nice. I remember an artist coming into Eleanor and Abigail's junior school and doing a mural in the assembly hall. Abigail helped paint an elephant. It was brilliant, of course, but then she's always been very advanced for her age, as you know. Eleanor too.'

'Hmm.'

'Ooh! Darling, speaking of the girls, there's been so much news! They came home last weekend with Klaus and Pietro.

You remember me telling you about their handsome boyfriends?'

'Er—'

'Klaus is a third-year medic in Munich and wants to go into anaesthesiology. Only the most intelligent specialise in that. Did you know he has to be able to fix the machine that keeps people alive?'

'No, I didn't.'

'Frightfully clever. Hugh approves, which is good. He also likes Abigail's boyfriend, Pietro. I've told you about him, surely?'

'Yes, you have. He's a lawyer from Milan, and met Abi at a charity event in The Hague.'

'That's him. Anyway, Pietro took Hugh aside and asked for his permission to propose! Isn't that exciting!'

'Wow! I mean, yes! Wonderful news.'

'Twenty-two does seem a bit young nowadays, but I was married and had you by that age. And Pietro is from the north of Italy, so quite progressive. He totally supports Abigail's career, which is reassuring seeing how far she's going to go.'

'Mum—'

'And, it goes without saying he looks like a model. Lovely long eyelashes—'

'Mum!'

'Yes?'

'Do you think you could visit this Christmas? I haven't seen you for so long, and you haven't been to Foxbrooke yet. There's plenty of room in the rectory to stay.'

'But darling, that's such a busy time with Hugh and the girls. And this year we'll have Klaus and Pietro too. You know you're very welcome to come to us anytime. And we've got that lovely sofa bed in Hugh's snug with your name on it.'

Eveline dug her nails into her palm. 'I would love to, Mum,

but Christmas is one of those times of year I really can't go on holiday.'

'You're right. Silly me. Well, you can come another time. Now, did I tell you that Abigail won a prize?'

TWENTY MINUTES LATER, EVELINE GOT OFF THE PHONE. She'd been fully briefed as to the recent accomplishments of her half-sisters, and shared nothing with her mother that was truly important to her.

Sitting at the kitchen table, she thumbed through the photos of Jack's father. The majority were from Nigel's late teens and early twenties—of him camping, fishing, mountain climbing and river swimming with a friend. They both looked happy and carefree. Were they still friends now?

A photo could tell a thousand stories, and at the same time, none at all. Who was Nigel Newton, *really*, behind the public face? Eveline had now learnt he was an abusive bully to his own children, but she would never have guessed that from looking at these pictures.

She put them back in the box. For the first time since Gracie's death, she wanted a funeral out of the way. She hoped it would bring some sense of closure for Jack and his family, even though it was only one step in the grieving process.

Jack kept his left hand behind him, touching the cold stonework of Saint Saviour's for support, as his right extended to greet the line of strangers. His mother was inside with his sister, Steph and Betsy, sitting in the front pew next to the coffin. Jack had made the executive decision not to carry it into the church at the start of the service, and he wouldn't be one of the pallbearers at the end, either.

On the other side of the large door stood Eveline, wearing a long white surplice over a cassock. An embroidered stole hung around her neck. Her sling was gone, and she didn't seem to be in any discomfort when she moved.

Whereas Eveline appeared in total control, Jack was the opposite. Over the last few days, he'd felt adrift in the middle of an ocean, as the sky darkened and a container ship in the shape of a coffin bore down on him.

He'd tried to focus on the Winter Ball, visiting Foxbrooke Haven, taking his mum for a check-up, and helping Finn replace Eveline's back door. But nothing worked. With each moment that passed, the air around him seemed to get thicker, until he felt like it was choking the life out of him. Sleep was only achieved with the help of a bottle of Scotch.

Jack knew he didn't have a problem with alcohol—this was just a stressful period in his life. But he didn't want Eveline to worry about him after what she'd shared about her past. So, he made sure what bits of work he did around the rectory were timed for when she was out, in case he still smelled of booze.

Being with Eveline was a double-edged sword. Jack craved her presence, but felt the weight of his own inadequacy when with her. And despite how much his body ached for her, his mind knew they could never be together.

'Mate, you look rough as fuck.'

He snapped back to the present as Finn hugged him. His friend pulled away, a frown on his face. 'If you want me to do the eulogy, I will. Honestly, you look like you're about to throw up.'

Jack managed a smile. 'If Mum and Emily weren't here, then I would have hired a kid's entertainer or a drag queen to do it. Something fun that Dad would have lost his shit over.'

'Shall I see if I've got any balloons in the back of the van? I could make a sausage dog or a pair of fake tits?'

'Don't tempt me.'

Finn glanced around. 'Looks like a good turnout. I didn't know your dad was this popular?'

Jack lowered his voice. 'Funerals aren't normally on a Sunday. I think Eveline suggested this day to ensure more than three people would show up.'

'That's the kind of thing she would do.' His friend reached into the inside pocket of his coat and showed him a silver hip flask. 'Thought you might need some of this?'

Jack let out a grateful sigh. 'You beauty.'

Finn handed it to him. 'Go and hide out in the sacristy for a few minutes. Fuck all this shit.'

'Sacristy?'

'Room at the back to the left of the altar. It'll be quiet there.'

Jack put the flask in his pocket and nodded, then looked towards Eveline, uncertain whether to go.

Finn pushed him through the door. 'I'll speak to her. Just go get your head together.'

Jack strode into the church, then left down the side aisle, keeping his gaze fixed ahead. Pushing open a door at the end, he found himself in a corridor. He tried a couple of doors before he found a small room with dark wood cupboards and a table with a couple of chairs. Hanging by the door was Eveline's coat.

Jack stared at it, filled with shame, feeling like a creepy little perve who'd found his way into the bedroom of a girl he was obsessed with. *You can stay here or go back out there.* He sat, his head throbbing, and unscrewed the cap of Finn's flask. Closing his eyes, the liquid burned a path to his stomach. *Just get through the day. Get through the fucking day.*

After a few minutes, there was a knock at the door. He put the flask away.

'Hello?'

Eveline entered the room and shut the door behind her. 'Finn said you would be in here. How are you holding up?'

Jack gazed at her. Even in an outfit designed for purity, not pleasure, Eveline's beauty was blinding. How the fuck was she a vicar? If God really existed, was this punishment for all his sins? A living hell where his dream woman would always be out of reach?

He stood. 'Is it about to start?'

'Yes.' She crossed the room towards him. 'You don't have to do this if you don't want to,' she said softly. 'I can do it all.'

Christ, she's so fucking lovely. He cleared his throat. 'I'll do it. It's not long.'

She held out her hands, and he took them. Her gaze was so filled with compassion, his heart cracked open.

'Would you like a hug?' she asked.

He nodded. What had happened to the man he was a year ago? The outer shell remained the same, but inside was a wasteland.

Opening her arms, she drew him in. Despite their height difference, Jack felt as if he was the one being held. He dropped his head to her shoulder and closed his eyes with a sigh.

Eveline squeezed him tighter, stroking his back as if soothing a child.

The warmth returned slowly to his heart. He took a deep breath in through his nose, and the scent from her hair sent heat flooding through him, straight to his cock. *What the fuck?*

He pulled away, disgusted with himself. Turning to the door, he averted his eyes from her.

'Are you ready?' she asked from behind him.

His cock twitched, and he almost laughed. *God, if you exist, you've got a sick sense of humour.* Opening the door, he held it out for her.

As she passed, she put her hand on his arm. 'If at any point you've had enough, I'll take over. Okay?'

Jack nodded, his gaze focused on the wall behind her.

Eveline squeezed. 'I'm here for you.'

Clenching his jaw, he followed her out into the church.

. . .

ORGAN MUSIC FLOATED ABOVE THE MURMUR OF THE congregation. Jack didn't want to know who was there. He wasn't getting married and therefore excited to see familiar faces in the crowd. Most of the people were strangers he didn't care about.

He sat at the front next to his mother. The pews were as uncomfortable as he remembered. Every memory of this place was negative. Jack allowed himself a quick glance at Eveline as she began her address. How different things would have been if she'd been the vicar when he was growing up. She would have made him a believer and inspired him to do something better with his life than fuck women for money.

The first hymn started, and he rose to his feet. He'd chosen *All Things Bright and Beautiful* because he knew his father hated 'children's hymns' and because he hoped Betsy would like it. He mumbled his way through the words on autopilot, then sat back, his hand moving to feel the outline of Finn's flask and needing to drain the contents.

Eveline was speaking again, but Jack didn't listen to her words, just to how she said them. So assured, yet welcoming and down-to-earth. She met everyone's eyes as if they mattered. As her gaze moved to where he was sitting, he ducked his head.

'Dack-Dack.'

He glanced right. Betsy was fidgeting on Steph's lap, her chubby arms extended towards him. Panic flared—a Pavlovian response to memories from childhood, when the previous vicar would lecture restless children about staying quiet and knowing their place.

Reaching across his mother, he took his niece. Betsy stood on his legs, grasping his cheeks as if to commandeer all of his attention.

'Dack-Dack,' she said solemnly.

Her sweet innocence felt like a punch to the chest.

'Dack-Dack, no cry.'

'Jack?'

He glanced up. Eveline was smiling at him, her hand extended to welcome him forward to give the eulogy. *Fuck!*

'I'll take her,' his mother said, drawing Betsy into her arms.

'Nana.'

His mother's face softened. 'Yes, Betsy. Nana.'

Jack stood, sucking in his stomach as he passed the coffin to avoid touching it. Eveline moved to one side like a proud parent, letting their offspring shine but being ready to catch them if they fell.

His hand went to the pocket with the hip flask in it first, then to the one with the notes he'd made. Pulling them out, he stared at the paper. He didn't want to raise his head and drown in the sea of black before him.

'Thank you for coming,' he began, his voice strange and thin. 'We're here today to celebrate the life of my—'

'Dack-Dack!' Betsy cried, excitedly.

Jack tensed and looked up, expecting to see his mother shushing her grandchild with disproportionate levels of disapproval. But she was opening her handbag and inviting Betsy to dive in like it was a lucky dip. He glanced at his sister and Steph. They looked bemused, and Emily gave him a thumbs up to continue.

'Er, we're here today to celebrate the life of Nigel Newton,' Jack continued, beginning with when his father was born and where he grew up. Writing the eulogy had been a stark demonstration of how little he knew about his father's life, and how much he hated him. He didn't want to stand there and tell people what a total shit his dad had been. But equally, he didn't want to lie and pretend Nigel Newton was an outstanding man who would be missed by everyone who knew him.

So his speech read like it had been bought off the shelf at a Poundshop and tweaked with the help of AI. There wasn't even one mildly amusing anecdote. Both his mother and Emily had declined the opportunity to do a reading, and when Simon offered, in a childish fit of pique, Jack said no.

The hip flask weighed heavily in his pocket, like Sauron's ring of power, demanding attention.

He cleared his throat. 'My father was a keen churchgoer, and Saint Saviour's was at the heart of his life. I'm sure he would have been pleased to see so many of you here today.' *Christ, this is a load of crap.* 'And celebrating his life. I hope that you can give my mother—' He glanced over to see his mum utterly ignoring him, as Betsy re-applied her lipstick with age-appropriate accomplishment. Emily and Steph were red-faced as they tried not to laugh. *What's going on?*

'I hope you can support my mother in her time of grief.'

'Nana! Funny Nana!' Betsy shrieked.

A ripple of amusement swept through the congregation and Jack's heart lifted a little.

'Thank you for coming,' he said, then quickly went back to his seat, his hand touching the pocket where the hip flask lay.

JACK WATCHED FROM THE SIDE OF THE ROOM AS FINN MADE his way through the crowds of people towards him, a glass of red wine in his hand. Estelle and Henry's parents had thrown open Foxbrooke Manor for the wake. Now, one of the drawing rooms was filled with people helping themselves to pastry-based finger food and expensive booze.

'Exchange this for my empty hip flask?' Finn asked as he reached Jack's side.

Jack took the flask from his pocket and swapped it for the glass in his friend's hand. 'You knew it would be empty?'

'If it'd been me, I would have tried to lick the insides.'

'Cheers,' Jack replied, then downed the wine in three gulps.

Finn patted him on the arm. 'You did good. Now you can relax.'

'That'll happen when I'm out of here. Do you know any of these people?'

His friend glanced around the room and shrugged. 'I've seen some of them before. Maybe they're your dad's old work colleagues?'

A waiter passed, carrying a tray of drinks.

Finn took it from him. 'Thanks, mate.' He carried the tray to a window alcove and Jack followed.

The men sat, and Jack took another glass. The knot in his stomach loosened. On the other side of the room was his mother, still carrying Betsy and talking animatedly to Eveline.

'I don't fucking get it,' he said to Finn.

'Get what?'

'Mum. Look at her.'

'She looks happy.'

'Yeah. It makes me sick.'

'Huh? You don't want her to be happy?'

'Of course I want her to be happy. It's not that.'

'Then what is it?'

Jack necked another glass of wine. 'You know what she was like with me and Em—always so ratty with us. We made too much noise, we made too much mess, blah, blah, blah. We were a constant irritant. But now look at her. She's acting like she's grandparent of the bloody year. She hasn't put Betsy down once since the service, and she's showing her off like some kind of prize-winning pony.'

'And...' Finn paused. 'You wish she'd been like that with you?'

Jack took another glass and nodded. 'Mum always seemed

embarrassed by us. As if our behaviour was a direct reflection of some failing of hers. But I think Betsy could smear the contents of her nappy on someone's face and she wouldn't bat an eyelid.'

Finn snorted.

'It makes me angry for what me and Em went through. And pissed off that she's had so little to do with Betsy for the last couple of years, but now picks her up as if they're best buds.'

'Honestly, mate, I know it's hard, but give her a break. Can you imagine how weird it is for her now that your dad's gone?'

Jack nodded and took a gulp of wine. Finn was right. He'd had over twelve years' worth of distance from his father. His mother had only had a couple of weeks.

JACK SAT WITH FINN, DRINKING STEADILY UNTIL HIS FRIEND had to go. Henry and Estelle had been buttonholed by locals, Connor was at work, and Jack didn't want to bother his sister and Steph when he was starting to feel drunk. The only other person he wanted to be around was Eveline, but in this state, he needed her at least ten feet away.

Grabbing a bottle from the makeshift bar, Jack left the Manor through the back door and wandered into the formal gardens. It hadn't changed since he was a child. The Duke of Somerset was a keen gardener, and the beds were filled with autumn colours. He made his way to a secluded bench inserted into a yew hedge and sat, the bottle at his feet and his head in his hands.

Memories swirled and heaved inside him, like a boat tossed on a choppy sea. He'd spent years believing his life was just the way he wanted it, and all it took was the death of his father and coming back to Foxbrooke for everything to unravel.

Spinning around at the centre was Eveline, pulling on the

threads of his very being, making him feel things he knew he shouldn't.

'Jack?'

He glanced up, instinctively pushing the bottle under the bench with his heel. It toppled with a crash and he grabbed it, stopping the rest from being spilled.

'Fuck!'

Eveline stood a few feet away, as if respecting his space. 'I haven't had a chance to speak to you since the funeral. How are you doing?'

How *was* he doing? Getting drunker by the second. Falling into the slippy, slidey state where filters disintegrated and thoughts became words.

'Why do people have kids?' Jack fumbled at his feet for the bottle and took a drink, only noticing when he stopped that wine had dribbled down his neck. He swiped it away clumsily with the back of his hand.

Eveline stepped a little closer. 'For all sorts of reasons, but I suppose because they really want them.'

He stared out at the garden as the flowers came in and out of focus.

'I don't,' he stated.

'May I sit down?'

Shrugging, he scooted to the far end of the bench, clutching the bottle to stop him from reaching for her.

'My parents can't have wanted kids,' he slurred. 'I don't think they even *liked* us.' Hot bile and nausea collided in his stomach. 'I could never have any. I'm a shitshow and the world's even fucking worse. How could I inflict that on a child?'

Eveline didn't reply, and he didn't meet her eye, refusing to allow her light to illuminate the darkness inside him. *We can never be together.* She needed to know he wasn't right for her.

'I know you want children and I hope you get them.' His head was spinning faster and faster. 'But it won't be with me.' He stumbled to his feet, the bottle dropping to the ground. 'It'll *never* be with me.'

Jack lurched to the right and staggered forward, only just making it to the first gap in the hedge before throwing up.

❧ 15 ❧

Eveline finished making a bacon sandwich for Simon, biting the inside of her cheek to keep her emotions in check.

God, please give me the strength to get through this meeting without crying.

Jack's words to her yesterday had smashed her dreams and trampled on her heart.

I was so certain that we were meant to be together. But now? I don't know what to do. And Simon seems so cross with me. What have I done to offend him?

She placed the sandwich in front of him as if it were a peace offering.

'Thank you, dear.'

He smiled as he took his first bite, and relief flickered like a tiny flame. Keeping Simon on her side was imperative if she was going to win the battle of the pews. He represented the section of her congregation Estelle called the 'Grey Army'. Simon shared their age, dress sense, values, and outlook on life. But, in the matter of the pews, he'd supported Eveline, and she hoped he could win at least some of the others over to her position.

Trying to keep her voice level, she opened her laptop and spun it around. 'I wondered if you could possibly look over my latest letter to English Heritage in advance of our meeting next week?'

Putting on his glasses, Simon peered at the screen, reading as he finished his sandwich.

'Hmmm... Hmmm...' He straightened, took his glasses off and tucked them in the breast pocket of his striped shirt.

'What do you think?' she asked.

He cleared his throat. 'It should hit the spot. You've certainly included the right type of buzzwords.'

'Buzzwords?'

'To tick the boxes on their politically correct forms.'

Her stomach prickled with irritation. 'What, like "community", and "accessibility"?'

'Yes, but it's more what those things might involve. You've mentioned yoga, and that has no place in a church.'

'Isaac teaches exercise and relaxation, not religion. I've been to his classes and they're wonderful. But he needs a better space to teach at the heart of the village.'

Simon drummed his fingers on the table. 'Eveline, it's the thin end of the wedge. Once you let one hippie in, the rest will follow. It'll be yoga one minute and gong baths the next.'

'I think a gong bath sounds like a perfect idea for the church. The acoustics are wonderful.'

He stared at her as if she'd suggested a broomstick-making workshop followed by a light orgy.

'Eveline, you cannot be serious?'

'Why not? It's just sound waves. We sing in church. What's the difference?'

'It's... I can't quite *believe* we're having this conversation. Have you seen what they look like?'

'What do you mean?'

'People who do that type of thing. Bangles up their arms, funny scarves, tattoos, *nose-rings*.'

'That sounds like a description of Dervla Foxbrooke.'

Eveline watched Simon's brain recalibrating, as the realisation hit that he'd just described the second wife of the Duke of Somerset.

He sighed. 'Eveline. I know you mean well, but Saint Saviour's is a *church*, not a community centre.'

'Simon. You're the treasurer. You know better than anyone how dire our financial position is. If we don't start bringing in money, then we might lose the church altogether. And I believe it should be at the heart of every community. I want to be able to help as many people as possible.'

'Like the Newton boy.'

'Jack?'

'Yes. Did you see him yesterday? Drunk as a lord at his own father's funeral.'

Pain lanced Eveline's chest again. After she'd smelled booze on Jack in the sacristy and at the wake, all her worst fears about his relationship with alcohol seemed to have been confirmed.

God, if you've brought Jack into my life to help him, then I promise I will do my best.

'Such a weak character,' Simon continued. 'Not at all like Nigel.'

'Simon, please show some compassion.'

'God helps those who help themselves, Eveline. I've known Jack since he was a boy. He may have lost the puppy fat and pimples, but he's still the same on the inside.'

Eveline dug her nails into her palms as fierce, protective anger surged through her.

Please, God. Help me stay calm.

'Weak. That's what he is. With no commitment to his family. You know—'

There was a knock on the newly installed back door. *Thank you.* She stood.

'And that's another thing', Simon continued as he followed her out of the kitchen. 'What on *earth* was he playing at, buying a door for the rectory? Did you fill out the correct forms? Ask the Bishop? This is church property, Eveline, and you need to follow procedure when altering the fabric of the building.'

She threw open the door.

On the other side was Jack, holding an enormous bunch of flowers.

'Eveline—' He stopped when he saw Simon behind her.

Her heart thudded faster and faster against her ribs.

'Jack,' she began breathlessly. 'How are—'

'I'll take those,' Simon said, reaching forward.

Jack pulled the bouquet away. 'No.'

'Why not? They're for the church, aren't they? I can take them over later.'

'No, they're for Eveline.' There was steel behind Jack's smile.

He's brought me flowers!

Simon barked out a laugh. 'Well, Eveline *is* the church, and she'll only take them over herself if I don't.'

She stared at the bouquet. It was stunning. The predominant colours were red, with roses, gerberas, dahlias and proteas. But there were flashes of gold, too. It must have cost a fortune.

Jack ignored Simon and turned to her. 'Eveline, I want to

thank you for all your help and support over the last couple of weeks, and to apologise for my behaviour yesterday.'

She heard a *harrumph* from Simon behind her.

'You can do whatever you like with these,' Jack continued. 'They're yours.'

Eveline took them from him, holding them close to her pounding chest, as if they were an extension of him.

'Thank you, Jack. Are you coming in?'

He glanced at Simon and shook his head. 'I was going to head over to Foxbrooke Haven.'

Jack made his feelings for you clear yesterday. You can't hope for more than that.

She swallowed. 'How's your mum doing?'

'Tired. Yesterday took a lot out of her.'

'I'll see if I can pop over to see her today. I can bring back the photos.'

'Thanks.' Jack gave them both a quick nod and left.

'Why don't I take those from you?' Simon asked as they returned to the kitchen. 'I can run them over in a bit.'

Eveline clutched the bunch tighter. If she couldn't have Jack, then she wanted the flowers. 'No, thank you, Simon. I'm going to keep them in the rectory.'

'But you've never done that before,' he blustered.

She smiled brightly to hide the light of her anger. 'Well, there's a first time for everything. And besides, people come and go all the time here, so I'll still be sharing their beauty.'

Simon harrumphed again. 'Well, let me arrange them for you.'

She knew her feelings were disproportionate, but she didn't want Simon touching the bouquet. She didn't want *anyone* touching it.

'No, thank you. I'll do it later.' She pulled a large jug from a cupboard, put the bouquet inside, and took it to the sink.

Despite the noise as the ancient tap turned on, the birds continued to squabble at the feeders outside.

When the jug was filled, she placed it on the counter. Simon eyed the flowers as if they were about to grow teeth and eat him.

He cleared his throat. 'Eveline. I haven't had you over for quite a while now. How about you come to mine tonight for a meal?'

How about you actually ask if I want to? She turned away and pretended she needed to check the tap had properly turned off. *God, I'm so angry with him and it's not fair. He's done nothing wrong.*

'Eveline?'

She faced him with a smile she didn't feel. 'I'm afraid tonight is not suitable.' *Not a lie, I just don't want to.*

Simon's face crumpled in on itself with confusion. 'But you don't normally have anything on a Monday evening.'

'Maybe another time?'

'Okay then, tomorrow. You can come after Evensong.'

'I think Isaac is popping over then.'

'Again?'

'I enjoy his company.'

'I don't trust him.'

'Simon!'

He held his hands up as if he was just the messenger carrying self-evident truth. 'He spends all day touching women in tight-fitting clothes. Take off the hippie pyjamas and he's just a man, Eveline.'

She took a deep breath. 'Isaac is a yoga teacher, not a sexual predator. He's one of the most upstanding men I know.' Angry fire scorched her insides. 'And besides, he would never pursue a romantic relationship with me or any other woman.'

'Gay, is he?'

'No, he's not. He's—' Eveline stopped talking. She didn't know who else knew about Isaac's vow of chastity, but she didn't want to be the first to spread gossip.

'A eunuch?' Simon shook his head. 'I know that kind of thing still goes on in India, but good grief. Is that what he did to himself over there?'

She briefly closed her eyes. 'No. He's not a eunuch.'

'Then what is he—'

'Tomorrow lunchtime. I'm free then. Shall I come over around twelve-thirty?'

'Er, yes.' Simon nodded. 'That would work.'

PATRICIA FIDDLED WITH HER WEDDING RING AS SHE perched on the edge of the armchair. Her gaze kept flicking to a tablet that lay on the table next to their mugs of tea.

'Jack said you were quite tired. Are you sure I shouldn't leave you to rest?' Eveline asked.

'No, I'm fine. Thank you for yesterday.'

'It was my pleasure.'

'I must apologise about Jack.'

'Jack?'

'His behaviour at the wake. I don't know if you saw, but he was—' Patricia swallowed. 'His friends had to help him home.'

Eveline's heart squeezed with compassion for Jack, feeling his pain as if it were her own. She would do everything in her power to help him.

'It was a difficult day for him.'

Patricia shrugged.

A thought came to her. *God. Did you also send Jack to me so he could help with the mural?*

'Has he told you about the project he's involved in at Foxbrooke Haven?' Eveline asked.

Patricia frowned. 'Simon says it's causing a lot of disruption.'

She put on her most reassuring smile. 'In the best possible way. The residents are very excited about it.'

'Gladys Little isn't.'

'I had no idea Jack had such a talent,' Eveline said, deflecting the conversation away from Simon's mother. The woman could meet Jesus and tell him his sandals were scruffy and his hair needed a wash.

Patricia looked confused. 'Talent?'

'At art,' she replied. 'He's gifted.'

'He liked doing it at primary school. But it wasn't what Ni —Jack didn't carry it on at secondary.'

Well, he's clearly been doing it since then. Eveline didn't know what to say without it seeming like a criticism.

Patricia glanced at the tablet again. 'I was wondering if you could give me some advice.'

'I'll do my best. How can I help?'

Patricia interlocked her fingers and squeezed, the knuckles turning white.

'I want to buy something for Betsy,' she said in a hurry. 'My granddaughter. But I don't know what she would like.'

'Maybe you could ask Emily or Stephanie?'

Patricia shook her head rapidly. 'No. I, er... No.'

Repentance came in many forms and maybe, now Nigel had gone, was Patricia trying to heal the rift between her and her children?

'Okay, so do you want to take a look online?'

GOD, I'M VERY HAPPY THAT PATRICIA IS MAKING MORE OF AN effort with her daughter's family. But did she not see the irony in denying her son access to art, then buying her granddaughter colouring books and pens?

Striding back to the rectory an hour later, Eveline flip-flopped between her internal rant and self-recrimination for her critical thoughts. As she neared the new back door, oinking and grunting drew her attention.

Please God, not again?

Running around the corner, she found both pigs eating their way through her flower borders. They noticed her and made happy snorting sounds, leaving the few autumn blooms for the promise of better food. Eveline dithered as they trotted forward. If she went back for her wellies, they would carry on around the house and onto the street.

Letting out a cry of frustration, she dashed to the feed shed to grab a bucket of pig nuts. Ruined shoes were better than ruined relations with her neighbours and a write up in the local paper.

'Pinky! Perky! Come on, this way.'

Slipping and sliding in the muck, she led them back into the pen, then set about mending the fence with galvanised wire. Icy rain was falling and making everything harder. Brushing water off the face of her watch, she glanced at it. Still plenty of time for a long soak in the tub before Evensong.

Upstairs, because God couldn't control everything, the boiler had stopped working again. Eveline left a message for the plumber, then stripped off and got under the electric shower.

Five minutes later, there was a loud bang, and it ran cold.

'Come on!'

She rinsed her body in the frigid water, then jumped out and rubbed her pink skin as dry as she could. Wrapping her bathrobe around her, she grabbed the brass door handle and gave it a tug.

It came off in her hand.

HALF AN HOUR LATER, HEAVY FOOTSTEPS THUMPED UP THE wooden stairs.

'Eveline! It's me,' Jack called. 'Which door are you—hang on, got it.'

'I'm s-so sorry to b-bother you,' she said through the door, her teeth chattering. 'I t-tried Estelle, F-Finn and Oscar, but none of them p-picked up.'

'It's not a problem at all. I'm glad you felt you could call me.'

There was a scraping sound as Jack picked up the handle from the other side of the door.

'Okay, I see the problem. When it came off on your side, the other one fell out this side with the spindle attached.'

'I t-tried to break the d-door down, but my shoulder's still a b-bit sore.'

'I'm very glad you didn't.' Jack pushed the spindle back through the hole and held it in place so she could reattach the handle on her side.

She tied her robe tighter around her, then opened the door. 'Thank you. I'll—'

'Fucking hell, you're blue!'

'I'm f-fine—'

'Has the boiler gone again?'

She nodded, her teeth clacking inside her head.

He held out his hands, as if wanting to rub her warm, then froze. 'What about the electric shower?'

'Stopped w-working.'

'Jesus, Eveline!'

Heat was radiating off him. All she wanted to do was curl up in his arms.

'Do you have a hot water bottle? What can I do to help?'

'Can you h-hug me, please? I'm so c-cold.'

He hesitated for a second, then drew her in, wrapping his arms around her and holding her against the hard heat of his chest. The effect of finally being near warmth caused her to relax a fraction, and the shivers became shakes.

'Eveline, I'm not a doctor, but you feel dangerously cold. Which bedroom is yours? We need to get you under some covers.'

'D-don't leave me.'

'I'm not going to, sweet—' He sighed. 'Just point me in the right direction.'

She shuffled with him to her bedroom and he threw back the bedcovers.

'C-can you keep hugging me p-please?'

He nodded and climbed in after her, tucking the duvet behind her, then pulling her against him, his hands rubbing up and down her back.

God, the only man I thought I'd ever have in my bed was my husband, but Jack made it clear he doesn't want me or children. Why did you send him to me now? To stop me from dying from hypothermia?

Eveline had never felt so cold before, and was shivering violently, but flashes of awareness punctuated the pain that had sunk through to her bones.

Jack shifted his legs. 'Put your feet on mine. If I can't get you warm, we need to get you somewhere with a hot bath.'

'I'll be f-fine,' she managed, moving her bare feet to find his.

He huffed across the top of her hair. 'Bloody hell. I've met warmer ice blocks.'

She laughed through her shivers. 'The p-pigs got out again, so I h-had to mend the fence. That's why I'm so ch-chilly.'

'Ah yes, I saw two lumps of mud inside the back door that

were vaguely shoe-shaped. I take it you didn't have time to get your wellies?'

She shook her head.

He sighed and held her tighter.

Closing her eyes, Eveline sank into Jack's warmth. As the chills slowly subsided, they were replaced with a slow-growing heat that moved languorously down inside her body to pool deep in her abdomen.

What's happening?

With a shiver that had nothing to do with being cold, she rubbed herself against him. The tie of her bathrobe had come undone, and as she moved, one side of the robe fell away. His shirt buttons and the top of his jeans grazed her bare skin. A shudder of pleasure ran through her.

'Are you okay?' he asked, his voice low.

She nodded, wriggling close and allowing the bathrobe to open fully. Her ear was resting against his chest and she listened to the thumping of his heart as it got faster and faster.

God, have I got it wrong again? Does he like me after all?

Her need for him grew stronger with every breath. She was filled with a heady desire to take as much as he was willing to give. More than a decade had passed since she'd been intimate with a man, and the dormant desire was now roaring, demanding to be fed. Rubbing her hardened nipples against the fabric of Jack's shirt, sharp spikes of pleasure shot down to the apex of her thighs.

Pressing her hips into his, she felt the rock-solid evidence that he was as much affected by their closeness as she was. His chest rose and fell faster, his breathing keeping pace with the speed of his heart.

He swallowed. 'Eveline?'

'Yes, Jack?'

'I, er...'

Raising her head to look at him, she ran the fingers of her hand up his back until her nails scraped into his hair.

He shuddered, his eyes squeezing tightly closed.

'Yes, Jack?' she repeated, her voice soft and breathy.

He opened his eyes, staring at her with such hunger, it stopped her heart. His pupils were almost completely blown out, the blackness encircled by tiny rings of golden light.

She moved her face a fraction closer. His lips parted and his ragged breaths mingled with hers. She'd never felt desire as powerful as this before—so potent it knocked out every logical thought.

One of his hands tangled in her hair and she whimpered.

Pressing her fingers lightly against the back of his head, she pulled him closer.

He didn't resist.

Trembling, she brought her lips to his, her tongue instinctively slipping into the wet heat of his mouth.

As the tip of her tongue touched his, he groaned, clutching her to him. He met her passion and increased it tenfold. This was no tentative first kiss. No delicate, closed-mouth testing of the waters. This kiss had been forged over a year of dreams and fantasies. It dragged her into an ocean of sensation and she clung to him as he swept her away.

Yes!

Hooking her bare leg over his, Eveline pressed her burning centre harder against him. Jack pushed the side of her robe away, sliding his hand down her back to cup her bottom, tugging her closer. She rubbed from side to side over the thick ridge of his cock, her heart tripping over itself as her tongue danced and fought with his.

His kiss rocketed her beyond the stars and his touch sent every cell spinning off its axis. She couldn't think. All she could do was feel as her body begged for everything he could give.

She shifted, reaching for his cock and stroking it through his jeans.

Suddenly, he broke away, his eyes scrunched closed, his breath hissing in and out through his clenched jaw.

'Jack?'

He leapt off the bed and covered her with the duvet.

Eveline sat, holding the covers around her as she stared at him. He looked in pain, one hand holding his head, his face contorted.

'I'm sorry,' he managed, his breathing laboured. 'I'm so sorry.'

'For what?'

'For kissing you.'

'But I kissed you first, and I'm not sorry.'

He stared at the floor and shook his head. 'It should never have happened.'

Confusion and disappointment swirled inside her, creating a cocktail of grief.

'Why not? What's wrong with me?'

His head shot up. 'Fuck! Eveline, there's *nothing* wrong with you.'

'Then what's the problem? Please, Jack. Help me understand.'

He shook his head. 'I'm the problem. I'm sorry, Eveline, but nothing can ever happen between us.'

He didn't wait for her to reply, but turned and fled.

She listened to his footsteps running down the stairs, then the sound of the back door.

God, please tell me what's going on?

❀ 16 ❀

Jack: Eveline said she rang you before me this afternoon after she got locked in the bathroom. She probably didn't mention the boiler's packed in again and the electric shower blew up. I'd put one in if I knew how to do it without killing myself, so that leaves you. Can you help?

Finn: Who am I? Bob the fucking builder? It'll have to be much later. I'm flat out today.

Jack: Thanks, mate. Add it to my bill.

Finn: Will do. Anything else you need whilst I'm at it?

Jack: Can you fix the bathroom door and find a plumber who knows his shit? If the boiler needs replacing, I'll pay.

Finn: Anything else? Redo the entire electrics? Chuck in underfloor heating? Nice extension out the back?

Jack: Ha ha.

Finn: You really want to pay for all this? A new boiler could be a few grand. The church should cough up for it.

Jack: I don't give a fuck about the money. Eveline shouldn't have to live in a place that's falling apart.

Finn: Is there something I need to know?

Jack: Yeah. If you've got time, can you check out the pigpen? They got out again.

Finn: About you and Eveline, dipshit.

Jack: Nothing's happening and nothing's ever going to happen.

Finn: Ah… This explains the back door.

Jack: Fuck off.

Finn: Does she know you fancy her?

Jack: Don't say anything.

Finn: You do know she rang me before you this afternoon?

Jack: Well aware.

Finn: Look, without meaning to sound like a dickhead, you need to stay well clear. Vicar stuff aside, she's the nicest of people and wants a husband, not a player. You can't fuck and run.

Jack: Player? How d'you work that out?

Finn: I've never known you to have a girlfriend, and if I looked like you, I'd be whoring it up.

Jack: No, you wouldn't.

Finn: Fair enough, but I'd dream about it.

Jack: I'm sorry about earlier. I've spoken to Finn about the shower and hopefully he's going to install a new one this evening.

Eveline: Can we talk face-to-face please?

Jack: I don't think that's a good idea.

Eveline: How about tomorrow?

Jack: I'm working on the mural in the morning, then have a planning meeting for the Winter Ball in the afternoon at the Manor.

Eveline: After that?

Jack: Sorry, I can't.

Standing in the main kitchen at Foxbrooke Haven, Jack stared at the kettle as it slowly came to the boil.

Every synapse in his brain fired, shutting down thought after thought of Eveline, but every cell of his body thrummed with awareness of her. He closed his eyes, falling back into the memories of her hot mouth, her soft skin, the needy, breathy sounds as she ground her pussy into his cock.

Jack glanced around, making sure the room was empty, then readjusted himself. For the past year, Eveline coloured every fantasy, every sexual encounter. But even the most lurid of imaginings didn't touch the technicolour brilliance of her reality.

After the first flush of his sexual awakening in Australia, no matter how attracted he was to the woman he was with, part of him always remained detached. The part that kept everything under control. *His* control. It meant he could focus entirely on his partner's pleasure—a skill that ensured his success as an escort.

But yesterday, Eveline had blown any control he'd had to bits. Jack knew he shouldn't have touched her, but when she pressed herself against him and brought her sweet lips to his, it would have been easier to cap an erupting volcano.

Hearing someone enter the kitchen, he forced a bland smile to his face and turned.

'Hi, Robert, isn't it?'

The elderly man gave a small salute. 'That's me.'

'Cup of tea?'

'If you're making one, that would be lovely, thank you.' He took a seat at a wooden table and rested his cane against it. 'Milk, no sugar, please.'

Jack made the tea, brought the mugs to the table, and sat.

'Have you come in here for a break?' Robert asked. 'I can leave you alone if you'd prefer?'

'Not at all. I'd enjoy the company.' *And it will help me stop thinking about Eveline.*

'The mural's looking good. Have you sketched it out completely now?'

'Almost. I wanted it to be pretty detailed in pencil before we start with the paints. Do you want to give us a hand?'

'I'd like to, but I don't want to take anyone's place, or get in the way.'

'You won't.' He glanced at Robert's cane. 'Would you rather sit when you paint?'

'If that would work?'

'Absolutely. I've put most of the fun stuff at a medium height, so it's accessible. I expect I'll be doing everything by the ceiling and the floor.'

Robert smiled. 'Sounds sensible.'

They sat in a companionable silence, but Robert was breathing as if he was about to ask a question, then bailing before the words came out. Jack tried to make his own posture as relaxed as possible.

'Jack,' Robert began tentatively. 'How do you do it?'

Do what? 'Er...'

'Talk to women.'

Jack paused, getting the sense that this was not the time for a flippant comment. 'In what way? Conversationally?'

'Yes. I've spent most of my life only in the company of men. Boys' boarding school, then working in remote areas around the world. You seem to be completely at ease around women and I wondered if you could share a few pointers?'

'Have you tried already?'

Robert nodded, frowning. 'It doesn't go very well. Either I don't stop waffling, or I clam up and don't say anything.'

Jack understood. From his observations over the years, most men talked too much and ignored the words or body language of the person they were speaking to.

'Well, I find the easiest thing to make a conversation flow is to ask questions,' he said. 'Maintain eye contact, listen carefully to what people are saying, and don't interrupt. Then ask another question based on the first.'

Robert was silent, his brow still furrowed. 'It can't be that easy, can it?'

'Oh, and if they hold strong opinions on something, be careful how you respond.'

'Like what?'

'Well, if they're very religious, it's fine to say that you're not. But don't say you think people who believe in God are deluded fantasists who need to stop believing in fairy tales.'

Robert laughed. 'I hope you didn't say that to the lovely vicar?'

Jack grinned. 'Definitely not. And I don't think that, anyway. It's just an example.' He took a gulp of tea. 'Is there anyone in particular you'd like to talk to?'

Robert's look of surprise was comical, but Jack kept a straight face.

'Er... Yes, as a matter of fact, there is.'

Jack leaned forward. 'And who is the lucky lady?'

'Well, I don't think I would describe her as "lucky".' Robert glanced around the kitchen, then lowered his voice. 'It's Shirley.'

Jack's heart lifted. 'She's wonderful. Good choice.'

Robert's cheekbones coloured. 'She *has* smiled at me a few times, but I tend to run away if I think she's coming to talk. I don't want to mess it up.'

'Do you think you can chat with her now? Or at least listen?'

Robert looked unsure.

'I could be your wingman?'

'*Wingman?*'

'A friend who has your back and helps you pull—get to know women.'

'Would it work?'

Jack shrugged. 'Who knows, but shall we give it a go?'

❧

EVELINE SQUARED HER SHOULDERS AND KNOCKED ON Simon's door. Normally, she wouldn't have questioned the lunch invitation. But since Jack had arrived, the status quo had been disrupted, and she knew Simon wasn't happy about it.

God, I trust you. But why did you bring Jack into my life? If it is to help him, then I promise I will accept that. But he kissed me back! So why did he then reject me? Please God, what am I doing wrong? I'm so confused right now.

Simon opened the door and beamed at her. 'Ah, there you are. Come in, dear, let me take your coat.'

Eveline smothered her feelings under a practiced and professional smile. 'Thank you, Simon. You're looking very smart. Are you off somewhere later?'

He hung up her coat and glanced at his coral pink shirt. 'No, no. I wore this for you.'

Why? 'Well, it looks lovely.'

He preened. 'Thank you. Why don't you go on through to the dining room? I've set up in there.'

Simon's Georgian house was not as big as the rectory, but was in far better shape. Simon's wife, Rosalind, had died just before Eveline had moved to Foxbrooke, but her personality and style were evident throughout the house. The wallpaper was pale green and pink stripes, and oil paintings of country scenes hung from the dado rail. The furniture was antique mahogany, and Denby China and polished silverware sat atop an embroidered white tablecloth.

'Oh Simon, this looks beautiful. What a treat.'

He held a chair out for her and she sat.

'Elderflower pressé with soda?'

'My favourite. Thank you.'

He turned to the sideboard, and Eveline failed to stop her mind from travelling back a year ago to a bar in London. She hadn't had the drink since that night.

Simon presented it to her. 'There we go. Now let me get the food. I've made belly pork.'

'Ooh, yummy!'

He chuckled and left the room.

Eveline sat back, the forced smile falling off her face. She was glad that Simon's mood seemed much improved. She didn't want anyone to be unhappy, and he'd been so out-of-sorts recently. But she still didn't want to be here. She wanted to be with Jack.

Taking a sip of her drink, she closed her eyes and replayed the previous afternoon. Shivers of pleasure ran across her skin. She wanted to believe that God would make things right, but he couldn't control everything. And despite Jack's physical reaction to her in bed, he'd made it crystal clear that he didn't want to be with her. Twice.

What can I do? I can't force him to be with me.

'Here we are!' Simon entered and placed a perfectly cooked pork roast in the centre of the table. 'You carve and I'll get the rest.'

Apart from the meals she'd had at Foxbrooke Manor with Estelle, Eveline couldn't remember the last time anyone had gone to this effort just for her.

Simon returned with a tray of apple sauce, gravy, roast potatoes, and vegetables. 'The pork is from Priscilla,' he said. 'I froze that joint you gave me.'

'How wonderful! Thank you, Simon and thank you, Priscilla.'

'Would you like to say Grace?'

'I'd love to.' Eveline bowed her head. 'Lord, we thank you for this meal and for filling our lives with blessings. May this wonderful food and the friends we share it with nourish us. Amen.'

They filled their plates and chatted amiably about church matters. Eveline kept up the happy façade, avoiding any talk of her supposedly radical plans for Saint Saviour's, but it all felt so facile. Guilt nagged at her. Simon was being lovely, but she wanted to talk truthfully and authentically about her ideas. She wanted to be herself. With Jack, she could be. But Jack didn't want her...

When their plates were empty, Simon brought out a trifle —another one of her favourite dishes.

'You're spoiling me,' she said with a smile. 'I'll be rolling home in a bit.'

'Help yourself. It's homemade. One of Rosalind's recipes that she got from her mother. Minus the sherry, of course.'

'Thank you. It's like an edible family heirloom.'

He put his head to one side. 'I suppose it is.'

'I think it's a wonderful way to remember her.' Eveline took a mouthful. 'And delicious. Thank you, Simon, and thank you, Rosalind.'

Simon's gaze turned serious, and Eveline suddenly worried that she'd been flippant about his late wife.

'I'm sorry. I didn't mean to sound irreverent. You must miss her terribly.'

'No, no, my dear, you're not speaking out of turn. Of course, I miss her. In fact, I often talk aloud to her as if she were still here. But life moves on.'

'That must be a real comfort.'

'Yes, yes, it is. Sometimes I wonder if I chat to her more now than I did when we were married.' He laughed at his own joke. 'I often get a feeling when I do it, as if she's answering me from heaven.' He cleared his throat. 'And I know she's given me her blessing.'

'Blessing for what? Are you selling the house and downsizing?'

'Well... Selling this place is part of the plan, but downsizing is not the reason.'

Eveline put down her spoon. 'This sounds exciting. Are you going to travel the world?'

Simon barked out a laugh and shook his head. 'No, I'm going to do what I really should have done a year ago but haven't got around to until now.'

'I'm intrigued. What are you only now getting around to?'

'Marrying you.'

Time seemed to fracture as Simon's words cut through her mind. He must have taken her silence as tacit approval because he continued.

'No need to be coy, Eveline. I'm sure the thought has crossed your mind many times before. I'm well aware of your desire for matrimony and motherhood, and even though I've been around that particular block already with Alan and Laura, I'm willing to make the personal sacrifice, and do it again for your happiness.' He frowned. 'I know you'll be concerned about a possible negative reaction from my children. But rest assured, the matter has been dealt with.'

'W-what?'

'I've already spoken to them about my intentions. After our marriage, I will, of course, move into the rectory with you, then sell this place and split the proceeds between Alan and Laura. That way we can have a fresh start and they won't think you're a gold-digger.'

God, is this a joke?

'I still have my pension, so I won't be marrying you completely empty-handed.' He chuckled. 'And, as you can see, I know my way around a kitchen. I'm a very modern man.'

The room wasn't cold, but Eveline was shivering.

Simon reached his hand across the table towards her.

She withdrew hers onto her lap.

'My dear, I appreciate when you've been a spinster for so long, marriage will be an adjustment. As will be the, er—' He cleared his throat again. '*Marital bed.* But please take comfort in the knowledge that I'm an experienced man of the world and will be gentle with you.'

Eveline was seconds away from being sick. Taking a deep breath, she pursed her lips and exhaled it slowly out.

'Simon. I'm, er, extremely flattered by your offer—'

He stood. 'Let me get the fizz. It's in the fridge. Back in a jiffy.'

'Simon! Wait!'

She stood, her heart thumping. She'd never received a marriage proposal before, least of all by someone she'd never had the slightest romantic feelings for.

'Yes?'

Be with me, God. She squared her shoulders. 'I am afraid I cannot accept.'

His mouth dropped open. 'Why on earth not?'

'Because...' *I don't fancy you? We're not in a relationship? You're older than my dad?* She fought to find words that wouldn't wound but kept coming up short.

He sighed. 'Eveline, *dear* Eveline. You have *such* a lot to learn about love. It's not like those silly books you read. It's about companionship, shared values, and friendship. Things the two of us have in spades. Marrying me is the sensible choice. Alan and Laura agree.'

Because it means they'll get at least half a million quid each!

He moved towards her, and she stepped back. 'I'm sorry, but my answer is no.'

His brow furrowed. 'But... We've had an understanding.'

What? No! We haven't! 'Simon, I deeply regret if, in any of my actions towards you, I've led—I have given you reason to believe we were anything more than colleagues and friends. I value you greatly, but have never viewed our relationship romantically.'

His chest puffed up. 'Has someone else stolen your affections?'

Eveline's mind snapped to Jack, flooding her cheeks with heat.

Simon's eyes narrowed.

'In order for my affections to have been "stolen",' she began, 'they needed to exist in the first place. You're my *friend*. That's all.'

An uncomfortable silence settled on the room.

He cleared his throat. 'Very well. I'll give you space to compose yourself and consider the many benefits our union would provide. I need not point out that your childbearing years are almost over. Nor that men your age are, for the most part, feckless and inconsistent...'

But you just did point those things out.

'... I hope you pray on this matter and seek appropriate guidance from God.'

She nodded. 'I should get back to the rectory.'

Simon stepped stiffly out of the way and Eveline went into the hall to get her coat.

As if punishing her unacceptable behaviour, he didn't help her put it on or open the door, but stood, his arms glued to his sides as she left.

17

As Jack approached Foxbrooke Manor later that afternoon, he found Jane Austen and Louis XVI on the front steps. They were waving goodbye to a large group of people dressed in century-appropriate clothes.

'It really has been most delightful to make your acquaintance,' said the woman wearing a pale-yellow Regency dress. This was Henry's girlfriend, Libby, who ran living history tours at the Manor. 'Godspeed on your travels and I pray we will have the pleasure of your company again soon.'

'Toodle-pip!' the man called out, waving a frilly handkerchief. Underneath the layers of make-up, and a wig consisting of birds attacking a two-foot-high, hairy fruit basket, Jack recognised Arthur, the Duke of Somerset, who was also Henry, Estelle, and Connor's father.

As the last of the tourists boarded their bus, Arthur strode forward and enveloped him in a bone-crushing hug.

'Jack m'boy!'

Jack recognised the familiar scent of patchouli under the

smells of face powder, rouge, and musty clothes. Arthur Foxbrooke was very different from his children.

Arthur pulled away, his hands still on Jack's shoulders as he peered at him. 'So glad to have you back. How are you holding up? I didn't want to bother you at the funeral. Well done, though, for the eulogy. You here for Henry? Estelle? And have you met our Libby?'

Without waiting for an answer, he took Jack's arm, propelling him towards her.

'Here she is! The reincarnation of Jane Austen herself. Our darling Libby, who runs these brilliant tours and allows me to dress-up and join in.'

Libby held out her hand. 'It's so nice to meet you at last, and thank you for everything you did.'

Jack took it. 'I didn't do anything.'

'Nonsense,' Arthur replied. 'By lending Henry and Libby your London flat, you helped their love grow. And you also inadvertently brought Mr Pussy into our lives.'

Jack bit back a grin.

'Arthur,' Libby said firmly. 'Our cat is now called "Mr P".'

'Is he around?' Jack asked. 'I'm happy to view him from a distance, but...'

'You're terribly allergic,' Libby finished, wincing as if remembering the damage the cat had inflicted on his flat. 'He's around somewhere, probably terrorising the dogs. He's not keen on new people—'

'The big bugger's not keen on *any* people,' Arthur grumbled. 'Apart from Henry and Libby, of course.'

'—and he never goes near the offices,' she continued, 'so you're safe there. Shall we walk that way now? Henry and Estelle are expecting you.'

. . .

Arthur went to get changed and Jack followed Libby through the ground floor of England's most scandalous stately home. Arthur, the Duke of Foxbrooke, had two wives, six children, was a committed naturist, and ran sex parties at the Manor. None of his children shared his passions, but they loved one another unconditionally, and welcomed Jack into the family as one of their own.

Turning down a corridor, Jack heard Estelle's raised voice coming from a room up ahead.

'But if they get bought out, who knows if the new owners will stick to the plans?'

Even though the door was half open, Libby still knocked.

Henry opened it, his face wreathed in smiles as he gazed at her. 'How did it go?'

'Brilliantly. Even when your father's wig flew off after he turned a quadrille into a country dance.'

Henry laughed and drew her into his arms. 'I love you.'

She sighed. 'I love you too.'

'And I love you three,' said Estelle, elbowing them out of the way. 'Are you aware that Jack's standing there like a lemon, not knowing whether to throw up or run away?'

They broke apart, and Henry cleared his throat. 'Sorry about that. Please, do come in.'

'And what's with all the formal crap?' Estelle asked her brother. 'Fuck me, it's like you've got no middle ground.' She pulled Jack in for a hug. 'He's either Sir Stiff-Upper-Lip, or Sir Soppy-Pants.'

Libby giggled. 'Or Sir Stiff-Pants?'

Jack grinned as Estelle made loud retching noises.

Libby kissed Henry's cheek. 'See you at dinner, my liege.'

'Yes, yes,' Estelle said, pushing her out of the door. 'Now bugger off before my brother breaks out into sonnets or something.'

'I love you, fair maiden!' Henry called as the door closed, a big smile on his face.

'I love you more!' Libby yelled from the corridor outside.

'Agh!' Estelle cried through gritted teeth, her hands on either side of her head.

Jack laughed.

Estelle pointed at him. 'Don't encourage them.' She stalked back to a desk on one side of the room. It was covered with papers, empty mugs, and bizarre ornaments. 'You see what I have to put up with?'

He ambled over. 'Are you talking about your brother and his girlfriend, or your messy desk?'

'This isn't a mess,' she retorted. 'It's a highly organised visual representation of my brain.'

Jack glanced across at Henry's desk. It held a laptop, a pad of paper, a pen and a picture of Libby. Each item was placed so precisely, Jack wondered if he'd used a ruler and set square.

Henry brought an extra chair to his side of the room. 'Why don't we sit here?'

Estelle folded her arms. 'This is it, Jack. Time to decide between me and my brother.'

He grinned. 'Stelle, I'm scared to go anywhere near—' he waved his hand at her desk '—that... I'm worried I'll accidentally touch something and get buried under a landslide of paper. Or a half-eaten sandwich from five years ago might crawl out and attack me.'

Henry snorted.

'Rude!' Estelle picked up something from her desk and threw it towards her brother.

Jack caught it mid-flight. It was a squishy Friesian cow with an angry expression on its face. 'What's this?'

'My Moody Cow. It's a stress ball Eveline got me.'

Jack squeezed, and the cow's head bulged. 'Does it work?'

Estelle hesitated, then said 'yes' at the same time her brother said 'no'.

'Stelle, you know I love you, but I'm going to sit at Henry's desk.'

She threw her hands in the air. 'Fine!' she huffed, then stomped to get her chair, accidentally nudging a stack of papers with her bottom and sending them sliding to the floor. 'That was meant to happen,' she said defiantly. 'It's called a brain dump.'

'*Dump* being the operative word,' Henry said under his breath. He went to a tall table at the side of the room, on which stood a coffee machine and kettle. 'Tea? Coffee?'

'Thanks, black coffee would be great.'

'Cappuccino for your older sister,' Estelle said, dragging her chair to Henry's desk. 'And make it a double shot.'

As the Foxbrooke twins bickered amiably, Jack reflected on how different Henry was since finding Libby and coming home. It wasn't just that he smiled more often and made jokes. He just seemed happier in his own skin.

Spending time with Estelle, Henry, Finn and Connor had made Jack realise how much he'd missed them. He'd been so fixated on keeping distance between himself and his parents that he'd lost sight of the other side of Foxbrooke, and the good times he'd had with his friends.

It didn't matter that they'd hardly seen each other over the last decade, or how their lives had changed since they left school. They knew each other on a fundamental level and clicked back together effortlessly.

Over the last ten years, Jack had always seen Foxbrooke as a black and white painting of a prison, and his life in France as a glamorous riot of colour and freedom. But now his flat in Monaco seemed cold and empty. There wasn't a single piece of well-used crockery or an item of well-loved clothing. Apart from his paintings, it was soulless designer perfection.

His mind flipped through images of his clients in feature-less hotel rooms. The endless faces turning over faster and faster until they blurred and made him nauseous. He'd give them all up in a heartbeat for Eveline. The thought shocked him like a bolt of electricity. He'd never had a long-term girl-friend before, but the thought of being with her forever made him excited, not fearful. Could he stay here? Be with her? *Love* her?

His stomach rolled. What was he thinking? His sordid past would always hang between them, like a clothesline dripping with his dirty laundry. Years of secrets and lies that would taint everything.

And even if he *did* give it all up, what did he have left? No qualifications. No career. Nothing to offer her.

'Earth to Jack.'

He blinked at Estelle. 'Sorry, I was miles away.'

Her face crinkled. 'How are you holding up?'

Huh? It took a few moments for him to realise she was referring to his dad. 'Um, not sure, really. It's a work in progress.'

'I bet. There's a lot to process.'

Jack nodded. His father was now just a tiny thought in a mind almost entirely consumed by Eveline. *Let her go. Focus on something different.*

'Yes,' he replied. 'That's why I'm grateful for the chance to help organise the Winter Ball. Even if there isn't a huge amount to do.'

Henry placed a mug of coffee on the desk in front of Jack. He centred it in the middle of a coaster, then turned it so the handle was on the right side.

His sister reached over and nudged it out of position.

'Estelle! For fuc—'

'Should I go through what I've done so far?' Jack interrupted.

Henry sighed. 'Yes, please.'

'That would be simply spiffing,' Estelle added in a posh voice. 'Most efficacious.'

Jack grinned, pulled his laptop out, and opened it up.

'Okay. I've gone through the health and safety forms, risk assessments and insurance, so we know the event is operating well within tolerance. Your mom wants to handle the VIP guest list, so I've allocated her five tables of eight. To maximise profit, I wanted to run an idea past you before I go ahead.'

Estelle leaned forward.

'How about we treat the Winter Ball like a wedding reception?' Jack continued. 'So, people pay top dollar for the whole event, which includes the formal dinner, then we can open up the rest of the night for those who will be paying less? If we use a few more of the downstairs rooms, we can easily fit in another couple of hundred people. And I spoke to Perry about catering. She said it wouldn't cost too much to have a buffet laid on for later in the evening.'

'What about booze?' Estelle asked. 'We can't put on a free bar for an extra two hundred guests.'

'The first group would have wrist bands so could continue to drink for free. The second would buy tickets that didn't include booze. Depending on how much they buy, the profit on that could also pay for the free drinks that the main ticket holders have.'

'That's a fantastic idea,' Henry murmured.

'Thank you,' Estelle replied smugly.

Her brother frowned. 'Huh?'

'Remind me who brought Jack on board? Could it be liddle ole moi?'

Jack laughed. 'And with the extra revenue, I wondered if I could use a proportion to increase the budget for decorations? I've sketched out some ideas I can show you.'

'Yes,' said Estelle. 'Do whatever you like.'

'Shouldn't we take a look first?' Henry asked.

'Why? It's bound to be stunning, and a million times better than anything our parents would come up with.' She turned to Jack. 'Does it involve naked men in gimp masks suspended from the ceiling by silks?'

'Er, no...'

'Does it involve naked women painted to look like floral centrepieces, seated in the middle of each table?'

He snorted. 'Definitely not.'

'Well, then.' Estelle gave her brother a glare. 'See what I mean? If you'd bothered to come to the ones over the last few years, you would have seen just how many variations of naked people Dad could come up with. Last year, I told him there was no way he was paying anyone to take their clothes off. And you know what he did?'

Henry rubbed his forehead as if he had a headache coming on. 'I dread to think.'

'Him and Mom undressed to be Adam and Eve, Mammy was the snake, and their gardening club all showed up—naked, of course—and pretended to be animals.'

Jack covered his mouth as he laughed. His parents may have been awful, but at least they kept their clothes on.

'Anyway,' Estelle continued. 'If I can persuade you to stay, or come back for a bit, I want you to organise next year's Winter Ball. If this music and arts festival I'm working on takes off and becomes a regular thing, then there's no way I'll have the time.'

'How's that all going?'

She puffed out her cheeks. 'Really well, kind of. There's a

big events company that wants to invest, but they're in the middle of a hostile takeover bid. If they're bought out, then I don't know if the new owners will still honour the contract. Hopefully, we'll know by Christmas.'

DARKNESS HAD FALLEN WHEN JACK LEFT THE MANOR. AS HE walked down the long drive, the lights from Saint Saviour's church shone from behind the tall trees. He kept his gaze on the stained-glass windows. What might Eveline be doing? As he passed between the stone gateposts into the courtyard which lay in front of the church, the lights from inside went out.

He stopped under a streetlamp. A few seconds later, Eveline exited through the heavy wooden door, locking it behind her. He froze. Should he wait for her, or turn quickly for home?

'Jack?'

He raised his hand as she approached.

'Were you waiting for me?' she asked.

He shook his head. 'I was coming from a meeting with Estelle and Henry.'

She smiled. 'Did it go well?'

He nodded, gazing at her. The streetlamp above had turned her pale skin golden and her hair was a halo of fire.

'Jack?'

He didn't respond. He was teetering on a knife's edge, caught between reason and desire.

She bit her lower lip. The sight sent a pulse to his cock. *Leave. Now!*

'Would you be able to come to the rectory for five minutes?'

No! Just say no!

'Just to talk.'

Fuck, fuck, fuck!

'Please?'

He nodded and followed her, his feet like lead.

She let them in the front door and locked it behind her.

'Would you like something to drink?' she asked, hanging up her coat.

He shook his head, the power of speech deserting him.

'Okay, let's sit in the living room.'

Eveline entered the first room on the left, turned on two small side lights, pulled the heavy curtains across the windows, then went to the fireplace and bent over.

Jack stared at the mantelpiece. 'Can I help?'

'I'm fine with the fire. Could you please close the door so we can keep the warmth in?'

He did. With the low lights and the flickering of the flames as they caught, the room was cosy and intimate. He felt trapped.

'Won't you sit?'

He chose an armchair, perching on the end and preparing to bolt at the first opportunity.

As the kindling took, Eveline carefully placed larger logs on them at an angle, then sat on the end of the sofa nearest to him.

'Jack?'

He forced his gaze to rest on her. The soft light from the fire caressed her cheeks and sent wave after wave of desire flooding through his veins. But her expression broke his heart. A mix of uncertainty and determination.

Whatever she throws at you, you can handle it.

'Do you believe in fate?'

'Er...' *Did* he? He thought back to his shitty childhood,

then to the series of events that led to his career. Some of them *did* feel like fate. 'I don't know.'

He didn't want to ask why. This was an occasion when he wanted to shut a conversation down, not let it grow.

'I believe in God's will. And that he has a plan for all of us.'

Okay. So we're back to Christian vs atheist.

'A year ago, I was waiting at a bar in London for Estelle. She was deliberately late, hoping someone might approach me.' Eveline cleared her throat. 'I was very uncomfortable and started praying to God.'

Jack's heart rate rose in anticipation as to where this was going.

'I asked God for a miracle. I asked him for...'—she swallowed—'...for the right person for me. And the very next moment, you said hello.'

'Eveline, that wasn't God. It was me. I made a mistake.'

Her lower lip trembled. 'Do you believe meeting me that night was a mistake?'

'No! Yes? Fuck!' He ran his hands through his hair, rapidly losing what little control he thought he had.

'Jack. I truly believe God sent you to me. Both on that night, and now.'

He shook his head. It couldn't be true.

'The moment I saw you,' she continued. 'I felt like my soul saw yours. I've never felt this way about anyone before. Ever.'

He hung his head. He couldn't take her raw and pure honesty. It only illuminated his own darkness and deceptions.

'I *know* you feel something for me. It may not be as deep as my feelings for you...'

Fuck!

'... But I know it's there.'

He was in hell. This beautiful angel was opening the door to her heart, and he had to shut it in her face.

'The day before yesterday, you said there was nothing wrong with me,' she continued, her voice wavering. 'But there has to be. Please Jack, tell me what it is?'

His head jerked up. Eveline was sitting poker straight, her knees pressed together and her hands on her lap. Her body language was poised, but her eyes were anguished.

'Is it because I'm five years older than you?'

He shook his head. That was nothing.

'Is it because your life is in France? Because I could always—'

'No!' He could never ask her to give up her calling.

'Is it the pigs? I know they're naughty and noisy and rather smelly.'

Shaking his head, he let out a bitter laugh.

'Is it because I'm a vicar?'

'No.' As he said the words, he realised he meant them. Eveline's career highlighted just how socially unacceptable his was, but it didn't mean he wanted her to change anything about herself.

'Do you feel *anything* for me?' she asked.

He dug the heels of his hands into his eye sockets and let out a strangled cry.

'Jack?'

He raised his head. 'Yes, Eveline, I do. I feel *everything* for you.'

A solitary tear ran down her cheek. It felt like acid dripping on his soul.

'Then why can't we be together?'

His throat was too full of emotion, but he forced the words out.

'I'm a bad—I'm not the right person for you. I'm not good enough for you—'

'But—'

'Eveline, please. I've done things in my life I can't tell anyone about. Not my friends, not my family, not even you.'

Her face paled.

'The Jack everyone thinks they know is a lie. I'm not who anyone thinks I am. And I can never be involved with someone like you.'

Silence.

'Are you a contract killer?'

He stared at her in shock.

She swallowed. 'Like John Wick?'

He huffed out an incredulous laugh. 'No. Jesus Chri—No.'

'Are you a serial killer?'

'What the f—? No, Eveline. I've never killed anyone. I've never even been in a fight before.'

She visibly relaxed. 'Are you a thief?'

'No!'

'On the run from the law?'

'No.'

'From the mafia?'

'What? No!'

'Loan sharks?'

'I'm not in debt to anyone. Neither have I broken any laws or, to my knowledge, pissed anyone off.'

'Have you abandoned your wife? Your ch-children?'

Jesus Christ. 'I've never been married. I don't have a girl-friend, or any children.'

'Are you addicted to d—illegal drugs?'

'No! I drink. That's it.'

'Are you dying?'

'What?'

'If you have a terminal illness, that might make you reluctant to be with me.'

He shook his head. 'I had a full health check last month. I'm fine.'

She wiped her eyes. 'Then what is it?'

They could never be together, but he could give her the truth.

He held her gaze. 'I'm not a party planner. I'm an escort.'

Her brow furrowed. 'Like a professional companion? You escort people to events?'

Jack shook his head, his heart breaking. 'No, Eveline. I'm a sex worker. I fuck women for money.'

❧ 18 ❧

For a brief second, there was nothing but ringing silence in Eveline's head. Then her brain went into overdrive, spitting out questions faster than fireworks. How did Jack start doing it? Did he enjoy it? Would he stop if he were with her? How many women had he slept with? Is this why he called himself Jasper? Was the woman in the bar a client? Did he even *like* the film *Groundhog Day*?

Jack was staring at her, his expression desolate, as if waiting for the axe of her censure to fall. But underneath the whirl of her mind, there was unbridled relief. *It's not me*. And, as for what he did to make a living? In her line of work, she'd met many people who'd done things a million times worse.

He must have taken her silence as an affirmation of his biggest fears, as he stood.

'I'll leave.'

She shot to her feet. 'No! Can I ask you a couple of questions?'

He shrugged, his posture slumped and defeated.

Grabbing his hand, she pulled him to the sofa. 'Please sit.'

He did, shifting his knee away from hers when she placed herself next to him. She smoothed her hands across her skirt, trying to remain composed, when her heart and brain were racing each other to win her attention.

'So,' she began. 'would you say your feelings for me are in the same, er... *ballpark* as the ones I have for you?'

He looked at her in astonishment. 'Eveline, did you hear what I just said? I'm a—'

'Do you feel romantically inclined towards me?'

He pinched the bridge of his nose. 'Yes! But that's not the point!'

Excitement flared in her chest. 'So, in the bar, it wasn't an act?'

His hand dropped to his knee. 'No! I...' He shook his head.

'Do you like *Groundhog Day*? *Galaxy Quest*? *The Princess Bride*? *Star Wars*?'

'*These* are your concerns? Seriously?'

She nodded.

'Yes.' He sighed. 'I love those films.'

Relief flooded through her. Somehow that fact made everything better, as if he hadn't lied about who he truly was.

Eveline cleared her throat. 'I know this is an unfair question to ask, but would you contemplate stopping your, er, *current* line of work if you were with me?'

Jack's eyes were wide. 'You're not considering it, are you?'

'Please, just answer the question.'

'Yes. I'd stop in a heartbeat.'

She smiled. 'Well then, we're all good.'

'What? I don't think you understand.'

Her hand snapped to her chest. 'Of course, I didn't think. I'm so sorry.'

'Sorry?' he repeated, as if she was now speaking ancient Greek.

'About payment. I don't have much, but—'

'Eveline! Jesu—' He ran his hands into his hair. 'No! Fuck's sake! You're not giving me anything.'

'Oh. Well, I have to say that *is* a relief.' She let out a short laugh. 'You don't become a vicar for the money.'

He shook his head. 'I don't think you get what I've been saying.'

Eveline held up her hand, ticking off each point in turn on her fingers. 'Your job is having sex with women in exchange for money. You would stop doing this if you were in a romantic relationship with me. You're attracted to me enough to pursue such a relationship, and I wouldn't need to pay you to sleep with me. Oh! And you like all my favourite films. Have I missed anything out?'

'But... But I'm a *prostitute*!'

'So?'

'And—' He gestured to her clerical shirt and dog collar. 'You're a vicar!'

She shrugged. 'Vicars are pretty forgiving types, but that's not the point. There's nothing *to* forgive. You haven't done anything wrong.'

'Huh?'

Reaching forward, she touched his knee. 'I believe there's a very big difference between you and the sex workers I know.'

'What the—You know sex workers?'

'Of course. Did you think being a vicar is just cucumber sandwiches and cake sales, with a bit of singing and light praying on the side?'

He looked utterly flummoxed. 'I, er... I hadn't really thought about it.'

'The women and sometimes young men I meet are in very different situations to you. I presume that you're not working under addiction, coercion or dire financial need?'

He shook his head.

'Are your clients abusive or controlling?'

'No, not at all.'

'And I'm guessing that due to the *nature* of the sexual act itself, you have to enjoy it? Or do you take pills to achieve an erection?'

He looked sideswiped with shock. Then his cheeks reddened, and he dropped his head. 'No, I do not need to take a pill.'

'Well, there we go. I presume the lady who arrived late to the bar that night was a client?'

He nodded, still looking down.

'She seemed very nice and also rather nervous. Was it her first time using such a service?'

He nodded again.

'Were you able to put her at ease and provide the pleasure she was seeking?'

Jack lifted his head, his eyebrows raised as if not quite believing the words that were coming out of her mouth.

'I apologise for questioning your ability to do your job,' Eveline said quickly, feeling her cheeks heating. 'I obviously have some experience in your, erm, *skillset*. And I'm sure you were able to, er, adequately satisfy her.' *Stop talking!*

He passed his hand over his face. 'Eveline. Are you seriously telling me you don't have a problem with the fact that I have sex with women for money?'

'Had.'

'Huh?'

'You *had* sex with women for money. You said that if you were with me, then you would stop.'

He nodded, his face cycling from shock to disbelief to something that looked like hope.

Taking her bag from the coffee table beside them, she

opened it up. 'I will freely admit that "former sex worker" is not one of the occupations I thought a prospective partner might have.' She rummaged about, trying to find what she'd bought earlier. 'But given the circumstances, I do not have a problem with it. Ah! There they are.' She held up a box.

'Condoms?'

'Yes. By your statement earlier about a health check, I'm assuming that you don't have any sexually transmitted diseases? However, we still need to use these as I am not on birth control.'

'You—you want to have *sex*?'

She nodded. 'With you, very much so. I haven't been intimate with a man for over thirteen years. And—'

'Thirteen *years*?'

'Yes, since I dedicated my life to God. I was waiting for...' She held his gaze. 'I was waiting for you.'

Silence. Had she been too presumptive buying the condoms? Too forward? Her confidence and bravado were rapidly disintegrating.

He swallowed. 'Eveline. I...' He shifted slightly, grasping the fabric of his jeans just above his knee and pulling it down. She glanced at his crotch and he shifted again, placing his hands over it. Was he aroused?

Before she could second guess herself, she reached out and touched his knee.

He sucked in a breath.

She moved closer, separating her legs so his right thigh was caught between hers.

'Jack,' she whispered. 'Do you want to have sex with me?'

He nodded.

Joy bubbled up inside her and she let out a nervous and excited laugh.

He smiled at her, his eyes full of love.

This is it! It's happening! Tugging her cardigan off, she threw it over her shoulder, then unbuttoned her clerical shirt.

'What? What are you doing?'

Her shirt joined her jumper on the floor. 'What does it look like? I'm taking my clothes off.' She faced him, goosebumps running across her skin despite the warmth from the fire. Only a bra remained on her top half. 'If that's alright with you?'

Jack stared at her breasts as if he'd never seen a pair before.

'I know it's not particularly fancy,' she said, nerves fluttering inside her tummy. She brought her arms up to cover herself and his hands shot out, lightly holding her wrists to stop her. His thumbs made hypnotic circles on her skin.

'Don't,' he murmured. 'You're beautiful.'

In her peripheral vision, she saw her breasts rising and falling as she breathed. Her nipples were hard and tingling, poking through the white cotton of her bra as if trying to break free.

He released her wrists, but his thumb kept contact with her skin, drawing lines of fire up her inner arms. His touch was so light, but it felt like a brand, searing down to her soul and marking her as his for life. She held his gaze, the fathomless depth of his pupils drawing her deeper and deeper.

When he reached the top of her arms, he swallowed, hesitating. She inched forward, willing him to touch her breasts. There was a beat. Then he moved inward, the pressure becoming firmer, as his large hands cupped her, the pads of his thumbs grazing over the tips of her nipples.

A lightning bolt of pleasure shot down between her legs and she gasped, her eyes fluttering as if to close. She forced them open, feeding from the fierce desire in his eyes. Hunger and need radiated off him in waves.

His thumbs continued to circle her nipples, pushing the

tips against the fabric of her bra, then releasing them. They sprang back with a snap of sensation that made her shiver.

The feelings were overwhelming, but at the same time not enough. She unhooked the clasp of her bra and shook the straps off her shoulders. He lifted his hands to let it drop between them, and she arched forward, offering herself to him.

'God, Eveline,' Jack murmured as he stared. 'You're so beautiful.'

Her heart was pounding faster and faster. She'd never felt so powerful before and yet so desperate to surrender her body to his. She moved to his lap, spreading her legs wide to straddle him, her skirt riding up her thighs. Holding the sides of his face, she kissed him, her tongue sweeping into the wet heat of his mouth, his groan tingling through her lips.

She could barely keep up with the feelings ricocheting around inside her, but when his hands found her bare breasts, she tore her lips from his with a gasp. Then his head dipped, and he sucked a nipple into his mouth.

'Oh, oh, oh!'

Blinding pleasure tore through her and she clung to him, her fingers lacing in his hair to tug him closer. As he pulled the nipple further in, the rough flat of his tongue rubbed across the tip. Sparkles of light rained down inside her, pooling between her legs, urging her to rock against the hardness of his cock. After so many years without physical intimacy, her body was crying out for him. She didn't want to take things slowly. She needed him inside her now.

Shaking, she fumbled to unfasten his jeans, yanking at the stiff button as if to punish it for getting in her way. His hand covered hers, capturing her fingers.

He raised his head, his gaze unfocused, his cheeks flushed.

She growled at him.

The corners of his mouth twitched, and he raised an eyebrow in question.

'I want to have sex,' she said, tugging her hand from his. She resumed her attack on his trousers. 'Now.'

He interlaced his fingers with hers, pulling them away. 'Can I pleasure you first?'

She stopped, startled. 'I, er, just want to get to the good bit,' she stammered.

'Hmm,' he replied, lazily stroking her nipple. 'So, this doesn't feel good?'

Her laugh was breathless. 'Yes, of course...' He maintained eye contact as he brought his mouth to her breast. 'Oh, oh my —Ah!' He sucked and nibbled until she was panting and writhing on his lap. 'But... Jack—'

'Hmm?' he replied. The vibrations from his voice trembled through her, amplifying every sensation.

'Oh! Er, ahhhhh!' She pulled away from him before she lost all control. 'But what about you?'

His lips were wet, and the sight tugged deep in her core. He licked her other nipple, then brought his fingers to the glistening tips, spreading the moisture in agonising circles.

'Me?' His voice was a dark rumble.

'Yes, this er—Oh! Oh!—' she gasped as he pinched the hardened nubs. 'I want—Ahh! You, I want *you* to enjoy it,' she finally managed.

His gaze was incendiary, his fingers still teasing her. 'Feel my cock, Eveline.'

A wave of heat barrelled through her at his words, lighting fires that scorched across her skin. 'I...'

He shifted his hips, pressing his hardness into her aching pussy. 'You don't think I'm enjoying this?'

Shifting against him, she was suddenly aware of how very wet she was.

He leaned in, nipping her neck. 'I want to give you more.'

More? She was a breath away from fainting. 'I don't think I c-could take it—' He rolled her nipples between his fingers and thumbs. 'Aah! I think, I think,' she stuttered. 'I'm pretty much maxed out about now.'

'Hmm?' He hummed into her neck. 'Don't you want to come?'

Her hands fluttered to his waist, trying to anchor herself in a storm of sensation. 'You don't need to worry about that. It's —it's not going to happen.'

He kissed his way to her ear, nuzzling the lobe. 'Can you show me how you touch yourself? I'm a fast learner.'

She shook her head. 'I don't.'

He raised his head. 'Never?'

Bringing her hands to his, she pulled them away from her breasts.

He raised another questioning eyebrow.

'I can't concentrate when you do that,' she said, gulping in a breath as if it would centre her. 'I've never touched myself or had an orgasm. It's completely normal. I can still enjoy sex.'

His lips grazed hers. 'Can I try?'

'Try what?'

'To make you come.'

Her laugh was breathless. 'I'm sure you're very competent at your line of work, but I assure you it won't work.'

His hands were now stroking her skin, passing from her neck down to her waist, but missing her breasts altogether.

'Have you ever tried?' he murmured.

She shook her head.

'Has anyone else?'

She shrugged. 'A bit?' She twisted to push her breasts towards his hands, but he continued to avoid them. It was utterly maddening.

'Will you let *me* try?'

A sob of frustration was inside her throat, pushing to come out. She didn't want him to try. It wouldn't work, and she'd only disappoint him. Why couldn't they just have sex and that be enough?

'Would it help if I told you how much I love touching you?' he said, his hands finally returning to her breasts, the darts of pleasure making her tremble. 'How much I love tasting you?' he whispered, before capturing her lips with his, his tongue sweeping fire into her mouth.

When she was breathless and boneless, he pulled away until his lips were barely touching hers.

'Please?' he asked.

'B-but it won't work.'

'It doesn't have to result in an orgasm,' he murmured. 'But I hope you'll enjoy it.'

He dipped his head to suck on her nipple and her hips jerked of their own accord.

'Will you stop if I ask?'

He brought his eyes back to hers. 'Eveline, the moment anything doesn't feel good, you just tell me. Okay?'

She nodded, biting her lip with insecurity. 'I don't want you to be bored.'

Both his eyebrows raised. 'With you? Never going to happen.'

'Can we set a time limit?'

'Will that make you feel more comfortable?'

She nodded, relieved.

'Okay. Four hours.'

'Four *hours*?'

'Yes.' His smile was sinful.

'I was thinking more like ten minutes?'

He laughed, then pressed kisses to her face, punctuating his words. 'I've been waiting for over a year to touch you. I've dreamed and fantasised about this moment. And as long as you're enjoying yourself, I don't want to be rushed.'

'But, but... What are you going to do?'

He tucked his finger into the top of her skirt. 'I thought I'd start by getting you naked.'

Yes! Just say yes! 'Oh, er... Okay then.'

In the blink of an eye, she was on her feet, the zip on the back of her skirt pulled down, and his hands working the fabric over her hips.

'Ah! That's, er... Quick?' she gasped.

He stared up at her, his gaze heavy with hunger. 'Over a year, Eveline...'

Her skirt fell to the floor, and she stepped out of it, her heart hammering in her chest. She'd had sex before, but her previous partners were clueless boys compared to Jack.

As if to further underline the difference, he tugged her hips forward, burying his face between her legs and breathing in.

Flailing at his head, she pulled him away. 'Oh my goodness! What are you doing?'

He raised an eyebrow as he smirked up at her. 'You're right. I forgot to remove your tights and underwear first.' He hooked his fingers inside the waistband. 'May I?'

Yes! 'Erm...' She stalled for time, suddenly unsure. Her many fantasies about being with Jack had never involved more than missionary sex. She was utterly unprepared for any of this. 'Only if you don't do *that* again,' she managed.

He nodded, his gaze inscrutable, then gently pulled her tights and underwear down. She stepped out of them, acutely aware she was now completely naked and he was still fully dressed.

His gaze raked unashamedly over her. 'Eveline,' he breathed. 'You're so beautiful.'

Electricity tingled across her skin, overriding her insecurities. 'Will you take your clothes off?' she asked shyly.

He hesitated.

'Please? I would... like to touch you.'

His eyes briefly closed, and he exhaled through gritted teeth. 'Eveline, if you do that, I might explode.'

She reached forward and popped the top button of his shirt. 'Compromise?'

He nodded, stood and allowed her to undress him. Jack Newton was by far the best present Eveline had ever unwrapped. She'd seen the magnificence of his chest once before when he'd dashed downstairs in his boxers, not expecting to find her or Simon in his mother's house. But now she was up close and very personal.

'You're very muscley,' she whispered as she pushed the shirt off his broad shoulders. 'Do you go to the gym a lot?'

He nodded, his jaw tense, as she ran her fingers across the hard planes of his pecs, then down the ridges of his abdomen. She reached behind him to pull the shirt from the back of his jeans, using the movement as an excuse to rub her nipples against his chest. His skin was so hot, the smattering of hair so soft. She placed a kiss over his heart.

He tugged the shirt completely off and encircled her with his arms, one hand cupping her bottom, the other cradling her head as he brought his lips to hers. She surrendered into his touch, opening her mouth to his tongue, parting her legs slightly to anchor the hard ridge of his cock between them. She gave herself to him, and in return, he overloaded her every cell with pleasure.

Then her feet were off the floor, and she was in his arms. He didn't break their kiss, and she didn't open her eyes. She felt the back of the sofa as he lay her down, his left arm cradling her and cupping her breast, his right stroking her abdomen, lower and lower.

She tensed, nerves fighting with desire.

His hand stilled, and he broke their kiss, his breathing almost as unsteady as hers. 'You okay?'

'I don't want to let you down,' she whispered. 'I don't want to be your only failure.'

His face was tight with emotion as he shook his head. 'You could never let me down.' He dropped his forehead to hers. 'Never in a million years did I think I'd meet someone like you, let alone be like this…' He kissed her cheek. 'You're my greatest success and the only outcome I want is your pleasure. Tell me with your words or your body what feels good. That's all I want. Okay?'

She nodded, her heart full to the brim with love. Then he smiled, and it overflowed. Reaching for his left hand, she guided it back to her breast and tilted her head to bring her lips back to his.

The energy shifted as his tongue slicked into her mouth. She arched off the sofa, pushing her body into his hands. His touch was no longer tentative. He followed her cues, his other hand trailing down her abdomen as she spread her legs to welcome him.

His fingertips brushed her clit, and with his other hand, he tugged her nipple. Electricity arced between the two points, and her hips bucked. She clung to him, eyes squeezed closed as the shocks continued. She'd never been touched so intimately before and with such intention. Sinking into the feelings, she let go of any thought or worry, as Jack circled her centre of her pleasure.

Fire was radiating out from his fingertips, through her lower abdomen. She instinctively squeezed her tummy muscles and tensed her thighs. His touch was assured and relentless, rubbing her nipple and her clit as if they were sparking off each other, preparing to combust. As the pressure built, she couldn't breathe fast enough and ripped her mouth from his, burying her face in his neck.

Everything within her was drawing up and up and up, building and intensifying like a kettle coming unstoppably to the boil. Above the pounding of her heart, she heard herself calling out—'Oh, oh, oh...'

Her muscles contracted tighter and tighter until she snapped with a high-pitched cry. An intense wave of indescribable pleasure pulsated through her, knocking out her breath, her vision, her knowledge of where she ended and the rest of the universe began. Wave upon wave of sensation crashed through her, pushed on by his touch. It was too much to comprehend, so she let go, losing herself to the feelings and losing herself to him.

❧ 19 ❧

As the tremors subsided, giddy emotion burst out of Eveline in pure, unrestrained laughter.

'It worked!' She gazed at him. 'Jack! Was that an orgasm?'

He nodded, grinning broadly, and brushed a kiss across her lips. 'How did it feel?'

She sighed contentedly. 'Like nothing I could have ever imagined.'

His fingers were still lazily stroking between her legs. 'Would you like another one?'

She blinked at him. Was it possible? Her body seemed to be humming at a higher frequency, waiting for another nudge to send it into the stratosphere.

'It's just...' Jack began, dropping kisses along the line of her jaw. 'I'm pretty desperate to taste you.'

Eveline's thighs instinctively clenched at the thought. It felt so decadently wrong, yet her body was screaming *yes!*

'I've never experienced that before,' she admitted. 'I don't know if I'll like it.'

'Can we try?' he murmured.

'And I'm not sure if *you* will like it.'

Lifting his head, he pinned her with a gaze that stopped her breath. His finger pushed gently inside her and she inhaled sharply, hot flushes rippling through her. He added a second finger, and she clenched around him, magnifying the sensations.

He slowly pumped in and out, each thrust making her gasp. Her inner muscles were tensing, already seeking out another rush like she'd just experienced. It was as if her body now knew what to do and wanted more.

Her hips rocked into his hand, pushing against him each time his fingers pressed deeper. Her heartbeat quickened. *Could* she have another orgasm? Suddenly, he pulled out, and she whimpered with frustration.

'Jack...'

His eyes trapped hers, the heat in them making her pause. She watched, her breath coming faster, as he brought his wet fingers to his mouth and sucked them.

She gasped as lust barrelled through her, scattering her thoughts.

He slowly withdrew his fingers, flicking his tongue over the tips. Everything deep inside her clenched.

'Please?' he asked.

She nodded, too stunned to speak.

He shifted, moving half off the sofa to kneel on the floor, settling himself between her legs and kissing the inside of her thighs.

Her hand unconsciously came to cover her heart as she stared at him. His hair was mussed up from where she'd been clutching it, and the gold flecks in his irises seemed to be glowing. He was otherworldly beautiful. And about to kiss her where no man had wanted to before...

His fingers parted her curls to open her to him. Holding her gaze, he dragged his tongue up the underside of her clit and flicked it over the top.

It was like being shot by Cupid. She arched off the sofa with a cry, intense pleasure rocketing through her.

Jack's palms pressed down, holding her in place. Then he did it again.

And again.

And again.

Sensations spun and sparked inside her like a thousand electric shocks. Just as she almost had a handle on it, he increased the speed or the pressure. She struggled to draw air in fast enough, her body trembling. Each time she caught her breath and gazed down at Jack, the sight of his eyes locked with hers sent another pulse of pleasure through her.

He raised his head. 'Touch your breasts,' he growled, before his tongue returned to licking her clit.

Shaking, she cupped them. Her muscles were drawing up again, gathering themselves for another climax. It felt like she was running full tilt towards the edge of a precipice.

Holding his gaze, she rubbed her nipples between her fingers and thumbs.

The climax crashed through her with such sudden intensity that her head jerked back and stars flashed against the blackness of her eyelids. The sharp stabs of sensation from her fingers and his tongue were the catalyst for breathtaking waves of pleasure that pounded through her, over and over. It was ecstasy beyond logical thought and comprehension, dissolving the boundaries of her body and mind.

As the feelings slowly ebbed, she pulled at his hair, desperately needing his body on hers.

He seemed to understand, moving up and stroking her hair from her face. 'Eveline,' he whispered.

Her heart was still beating double time, her chest heaving as she stared at him. Just like at the bar over a year ago, her soul left her body to dance with his. But now everything was even sweeter and more beautiful because she knew to the depths of her heart that she loved him. Any stress, anxiety or flickers of doubt had left his face. His expression was relaxed and happy, showing her the real Jack that she knew was inside.

He kissed her. 'Thank you.'

She giggled. 'I think the thanks should go the other way.'

He shook his head. 'You've given me the greatest gift.'

'And you've given me my first ever orgasms. Honestly, I feel so happy right now, I want to run down Foxbrooke high street naked and tell everyone.'

He laughed. 'Estelle's dad would approve.'

'Very true.'

They stared at each other for a moment, grinning like idiots. Then she raised her hips to press against his. 'Can we have sex now?'

He hesitated.

'Please?'

'Are you sure?'

'Yes! I don't know if you've noticed, but I've been practically begging you for it.'

He looked relieved. 'Well, in that case.'

'Hallelujah!' She pushed on his chest and he knelt between her legs. This time, when her fingers went to undo the buttons of his jeans, he didn't protest. Her heart leapt off the blocks, nervous excitement making her fingers tingle as she reached inside his boxers and pulled out his cock.

She swallowed. 'And it's meant to fit in, er, me?'

He huffed out a laugh. 'That's the general idea.'

'Inconceivable...'

He laughed again at the line from the *Princess Bride*, but stopped as she swept her hand up his length.

It had been so long since she'd seen a cock, and her experience back in her early twenties had mainly consisted of drunk fumbling in the dark with strangers. She couldn't get over how hard he was underneath such soft skin. The head was wet and sticky, and she swiped her thumb across it.

'Is this okay?' she asked, glancing up. 'I don't really know what I'm doing.'

His lips were parted, his cheeks darker, his gaze more intense. 'It's incredible.'

Emboldened, she swept her hand from base to tip, twisting when she got to the head. With the other, she cupped his balls, feeling their weight.

He let out a long slow breath through pursed lips, the muscles of his abdomen tight, his hands formed into fists by his sides.

'Can I suck it?'

His eyes widened, and he opened his mouth as if to speak, but then started coughing, pulling away from her.

'Are you okay?'

He held up a finger as if to ask for a minute, his eyes streaming.

She got off the sofa. 'Do you want me to get you a glass of water?'

He shook his head. 'I'm, I'm okay,' he finally managed, the coughs turning into laughs.

'What did I do wrong?'

He wiped his eyes, shucked his jeans and boxers and reached for her, drawing her into his arms and laying her back on the sofa.

'You took me by surprise,' he murmured, brushing her lips

with a kiss. 'It was like one of my fantasies coming to life. Unexpected and a little overwhelming.'

'Oh, thank goodness for that.'

She ran a finger down the indentation of his spine to his firm backside. Now all of *her* fantasies were coming to life. Jack was naked and on top of her, his body hot and hard. She ran her toes through the hairs on his legs, moving her wet centre back and forth across his solid length.

He groaned into her neck, one hand coming between them to roll her nipple between his fingers and thumb. Desire lit her up from the inside out and she turned her head, her mouth seeking his. His lips found and claimed hers, his tongue stoking the fire that burned deep between her legs. She undulated her hips, desperate to feel him inside her.

He broke the kiss, reaching for the packet of condoms on the table.

Captivated, she watched him sheath himself, her heart racing with anticipation.

He grabbed a sofa cushion. 'Lift,' he said, tucking it under her when she raised her hips.

She opened her legs wider, her pussy clenching unconsciously, as if trying to draw him in. Reaching for him, she pulled him down, squirming to find the head of his cock.

He held back, his expression serious. 'Are you sure?'

'Oh, for goodness sake!' She slapped his bottom. 'Enough already! Get on with it!'

He laughed. 'As you wish...'

Settling above her, he bracketed her head with his forearms, holding her gaze as he nudged at her entrance.

She tensed, suddenly worried how he would fit.

His hips stayed still, but his lips coaxed hers apart, his tongue licking fire into her mouth. She melted into the sensations, her fingers running down the expanse of his back, revelling in the feel of him. Keeping their kiss, he shifted his weight to one side, his free hand coming between them to rub the tip of her nipple.

Pleasure zinged down to her clit, and she bucked her hips, feeling the delicious stretch as he filled her another inch. Even though she'd had sex before, it had been years ago and bore little comparison to this. With Jack, the feelings were monumental and all-encompassing, as if they were rewriting the playbook and creating something completely new.

With every sweep of his tongue and stroke of his fingers, she softened to let him in deeper. Prickles of light filled her abdomen, flaring each time she pushed up to take more. Love and lust looped and spun inside her, twisting around each other until they were one thread of pure pleasure.

As his cock filled her completely, she squeezed.

He groaned into her mouth.

'Does that feel nice?' she asked, pulling her lips from his.

He stared down at her, his expression dark with desire. '*Nice?* It's...' He huffed out a breath as he smiled. 'It's beyond.'

'Beyond what?' She squeezed again, biting the inside of her cheek with glee at the tension that flickered across his face.

'Beyond everything,' he growled, thrusting his hips forward.

'Oh!' she cried at the sudden shock of pleasure.

'You, Eveline Shaw,' he said, withdrawing an inch. 'Are a minx.' He thrust again, and she gasped, sensation shooting through her core.

'I don't know what you mean,' she replied, feigning innocence. She squeezed tightly around him and he raised an eyebrow.

'I said...' He pulled out a fraction. 'You are a naughty, naughty, minx.' He underlined the last three words with a jerk of his hips and a tweak of her nipple.

She threw back her head, crying out. Gulping in air to ground her, she met the fire in his eyes with her own.

'I don't know—What... You... Mean...' she replied, squeezing and bucking her hips up to his to punctuate her words.

His eyelids fluttered as if to close, then he took a deep breath. 'That's fighting talk.'

Heart hammering, she brought her hand up and crooked her index finger as if beckoning him forward.

'Bring it.'

He smiled with devilish delight. 'Oh, I will.'

Shivering with anticipation, she squeezed around his cock as he slowly dragged it out of her, further than before. Without any change in his breathing or expression, he thrust forward, taking her by surprise.

She clung to him, sensations shuddering through her. 'Oh my goodness!'

His lips found her ear as he withdrew again. 'What are you, Eveline Shaw?'

'Um...'

He thrust again, and she bucked her hips to meet his.

'Shall I tell you what you are?' he growled, bending her leg then holding her backside, pulling her to him.

'Yes, please.'

He nipped her earlobe, and she squeaked.

'You are...' he began, sliding out.

She held her breath.

'... A naughty, naughty, minx,' he rumbled, plunging into her with every word. 'Haunting my dreams, owning my cock, driving me insane...'

Thrills raced through her—prickling sparkles of light that collided with each other, setting off chain reactions until she couldn't keep track. Everything was urgent, chaotic pleasure, with the only points of reference being his thick cock filling her pussy and his thrilling words filling her ear.

'And you're a minx...' *Thrust.* 'Because you know...' *Thrust.* 'Exactly...' *Thrust.* 'What you're...' *Thrust.* 'Doing to me...' *Thrust.* 'You make me...' *Thrust.* 'Lose my—' *Thrust.* 'Mind...' *Thrust, thrust, thrust.*

She clung to him, urging him on as a swell moved deep within her. He circled his hips as he pounded, pushing the feelings on until she had no choice but to lose herself to them, gasping for breath as the wave carried her unstoppably on.

'Eveline... God, Eveline...'

Her muscles coiled tighter and tighter as the wave reached its peak, pushing out her breath in one last desperate cry. Then it broke, crashing through her with blinding pleasure. She clung to him, convulsing around the thickness of his cock, his thrusts multiplying every sensation.

He cried her name again, his hips jerking faster, then he shuddered above her, holding her tightly, his breath ragged.

Her heart bloomed with emotion until she didn't know whether to laugh or cry with joy. All the years of loneliness, all the waiting for her perfect man, had been worth it.

Thank you, God. Thank you for bringing me Jack.

He was still breathing hard in the crook of her neck, but she turned her head, kissing as much of him as she could reach.

He raised onto his elbows, staring down at her with drowsy eyes.

I love you, Jack. I love you with all my heart and soul.

'How did I get so lucky?' he murmured as if to himself.

Her cheeks hurt from smiling so much. 'I'm the lucky one. If I hadn't met you, I would still be orgasm-less.'

He kissed her. 'And that would be a terrible shame.' He shifted to his side and ran his fingers down her chest, circling her nipples. 'I'm going to enjoy helping you make up for lost time.'

'Not as much as I will,' she replied, shivering with excitement.

Palming her breast, he grinned. 'I reckon you're going to have to have at least ten a day for the foreseeable if we're going to play catch up.'

'*Ten?*'

'Yep. I know I'm not the sharpest tool in the box, but even *I* can figure out you need to have another seven before the clock strikes midnight and I turn into a pumpkin.'

The mention of the time brought reality seeping in like a bad smell under the door. Eveline looked at her watch and frowned.

He kissed her. 'It's going to be okay.'

'Do you need to get back to your mum's?'

'At some point, yes. I don't want her to worry. But I don't have to leave right now.'

He held her close, and she kissed his cheek. 'Is it terrible of me to wish the whole of the world would go away for a bit?'

She felt his smile. 'Not at all. You spend your life putting everyone else first. It's about time you went to the front of the queue.'

'Jack...'

'Yes, angel?'

She jiggled with joy at the endearment, and he raised his head.

'What was that?'

'My happy dance because you called me "angel".'

His expression faltered for a second, before his smile returned. 'And what happens when I call you "minx"?'

She felt heat bloom across her skin.

'You blush,' he stated, dropping a kiss onto each cheek.

From his jeans pocket on the floor, his phone buzzed. He didn't move.

'Do you need to get that?' she asked.

He shook his head. 'Nothing good seems to come from answering it when I'm with you.'

'It might be important?'

'Nothing's more important than you.'

She squealed with excitement inside, but externally tried to hide it.

He raised an eyebrow. 'Is that meant to be your "stern vicar" face?'

She giggled. 'Might be.' Reaching to the floor, she snagged his jeans with her hand as the buzzing stopped.

'Kicking me out already?'

She took the phone from the back pocket and gave it to him.

He glanced at the screen and sighed. 'It was Mum. I should call her back.'

'Jack... Are you going to tell anyone about us?'

She could see the uncertainty in his eyes. 'Would you rather I didn't?'

'It's not what you might think, really. I just want the beginning of our relationship to be special. And just about us. I don't want people to gossip.'

'You're not going to tell Estelle?'

She shook her head. 'Not yet. My whole life is public and I want us to have privacy.'

'You know you're going to have to start locking your doors? Or, at the very least, teach people to knock before barging in?'

Eveline frowned. Jack was right, but how could she change the status quo without upsetting anyone? And what on earth was she going to say when she next saw Simon?

❦ 20 ❦

Jack: I'm home now and wishing I was with you X

Eveline: I wish you were here too. I don't think I've ever been this happy before xxx

Jack: Me neither. Sweet dreams and I'll see you in the morning XXX

Eveline: Don't forget I've got Matins first thing at the church, then I'm at Foxbrooke Primary for assembly. I should be back by ten fifteen. You've got a key for the back door, so come and go as you please xxx

Jack: Are you locking your doors now? X

Eveline: If you're with me, then they'll be bolted as well… xxx

The next morning, the sun was still an hour and a half away from rising when Jack's alarm went off. He lay in the darkness, aware of just how different everything inside him felt. His heart wasn't just lighter than it had ever been before. It was bouncing around with excitement like a kid on their birthday. Stretching, he noticed the changes in his body. It had been three days since the funeral—and his last drink—and for the first time in as long as he could remember, everything felt clean and clear.

Swinging himself out of bed, he quietly padded to the bathroom, not wanting to wake his mother. Maybe he *had* been drinking a bit too much recently. A few weeks ago, he would have dismissed any suggestion he had a problem, but Eveline had given him pause for thought. So he'd decided to stop completely for a bit and prove to himself—as well as everyone else—that he could. So far, any niggling thought about wanting alcohol had been hidden under thoughts of wanting Eveline.

Outside, the sky was still dark above him, low clouds hiding the first reaches of the sun as it crept towards the horizon. With no traffic or early morning dog walkers on the roads, his footsteps felt louder than normal. He sped up.

With the late nights of his job, Jack usually didn't wake until ten, but he didn't want to wait until late morning before he saw Eveline again. The previous evening had truly been 'beyond', and still felt shockingly unreal. Seeing her as soon as possible would confirm it hadn't been a fever dream.

Passing the side of the rectory towards the back door, he heard the birds already squabbling at the feeders and the happy oinks of pigs being fed. Continuing into the garden to the far end, Eveline's hair was shining like a beacon in the grey half-light.

One of the pigs noticed him and snorted loudly.

Eveline raised her head. 'Jack!' She looked so happy to see him.

His smile felt like it might split his own face in two.

'What are you doing here?' Her hand smoothed her hair, as if conscious she hadn't prepared herself for his arrival.

The gesture tugged at his heart, and he closed the distance between them. 'I wanted to see you.' He cradled her head and brushed a kiss across her lips.

'Ohhhh,' she replied, turning the word into a breathy sigh.

Jack kissed her again, his lips pressing firmer. She opened to him, her tongue darting out to meet his, and a pulse of heat shot down to his cock. Memories from the previous evening slammed into him with visceral intensity. Having sex with Eveline hadn't taken the edge off his desire. It had only sharpened it to a point where everything else in life seemed utterly superfluous.

She seemed to think the same, pressing herself into him, pulling on his hair almost to the point of pain, her kiss greedy and demanding.

A sudden squeal from the pigs broke them apart.

She laughed nervously, touching her reddened cheeks and glancing around the empty garden.

'I think we're safe,' he said. 'The sun hasn't risen yet.'

Her eyes darted down to his crotch.

'But yes,' he continued. 'That *has* risen.'

The colour in her face heightened, and she giggled. 'Is your cock about to crow?'

A laugh burst out of him, and he tugged her into his arms, gazing down at her. 'Eveline Shaw, you're a minx.'

She looked delighted at his words and pressed her hips into his. 'I think it wants to doodle-do.'

Jack laughed again, happiness bubbling out of him. 'Eveline, whenever I think of you, that's all it wants to do.'

An oink and a thud drew her attention, and she frowned. 'Not again.'

She pulled away from him to the pigpen. Pinky and Perky were using their force to shoulder one of the fence posts. It was already bent from the vertical and looked like it wouldn't take much more to bring it down completely.

Eveline let out a growl of frustration. 'You little monsters. The sooner you're in my freezer, the better.'

'When's that happening?'

'Not for a couple of weeks. I had to book them in months in advance and I didn't know they were going to get quite this big.'

Jack moved the top of the fence post. 'It doesn't feel that sturdy.'

She nodded. 'It's been loosened over the last couple of years. I've been meaning to install an electric fence that I got cheap off one of the local smallholders, but haven't found the time.'

'Can I help?'

She stared at him in astonishment, as if someone offering to help was still a foreign concept to her. 'But don't you have things to do?'

Jack swallowed his irritation at Simon—and all her other parishioners—who were happy to eat the fruits of her labour, but not help in the production of it.

'Top of my to-do list is you,' he replied, her excited gasp helping to soothe his annoyance. He leaned forward and brushed a kiss across her lips. 'So if you're not around to be thoroughly "done", then I need to find something else to occupy my hands.'

'Oh...'

He kissed her again. 'I don't think we've got enough time

now for you to be properly "done", so why don't you show me where the fencing is and I can make a start on it?'

She glanced at her watch, holding it up to catch the growing light. 'That would be amazing. I've got a bit of time before Matins.'

Jack changed into welly boots, then helped Eveline manhandle netting from the back of the shed. They then began the laborious task of attaching it to the inside of the existing pen with a hammer and fiddly staples that were difficult to use in the cold.

AFTER EVELINE LEFT FOR CHURCH, JACK CONTINUED WITH the fence and thought about what he'd be doing if he was back in his flat in the south of France. There, he would have still been asleep, waiting at least another hour before leisurely waking and ambling towards his balcony to take in the morning sun.

Now he was tramping about in a stinky pigpen and wasn't sure he'd ever felt quite as content. Back in his Monaco apartment, the first coffee of the day would be accompanied by the sounds of toots and engines from cars and mopeds, shouts from people, yaps from expensive dogs, and the low horns from the mega-yachts in the harbour. Monaco was the subjugation of the natural environment into a carefully curated playground for the über rich. It wasn't messy, and it certainly wasn't muddy.

But here, in the ancient rectory garden, the natural world was doing its own thing, no matter how Eveline attempted to tame it. Autumn leaves fell with no consideration for the tidiness of the paths, weeds elbowed their way between the flowers she'd grown, birds whirled past as they fought and chattered, and the pigs churned the ground and defecated at will. But even though nature was noisy and chaotic around him, the morning held a stillness about it.

He finished attaching the electric netting to the existing fence, then connected the battery, which luckily Eveline had kept charged. Back inside the house, he put the kettle on and cracked eggs into a bowl, knowing she would be back from school soon and likely to be hungry. Contentment seeped down to his bones. Doing these small tasks for her, helping her day run a little smoother, gave him such satisfaction. Maybe this *was* where he was meant to be.

A small sound from outside the kitchen made him pause. It wasn't loud enough to be the back door unless Eveline was trying to creep in and surprise him? He turned with a smile as the kitchen door quietly opened.

Simon entered the room, his face contorting from confusion to annoyance.

'Where's Eveline?'

Jack forced himself to take a breath. 'Assembly at Foxbrooke Primary school.'

'She should have been back by now,' Simon replied, as if it were Jack's fault that she was not.

He shrugged. 'Can I help you?'

Simon's eyes narrowed. 'What are you doing here?'

Jack glanced at the work surface. 'Eggs are ready to be scrambled, then I think I'll make some toast and possibly fry up some bacon if there's some to hand.'

'This isn't your house. You can't just help yourself to what's not yours.'

'True,' Jack replied, forcing his features into a smile, whilst his right fist itched to be planted in the middle of Simon's pompous face. 'That's why I always knock when I arrive and wait to be let in.'

Simon opened his mouth, his lower lip quivering, but Jack didn't let him speak.

'As for what I'm doing at the rectory, I'm working from here to organise Foxbrooke Manor's Winter Ball, and the food I'm about to prepare is for Eveline, not me. Do you have any other questions?'

Jack leaned back against the Aga, his posture relaxed as Simon drew himself up.

'Now listen here, *boy*...'

Images of Jack's bullying father flashed across his mind, tearing apart the scar tissue from memories he thought had healed over. Folding his arms across his chest, he raised an eyebrow, feigning nonchalance even as his heart rate rose.

'... I don't know what your game is, but you need to leave Eveline alone. I—*She* doesn't need anyone like you getting in the way and ruining everyth—her reputation.'

What the fuck? 'And tell me exactly *how* my presence "ruins her reputation"?' Jack asked scathingly, even as the icy fear that Simon knew his secret dripped down his spine.

'May I remind you that Eveline is Foxbrooke's vicar, as well as an unmarried spinster—'

'What is this? Seventeen eighty-two?'

'You can't just waltz into her life like you're cock of the walk, sticking your oar in where it's not wanted—'

Jack pushed off the Aga, fury roaring through his veins. He'd presumed Simon had a crush on Eveline, but this reaction was off the charts. He raised his hands, ticking off each point as he spat it out. 'Not your life. Not your house. Not your little woman to boss about.'

Simon's face was puce. 'And you think she's *yours*, do you?'

Yes! I fucking do!

The back door slammed, cutting through the silence.

'Hey, honey!' Eveline called out in an American accent. 'I'm home!'

Simon's eyes bugged out and Jack briefly wondered if this is what his father looked like just before dropping dead of a heart attack.

'In the kitchen with Simon!' Jack yelled before she said anything to incriminate herself further.

Another silence, then Eveline opened the door, her face bright red and an over-the-top smile in place.

'Simon! What a lovely surprise! We missed you at Evensong last night and Matins this morning.'

'Yes, well—' He cleared his throat, his eyes flicking to Jack. 'I thought I'd... I was busy.'

'I was just about to make you eggs on toast if you were hungry?' Jack asked Eveline, trying to keep his tone mild.

Her gaze moved uncertainly between the two of them. 'Thank you, that would be, er, lovely.' She turned to Simon. 'Would you like to join us?'

'Yes, thank you, dear,' he replied, shooting Jack an oily smile. 'It will be interesting to see if Nigel's boy can handle a kitchen as skilfully as me.'

A sudden image of Simon 'handling' Eveline slapped Jack in the face and he flinched.

Simon noticed, and his smile became slyer. He pulled a chair out for Eveline. 'I thought we could spend a few hours going over the church accounts.'

Her dismay was obvious as she sat. 'Now?'

'Well, you don't have any other plans this morning, do you?'

Jack turned his back on them, not wanting her to glance his way and give Simon any ammunition. He broke more eggs into the bowl and beat them with a fork.

'I was planning on going to Foxbrooke Haven to see how the mural was getting on,' she replied.

'No need. I popped over to see mother yesterday afternoon and had a look. Not much progress from what I can see.'

The fork fell from Jack's grip into the bowl as ancient memories sprung from their graves. He saw himself running out of school with a picture he'd drawn. His pride when his mother stuck it to the fridge. Then the confusion and hurt when his father ripped it off and told him art was for 'pansies'.

'Need a hand?' Simon asked.

Jack shook his head, his eyes tightly closed. *I need a fucking drink*. The immediacy of the thought shocked him. He took a slow breath in and out. *Calm down. Don't react and make things worse.*

'Do you have any bread left?' Jack asked Eveline.

'Yes—' she began.

'Cupboard over there,' Simon interrupted, waving his hand towards it.

Jack glanced at Eveline. Her lips turned down, and she gazed at him with a dejected expression. He wanted to kick Simon out on his arse, but that move would play right into the man's hands, so he bit his tongue and took the loaf out.

'So, dear,' Simon said behind him. 'I met Jennifer Woodley on the high street and she told me some interesting developments in our plans to get Foxbrooke a "Britain in Bloom" award.'

Jack focused on cooking, trying to tune out Simon's monologue—the point of which seemed to be to show how interwoven Simon was with Eveline's life.

Placing plates of food in front of them, Eveline looked at him in surprise. 'You're not eating with us?'

He forced a smile. 'No, I'm going to head over to Foxbrooke Haven and spend a few hours there. Then I've got some calls to make about the Winter Ball.'

'Best he clears off,' Simon said to her. 'We shouldn't be

discussing confidential church matters in front of him, anyway.'

JACK'S STOMACH GROWLED AND HIS MOUTH WAS SOUR AS HE strode towards Foxbrooke Haven. The five hours he'd been up so far had included unexpected manual labour without the sustenance to underpin it. But there was no way he was going to make the uncomfortable situation for Eveline worse by sitting down with that prick, Simon.

What's his fucking problem? But even as Jack asked that question, unease stabbed at his gut. *Would* Jack Newton ruin Eveline's reputation? *Was* he bad for her? As he passed a small supermarket, his feet itched to take him inside, straight to the aisles of booze. He ground to a halt outside the entrance as the automatic doors opened to welcome him.

His head was ringing, and he kneaded his scalp, trying to soothe it away. *Do I really have a problem?* He let the question sit, listening to the excuses and explanations that popped up, already perfectly formed in his mind. He knew he'd been under intense stress, but was alcohol now a crutch?

'Excuse me?'

'Sorry!' He leapt out of the way as a woman pushed a double buggy through the doors.

That was what Eveline wanted. Marriage and kids. Two things he never saw in his life.

Turning away from the supermarket, he walked on, faster and faster, as if he could outrun his thoughts. He could leave his job and life in France behind for her, but could he ever provide the happy-ever-after she deserved? Each day he was back in Foxbrooke, old memories flashed up, reminding him with brutal clarity how crappy his upbringing had been. How could he take the risk that he might turn out even a little bit the same?

'Jack! Has the world ended?' Erica greeted him as he pushed through the front doors into the warmth of Foxbrooke Haven.

'Do I look that bad?' he asked with a smile.

She drew him in for a hug. 'Just a touch cold and thunderous, but nothing we can't solve.' She pulled back. 'Is everything alright? Eveline?' His stomach grumbled loudly and her eyes widened. 'Aha!'

'I'm afraid I haven't had breakfast yet.'

'Bugger breakfast. It's almost lunch.' She grabbed his arm, propelling him along the corridor towards the kitchen. 'A strapping young man like you can't go that long without food.'

He smiled, his heart lifting. 'A couple of biscuits will do me fine, honestly.'

'Nonsense.' Erica entered the kitchen, where one of the staff members was chopping vegetables. 'Hi Lacey, love, I'm just feeding up our resident starving artist before he dies of consumption or cuts off his ear in desperation.'

The young woman giggled. 'Hey, Jack. Help yourself to anything in here.'

'Except the staff!' Erica said, as Jack's cheeks warmed.

She pushed him into a chair. 'Don't mind us, it's nice having a bit of man candy around. Now let me see what I can rustle up for you.'

Half an hour later, Jack's stomach was full, and his mind had settled. Being at Foxbrooke Haven felt like a hug from the perfect grandmother. It was warm, cosy, and smelled of cornsilk powder, cleaning products and overcooked food.

Simon's mother, Gladys, may have been watching him from across the main lounge like a fossilised hawk, but her presence was almost entirely negated by the other residents. They'd arranged their chairs in a semi-circle around him, facing the mural.

'You know,' Jack said, raising his eyebrows. 'I thought you all wanted to help?'

'Oh, we do,' Shirley replied. 'But it's almost lunch so we're watching the master at work first, then we'll eat and come back, raring to go.' She gazed along the line of women. 'Isn't that right, girls?'

They nodded.

'This is like the television, but better,' Doris added.

'It's *interactive*,' said Ada.

'Ooh, get you with your fancy words,' Shirley said, and the women dissolved into laughter.

The door to the lounge opened and Robert entered, glancing towards the women. Shirley smiled at him.

'Robert,' Jack said, beckoning him forward. 'Will you join us?'

He nodded, casting his eyes around for a spare chair.

'Hang on.' Jack grabbed one from the side of the room. 'Now ladies, Robert needs to be in a particular position in order to see the section I'm about to paint.' He put the chair at one end of the semi-circle. 'Enid and Ada, would you mind moving along one place so he can sit here?'

They complied and Robert sat next to Shirley, colour rising in his cheeks. Jack hid his smile, deflecting the other women's attention as Robert and Shirley murmured hellos to each other.

'Right then, ladies and gentleman, the art channel is now

beaming live into your living room with your host, Mr Jaccccc-ccck Newton!'

AN HOUR LATER, JACK HAD NEARLY OUTLINED ALL THE major details of the mural, as well as given an impromptu lecture on perspective, composition, and colour. When Erica announced lunch was served, his audience burst into rapturous applause and made their way slowly to their feet for a standing ovation.

As they left the room, Robert hung back.

'How's it going with Shirley?' Jack asked, dropping his voice.

Robert looked ten years younger, his eyes alight. 'Very well, I think. Your advice was spot-on.'

Jack's chest warmed. 'That's brilliant. See, I knew you could do it.'

'It's been simply wonderful getting to know her, it's just that...'

'Yes?'

'It's all very *public*.' Robert frowned. 'I'd like to invite her to my flat for a meal, but I've never learnt to cook anything beyond the bare minimum. I want to do something special.'

Across the room, Gladys the gorgon's eyes were closed, but Jack still lowered his voice further.

'That's easy. You can get some really high-quality ready meals nowadays.'

'Would you help me choose a menu?'

'Of course.'

'And...' Robert's frown deepened.

'Anything you need, just ask.'

'It's my leg. I can't walk far. If I gave you some money, would you be able to do the shopping for me?'

'Absolutely.'

'And pick out a good wine? You know far more than I do.'

Only because I seem to have drunk more of it than water over the last few years... Jack nodded. 'Yes, not a problem.'

Robert's face relaxed into a relieved smile. 'Thank you.'

'When's date night?'

'Next week maybe? I'll let you know if she says yes.'

'She will, I promise you.'

As the room emptied, Jack took out his phone just as a message pinged in.

> Eveline: I'm so sorry about Simon earlier. He's still here but just popped to the toilet. Are you free later? xxx

> Jack: Yes. What time works for you? XXX

> Eveline: Not sure yet, sorry. I'll message you as soon as he leaves xxx

> Jack: No worries. Don't be shy about kicking him out XXX

By mid-afternoon, Jack called it a day. His helpers were beginning to flag, and he was desperate to get back to Eveline. A message from her saying she was on her own and missing him was the cue for him to pack up the paints until tomorrow.

Striding back through Foxbrooke, Jack felt a stone lighter. Simon was a minor inconvenience. He couldn't monopolise Eveline twenty-four-seven. As excitement sent blood flowing faster around his body, a significant amount decided to stay in his cock. He smiled to himself. The things he wanted to do to Eveline. The ways he wanted to make her come...

His ringing phone jolted him back to the present. It was Steph, his sister's wife.

'Hi Steph, everything okay?'

'Dack-Dack!' came an excited cry on the other end of the line.

'Hey Betsy-Boo! How are you?'

'Mummy baby! Mummy baby, Dack-Dack!'

❧ 2 1 ❧

'Jack! Are you on your way?' Eveline asked.

He shook his head, even though she couldn't see him over the phone. 'Emily gave birth a couple of hours ago.'

'Oh, what wonderful news! You must give them my very best. What did she have?'

He smiled at her excitement. 'A little boy called Alfie.'

'Awww. Do you have any pictures?'

'Yes, although his face is all red and scrunched up, so he's not exactly what I'd call cute. I'll send them through in a bit.'

There was silence as Eveline digested the meaning of his words.

'You're going up there,' she stated.

Jack sighed. 'As soon as we're packed.'

'Okay.'

'Mum's acting like if we don't go right this minute, he's going to disappear or something.'

'Do you know when you'll be back?'

'Not sure. Couple of days?'

'They're in York, aren't they? How long will it take to get there?'

'Four and a half hours if we don't stop. It's nuts. We're going to get there so late.'

'Will you message me when you arrive?'

'Of course, but promise me you won't wait up.'

'I'll see how tired I am.'

Jack smiled, even though her words made his heart squeeze. Eveline was going to be thinking of him. Maybe as much as he would be thinking about her.

Jack: Finally got here. Alfie's in with Steph and Emily, Mum's sleeping in Betsy's room and I'm in the nursery. I forgot how thin the walls are, or I would have left you a voice message. I hope you're asleep XXX

Eveline: I'm trying to imagine you in the nursery. Can you fit in the cot? xxx

Jack: Minx, it's nearly midnight... Go to sleep XXX

Eveline: Will do. Glad you've arrived safe and sound. Sweet dreams and hope to speak tomorrow xxx

Jack: Definitely XXX

'Dack! Dack!'

Jack's navigation out of dreamland started with a high-pitched version of his name, followed by excruciating pain as his niece jumped onto his airbed and landed straight on his junk.

'Fu—aaggghhh!' he yelled, rolling onto his side.

Betsy giggled and patted the side of his face. 'Wakey-wakey, Dack-Dack.'

He opened his eyes to see his mum's slippered feet in the doorway.

'I've made you a cup of tea,' his mother said.

'Nana!' Betsy slammed into Patricia's legs and hugged them.

Jack sat, the bed squeaking and shifting uncomfortably beneath him, and took the mug from his mother. 'Thanks. What time is it?'

'Almost seven-thirty. We let you lie in.'

Seven-thirty is a lie in? His mind went to Eveline. She would have been up an hour and a half already.

'I'm going to help with Betsy's breakfast,' Patricia said. 'Can I make you something?'

Jack blinked. His mother was behaving very, *very* strangely. 'How are you feeling?'

'Fine, thank you. I slept very well.'

Betsy toddled back to him. 'Nana sleep with me!'

'Come along, darling,' his mum said to her. 'Let's leave your uncle to get dressed and we'll help with breakfast.'

'Pantakes?'

His mother took her hand. 'Let's see what your mummy says, shall we?'

As the door closed, Jack stared at it, wondering if the house had teleported to an alternate universe. He wasn't going to jinx it by asking his mum why she'd suddenly turned into grandparent of the year, but it was weird as fuck and picked at the edges of his painful childhood memories.

He turned on his phone.

Eveline: I hope you slept well. I also wanted to say thank you for putting up the electric fence. It seems to be doing the trick! xxx

Jack: Glad to hear it. Let me know when you're free today and I'll take a walk and give you a bell XXX

Jack put his phone down and got washed and dressed. His sister's bedroom door was closed, so he crept downstairs. Steph was coming out of the kitchen, hissing into her mobile.

'Fuck's sake, Andy, *you* handle it. Em only gave birth yesterday—' She nodded at Jack and rolled her eyes as she passed him to enter the living room. 'And I'm legally allowed two weeks of parental leave.'

The door shut behind her and Jack carried on into the kitchen. Inside, Betsy was kneeling on a chair at the kitchen island holding open a cookbook, whilst his mother stirred a bowl of pancake batter.

'Can I help?' he asked.

His mum looked up. 'Can you get me some more milk from the fridge? It's looking a bit thick.'

Jack's hand stilled on the fridge door. It was covered with photos of Betsy, including several of him, holding her at various stages of her life. There were none of his mum or dad. It couldn't have been clearer that Jack had been in the UK and stayed here many times before. Not one of those trips had included a visit to Foxbrooke.

He passed his mum the milk. Her smile was tight as she took it. 'Thank you.'

'Dack-Dack, look! Mouse!'

Betsy pointed at the picture in the recipe book, where two smaller pancakes had been joined to a bigger one, giving the impression of a head with ears. Chocolate buttons had been used to make eyes, with a squirt of chocolate sauce to make a smiley mouth.

He frowned at it. 'Dog?'

'Nooooooo! Mouse! Eek, eek!' she squealed.

Both Jack and his mother winced as the sound shocked their eardrums.

'Eek eek!'

'Betsy-Boo,' he said, bringing his head level with hers. 'Want to play a game?'

She nodded.

'Okay, this is a special game for you and me, and Nana is going to decide on the winner.'

Betsy's eyes widened.

'The game is called "quieter than a mouse". Me and you have to be so quiet that Nana can't hear us. The first person to say anything loudly, loses. Okay?'

Her head bobbed up and down and she slapped a hand over her mouth.

Jack gave her a thumbs up, then caught his mother's eye.

'*Thank you*,' she mouthed.

TEN MINUTES LATER, BETSY HAD FORGOTTEN ALL ABOUT THE game as she tucked into her pancakes. Steph entered the kitchen, her features pinched.

'Thank you, Patricia. I really appreciate you looking after Betsy.'

'Is everything alright?' his mother asked her.

'Oh, er...' Steph seemed taken aback. In their past interactions, his mum had barely managed to be civil. Steph went to Betsy's side, running her hand through her daughter's hair. 'That was my boss. One of my clients is having issues and won't accept anyone else at the office dealing with his case. I've told him I've got to have this time off to allow Em to rest, but he's not having it.'

His mother swallowed. 'We, er, I could help?'

Steph glanced up, her eyes wide.

'With Betsy,' his mother continued quickly. 'And cooking for Emily. Cleaning. Whatever you need.'

'Oh, um, thank you, Patricia, that's incredibly generous. I'll speak to Em, but that could be really amazing. Thank you.'

His mum let out a breath and gave a tentative smile.

Betsy pushed her plate away. 'Park?'

Steph turned to her daughter. 'How about you go with Nana and Uncle Jack?'

'Yes!' She slid off the chair and grabbed Jack's hand. 'Dack, Nana, park.'

FIVE MINUTES FROM THE HOUSE WAS A NEWLY-BUILT children's playground. Jack had been here several times before and his mother didn't make any comment as he led the way. Inside the fenced-off area, Betsy saw a friend, and the two of them chased each other around a small fort.

Jack stood, his hand in his pocket, fingering his phone and wishing he could call Eveline. It wasn't just that he missed her down to his bones, he wanted to talk to her about his mum, even if just to share the strangeness of the situation.

'There was never anything this fancy when you and Emily were young,' his mother said, pressing at the rubberised ground with the toe of her shoe. 'It used to be a seesaw, swings and a merry-go-round, all set in concrete.'

'And don't forget the chipped lead paint.'

She nodded. 'When your father and I were growing up, we didn't even have that. Your dad's mum used to send him out the door after breakfast with a sandwich and tell him not to come back until suppertime.'

Jack thought back to the photos he'd found in the loft—of his father and his friend. From their late teens to early twenties, every photo was taken outside. They were climbing trees, jumping into the river Foxbrooke, fishing, camping, hiking. He'd brought some of the pictures with him, meaning to ask his mum more about them.

'Dad's friend, the one in all the photos with him. You said he was dead?'

'Yes. Will was your dad's best friend all the way through school. They were closer than brothers.'

'How did he die?'

She sighed. 'He fell whilst rock climbing out at Cheddar Gorge.'

'Did you know Dad then?'

'No, not really. Our parents introduced us properly at the cricket club a year after Will died. His death hit your father very hard. He wasn't the same afterwards.'

'In what way?'

Patricia shrugged, as if trying to dislodge an itch. 'When Will was alive, I remember your father being, I don't know, happier? Whenever I saw them both at school, they were always smiling.'

Jack thought about his parent's wedding photos. His mother looked excited, but his father looked like he'd learned to smile from a manual.

Betsy ran towards them and his mother held out her arms. Betsy ignored her, grabbing Jack's hand from inside his pocket. 'Dack! Swing!'

He knelt down. 'Do you know who is best at pushing little girls on swings?'

She shook her head.

'Nana,' he whispered in her ear.

WHEN THEY GOT BACK TO THE HOUSE, STEPH WAS ON A CALL in the living room and his mother took Betsy to her room for a nap. Jack went to check on his sister. She was in bed, propped up with pillows, Alfie lying asleep beside her.

'Do you need anything?' he asked.

'A new vagina?' Emily snorted with laughter as Jack winced. 'Joking! Well, kind of. Come sit down and talk to me.' She gestured to the glass of water and a packet of biscuits on her bedside table. 'I'm self-sufficient for a few hours.'

Jack sat gingerly on the end of the bed, trying not to disturb his new nephew.

'Seriously, don't worry,' his sister said. 'He's a day old. He'll sleep through pretty much anything. Do you want to hold him?'

He shook his head. Babies were way too fragile. 'He's so small.'

'He's not that bloody small. You try pushing that out of your backside.'

His sister cackled at his grimace. 'Your face. It's the gift that keeps on giving.'

Jack rolled his eyes. 'You sure I can't get you anything?'

'Nah, I'm all good, just tired... And surprised. I didn't think Mum would come up.'

'She's taken rather a shine to Betsy.'

'So it would appear. She sent her a ton of art stuff in the post.'

'Really?'

'Yep, I don't think she saw the irony.'

He huffed. 'She's been so weird since Dad died.'

'What, as in being nice?'

'Yeah, but it's other stuff. She's been watching CBeebies.'

'Seriously?'

'Yep.'

'Well, she can watch it with Betsy, then. It does my head in.'

'Em, if you need us to get out of your hair, you need to say. Okay?'

She patted his hand. 'I will, but to be honest, it's cool if you stay a few days. Steph's stressed out with this muppet client of hers, so if you and Mum can help out with Betsy, that would be amazing.'

'No worries.' He smiled at his sister, but he was already counting how many days it would be before he was back with Eveline. He stood. 'Em, can I show you something?'

'This sounds interesting.'

'Maybe. Hang on a sec.' He went to his room and returned with an envelope, closing his sister's bedroom door behind him.

'The plot thickens! What have you got there?'

He handed it to her. 'Take a look.'

She opened it. 'Oh, these are those photos you found in the loft of Dad and his friend. Didn't he die?'

'Yeah, Mum said it was when they were about twenty.'

His sister flicked through them. 'What am I meant to be looking at?'

Jack cleared his throat. 'I chatted to Mum about him earlier. She said that they were closer than brothers growing up, and that Dad was different before Will died. Happier.'

'O-kay. And?'

'Well, every photo is of either Dad or him taken at the same spot. Look, here's one of Dad taken by the river, and this one is of Will in the same place. So they took photos of each other. There's only one of them actually together—the one they took by turning the camera around.'

Emily rifled through until she found it. Will was holding the camera and grinning down the lens. His father was looking at his friend.

Jack held his breath as his sister stared at the photo, then went back through all the others.

'Oh,' she said softly. 'Do you think...'

'We can never know for sure, but if you look at the way they're looking at each other in the photos, and how cut up Dad was about his death...'

'Not to mention the rabid homophobia.' Emily lay her head back on the pillows and exhaled a long breath. 'Holy shit, Jack.' She stared at him. 'Holy fucking shit! You think Dad was *gay*?'

He shrugged. 'Like I said, we'll never know, but it kind of explains him and Mum being in separate bedrooms all our lives, and the obsession with me doing "manly" stuff.'

His sister snorted with laughter, then suddenly teared up.

Jack passed her a box of tissues.

'Thank you. It's mainly hormones, but if Dad was hiding who he really was the whole of his adult life, then it's just so fucking sad. What a waste of a life.'

'He did produce us.'

Emily blew her nose and gazed down at Alfie. 'Yeah, and if he hadn't, then Betsy and this little poppet wouldn't be here.'

AFTER DINNER, JACK'S MUM WANTED TO HELP STEPH WITH Betsy's bath and story time, so he slipped out of the house, wandered back to the park, and rang Eveline.

She picked up after only one ring. 'Hello?'

He couldn't keep the smile off his face. 'How was your day?'

'Fine, thank you, and yours?'

The conversation with his sister flitted across his mind, but he let it go. Discussing his conjecture about his dad might help him understand the past, but it wouldn't change anything. And he didn't want to think of anything to do with his dad anymore. He wanted to think of Eveline.

'Today was full-on,' he told her. 'Pancakes, the park, nap time, lunch, playdate, CBeebies, dinner, bath, story, bed. Yeah, I think that's it.'

She giggled. 'You have been busy.'

'I'm exhausted. I've got a jingle about a jungle going around my head non-stop, and have PTSD from this afternoon's visit to a soft play.'

Her laugh made his heart flip-flop in his chest. 'It can't have been *that* bad?'

'It was the seventh circle of hell. A thousand screaming banshees mushing food into their faces or trying to kill each other, and more green snot than *Fungus the Bogeyman*. Have you ever *been* to a soft play before?'

'No, but I know what they are.'

'When there was a call over the tannoy for a cleaner to deal with "an incident in the ball pit", even Mum thought we should get Betsy out of there.'

'How's she doing?'

'Mum?'

'Yes.'

He paused. 'Different. Still auditioning for "Britain's Top Nana" competition. She's got through to the final three.'

A laugh spilled out of her. 'Jack!'

'Do you miss me?'

Her soft sigh ran across his skin like a caress. 'Very much so.'

'Do you think about me?'

'Every moment of the day. I was in a meeting earlier with

one of my parishioners and just drifted off into Jack-land. I didn't listen to a word they were saying. It was mortifying.'

He laughed. 'I bet it was boring.'

'Jack!'

'Go on, what did you tune out?'

She hesitated before replying. 'It was a ten-minute monologue about repositioning the parish council noticeboard.'

'Thrilling stuff. I would have snored.'

'*Do* you snore?'

A zing of awareness shot through him. 'I don't think so. Would you like to find out?'

There was a pause. 'I have been imagining you... in my bed.'

He closed his eyes as a kaleidoscope of images passed through his mind on the way to his cock. 'Is that an invitation?' he asked, his voice almost a growl.

'Yes.'

Jack stared across the park, wishing he was two millimetres from Eveline, not over two hundred miles. 'I think about you all the time.'

She sighed, and a bolt of electricity made his dick twitch. 'I think of you, too. I imagine...'

His ears pricked. 'Tell me.'

Her voice lowered. 'When I'm in the rectory on my own, usually when I'm cooking or doing the dishes. I imagine I'm standing at the sink staring out at the birds on the feeders... And I hear the back door...'

He closed his eyes. 'Go on...'

She took a breath. 'I look up, and you're standing in the doorway. But you don't say anything. You're just staring like you're hungry for me.'

'I am.'

'And I don't move. It's like I can't even if I wanted to. Then you come up behind me, and...'

'Go on.'

'You, er... We, er... You know?'

His cock was straining uncomfortably in his jeans, so hard it could hammer nails. 'What are you wearing in this fantasy?'

'A dress with buttons down the front.'

'Underwear?'

'No,' she whispered.

'Fu—Eveline, you're killing me.'

'When are you coming home?'

Home? Was Foxbrooke his home now?

He huffed with frustration. 'I don't know. It all depends on Mum.'

$\maltese$ 2 2 $\maltese$

'**I**'ll speak to her.'

Jack glanced at his sister. Four days had passed and their mother had not once mentioned returning to Foxbrooke. He was sitting in the living room with Emily as she fed Alfie. Betsy was 'helping' Nana make cakes in the kitchen, and Steph was out food shopping.

'About?'

Emily gave him a look. 'Jack, I know you've got shit to do and daddy daycare was never going to be on the list.'

'I don't mind—'

'It's not a criticism. You're amazing with Betsy, but it's like you've got itching powder up your butt crack and the relief cream is back in Somerset.'

He laughed. 'That obvious?'

'Party-planning is your job, but it's a different kettle of fish when it involves the Foxbrookes. When is the Winter Ball, anyway?'

'Just under a week away.'

'Then what the fuck are you still doing here?' she hissed.

'Honestly, Em, it's fine. Most is in hand, but I could do with being back at least four days before to help decorate.'

Emily took Alfie off her breast and laid him over her shoulder. 'I'm feeling tons better and Steph has pretty much finished sorting out her twat of a client. We'll be fine, I promise.'

Relief poured through him. 'Thank you.'

She smiled. 'I know you don't want a family, but I wish you could find someone to share your life with. Someone who makes you as happy as I am with Steph.'

The invisible cord that seemed to connect Jack perpetually to Eveline tugged on his heart. He wanted her with every part of him, but could he ever give her what *she* wanted?

He stared at Alfie, crumpled up over his sister's shoulder. 'How did you do it?'

'Make him? Do you need a biology lesson?'

The corners of his mouth twitched, and he got up to close the living room door. 'No, I mean, how did you get over what our upbringing was like? How did you trust yourself not to fuck it up?'

Emily sighed, her face creasing with compassion. She held her son out to him. 'Go on, take him.'

'What?'

'Come on, you held Betsy when she was a baby. It's not rocket science. Just make sure his head is supported.'

Jack took Alfie from her, cradling him in his arms. His eyes opened—deep dark holes into his little baby soul, then closed as he fell back to sleep. Jack stared at him, feeling again a sense of helplessness. How could you protect something so perfect and so fragile, both from the world and from yourself?

'Jack, I had it way easier than you when we were growing up. I could keep my head down, my mouth shut, and plan a future that was far away from Foxbrooke. I always wanted to be a mum, and by the time I reached my teens, it didn't seem to matter that our parents were shitty role models.'

He glanced up, surprised.

'Honestly, it was mostly irrelevant. I spent so much time in my head, thinking about who I was and what I wanted. And the knowledge I was gay solidified everything, because I knew my forever home would never be anywhere near Dad. If anything, how they were with us crystallised how I was going to be a mum. I just do the opposite of whatever they did.'

Jack stroked the softness of Alfie's head. 'I don't know if I could trust myself.'

'Bollocks. You're the best of men, Jack. You protected me when I was a child and I know you'd look after and love your own kids the same way. You're just scared, that's all, and waiting for the right person. When she comes along, you'll know.'

Jack: We're coming back to Foxbrooke today. Not sure when. Can I see you when I get back? XXX

Eveline: Yes!!! Come over whenever you can. You've got a key, so let yourself in if I'm not at home. Can't wait to see you! xxx

CRUISING SOUTH ON THE MOTORWAY, PATRICIA FELL ASLEEP and Jack mulled over his sister's words. Emily had always seemed so sure of herself and what she wanted, whereas he'd just run away from everything. Foxbrooke, family, friends, a girlfriend, societal expectations and a normal career. He'd avoided all of it, creating a secret life in the shadows.

Eveline was the complete opposite. Living a public and spiritual path, she was the brightness of sunshine through rain, turning every droplet into a rainbow and washing everything clean. But no matter what she thought of him and how he tried to convince himself he was worthy of her, the fear still remained that his past would somehow sully her life.

HIS MOTHER CONTINUED SLEEPING AS THE CAR ATE UP THE miles, so Jack didn't stop, pressing on until they reached Foxbrooke and the family home. He dumped his bags, had a quick shower, then headed straight for the rectory, his heart matching the speed of his step. It was mid-afternoon, so still light, the sky a cold blue and the low autumn sun sending slivers of gold through the bare branches of the trees.

Outside the back door, he hesitated. Should he knock? Was she even home? He opened it and paused, listening to the sound of Eveline humming to herself from the kitchen. His stomach turned over with excitement, sending butterflies scattering. Closing the door firmly behind him, he locked it.

The humming stopped.

Striding forward, he pushed the kitchen door open. Eveline was at the sink, her hands in a pair of yellow rubber gloves, her hair piled up in a messy bun at the top of her head.

Jack gazed at her, watching surprise, excitement, joy and desire flit across her features. None of his memories or fantasies of her had been accurate. They were pale imitations of the vibrant woman in front of him. He raked his eyes down her body, his mouth watering with anticipation.

The colour heightened in her cheeks. 'Jack! I—'

He held a hand up and she stopped, her mouth still open as she breathed.

Eveline went to take off her gloves, and Jack shook his

head. She swallowed, her eyes wide, and replaced her hands on the edge of the porcelain sink.

Nodding his approval, he closed the distance between them, standing behind her but not allowing their bodies to touch. A wild pulse was jumping at the base of her neck. He brushed his lips over it and her breathing hitched.

'Did you miss me?' he murmured.

'Ye-es,' she stammered.

He moved a little closer, his lips ghosting across her skin as he ran his fingers up her bare arms. The kitchen was warm from the Aga, and she was only wearing a patterned dress. Fire surged through his veins as he remembered her fantasy.

'Did you wear this for me?' he asked, gently biting into the soft flesh of her neck.

She jumped, nodding as if words had deserted her.

'Good,' he said, sucking her skin. His cock throbbed with every beat of his heart.

He found the buttons running down the front of her dress and flicked the top one open.

'J-Jack,' she gasped. 'The window.'

He glanced up. The light was fading, but birds still chattered away around the feeders outside. Although he could still see the small garden enclosed by the thick hedge as it got darker outside, their reflection in the glass was getting clearer. The sight of Eveline in his arms was unbearably erotic.

'Unless someone comes around the back and sticks their head through the hedge, no-one can see us.' He kissed her neck again. 'And I locked the back door.'

'Oh...' Eveline was staring at her reflection, her lips parted, her eyes drowsy with desire. Holding her gaze, he cupped her full breasts, rubbing the hardened tips through the cotton of her dress.

She gasped, her head falling back to his shoulder. Jack held her tightly, pressing his cock into the crease of her backside, touching and tweaking her nipples as her breath came faster.

Clasping his left arm around her body, biting and sucking her neck, his right hand lifted the fabric of her dress, his fingertips finding the skin of her thigh.

'Are you wet for me, Eveline?'

She swallowed, nodding, her spine arching to push her breast into his hand and her bottom into his cock.

His own desire was raging inside him and he fought to keep control, desperate to bury himself inside her tight heat.

His fingers inched up her leg. 'Shall we see?' he asked, his voice rough.

She nodded again, and his hand moved higher to the outside of her hip.

'God! Eveline!' He gritted his jaw, his forehead falling to her shoulder as he felt the expanse of bare skin. She'd taken her fantasy and run with it. Prim and pretty dress on the outside, but no underwear underneath.

A lightning bolt of need shot through him, earthing itself at the base of his cock. With a growl, he cupped her pussy, his middle finger pushing through her seam into the liquid core.

'Oh, oh, oh!' she cried, bucking into his hand.

'Minx,' he exhaled through gritted teeth, spreading her slickness over the bud of her clit. 'Naughty, naughty, minx.'

He could feel her climax building as if it were his own, the swells of pleasure moving through her body as she pushed into his touch.

At the top of each breath, she held it, her body trembling as she chased her orgasm. He pushed his pelvis forward, anchoring her between his cock and his hand. His own release was on a hair trigger, and any more friction would send him over the edge. He wasn't going to spin this out. Now he knew she could climax; he was going to get her there as fast as he could.

'Oh, oh, oh...'

'Are you going to come, Eveline?' he whispered in her ear.

She nodded, her gasps turning into keening cries.

He bit down on her lobe and lightly pinched her nipple, his fingers thrumming faster over her clit.

She stiffened in his arms with a scream, her body bucking into his hand.

'Eveline, Eveline, Eveline,' he groaned, drawing the pleasure out of her in shuddering waves until she sagged in his arms with a sigh.

Kissing and nuzzling her neck, he inched two fingers inside her.

She clenched her inner muscles. 'Jack...'

'Yes, angel?'

She clenched again. 'I want...'

His cock twitched in his jeans, desperate for release. He slowly pumped his fingers in and out. She moaned.

'Do you want my cock, Eveline?'

She squeezed so hard he could hardly breathe. 'Yes, Jack, yes.'

He released her breast, bringing his hands to the front of his jeans. Freeing his length, he grabbed a condom from his back pocket, ripped it open with his teeth, and sheathed himself.

Keeping his fingers inside her, his thumb circling her clit, his other hand bunched the fabric of her dress in his fist, drawing it up.

'Spread your legs for me,' he whispered.

She did, and he pulled the skirts to her waist, exposing her completely.

He gripped her hip as she angled back towards him,

sucking in a harsh breath as he stared at the perfect plumpness of her backside, and his swollen cock—bobbing as if demanding entry.

With every breath, she was tightening around his fingers, circling her pussy into his hand.

'Jack... Please...'

He was the master of restraint, able to hold back his orgasm until he had wrung the maximum amount of pleasure out of his clients. But here, with Eveline, that restraint was being tested beyond all tolerance.

He withdrew his fingers, replacing them with the thick head of his cock, and rubbing her arousal over her clit.

'Oh!' she cried. 'Yes!'

He pushed an inch into her pussy, squeezing his eyes shut and gritting his teeth as he forced his climax down. She was so hot, so tight, so mind-numbingly, body-blowingly perfect. The pleasure was so intense it was almost painful.

He stroked her hardened bud faster and her breath came quicker.

'Jack! Jack, I'm going to come,' she gasped, pushing back onto his cock. 'I need...'

He jerked his hips forward, burying himself inside her to the hilt.

She threw her head back and screamed, convulsing around him as his fingers rubbed her clit.

He held still as she shuddered, straining to hold back the tide of his pleasure, refusing to give into his release until she'd come again.

The contractions around his cock slowed, but he didn't let her come down fully. Still circling her clit, he withdrew a couple of inches, then thrust hard back into her.

She cried out.

He tensed, his heart pounding. 'It's okay, angel?'

'Yes!' She nodded. 'More.'

Crackling pleasure arced through his veins and fired through his muscles. He glanced between them, watching his cock slide out of her glistening pussy, then pumped deep again.

She grabbed his hand and pulled it from her hip to her breast, folding his fingers around her nipple.

'Fuck! Eveline!' he growled, pinching the tip as he thrust again.

And again.

And again.

Each time he withdrew, she inhaled, squeezing around him. And when he buried himself inside her, she exhaled with a cry.

He kept the rhythm steady, building the pace to match the tempo of her breath. Tremors flickered through his body like seismic shocks, warning of what was to come. He pushed back against the force of his onrushing climax, his hips pistoning faster and faster as he lifted her higher.

As his control stretched to the point of snapping, she stiffened in his arms, her back arching, screaming again as her release shuddered through her body.

Lights flashed in his eyes as he let go with a roar, pleasure rocketing up from the base of his spine out through the top of his head.

He emptied his body and soul deep into the heart of her, clutching her tightly, waves of sensation continuing to move through him, pounding against the inside of his skin.

As soon as the shocks began to subside, he pulled out, spinning her around and lifting her onto the edge of the sink.

She spread her legs and clasped around the back of his head as his mouth fell on hers, their tongues clashing as if nothing would ever be deep or close enough. Jack clutched her to him, running his fingers into her hair. Nothing had ever felt so all-encompassing. If Eveline had God, then he had her. She was his everything.

Eventually, their kisses softened, and she giggled.

He lifted his head, arching an eyebrow in question.

Eveline brought her hands from behind his head, showing the yellow washing-up gloves she was still wearing.

'Well,' he said. 'It's important to use protection.'

The laughter bubbled out of her until she was gasping for breath. Her joy was infectious, and he laughed with her, feeling lighter than air.

As her giggles subsided, she glanced over her shoulder. 'I think we've finally scared the birds away. That, or they've gone to sleep early.'

He nuzzled her cheek. 'I like making you scream.'

She shivered as she turned back to him. 'That was...' she began shyly.

'Did it fulfil your fantasy?'

Her cheeks flushed. 'It was beyond anything I could have imagined.'

He ran his fingers over her brow and down her cheeks. '*You're* beyond anything I could have imagined.'

❧ 23 ❧

Eveline stood in the doorway of Saint Saviour's, sheltering from the wind as she waited for Amanda Haynes from English Heritage to arrive and decide the fate of the pews. Butterflies fluttered with excitement in her stomach as she ran her speech over in her head.

God, I know it's almost a done deal, but I'm still super nervous. Please give me a little more courage so I don't fluff up this chance.

She waved her hand as she spotted Simon crossing the car park towards the church grounds. His hands were deep in his pockets and he didn't wave back. The butterfly wings began to sting as they flapped faster.

Since his proposal, Simon had been avoiding her, and what little time they did spend together, Eveline couldn't shake a feeling of unease. Yes, she'd hurt his feelings with her rejection, but his coldness was uncomfortable and pushed her off balance when she was happier than ever.

Jack. A few days had passed since he'd returned from his sister's, and they'd spent as much time as possible together.

When she was working, he went to Foxbrooke Haven to work on the mural, or to the Manor to prepare for the Winter Ball. He still hadn't stayed the night, but Eveline felt more and more confident they would soon take that step and make their relationship public. She tried to ignore the scratching at the back of her mind, reminding her that Jack didn't want children. If that wasn't part of God's plan for her, then so be it.

'Good morning, Simon!' she said brightly as he approached along the flagstone path.

'Eveline.'

'Thank you for doing this with me. I really appreciate your support.'

He nodded his head.

An awkward silence descended. Once again, she prickled with hurt and anger. His marriage proposal had come out of nowhere, presented as a done deal that benefited him and his children, and without any true consideration for her feelings or the reality of their relationship. Why couldn't he see that? Why was he making this *her* fault?

'Eveline?'

She forced herself to smile. 'Yes?'

'I've given you space since our lunch last week so that you could pray on the matter and seek counsel from our Lord.'

Silence. Was she meant to respond?

He cleared his throat. 'Are you aware that Nigel's boy has been drinking to excess again?'

Adrenaline flashed through her. What? Why this sudden and strange segue? How dare he talk about the man she loved like that?

'By "Nigel's boy", do you mean Jack Newton, the thirty-year-old *man*?' she replied, before any of her filters could moderate her words. It was true she hadn't spent each night with Jack, but she hadn't seen him touch a drop of alcohol since the funeral, and when he was with her, he seemed as happy as she was. 'And what is your evidence that he's been drinking?'

A thin smile stretched across Simon's face. 'I was in the supermarket two days ago and saw him deliberating over the wine selection. He left with two bottles. I take it he did not share them with you?'

Heat flooded Eveline's cheeks. 'What are you trying to insinuate?'

'I'm well aware of your infatuation, but it's naïve and immature.'

Nausea lurched in her gut. Did he know what had been going on? Or was it jealousy and conjecture after she'd turned him down?

'In so many ways, Eveline, you're an innocent,' he continued. 'Unprepared for someone like him, who'll toy with your affections, then leave. Patricia confirmed that he has no plans to stay in Foxbrooke after the event at the Manor, so you're only setting yourself up to fail by continuing this dalliance.'

'I, I don't know what you mean,' she blustered.

He sighed. 'My dear, I'm only concerned with your happiness. You'll find companionship and contentment with me, not him. So, I'm giving you a second chance. Will you marry me?'

No! No! A thousand times, no!

'Hi!'

Eveline's head whipped around to see a woman waving at them from the car park. *Amanda Haynes.*

She turned back to Simon. 'I'm sorry, but my answer remains the same.'

His face hardened. 'So be it.'

She stared at him, shocked by his tone. Who was he, Emperor Palpatine?

'I'm Amanda,' the woman called out as she made her way towards them. 'You must be Eveline?'

She shook Amanda's hand. 'Yes, and this is Simon Little, the church treasurer. He's been helping with the application and speaks for most of our congregation.'

'Fantastic! Nice to meet you, Simon.'

'A pleasure, Amanda,' he replied. 'Shall we go inside?'

Eveline followed them in, her pulse pounding in her skull. *God, please help me. I need to remain calm. This is too important.*

Amanda smiled as she looked around the space. 'This is fabulous.'

Simon cleared his throat.

'Yes, we are very proud of Saint Saviour's,' Eveline interrupted. 'And the main purpose behind the removal of the pews is to ensure it continues as a church for the foreseeable.'

Amanda pulled the application from her bag. 'You've gone into detail about the financial benefits of replacing the pews with chairs, and your arguments are strong. My concern today is to assess the aesthetic impact, as well as community concerns.'

'Yes, of course. The chairs we wish to buy have worked well in other churches and can be stacked to leave the centre space free for other activities. As for community concerns, yes, there has been some opposition, but the vast majority of people we've polled are in favour of our plans.'

'Well, that's not exactly true,' Simon said.

Huh?

He reached inside his coat pocket, drew out a tri-folded sheaf of paper, and handed it to Amanda.

'I've had my own personal reservations regarding Eveline's plans but have remained open-minded.'

Amanda looked through the papers. 'This is a signed petition from locals, opposing the removal of the pews?'

'Indeed. I'm concerned the Vicar has not been diligent in publicising her plans, nor truly canvassed the community for their thoughts.'

'Wha—'

'So, over the last week I've reached out myself and found that public opinion is unwaveringly against the removal of the pews from Saint Saviour's.'

A lump pushed against the inside of Eveline's throat. 'I don't understand,' she said, her voice cracking. 'Why didn't you tell me this? You've been so supportive of this initiative. You helped me write the application!'

Amanda glanced between them, her eyes widening.

Simon drew himself up. 'Yes, that is true. However, new evidence has come to light, and the situation has changed. I cannot in good conscience support you.'

Slamming the back door of the rectory shut behind her, Eveline shook with rage. After Simon had stabbed her in the back, the meeting was over. They'd walked Amanda back to her car and Simon had left before Eveline could talk to him.

Stalking through the house to the kitchen, she stood at the sink, staring out of the window as rain hit the glass. *What now?* She didn't want to give up, but the battle was lost. And all because she'd turned down a marriage proposal.

Closing her eyes, she dropped her head. *God, I'm praying for compassion towards Simon, because right now all I feel is anger and disappointment. Please—*

A loud 'oink' came from outside.

'No, no, no, no, no!' Dashing to pull on her wellies, Eveline ran into the garden. The pigs were out again and turning her vegetable patch into a mud bath. *How?*

She got the food bucket and rattled it, calling them back to the pen. Glancing at the battery for the electric fence, she saw it was almost flat. Not used to having one, and with the delicious distraction of Jack, she'd completely forgotten to keep it topped up. Now she needed to make their pen secure enough whilst it re-charged.

Swiping her wet hair from her face, she looked at the time. Jack was at the Manor and she didn't want to disturb him when he was working so hard to prepare for the Winter Ball. She'd done jobs like this on her own countless times and she could do it again.

AN HOUR AND A HALF LATER, EVELINE WAS BACK IN THE kitchen and heard the back door open.

'Hi! It's me, you in?' Jack called out.

'In the kitchen,' she shouted back, running her hands over her wet hair.

He opened the door, a huge smile on his face. 'Any of your acolytes about?'

She suppressed a giggle. 'They're called *parishioners*. And no, the coast is clear.'

'Excellent.' He crossed the room, gathered her in his arms and kissed her.

'But I'm all wet,' she protested.

'Just the way I like you,' he murmured into her neck.

She sighed, arching closer to him. 'Well, if you insist...'

His head jerked up. 'I totally forgot to ask! How did it go?'

All Eveline's excitement at seeing Jack crumpled, and she bit the inside of her cheek.

'Angel?'

She shook her head.

He frowned. 'I don't understand. I thought this was a done deal. What happened?'

'It seems the opposition from the locals is greater than I thought.'

'In what way? Were they standing outside the church with pitchforks?'

Eveline shook her head, not wanting to throw Simon under the bus, even though that was exactly what he'd done to her.

'But the meeting was just the woman from English Heritage, you, and...' She saw the penny drop. 'What did he do?'

Jack was staring at her with such intensity, and she didn't want to lie. 'Simon changed his mind about my ideas and has spent the last week creating a petition against it. There were almost a hundred signatures. Far more than on the one your fath—on the other one.'

His hands tensed on her arms. 'Why did he do that?'

Eveline didn't want to tell him about Simon's marriage proposal. She'd hurt him with her refusal and didn't want Jack turning up at his door, rubbing salt into the wound.

'It's because of me, isn't it?'

'No, Jack, it's me that's caused this, not you.'

He shook his head. 'Simon was your friend before I showed up.' He ran his hands through his hair. 'Fuck!'

She reached for him. 'Jack, please. It's not your fault.'

His gaze fell to her arm. 'What happened?'

She glanced at the bandage. 'Oh, nothing much, just a scratch mending the pig pen.'

He raised his eyebrows. 'What about the electric fence?'

'Battery ran flat.'

'Shit! Sorry, Eveline.'

'It's not your responsibility.'

'I should have remembered. How bad is the cut? Do you need stitches? Tetanus shot?'

It *had* been deep, but she didn't have time to go into Bath and wait in A&E. Steristrips were holding the wound closed perfectly well. 'Honestly, it's fine. I promise.'

24

The next day, Jack hurried to Foxbrooke Haven, wanting to get at least an hour's work in on the mural before returning to the Manor to work on the decorations for the Winter Ball taking place that Saturday. But no matter how positive the two projects were, they didn't outweigh the damage that he'd inflicted on Eveline's life.

No matter what she said, he knew to his bones he was the reason for Simon's about-face. The man was as petty as Jack's father had been and clearly saw Eveline as somehow belonging to him and him alone. But why? He wasn't in a relationship with her. It made no sense.

Outside the entrance to the main building at Foxbrooke Haven, he inputted the code for the door.

It didn't work.

After the third try failed, he rang the intercom.

'Hello?'

'Hey, Erica, it's Jack. The code for the door doesn't work.'

There was a pause. 'Hang on, I'll come and let you in.'

When Erica opened the door, her face was grave. 'Hi Jack, do you mind if we have a chat?'

'No, not at all. Is everything okay?'

She didn't reply, leading the way down the corridor, ushering him into her office and shutting the door behind him.

His heart hammered. Something was seriously wrong. 'Erica, has someone died?'

She shook her head. 'Please, take a seat.'

Sitting opposite him, the lines on her face that were usually animated by laughter were now pinched with stress.

'Jack, I wanted to speak to you privately before the other residents. I'm afraid there's been a serious complaint against you.'

'What?' They couldn't know he was an escort. No-one except Eveline knew, and he would swear on his own life she would never break his confidence.

Erica rubbed her forehead as if to erase the lines. 'You've been accused of—' She gave a bitter laugh, as if she couldn't believe she was saying the words. '—peddling drugs, supplying alcohol, and being sexually inappropriate.'

Jack's jaw dropped as he reminded himself he was actually awake and on the same planet as yesterday. 'What the f—? Erica, this is insane. What drugs? *Sexually inappropriate?* Is this when I danced in the lounge with the residents? You were there the whole time! Do you think I acted inappropriately?'

She shook her head.

'Then what exactly have I been accused of? And by whom?'

Erica sighed. 'I'm afraid I can't disclose who made the complaints, but I can give you the substance of them.'

Okay, so only one person. This is a start.

'Apparently, you have given them alcohol, erectile dysfunction medication, and lessons on sexual performance.'

Jack blinked as the pieces fell into place, creating a picture of a wizened old woman with a shrivelled-up heart and ears that functioned better than bats. He sagged with relief and started laughing.

'Jack?'

'Sorry, Erica.' He took a breath. 'I take it this complaint has come from Simon Little on behalf of his mother, Gladys?'

Her eyes widened slightly and her nostrils flared.

Bingo.

'I'm afraid I cannot confirm or deny that.'

Jack ran his hands through his hair. 'Okay, before I tell you what *actually* happened, I need you to know that yesterday Simon scuppered all of Eveline's plans to remove the pews from Saint Saviour's.'

'But why? He was supporting her!'

'Because of me.'

Erica paused, reading his expression as he stared intently at her. 'Ah,' she eventually replied.

'And as to those ridiculous accusations, Robert has been courting Shirley and gave me money to buy food and wine for a special meal he wanted to prepare for her. He's unable to walk far because of his injury, let alone carry heavy bags, so asked if I could do it. The other day, he made a joke about Viagra, asking if I could pick it up at the supermarket. At the time of the conversation, I believed we were alone in the lounge. This was clearly not the case.'

Erica let out a breath.

'But don't take my word for it,' Jack continued. 'Please speak to Robert.'

She nodded. 'Do you mind if you stay here whilst I do that? I'll just see if I've got a spare member of staff who can sit with you.'

'Not at all.'

Hurrying out of the room, Erica returned shortly with

Lacey, one of the care assistants, who looked confused as to why she had to babysit Jack in her boss's office.

'Thank you, Lacey,' Erica said. 'I won't be long.'

After she left, Jack sat in silence, wondering what to do. Confronting Simon might feel satisfying in the short term, but was likely to bring more stress down on Eveline. And if Simon *could* get away with accusing Jack of this bollocks, then he didn't trust what the man might accuse him of if they spoke alone.

Since finally getting together with Eveline, Jack had been in a bubble where nothing about him or his past could hurt her. But now that prick, Simon, was bursting it, and the poison was spreading everywhere.

Fifteen minutes later, Erica returned and ushered Lacey out. As soon as she'd shut the door, she turned to him.

'I must offer my sincere apologies for this situation. Robert has indeed corroborated your version of events, and, moreover, told me that thanks to you, he's had the confidence to start a relationship with Shirley and has never been happier.'

Relief flooded Jack's chest.

'Unfortunately, due to safeguarding concern for our residents, any accusation has to be taken extremely seriously.'

'I understand.'

Erica hesitated, her jaw working as if she wanted to say something, but wasn't sure if she should.

'One of the persons who made these claims,' she began. 'Also told me that you had a problem with alcohol, and had most likely been inebriated whilst at Foxbrooke Haven, however I've never seen any evidence of this.'

Jack's fingers clenched on the arms of the chair, his mouth dry. Simon may have been toxic, but *he* was the one who got publicly wasted at his own father's funeral.

'I've never been under the influence here, and the last alcoholic drink I had was at my dad's wake nearly two weeks ago.'

Erica frowned. 'I'm truly sorry, Jack. I'll be having words with two *little*-minded people about their claims.'

He nodded at Erica's subtle reference to Simon and his mother.

'Let me give you the new code for the front door,' she continued. 'And then you can carry on with the mural.'

Jack nodded, but felt tired and washed out. *Did* people think he had an issue with alcohol? Did *Eveline*? And to think he was worried about people finding out about his job... Now it seemed there were so many other ways he could disappoint people.

AT LUNCHTIME, JACK PACKED UP HIS PAINTS AND HEADED back towards Foxbrooke, his feet slow and his heart heavy. The grey clouds seemed to press on him, so different from the open skies he was used to above the Mediterranean.

His phone rang.

'Putain!' Cyrille cried. 'Did you forget about me?'

'No such luck. How's it going?'

'Pah, you know, busy, busy, party, party. People keep asking where you are.'

'People?'

'Oh, putain, you know... Your ladies, they are so demanding...'

Memories that once used to excite Jack now left a bad taste in his mouth.

'You know you're welcome to them?'

Cyrille snorted. 'I haven't played with pussy since the noughties. And your women are so old.'

'They're the same age as you!'

'Putain! I'm only thirty-nine!'

'Yeah, well, then I must be a foetus.'

Cyrille laughed. 'All the ladies love cute baby Jack.'

He paused, thinking about his life in France. There was such a dissonance between Jasper that slept with any woman for cash, and Jack who could only get it up for one. His life as an escort was completely divorced from his present reality, yet only a month ago he'd been balls-deep in Antoinette Lavigne— a bored socialite with too much time and money on her hands.

'Cyrille, can I ask you a question?'

'Of course, mon chéri.'

'Do you think I drink too much?'

'Quoi? Of course not. Wine is life!'

'But have you ever seen me without a drink?'

'No, but so what? It's part of la culture. We drink, we party, we fuck, we sleep, then we do it all over again.'

'But—'

'Putain, what is wrong with your head?'

'I—'

'When's your big party?'

'Saturday.'

'Bon, then you can come home. England is so cold and damp. There is nothing for you there.'

WHEN JACK GOT OFF THE CALL TO CYRILLE, HE DIDN'T FEEL any better. Speaking to his friend brought back all the visceral memories of his life. Nearly ten years of parties, wining and dining, with alcohol as the social lubricant that helped him and his clients relax enough to have sex when they knew nothing about each other.

God? Okay, now I don't believe in you, but Eveline does, so I'm putting my faith in you via her. I don't know what I'm doing anymore, and I sure as shit don't know where I'm going. I just can't see myself ever returning to France or doing anything without Eveline by my side. If you're listening and give even the tiniest shit, then please give me a sign. Show me what I need to do.

Up ahead, a woman was getting out of a car, speaking on her phone. She slung a bag over her shoulder, locked the car and went to drop the keys into her bag. They missed, falling onto the pavement. She didn't notice, running up a small flight of stone steps into a Baptist Chapel.

Jack ran forward and scooped up the keys. 'Excuse me? Hello?'

The door closed behind the woman with a bang.

He followed her into the building. There was an entrance hall with stairs on the left leading to the balcony. In front of him was another door. He pushed it open.

'Hello?'

Inside was a group of people sitting on chairs in a circle. A man stood and came to greet him. Jack frowned. He seemed familiar.

'Hi, I'm Kieran,' he said, holding out his hand.

Jack passed him the keys. 'That lady over there dropped these outside.'

Kieran turned and held them up. 'Sal, these yours?'

The woman pushed her chair back with a screech and came over. 'Thank you, love. You're an angel.' She took the keys and went back to her seat.

Kieran smiled at him. 'You want to join us?'

'Er, what is this?'

'Alcoholics Anonymous, also known as AA or the twelve-step program.'

Jack closed his eyes, remembering Kieran from the church a couple of weeks ago. *Okay, God, you've made your point.*

When he opened them again, Kieran was smiling at him. 'You don't have to speak,' he said. 'Is this your first time?'

He nodded.

'Want to come in?'

There was a moment of silence whilst his internal universe rearranged itself. Then he nodded again. 'Yes.'

Jack followed Kieran and joined the circle, wondering if he was having an out-of-body experience. He glanced around the group as Kieran spoke. Everyone seemed so normal. *What did you expect?* His mind wandered to Eveline, and how she might have experienced her first meeting.

'... And we have a new face today,' said Kieran. 'Would you like to introduce yourself?'

Jack felt all eyes on him. But they weren't questioning or judgemental, they were empathetic and supportive.

Come on. You've got nothing to lose. He cleared his throat. 'Hi, I'm Jack. I didn't plan on being here today, but, er, five minutes ago, I asked God to give me a sign and show me what to do. That's when I saw Sal drop her keys and I followed her in here.'

That was the easy part of the story. Where he went next was anyone's guess.

'I haven't had a drink for eleven days, and never thought I had a problem...' He rubbed his hand over his face and sighed, realisation and acceptance sinking like a stone into the deep well of his chest. 'But now I'm coming to see that I've been using alcohol as a crutch for a very long time, and I need to know that I can live without it. So, er... My name is Jack Newton, and I'm an alcoholic.'

25

Standing outside the rectory's back door, Jack knocked. The heavy weight had gone from his chest, leaving only emptiness behind. He had no energy left to fill the void and couldn't expect Eveline to do it, even though he ached for her.

She opened the door, a look of surprise on her face. 'Why did you knock? It's not locked.'

She was so beautiful. So good. His heart hurt.

'Jack? What's happened?' She reached out and took his hand.

'I think—' *I'm not good enough for you? I'm not the man you deserve? I can't give you what you need?*

She pulled on his fingers to bring him into the house, shutting the door behind him.

'Do you need a hug?'

He nodded, and she drew him into her arms.

Exhaling some of the sadness away, Jack breathed in deeply, filling his lungs with Eveline's sweet scent. She didn't let go, continuing to hold him, as his brittle edges softened, and warm honey filled his veins.

'I'm not good enough for you,' he whispered, only aware he'd externalised his thoughts after he'd spoken.

She pulled her head back to look at him—her gaze full of compassion. 'I thought I'd kissed all those silly ideas out of your handsome head.'

He smiled. 'They keep on coming.'

'What happened today?'

He didn't want to tell her about Simon's fuckwittery, nor yet about his first AA meeting. He didn't want her to worry, and his admission to himself about his alcoholism felt too raw to share right now. Eveline would never say the words, 'I told you so', but his subconscious supplied them for him.

'It's been an intense few weeks,' he eventually said. 'And I think it's just all coming to a head. The differences between you and me just feel...'

She drew herself up. 'Right, that's it.' She pulled his jacket off his shoulders. 'Take off your shoes.'

When he did, she grabbed his hand and marched him through the house and up the stairs to her room.

'You don't have to—' he began.

'I'm going to show you my darkest secret.'

'In your bedroom?'

'Yes. In all the kerfuffle since you returned to Foxbrooke, I'd totally forgotten about my shameful habit.'

Huh? 'Do you smoke?'

She shook her head.

'Vape?'

'Good gracious, no.'

Entering her room, she sat him on the wrought iron bed. The bedspread was printed with blousy pink roses. A white bookshelf was set against one wall, containing every romance novel ever written by Polly Hart, and a pink and white rag rug lay on the floor.

Crossing to her wardrobe, she took a small box from the back of the highest shelf. She held it to her chest as she faced him.

'Now, am I right in thinking you have this over-inflated opinion of my saintly goodness?'

He smiled. 'My opinion of you is pretty much in line with how Estelle, Finn, Isaac, and all your other friends would describe you.'

'And how does your opinion differ?' she asked, a cheeky look on her face.

He held her gaze. 'I know you're a minx.'

The heat rose in her face and his cock woke up.

She cleared her throat. 'Well, I am far from perfect, and in this box is the evidence of my greed, competitiveness and duplicity. The only reason I haven't shown it to you already is that my subconscious was ashamed and made me forget.'

Jack's eyes widened as he stared at the box. What the fuck was in it?

Eveline sat beside him. 'I try my best to be a good person, but unfortunately I am also extremely competitive and this leads to some not-great decisions.'

Her fingers were rubbing the top of the box. Was a genie about to appear?

'I started doing this in my last posting and swore blind that I wouldn't do it when I came to Foxbrooke.' She pulled a face. 'But in my first month, one of my parishioners rubbed me up the wrong way...'

'What did Simon do?'

Eveline let out a peal of laughter. 'It wasn't him. It was a lady who shall remain nameless. She came around for a cup of tea and asked where I had bought the cake she was eating.'

'And...'

Her look of indignation made the corners of his mouth twitch. '*I* made it! It was a perfectly cooked Victoria sponge, and she knew it!'

His smile widened. 'So, she asked where you'd bought it to fu—mess with you?'

'Yes. She's very active in the Women's Institute and wins most of the prizes at the village fete each summer. She also made it clear on another occasion that it would be a conflict of interest if I ever entered.'

'Are you one of the judges?'

'No, I declined the offer.'

'Why?'

She passed him the box. 'You can open it.'

He lifted the lid. Inside was a stack of coloured cards. He picked up the first one and read the words '*First place, sponge cake category, Daisy Spring*'. He took another. '*First place, straw-berry jam category, Posie Parrot.*'

He glanced at her. 'Posie *Parrot?*'

Her eyes flicked towards the bookshelf. 'They're all character names from Polly Hart books,' she said quietly.

Fireworks went off inside his chest and he laughed. 'You're brilliant, Eveline. That's fuc—epic!'

She was staring at the bedspread, her cheeks pink and her fingers picking at the patterned flowers.

'Does anyone else know?' he asked.

'Estelle,' she said quietly. 'She swipes the cards for me after the event.'

'Legend.' He took her hands. 'Eveline? Look at me, love.'

She slowly brought her gaze to meet his.

'You're amazing. Don't hide your light. Let it shine. Isn't that what God wants you to do?'

She blinked. 'But you don't believe in God.'

He huffed. 'Let's just say that God and I have reached an understanding.'

Her eyes widened until he could see all the whites.

'Look, it doesn't matter what I believe or not,' he continued. '*Your* God loves you and wants the best for you. You've worked hard to earn these prizes and deserve the recognition. Next year, promise you'll enter under your own name?'

She frowned, chewing on her lower lip, and Jack remembered her telling him about her family—the unsaid message that her mother and accomplished younger half-sisters didn't visit the UK. Had Eveline been so marginalised that being taken for granted felt like her natural position in life? It certainly fitted the pattern of never putting herself first.

She glanced away.

'Eveline?'

'I don't know.'

'Are you going to the Winter Ball this Saturday?'

'Um?'

'I know Estelle's given you a seat at her table and has been badgering you to go. This is a chance for you to shine as *you*, not just Foxbrooke's vicar.' He squeezed her hands. 'When I first saw you in that bar, the rest of the world just faded away. You're so beautiful, Eveline, in every way.' He swallowed, his mouth suddenly dry. 'Would you consider going to the ball... With me?'

She looked up. 'Oh...'

'You don't have to, it's just a thought,' he said quickly.

Colour bloomed in her cheeks. 'Well, after what's happened now with the pews...'

Simon Little. Had she been holding back not to piss off that fucker?

She took a breath. 'Yes, Jack. I would love to go to the ball with you.'

He smiled at her, giddy with excitement. He could leave his past behind in France *and* find a way to make it work with Eveline in Foxbrooke.

'Jack...'

'Yes, angel?'

'You understand now how competitive I am?'

He nodded.

'Well, something has been playing on my mind...'

'Go on.'

'I, er—' She cleared her throat and sat a little straighter. 'I want to be the best.'

'At what?'

'Pleasing you. Sexually.'

His brain froze, then was shocked back to life. 'But you *are* the best.'

She frowned. 'That simply can't be true. I'm woefully inexperienced. I don't know any tricks—'

'Tricks? Eveline, you don't need any. Just by being you, it's the best I've ever had.'

She didn't look convinced. 'Well, I want to try something a little different...'

Different?

'... And I would really appreciate if you would let me do it to you.'

Do what to me? His mind boggled. Did she want to peg him?

'Please don't look so concerned. I've been doing some research—'

Whaaaaaat?

'—I didn't watch any videos, but I found some very illuminating articles online.'

Breathe. Whatever she wants to do, you can take it.

'And I hope you'll like it.'

His butt cheeks tensed.

She lay her hand on his leg and he tried not to flinch. 'Jack, I promise I'll be gentle.'

Please tell me she's bought some lube.

'And if anything doesn't feel good, you just tell me.' She shook her head as if shaking off her words and huffed. 'Look. The whole point of this exercise is for me to learn because I want to be the best. So it's imperative you teach me. Understand?'

Not really. 'Uh-huh...'

She smiled. 'Marvellous. Can I start?'

'Eveline...' He swallowed. 'Can I just clarify what you want to do to me?'

She frowned. 'I want to give you a blow job, of course.'

His body sagged as he failed to hide his relief. 'Thank fuck for that.'

'What did you *think* I wanted to do to you?'

He laughed as he shook his head. 'I thought you wanted to peg me.'

'*Peg* you? What on earth is that?'

Fantastic. Now you have to explain it to a bloody vicar. Way to go, Newton.

'Jack?'

He felt his face flushing. 'It's where...'

'I'm listening...'

'The woman, er, penetrates the man anally, using a strap-on dildo.'

Her mouth fell open. 'That's a *thing*?' she squeaked.

He nodded. This was all going horribly wrong.

'Have you ever done that before?' she asked, her voice now audible only to dogs.

He shook his head. 'No.'

She let out a breath. 'Oh, thank goodness for that. I'm sure it's a delightful experience for those who choose to do it, but it really doesn't sound like my cup of tea. And I have to say how relieved I am you haven't already done that particular act. If you had, then I would have also had to have a go in order to ensure I was your best, er, "pegger"? Am I using the correct terminology?'

Jack sank his head into his hands.

'So, can I give it a go then?'

He made an anguished noise. He couldn't think of anything more mind-blowing than Eveline's lips around his cock, but something in him held back.

She peeled his fingers from his face and lifted his chin. 'With your customers, do they do this for you?'

'Sometimes.'

'Often?'

'No.'

Most of his clients came from disappointing and sexless relationships. When talking to them, he was always staggered at just how incompetent and selfish men could be when it came to sex. Jack's job was to ensure the women who paid for his services received pleasure without any expectation of having to give it. And even if he climaxed, he always remained in control of himself and the interaction.

'Jack, I want to touch, and lick and suck you until you have an orgasm...'

His breath caught in his throat, his cock thickening.

'... And I don't want you to feel it has to be transactional. Does that feel strange to you?'

'Eveline, you can't—'

'Why not? I really want to. It's one of my fantasies.'

He blinked at her, struggling to comprehend what she was saying.

She placed her hand over the hard bulge in his jeans. 'I

fantasise...' she began, her cheeks pink. 'That you're tied up and completely at my mercy...'

Holy fucking shit.

'... And I drive you so wild with passion that you lose control. You can't think anymore, you can't hold back. All you can do is let go.'

His brain had suspended operations, ceding all power to his cock, which had no issues accepting any of her suggestions.

'Jack, please, can I do this?'

Could he? Even in his most lurid fantasies of Eveline, such a scenario was never in the playbook. Just the thought of it blew his mind. She was staring at him, her eyes bright and excited.

He nodded.

26

'Eek!' Eveline clapped her hands, then shimmied off the bed. 'Don't move!'

She opened her wardrobe door. Over the back was a metal bar with hooks, each holding a long, patterned scarf. She ran each through her fingers, her forehead furrowed slightly as she assessed them for suitability.

Jack swallowed, his heart thumping.

Selecting two, she bounced back to the bed, kneeling beside him and pulling the bottom of his t-shirt out of his jeans. He raised his eyebrows but didn't try to stop her.

'I want you naked,' she said.

He allowed her to pull it over his head. 'And you will be...?'

'Would it enhance your experience if I also removed my clothes?'

'Everything's better when you're naked.'

She giggled. 'Okay, but you first.' She touched his bare chest and sighed. 'You are so very beautiful.'

He flexed and she let out a shriek of laughter.

'I've never seen that before!' She lay her hands on each pec. 'Do it again.'

He did, grinning at her excitement.

She ran her fingers across his nipples. 'Are they sensitive?'

'Not in the same way yours are, but it still feels good.'

Leaning forward, the tip of her pink tongue darted out to lick the tip.

He sucked in a breath, blood rushing south.

'How does that feel?'

'Even better,' he managed. 'But it's the sight of you that makes it.'

She stared up at him as she deliberately flicked her tongue back and forth across his nipple. 'Like this?' she asked.

'Minx,' he exhaled roughly.

She looked so happy his heart swelled. Sitting, she unfastened the top button of his jeans.

'These next. You'll have to help me as you're quite heavy.'

He lifted, and she pulled his jeans and boxers down and off, along with his socks. His cock bobbed with the excitement of freedom and the promise of what was to come.

'Now you,' he said, nodding his head at her clothes.

'Oh no,' she replied, a mischievous look in her eyes. 'I'm the bossy one today.'

'You think I'm bossy in bed?'

'Sometimes...' Her cheeks flushed. 'And I like it.'

Fuck me... File that one away for another time. He cleared his throat. 'So then, what are you going to do with me now?'

She eyed his cock as if it were the pudding she wanted to skip straight to, then took one of the scarves and fastened it around his wrist. She tied the other end to the far post of the bed frame, then attached his other wrist the same way so his arms were spread.

'Shuffle down, so you're comfortable,' she said.

'But I want to see you.'

She piled her pillows behind him. 'Try that.'

He lay, his head propped up, his cock twitching as if waving to attract her attention.

Grabbing two more scarves, she tied his ankles to the frame at the other end of the bed.

'I have you at my mercy,' she said, clapping her hands with glee.

'Minx, I've been at your mercy since we first met. Now take off your clothes.'

She pulled another scarf from the wardrobe and held it out. 'Do we need this for Mr Bossy-Pants?'

He laughed. 'I would mime zipping my lips shut, but as you can see...' He glanced at the restraints.

'Hmm...' She dropped the scarf on the bed and crawled between his legs. 'I'm going to leave that there just in case I need it.'

'What are you—'

She raised an eyebrow, stopping him in his tracks. 'Who's driving the coach to Climax City?'

'But your clothes—'

'Will come off when *I* decide.' She picked up the spare scarf and waved it at him, a questioning look on her face.

'Minx,' he huffed.

'Correct.' She grinned. 'Now stop talking unless it's instruction. I need to concentrate.'

Placing her hands on the inside of his thighs, she brought her face to his cock and nuzzled the base of his shaft, breathing in.

'Ghhhnnnnn...'

'You smell so good,' she whispered.

Fuck! Fuck! Fuuuuuuuckkkkkkkkk!

His cock was twitching along with his muscles, desperately

seeking more of her touch.

She held the base to keep it steady, then, without any preamble, sucked the head into her mouth.

'Jesu—Fu—!' His hips jerked off the bed as if hit by two hundred and forty volts of electricity.

She took him deeper.

'Oh, my, chri—!' It was overwhelming. It wasn't just the feel of her sweeping tongue and hot wet mouth, it was the sight of her sucking his cock, her eyes locked on his, that was his complete undoing.

She lifted her head, breathing heavily. 'Was that okay?'

He tensed against the restraints, struggling to catch his breath. 'It was... It wa—Fuuuhhhhhhhggghhhhhh!' he cried, as his cock vanished again.

Sharp rushes of sensation shot through his legs and abdomen. He wasn't sure what articles Eveline had been reading about giving the perfect blow job, but she'd clearly paid attention. One hand was now sweeping up his shaft, following her lips, the other gently tugging his balls.

'Oh fu—Jesaaaagghhh! Eveline!' Jack was panting now, blinking as the edges of his vision sparkled, leaving just her at the centre of his universe. 'Wait, wait!'

She raised her mouth, her lips puffy and wet. 'Am I doing it wrong?'

Jesus fucking Christ. 'No! God—No!' He drew in a ragged breath, closing his eyes and gritting his teeth. He was the king of control in the bedroom, but right now, he was about to blow faster than a teenager. His heart was pounding in every part of him, pulsing against the inside of his skin, pressing on his skull, and pumping with urgent beats in his throbbing cock.

He took another deep breath, pursing his lips as he exhaled, then opened his eyes.

'Eveline, it's incredible. You're driving me insane and I'm not going to last much longer if you keep doing that.'

Her face lit up. 'Well, in that case…' She let go and stepped off the bed.

Where are you going?!

She laughed. 'Don't look so panicked. I'm not doing a runner. I just thought I might now take off my clothes?'

He nodded so fast she became a blur. 'Yes, yes, definitely, one hundred per cent yes.'

She smiled at him, slowly undoing the buttons of her shirt.

Off! Off! Off!

Underneath was a white lacy bra, her nipples poking through, pink and hard. She stopped moving and his eyes flicked to hers. Running her fingers down her throat towards her breasts, she watched him intently. He tracked the movement with laser focus, holding his breath until the tips of her fingers grazed across her nipples and her breath caught.

'Eveline,' he choked, his mouth watering, wishing he was free to grab her and suck the tight buds into his mouth. 'I need to touch you.'

Unhooking her bra, she tossed it to the ground, and cupped her breasts as if presenting them to him. 'Not yet,' she replied, her voice unsteady. She rolled her nipples between her fingers and thumbs, sucking in another short breath, her eyelids fluttering.

'One day, soon,' he growled. 'You're going to make yourself come for the first time and I'm going to watch.'

Her nostrils flared slightly and her cheeks flushed.

'And then I'm going to tie *you* up and drive you as fucking insane as you're making me.'

She gasped, tugging on her nipples as she stared at him.

'Would you like that, Eveline?'

Her nod was tentative, then definitive.

'Good. Now get the rest of your clothes off. I want to see you.'

He could see how turned on she was—any earlier sass replaced with yielding need. She shimmied out of her skirt, then hooked her thumbs inside the edge of her pants, pulling them away from her hips and letting them drop to the floor.

'Pick them up.'

She looked shocked, but did as he asked.

'Are they wet?'

Running her thumb across the gusset, she nodded, her blush deepening.

'Bring them here.'

'W-why?'

'You've got two choices, Eveline. I want to see. Or preferably, you can sit on my face and I can get what I need straight from the source.'

Her mouth dropped open into a perfect 'O' and she sucked in a sharp breath.

'What's it to be?'

Holding the knickers in her fist, Eveline crawled onto the bed and straddled his torso. He stared between her legs at her swollen pussy, the cherry red nub of her clit. His cock bounced angrily against his stomach, demanding entry to the party.

Jack held her gaze as she shifted forward.

Come on, angel, higher. I need to taste you.

Shuffling closer, she held out her knickers, then dropped them to the bed, shunting her pussy to his mouth.

Fuck yes! Groaning, he dived into her salty sweetness.

'Ahhh! Jack!'

He sucked her clit, then flicked his tongue over it, feeling her tremble as he lost himself in her hot perfection. Desire roared through him, heady and intoxicating, as he pushed her pleasure forward, faster and faster.

Then she was gone. 'No!' she gasped. 'This is meant to be about *you*!'

'It *is* about me,' he growled. 'I want to lick your pussy until you come.'

She scooted back down the bed, kneeling between his thighs. 'Well, Mr Bossypants,' she said, breathing heavily. 'I want to suck your cock until you come.'

His brain overloaded, then exploded, leaving his mind empty and blank.

A delighted smirk tugged at her lips, then she lowered her head and sank onto him.

'Fu-fu-fu-fu-fuccccccck!'

She hummed around him, her hands now back in play, working on his shaft and balls in tandem with her mouth.

The whole of his being was concentrated on his cock. It was the centre of a storm, sending flashes of light shuddering through him and goosebumps prickling across his skin.

Jack watched as she took him deeper, his cock slick with his arousal and her saliva. Grinding his teeth to dust, he tried to push back against the inevitability of his orgasm as it thundered unstoppably towards him.

'Eve—Eveline!' he panted, his wrists and ankles pulling against the restraints.

'Yes?' she asked, her hand still twisting up his length.

'I can't hold on... I'm going to come... Move your head.'

She did, but not in the direction he was expecting.

'Fuuuuuuccck!' he yelled as his cock disappeared deep into her mouth.

She hummed her approval, bobbing her head faster.

Fighting to hold back the oncoming rush, pleasure spiked through him, agonising in its intensity. He strained against the scarves as they bit into his skin, his hips shaking, desperate to thrust up.

She released the head of his cock with a sucking pop. 'Let go, Jack,' she breathed. 'I've got you.'

A wave of emotion crashed through his chest and he sank into it, giving every part of him up to her—his body, mind, feelings, soul. His past, present and future. All the strands that made up his being were being drawn together by her, tighter and tighter until everything concentrated into a perfect singularity.

At the edge of his consciousness, he was aware of his voice, crying out incoherently as the climax roared up his spine, torching everything in its wake. Every cell was on fire, each ragged breath fuelling the sensations. Blinding light shattered through him, his cock emptying deep in her mouth as she sucked him dry.

As the intensity ebbed, her touch became softer, gently drawing every last bit of pleasure out until he was empty, floating in a sea of bliss. She released him, and he watched, his head still filled with light as she untied the scarves, then lay her body over his. He kissed her, clutching her to him, his tongue sweeping into her mouth to tangle with hers.

She broke the kiss with a breathless laugh. 'How was that?'

He blinked as another swell of emotion bumped against his heart and filled his throat.

'Do I win first place?'

He nodded, speech impossible.

She nuzzled the end of his nose with hers. 'Jolly good. I do like coming first.'

He took a breath and raised an eyebrow. 'You haven't come at all yet...'

'It doesn't matter,' she replied with a grin. 'I'm ridiculously happy right now.'

'Only ridiculously?' He rolled her off him, pinning her to the bed. 'I think we should at least aim for *ludicrously*. What do you think?' She smiled, and he kissed her again. 'Or *preposterously* happy?' He peppered kisses down the soft skin of her neck and she writhed beneath him. '*Insanely* happy?'

She sighed. 'I think I'm all those things and more right now.'

He shifted to the side and ran his fingers down her torso, through her curls, into the wet heat of her pussy.

She arched off the bed into his hand. 'Jack!'

Brushing his lips across her nipple, he felt it tighten under his touch. 'Let's see if we can work through the thesaurus,' he murmured. 'We'll start with *ridiculously* happy, and end when you run out of words and forget your own name...'

❄ 27 ❄

Estelle: So sorry I haven't been around recently. The Winter Ball is taking more of my time than I thought thanks to Jack's extravagant decorating ideas. And the company investing in the summer festival has been bought out so I'm stressing about who the new owners are and if they still want to do it. Anyhoo, are you free today at all for a catch up? You need to tell me what the fuck's happening with the pews. Miss you xxxx

Eveline: I miss you too. I'm in Wells seeing the Bishop tomorrow morning, but if you had some time, you could meet me afterwards at the Italian place? I have BIG news… xxx

Estelle: What BIG news? Tell me NOW!

Eveline: Patience is a virtue…

Estelle: You have got to be SHITTING me! I can hardly wait for handmade chocolates and gelato, let alone your gossip. TELL ME NOW!

Eveline: Can you do eleven?

Estelle: You're not leaving Foxbrooke, are you?!

Eveline: Never. Not going anywhere xxx

Estelle: Thank fuck for that. Okay, I'll be there from ten thirty. I have to sample every flavour of ice cream before making my decision, and these things can't be rushed.

Eveline: Fantastic! See you there xxx

Estelle: Can't wait for your BIG news. Love you XXX

Eveline: Love you too xxx

Eveline stood outside the Bishop's Palace, watching the morning sunshine reflecting on the surface of the moat. Despite the fact it was officially a city, Wells had a population smaller than that of Foxbrooke. It was ancient and pretty, and Eveline always tried to arrive early for her meetings so she could pray in the cathedral, then say hello to the ducks and swans that glided around the palace moat.

God, thank you for this beautiful day and thank you for Jack. I don't think I'm ever going to stop thanking you for bringing him into my life. He is a blessing beyond blessings.

Despite the unsettled nature of her upbringing and feeling that she didn't really belong anywhere, since finding her calling, Eveline had found her place in the world. But now she was together with Jack, she felt a different kind of contentment, one bursting with excitement for the future.

Her gaze moved from the sparkling water to a woman with a tiny baby strapped to her chest. Eveline's hand instinctively moved over her stomach. Had she missed the window for having her own child? Would Jack ever change his mind about being a father?

Even though they hadn't yet discussed marriage, Eveline knew that was a certainty. She wouldn't have slept with him unless she was sure he was the one. But as for children?

I trust you, God. I know you will find the right path for me.

Checking the time, she walked across the moat into the grounds of the palace and through to the offices of Jonathan Palmer, the Bishop of Bath and Wells.

He opened the door and welcomed her into the ancient room. The solid stone walls had been built over eight-hundred years ago, and the room always had a peacefulness about it that she loved.

'Take a seat, Eveline, and I'll make us a cup of tea.'

Jonathan was in his sixties and she'd known him for over ten years. Even though he was her boss, he was also a father figure and a friend.

She took a tupperware box from her bag. 'I brought cake.'

His eyes lit up. 'It's my lucky day.'

'Carrot and citrus. I soaked the sultanas in orange juice, added orange and lemon zest to the mix, and lime juice and zest to the cream cheese topping.'

'Sounds marvellous. Let me get a couple of plates.'

Jonathan placed them on top of his desk in front of her, along with another empty plastic box.

'From last time. Hattie said it was the best lemon drizzle she'd ever tasted.'

Eveline preened. 'I'm leaving this cake for her to try. I'll pick up the box when I next visit.'

'Thank you, but you know you don't always have to bring treats like this?'

She grinned. 'I know, but I'm a terrible show-off and I like making people happy.'

Jonathan's face crinkled as he smiled. He placed a cup of tea in front of her and she doled out pieces of cake. They sat opposite each other and ate in a contented silence.

'What happened to your arm?' he asked.

She absentmindedly rubbed at the bandage. It was still annoyingly itchy and red. 'I cut it on the pigpen when I was mending it the other day. Pinky and Perky are the strongest pigs I've ever reared and keep getting out. They've got brains *and* brawn, which is never a good combination in a pig.'

'Are they going to slaughter soon?'

'Before Christmas, hopefully. They're definitely big enough.'

Jonathan put his plate down and took a sip of tea, his expression sombre.

'Is everything okay?' Eveline asked.

He took his glasses off and rubbed his eyes before putting them back on and meeting her gaze.

'Eveline, I'm afraid this meeting is quite serious, but I wanted it to be completely off the record so we could talk as friends.'

Her heart beat faster, and she put her plate on his desk. 'Is it about the pews?'

He let out a sigh. 'Not really, although that may be part of the bigger picture. I received an email from Amanda Haynes at English Heritage this morning, confirming what you no doubt suspect. Without the support of the community, they cannot get behind your plans.'

Despite knowing this would happen, the confirmation still

felt like a punch to the guts. She nodded, not knowing what else to say.

'I'm deeply sorry, Eveline. I know how much this meant to you.'

Meant. It was now in the past tense, possibly beyond all hope of resurrection. With her congregation so small and ageing rapidly, how long could Saint Saviour's continue as a church?

'But that's not what I wanted to talk to you about.'

Huh? Jonathan looked troubled and her stomach cramped with anxiety. 'What is it?'

He sighed again. 'I received a letter of complaint from one of your parishioners about your conduct.'

'My *conduct*?'

He nodded and picked up several pieces of paper from his desk. 'It's quite the laundry list.'

'Is it from the Dowager Duchess?'

'No, she seems to have quietened down. I haven't heard from her for over a year now. Is your relationship with her any better?'

Eveline puffed out her cheeks. 'I think she finally tolerates me and has accepted my presence in the village.'

'Good. She can be a little *challenging*, but her heart's in the right place.'

'I know. But if it wasn't her, then who complained and what have they said?'

Jonathan lifted his glasses to rub his face again, then replaced them and looked at her.

'The complaint is from your treasurer, Simon Little.'

'Simon? But what has he got to complain about? He changed his mind about the pews and won.'

'He still has issues with the pew situation, but mainly

because he claims you didn't consult the village about your plans.'

'Jonathan, that's absolute nonsense. He was my ally right from the idea's inception and knew the work I put in. I truly believe I canvassed local opinion, and if he disagreed, then he had months of opportunity to tell me.'

'Yes, I would agree. And I still have absolutely no idea why he would turn around and stab—change his mind without telling you first. And going behind your back like that to create another petition?' He shook his head. 'I don't understand it.'

Eveline kept quiet. She didn't want to surmise Simon's motivations or gossip about her theory with Jonathan, no matter how clear the correlation appeared between her refusing his proposal and his change of heart.

'But unfortunately, that's only the start of his grievances against you. I'm afraid he's requesting you be suspended from your position immediately pending a formal enquiry.'

'What? Why?'

Jonathan shifted in his chair, looking increasingly uncomfortable. 'He claims you violated health and safety legislation and the law by providing your own sausages in the church. You modified the rectory without permission, sublet it for your own financial gain, and...'

Her head was spinning. 'And? And what?'

'Performed carnal acts during the day in front of the rectory windows.'

'OH MY GOD, WHAT HAPPENED TO YOU?' ESTELLE PUSHED back her chair and stood as Eveline approached. 'Did he cut you from the next round of *Britain's Next Top Vicar*? Smite you for being too hot?'

Eveline opened her mouth but nothing came out, her mind

stuttering like a stuck record, replaying the last half hour over and over again.

Her friend frowned and sat her down at the corner table of the café, facing the wall. 'If you need to cry, go right ahead. No-one can see you.'

Eveline nodded in response, nausea rolling in waves from her stomach to her throat.

Estelle reached across and took her hands. 'There's chocolate ice cream, chocolate cake, hot chocolate, and fancy chocolate truffles. You can have any or all of them. Or we can sit for a bit and you can have me?'

'You.'

'Done. And they won't bother us to place an order. I've already spent nearly a hundred and fifty quid whilst I was waiting.'

'Sorry—'

'Shut-it, Shaw. I came early so I could stuff my face and get a jump on buying Christmas presents. You're all good.'

Eveline stared at her cold white hands held in her friend's warm brown ones. Everything inside her was frozen.

God, are you there?

'It's okay if you don't want to tell me what's going on,' Estelle said, squeezing her hands. 'But I'm not going to lie. I'm freaking out at the moment. I've never seen you like this before. Ever.'

Eveline raised her head and gazed at her friend. 'It's likely I'm being suspended from my post.'

Estelle's jaw dropped. 'What?' she screeched, then lowered her voice to a hiss. 'What the actual fuck for? Being too nice? Working too hard?'

She shook her head. 'I need to tell you a few things, but I would appreciate if you kept them to yourself.'

'Yes, of course. I won't tell anyone.'

'Simon Little asked me to marry him.'

Estelle's eyes bugged out. 'Simon *Little?*'

Eveline nodded.

'Please, for the love of god tell me you said no?'

She nodded again.

'Thank fuckity-fuck for that.' Estelle sighed loudly, her shoulders sagging, then narrowed her eyes. 'Why did he propose? Don't get me wrong, you're a total catch, but he's older than your fucking dad. Was he having a funny five minutes?'

'He believed I shared his feelings. He said we already had an *understanding...*'

'What. The. Actual. Fuck?'

'He presented it as a done deal. He'd already spoken to his children about it.'

'Alan and Laura? I bet they were as appalled as you were.'

Eveline shook her head. 'No, they were very much in favour.'

'Why? Are they out of their minds too?'

'Simon is going to—*was* going to sell his house, split the proceeds with Alan and Laura, then move in with me.'

'What?' By now, Estelle's whispers were loud enough to be heard in Shepton Mallet.

'He said if he did that, his children wouldn't think I was a "gold digger".'

Her friend's curly black hair was vibrating as she trembled with righteous anger. 'I... I... MotherFUCKER!'

'Estelle! Shush!'

'Sorry, sorry, I just...' She shook her head as if to throw off some of her fury. 'What a presumptive arsehole,' she spat. 'Did he think he was doing you some kind of favour?'

'He said he was willing to make the personal sacrifice to provide me with children...'

Estelle's face froze, then she shuddered and retched. 'Can you imagine how hideous making babies with him would be?'

A small laugh hiccupped out. Eveline hadn't realised how much she needed to speak to her best friend about this. Estelle's reaction made her feel better about her own feelings.

'He also said that he was an "experienced man of the world" and would be "gentle" with me in the marital bed…'

Estelle blinked, then threw her head back and roared with laughter. 'Good grief. Does he think he's the Casanova of Foxbrooke and you're some doe-eyed virgin?'

Eveline smiled, the sensation strange on her face, as if she'd forgotten how it felt.

'But… What has this got to do—Oh god, the fucking pews! Is this why he stuck the knife in?'

She nodded. 'When he realised I wasn't going to change my mind about him, he changed his tune about supporting me.'

'What a total cun—*wanker*, sorry, Eveline. But this can't cost you your *job*?'

She clutched Estelle's hands tighter, trying to anchor herself in a swelling sea of sickness. 'He's made a series of complaints to the Bishop about me.'

'Seriously? About what?'

'Apparently, I've broken the law in using my pork for "Sausage Saturdays", broken church law by fitting a new back door and shower without permission, sublet the rectory for financial gain—'

'Sublet? To whom? Jack? But you're giving it to him for free, aren't you?'

She nodded.

'These are all minor things.' Estelle let go of Eveline's hands and pulled her phone from her bag. 'I'm ringing the family solicitor. He'll—'

'Estelle, no. I can't afford it—'

'You're not paying a fucking penny, Eveline.'

'Stop! Wait, that wasn't all of it.'

Estelle put her phone on the table. 'Ah, so now we get to the part where you tell me you've been running drugs out of the rectory and selling off the church candlesticks?'

Fire stung her cheeks, but the desperate need to share what had happened with Jack burned just as strongly.

'I'm, erm, in a relationship. I have a boyfriend.'

'And you didn't *tell* me? Fuck! It's not that dweeb from the dating site, is it?'

Eveline shook her head.

'Isaac? Look, I know I called first dibs, but I love you more than I lust after him, so I give you my blessing.'

The corners of Eveline's mouth lifted. 'It's not Isaac.'

'Phew-be-doo. He's the only hottie in the village and I swear to God I'm going to make him mine.' She frowned. 'Finn? *Connor?*'

'No.'

Estelle appeared completely confused. 'Do I know him?'

'It's Jack.'

There was a brief pause, then Estelle's face snapped from surprise to excitement. 'Oh, my god! When did this happen? Is he staying in Foxbrooke now? Why didn't you tell me sooner? Is he good in be—no, don't answer that. Does anyone else know? His mum?'

'You know... And one other person.'

'This is so cool! It means he'll stay in Foxbrooke and won't fuck off back to France!'

'We don't know that for sure.'

'Bollocks. You're a total babe and the nicest person I know. Of course he'll stay.' Estelle sighed happily, then her forehead creased. 'But what has that got to do with Simon—oh fuck. Does he know? Is this why he's trying to get you sacked?'

She nodded, swallowing bile as she imagined Simon watching her and Jack. She felt utterly violated.

'But how?' Estelle continued. 'You and Jack are both single. What's the fucking problem here?'

Eveline dropped her head. 'We made love in the kitchen in front of the window. And Simon saw everything.'

'What a fucking perve!'

'No, Estelle, he's not. He's so lovely.'

'Not Jack, doofus, *Simon*. Once Jack finds out about this, that sleazeball is going to get what's coming for him.'

'No.'

'Come on. If anyone deserves a good smiting or a punch in the face, it's him.'

'I know Simon hasn't behaved well, but I'm not going to tell Jack. I'm worried if he finds out he might do something terribly rash...'

28

On the morning of the Winter Ball, Jack awoke in the single bed from his childhood, in a room that contained no other evidence he'd occupied it for eighteen years. By leaving home and rarely returning, he'd sought to divorce himself from one life and create another. Staring up at the clean white ceiling where his glow-in-the-dark stars used to stick, it felt like his parents had done the same when they redecorated and removed every trace of him from the room.

He stretched, wincing at the dig of a lumpy spring in his back. Hopefully, this would be the last time he would ever sleep here. Tonight was the official 'coming out' of him and Eveline as a couple, and he wanted to wake up tomorrow morning next to her.

Despite his contentment, a niggling unease lurked. Was his happiness nothing but a house of straw on the surface of an iced-up lake facing rising temperatures and a hurricane?

If he stayed, what would he do for work? Would Eveline think he was sponging off her? He dismissed that thought. She was far too nice for that, but it wouldn't stop everyone else from coming to that conclusion.

And no matter how much he tried to rationalise it, he felt responsible for Simon changing his mind about the pews and ruining her plans. If he hadn't wound the man up, Simon wouldn't have felt the need to stab her in the back.

Eveline was putting a brave face on the situation, but he could sense her deep disappointment. Over the last couple of days in particular, she'd been distracted, and when she thought he wasn't looking her way, her expression was absolutely miserable.

Was it just the situation with the pews? Or was she having second thoughts about going public with their relationship?

Swinging himself out of bed, he went to the bathroom. So much needed to get done before the ball. But before tackling any of it, he wanted to see Eveline, hold her close and check everything was okay.

'DO YOU WANT A CUP OF TEA?' HIS MOTHER ASKED AS HE entered the kitchen. 'The kettle's just boiled.'

'Er, yes, thank you. I didn't know you were up.'

She put a tea bag in a mug and poured water over it. 'Yes, I have a lot to do.'

He noticed her make-up. 'Is wearing mascara okay with your eye?'

She nodded. 'It all feels fine.'

He sat at the table and she joined him, placing the mug on a coaster.

Silence. Should he tell his mum about Eveline now? Get it out of the way?

'Mu—'

'I'm selling the house.'

'Huh?'

'Two different estate agents are coming around today to value it.'

'Er... Okay.'

'I'm going to move to York to be closer to Betsy and Alfie.'

So, not to be closer to your daughter then? 'Have you spoken to Emily about this?'

'Yes, last night. She's going to need more support, especially when she goes back to work. I can look after the children. It's much better for them to be with family than a nursery and will save Emily and Steph a great deal of expense.'

Jack glanced through the window at the sky, as if expecting Pinky and Perky to fly past.

'I can get a lot for my money up there,' his mother continued. 'So there will be room if you... If you wanted to visit.'

Sod pigs flying, he was now expecting to get to the rectory and for Eveline to tell him hell had frozen over.

'That sounds...' *Like you've had a complete personality transplant?* '... lovely.'

'Of course, it won't happen immediately. You've still got a place to stay before you return to France. Were you still planning on leaving next week?'

Okay... Here goes. He took a mouthful of tea. 'Actually, Mum, I think I'm going to stay in Foxbrooke.'

Her eyebrows raised. 'Oh. But when I'm gone, where will you live? With one of your friends?'

'I'm going to stay at the rectory.'

She frowned. 'I know it's big, and you've been working there, but it's not a long-term option.'

Er... 'Why not?'

'Well, you can't guarantee the new vicar will be as *accommodating* as Eveline.'

Icy knives stabbed at his skin. 'What new vicar?'

His mother's cheeks coloured, and she lowered her voice. 'I don't want to gossip, but as it will affect you, I think it's only fair to let you know what's been going on.'

Jack tried to keep his voice level. 'What *has* been going on?'

She sighed. 'Eveline is being suspended. After a formal investigation, her case may go to a tribunal. She'll either be barred from practising or moved to another parish. Whatever happens, she won't stay here.'

Heat flared inside his head, white hot pressure pushing against the inside of his skull.

'What are you talking about?'

'There's no need to shout. I'm as disappointed as you are. She's been very kind to me.'

Jack gritted his teeth, forcing the panicked fury back inside. 'Mum. What is it that Eveline is supposed to have done wrong?'

'Well, not properly consulting the village about the pews for one, but she's apparently broken the law in relation to what she does with her pigs, and she's been making illegal alterations to the rectory.'

Is this bullshit for real?

'But that's not the worst of it...' His mother's voice dropped to a whisper. 'She was seen... *Fornicating...*'

Jack gripped the edge of the table. 'With whom?'

'He didn't—I don't know for sure, but I'm pretty sure it was that hippy chap who teaches yoga. Or it could be Finn? Apparently, he's been hanging around there a lot recently.'

'And where was she seen doing this?'

'At one of the rectory windows! Can you imagine? Anyone walking past could have seen them!'

'Who told you this?'

'Simon Little.'

Jack stood, his chair scraping across the lino floor. 'Of course he fucking did.'

'Jack! Language!'

He ignored her, heading for the front door.

She followed. 'Where are you going?'

Jack bit his tongue. The last thing he wanted was to make this any worse for Eveline. He forced a smile. 'I'm going to the Manor. Got a lot to do before the ball tonight.'

'Ah yes.' His mother looked relieved. 'Good luck.'

THE WALK TO THE RECTORY DID NOTHING TO CALM JACK'S anger. Every step merely fuelled his rage. But under the layers of fury levelled at Simon lay the unshakable core belief that this was all his fault. Simon was merely the messenger. Jack was the general and the army, laying waste to Eveline's life.

He paused, his hand on the back door, then knocked.

Opening it, Eveline's friendly smile lit up into one of joy when she saw him, then crashed and burned at his expression.

'When were you going to tell me?' he asked.

He saw the shock on her face, then the soul-crushing realisation that he knew.

'When you were packing your bags to leave?' He ran his hands through his hair. 'Christ, Eveline, why didn't you tell me?'

Her lower lip wobbled, shooting a dagger into his heart.

'God, Eveline, I'm sorry.' He drew her into his arms, nuzzling the top of her head. 'I'm so sorry, angel. Can I come in?'

She nodded into his chest, then disengaged. 'Of course, you don't need to knock.' Her smile was bright, but her eyes glistened with tears.

'Eveline—'

'It's fine,' she said, and started towards the kitchen. 'Would you like a cup of tea?'

'Eveline, it's clearly not fine. Please, can we talk about this?'

Entering the kitchen, her eyes flicked to the sink by the window where they'd had some of the most mind-blowing sex of his life.

She turned back to the door. 'Can we go to the living room instead?'

He followed her.

Inside, her gaze fell to the sofa where they'd first had sex.

'Actually, let's sit in your office,' she said, striding out and along the corridor.

Pushing open the door, she went in and sat on a chair, her knees pressed together as if she was a schoolgirl in trouble with the headmistress. The tightness around her face twisted the dagger in his heart.

He approached. 'Up,' he said, holding out his hand.

She stood, taking it.

'Come here.' He walked her to an armchair and sat, pulling her onto his lap. She flinched when he touched her arm and he noticed the bandage was still there. 'Sorry, angel. How is it?'

She rubbed at the edges where the skin was red and inflamed. 'It's fine. Annoying more than anything else.' She lay her head on his chest. 'Are you sure I'm not too heavy?'

He shook his head and wrapped his arms around her. 'You're not going anywhere.' In the silence, he stroked her back until she softened. 'Eveline, what happened?'

She took a breath as if it was an effort. 'That time, after you came back from your sister's, and we...' She took another breath, this one catching in her throat to become a sob. 'Simon was... He was watching.'

Jack willed his body to stay still as the need for vengeance ran through his veins. 'Angel, we did nothing wrong. We were in the privacy of your home and he's a disgusting pervert who spied on us and trespassed on your land to do so.'

'That's what Estelle said.'

He stiffened. Eveline told Estelle before him? *Calm the fuck down.* 'So, there's no need to worry then, is there?'

She shrugged. 'He's claiming the rectory is church property and, as treasurer, he can come and go as he pleases. He also said... that I invited him for a meeting at that time and did it deliberately to—I don't know... Show off?'

'If you invited him for a meeting, then why didn't he knock or come to the window, rather than peering through a fucking hedge?'

'He said he knocked and got concerned when he heard "cries that sounded like pain".'

Jack squeezed his eyes shut, trying not to lose control. 'If he was concerned about your safety, why didn't he call out? Ring the police? Eveline, he's full of shit. Please tell me the Bishop isn't taking any of this seriously?'

'He's going to gather more evidence about the other issues, then let me know next week if it's going any further.' She wiped her eyes and sniffed. 'I just feel so violated. Every time I think of him looking at us, I feel sick.'

'This is all my fault.'

She raised her head, her face streaked with tears. 'No, Jack it's not.'

'Yes, it is. If I hadn't come back, none of this would ever have happened. He's doing this to you because of me.'

'No—'

'He is. He tried to get me kicked out of Foxbrooke Haven the other day. Accused me of being "sexually inappropriate" with residents and supplying them with drugs and alcohol.'

'I know,' Eveline replied softly.

She knew? But why didn't she say anything? Did she think it might be true?

'Erica told me. I didn't want to say anything to you because...'

He tensed. *Because you think I would do that? You know I've got a problem with alcohol?*

'... Because it was nonsense, and I didn't want you to pay any more attention to it than you had to.'

'But don't you see? When attacking me didn't work, he came after you. This shitshow is my fault.'

'No. And this is why I didn't want to tell you. I didn't want you to worry—'

'Why can't I worry? Why—'

'And think you were to blame.'

'But I am!'

She got off his lap, pulling a handkerchief from her pocket and blowing her nose.

'Jack. The way your parents treated you when you were growing up was not your fault. Simon Little's cruelties and presumptions are not your fault.'

'Presumptions? What do you mean?'

She froze. 'Um, nothing.'

The hairs on the back of Jack's neck rose, prickling his skin. He got to his feet, his hands forming fists. 'Did he say anything to you? *Do* anything?'

Guilt followed by panic flashed across her features and his pulse rocketed.

If he's laid so much as a finger on her, I'm going to fucking kill him.

'No, Jack, no, Simon hasn't touched me.'

'Does he have a key for the rectory?'

She nodded.

Jack pulled out his phone and fired off a text to Finn.

Jack: I know it's the weekend, but it's urgent. Eveline needs new locks on the front and back doors of the rectory. Will explain why when I see you. Can you help? I'm meant to be at the Manor now doing the final prep, so if you can't help let me know and I'll think of something else. Thanks, mate.

'What are you doing?' Eveline asked.

'Seeing if Finn can fit new locks today. If he can't, then I'll try to do it myself and sack off setting up the ball.'

She looked wretched. 'You're already late going over there, aren't you? Please, just go. Honestly, I'll be fine. Now he's made his complaint, he won't come back.'

'Eveline, you don't know that! The man's a vindictive little shit! I know you're self-reliant and incredible and used to doing everything on your own, but he's still physically stronger than you, and you can't predict his behaviour. Please, I need to know you're alright.'

'I'm okay, I am!' She rubbed the bandage on her arm. 'I'm off to the church now, anyway. Then Estelle is coming around and we're going to get ready together. We'll see you at the Manor, later?'

He took a deep breath and held it. He trusted Estelle completely, not only as a friend to Eveline, but also as someone able and willing to punch Simon out cold.

'Okay,' he managed. 'But I'm walking you over to the church.'

THEY CROSSED THE SHORT DISTANCE FROM THE RECTORY TO the church in silence. Entering the building, Jack remembered meeting Kieran for the first time, setting up the AA meeting. He had yet to tell Eveline that he'd started the twelve-step programme. It felt like another personal failure, and he wasn't ready to go there yet.

By the time Jack had searched the whole of the church, two of Eveline's female parishioners had arrived, putting a stop to any personal conversations.

'I'll see you at the ball later?' he asked her.

'Ooh, Eveline, are you going tonight?' one woman asked.

'Of course she is. She's going with Lady Foxbrooke,' the other replied. 'They're BFFs.'

'What's a BFF?'

Jack nodded at Eveline and left them to it.

OUTSIDE THE CHURCH, JACK WENT TO THE MANOR VIA THE dilapidated church hall and stopped to take a closer look. The roof wasn't clearly visible, but through the dirty windows, he spotted buckets set up with towels around them. Those towels were from Eveline's house. Was this yet another job she had to keep track of?

His phone pinged with a message.

Finn: Foxbrooke's fourth emergency service here. I'm on it. I'll let you know when it's done.

Jack: Thanks mate, I really appreciate it. You coming to the ball later?

Finn: I'd rather sandwich my nuts in a waffle iron.

Jack: Whatever floats your boat on a Saturday night.

Finn: Anything's better than having to tidy my beard, then dress up like a penguin. You going to tell me what's going on with Eveline?

Jack: You free Sunday?

Finn: Only if you don't press-gang me again into assisting your lady love.

Jack: I'll let you have one day off.

Finn: You're too kind. Now fuck off and let me buy some new locks.

Jack. Will do. Don't forget to bill me.

Finn: Oh, I won't. You're turning into a right little earner.

Jack smiled at his phone and turned towards the Manor. Now that changing Eveline's locks was in hand, he could focus on making sure the ball went off without a hitch. Everything else could wait until tomorrow.

29

'Y ou have to wear the red one,' Estelle said. 'It's your favourite colour.'

Eveline held up the dress and looked at herself in the mirror. She'd worn it twice before. The last was at Estelle and Henry's thirtieth birthday and the time before had been in London the night she'd met Jack.

'And you also look hot as fuck in it,' Estelle continued. 'Plus, I'll always be able to find you. I just have to scan across the room of little black dresses until I see red.'

'Don't you always see red?'

'Ha! Only when I'm dealing with fuckwits.'

'Which is on a...'

'Daily basis, yeah, yeah. Oh, did I tell you the people that bought out the events company still want to invest in the music and arts festival next year?'

'That's wonderful news!'

'I'm so fucking relieved. They want me to work out of their offices, but they're only in Bath, so that's easy, and it means Henry can have ours to himself for a while.'

'Will he miss you?'

Estelle snorted. 'Like a hole in the head. He can't stand my brand of chaos and says that having to look at my desk "offends his eyes".'

'Maybe you can lend him your Moody Cow stress ball?'

'It'll take more than that to unclench the stick he's got wedged up his butt.'

'Estelle!'

'Okay, I'll admit he's fifty per cent more chilled since going out with Libby. Thank god he found her.' She sighed happily. 'Anyway, I'm going to Bath the week after next to meet the new owner. I'm going to be working under them, which will take some getting used to. You know I'm a top, not a bottom.'

Eveline frowned at her friend. 'Are you making a sexual reference?'

Estelle gave her a sly grin. 'Might be...'

'Can you please explain it? I'm trying to expand my sexual vocabulary and awareness.'

'This is just too weird!' Estelle screeched. 'I'm not used to "getting it regularly" Eveline.'

She smiled. 'The other day I learnt what "pegging" is.'

Estelle's jaw dropped. '*Whaaaaat!* Please, for the love of god tell me you didn't try it!'

Eveline's hands flew up, batting the air as if putting out invisible fires. 'No, no, no! Absolutely not! That's really not on my to-do list.'

Estelle fell back on the bed. 'Thank fuck for that. One of the reasons I'm friends with you is because you're the absolute opposite of my sexually incontinent parents.'

She grinned. 'So, do you know who your new boss is?'

'All I know is that they're rich and have just relocated from London. As long as they hand over the cash and let me do my thing, we'll get on.' Estelle rolled onto her tummy, her head propped up on her hands. 'Anyway, enough about that. Did you tell Jack about sleazeball Simon?'

Eveline sat next to Estelle and nodded, her good mood evaporating. 'He blames himself.'

Estelle reached across and squeezed her hand. 'That's because he's a good man and you're a saint.'

'Hardly.'

'Well, a sexy saint then. As soon as the Bishop tells Simon to fuck off, it'll all come good. Jack's just been through a lot recently.'

Eveline remembered Jack's barely contained rage from earlier, the anguish in his eyes. She hadn't seen him drink since his father's funeral, but tonight might be a different matter.

'Is Jack going to stay in Foxbrooke, then?' Estelle asked.

'I hope so. We haven't really talked about the future. I think he wanted to get tonight out of the way first. But...'

'Yeah?'

'He's the one, Estelle.'

'Your Wolf Deadwood.'

She snorted. '*Redwood*. Yes. Jack's my hero.'

'I'm not quite sure whether to swoon or barf.' Estelle pushed off the bed. 'But at least Jack doesn't wear mustard-coloured corduroy trousers or own a Lab called Bunty.'

Eveline fanned her face.

'Please tell me you're not getting hot and bothered thinking of Jack cosplaying as a Young Conservative?'

She shook her head. 'Is it me, or is it a little warm in here?'

Estelle waved her arms through the air. 'No, still got that lovely draft coming from the dodgy old windows. You feeling alright?'

'Absolutely fine.'

Estelle put her hand on Eveline's forehead. 'You're burning up. Are you coming down with something?'

'I don't think so. Maybe it's hormonal?'

'Oh my god, are you *pregnant*?'

The heat coursing around Eveline's body intensified. 'No! Definitely not! We've been extremely careful.'

Estelle frowned. 'Well, something's up. You sure you want to go tonight?'

She nodded. 'I wouldn't miss it for the world.'

At seven o'clock they left the rectory and Eveline locked up with the new key Finn had given her.

'I'm glad you've done this,' Estelle said.

'Well, Jack was most insistent.'

'Good. It pissed me right off when that twat, Simon, treated this place like he already lived here. Plus, it's not safe.'

'It's Foxbrooke. Most people don't lock their doors. *You* don't lock your doors.'

'That's because everyone knows I'm a light sleeper and keep a shotgun by the bed.'

'Estelle!'

Her friend shrugged and lowered her voice. 'They call me Redwood. Roxy Redwood. I'm like my cousin, Wolf, only I actually have balls.'

She laughed. 'You are very naughty.'

'And you bloody love it.' Estelle took her hand. 'Come on, let's go have fun with a completely different kind of ball.'

The car park in front of the church was full, and new arrivals were now parking either side of the long drive to the Manor on temporary hard-standing laid over the grass.

'This seems busier than last year,' Eveline said.

Estelle nodded. 'Nearly two hundred per cent. More people at the meal and a couple of hundred extra coming later. Thanks to Jack, we're going to turn a large profit.'

Eveline's heart swelled with pride. 'I'm pleased it all worked out so brilliantly.'

'Well, it *is* his job.'

Her pulse quickened. She couldn't forget that everyone knew Jack as a party planner, not a former sex worker.

'And it meant we could also mollify Mom by letting her invite more of her fancy friends. Did I tell you Aunt Simone has come over for it?'

Henry and Estelle's aunt was a famous designer who had her own label in Paris. Eveline glanced at the coat over her dress.

'Relax. She's not the fashion police,' Estelle said.

'I'm not used to dressing up.'

'Well, you should do it more often. You look incredible.'

She squeezed her friend's hand. 'As do you.'

Estelle grinned. 'Thank you. I'm hoping Isaac is going to show up so I can finally seduce him.'

Eveline's tummy knotted. Not only had Isaac taken a vow of celibacy, but she also knew that if he was ever tempted to break it, it wouldn't be with Estelle. Isaac liked her, but only as a friend.

'Estelle... It has been a while now without him accepting any of your invitations.'

Her friend let out a growl of annoyance. 'And even when I wave my arse in the air like a muppet in yoga, he still refuses to correct my downward doggy-style... Are you sure he's not gay?'

Eveline nodded. 'It might be time to let this one go.'

'Humph. I don't think so. What do you always say? "Never give up, never surrender?"'

She grinned. 'Well, maybe this should be an exception?'

Estelle stuck her tongue out, then shrugged. 'Well, tonight there might be some hotties. I just wish my brothers had fitter friends.'

'Finn's very handsome?'

'Eww! I feel more related to him than to my bloody cousins! And anyway, that beard is...'

'Rugged? Manly?'

'I was going to say "gross".'

Eveline stopped abruptly, heat flaring through her, lights flashing on and off behind her eyes.

'You okay?'

She nodded. 'I just suddenly went all woozy.'

Estelle was frowning with concern. 'Are you sure I shouldn't take you home? Call a doctor?'

Eveline forced a laugh. 'No, I'm fine, I promise. There's no way I want to miss this.' She pulled her friend towards the Manor. The façade had swirling snowfall projected onto it and looked otherworldly.

'Cinderella shall go to the ball?'

'Something like that.' Eveline wasn't feeling herself, but she wanted to be by Jack's side to celebrate his success and show the world the two of them together. 'And anyway,' she continued. 'I don't think I've ever been to an event like this before.'

'Didn't you have a prom when you left school?'

Unpleasant memories flooded in and she pulled a face. 'I did, but I spent most of the night crying in the toilets.'

'Why! What happened?'

'I was totally in love with this boy in my year, but it seemed he only invited me as his date because his first choice said no.'

'Bastard!'

Eveline smiled, loving how fiercely loyal her friend was. 'When I arrived on his arm, the other girl looked like she'd sucked a lemon. She changed her tune about rejecting him and made a beeline.'

'Fucking bitch!'

'He ditched me immediately and within ten minutes, the two of them were snogging in the middle of the dance floor.'

'Twats!'

'Needless to say, I looked like a total fool and was the object of everyone's gleeful pity. It was mortifying.'

'I hope they gave each other venereal diseases.'

'Estelle!'

She shrugged. 'I was going to say something worse, but then remembered how bloody lovely you are. He didn't deserve you.'

'And it all worked out in the end. I'm here now... And I have Jack.'

Her friend smiled. 'That you do. Now come on, let's go find him so you can blow his...'

'Estelle...'

'Mind! Blow his mind!' Estelle gave her the side eye. 'What did you *think* I was going to say?'

Eveline rolled her eyes. 'Come on.'

THE ENTRANCE HALL WAS FULL OF PEOPLE AND THE CHANGE in temperature from outside was unbearable. Eveline pressed her hands to her burning forehead and cheeks as Estelle hung their coats on a long rail, then summoned a smile when her friend returned.

'Let's go to the larger of the drawing rooms. I want a drink and we can see if Jack's there,' Estelle said, interlocking her fingers with Eveline's and pushing people out of their way with polite efficiency.

Gauzy white silk fabric was suspended along the ceilings, twinkling fairy lights behind. The effect was stunning.

Eveline sighed. 'It's so beautiful.'

Estelle paused, a soft smile on her face. 'Yes, it's magical. And you should see the dining rooms. You know that projection of snow across the front of the Manor?'

She nodded.

'Well, Jack's put the same thing in the other main rooms. It's like being in the middle of a snowy day in Narnia, but without the cold and being turned to stone if you look at Mom the wrong way.'

'Your mom's not that scary.'

'She's rich, famous, titled, and let's not forget, American. She's super sweet to you because you've got a direct line to God.' Estelle led her to the back of one of the drawing rooms, where a temporary bar was set up at one end. 'The usual?'

'Thank you, that would be lovely.'

As Estelle ordered the drinks, Eveline glanced around the room, hoping to see Jack. She was feeling increasingly light-headed and thought back to what she'd eaten that day. Had it been enough?

'Here we go,' Estelle said, passing her a tall glass. 'Bottoms up.'

Eveline clinked her glass against Estelle's, then gulped down the cool liquid.

'Woah girl. You're reminding me of Duke at his water trough.'

'I'm not sure I've drunk enough today.'

'Are you *sure* you're alright?'

'Estelle! Eveline!'

Henry had his hand up in greeting as he moved through the crowds towards them.

'You look absolutely beautiful, Eveline,' he said as he reached them. 'I'm so glad you came.'

'Thank you, Henry. I'm very grateful for the invitation and to your sister for lending me her wardrobe again.'

'And what about me, little brother? Haven't I scrubbed up well?'

He hugged Estelle. 'As always.'

The eldest Foxbrooke siblings were stunning on their own, but when you put the twins together, they were jaw-dropping. Much to their mother's dismay, neither of them wanted to follow her into acting and modelling, although Henry had done his 'one and only' photoshoot for his aunt's fashion house a few months ago to help Libby out of a tight spot.

'Estelle,' Henry said, a frown on his face. 'I don't mean to put a downer on the evening, but have you seen who's here?'

'I've only just arrived. I haven't been taking inventory. Who's got your boxers in a twist?'

'Hunter-Savage.'

'What? You're fucking *joking* me. How?'

'Who is Hunter-Savage?' Eveline asked.

Estelle faced her, a look of pure disgust on her face. 'James Hunter-Savage. He went to school and uni with Henry and is a complete arsehole. They worked together in the City before Henry left. He stole Henry's girlfriend, his clients, his commission, and nearly got him sacked. Oh, and he tried to cop off with our littlest sister, Summer. He's a pig.'

'Oh.' Her friend was prone to drama and exaggeration, but her expression was fierce.

'And now he's moved to Shoscombe Manor on the other side of the Foxbrooke river,' Henry said.

'How did he manage to get a ticket for tonight?' Estelle asked her brother. '*Please,* can I kick him out? Pretty please?'

'He's one of Mom's VIP guests.'

'What the fuck?'

'Apparently, she thinks he's "highly entertaining" and "easy on the eye".'

'Traitor! Where's Summer? We need to keep him away from her.'

'Done. I rang Finn and begged him to babysit.'

Estelle pulled a face. 'I bet that conversation went well.'

Henry rubbed his forehead. 'It actually went better than expected. His older-brother-by-proxy instincts kicked in when I told him about Hunter-Savage. Finn arrived twenty minutes ago, and I lent him one of my suits.'

Eveline tried to imagine the burly Finn fitting into any of Henry's clothes, as Estelle sniggered, clearly thinking the same thing.

'Ugh,' said Henry. 'There he is.'

Eveline glanced to the doorway as an extremely good-looking man entered the room. He was at least a couple of inches taller than everyone else, with short, jet-black hair, artfully tousled.

'Where's Willow?' Estelle asked Henry, naming their other sister.

'With Leo. And she's not interested in anyone like Hunter-Savage, so we're safe.'

'God, just look at him,' Estelle muttered. 'He's absolutely vile.'

Eveline took another gulp of her drink. James was surveying the room as if he already owned everyone and everything in it. His cool gaze snagged on the three of them and his eyes gleamed.

'Don't look at him!' Estelle hissed. She grabbed Eveline where her bandage was, to turn her towards the bar.

White hot pain shot up her arm and she cried out, her drink falling from her hand.

'Oh, my god! Sorry! Shit, are you okay?'

Henry picked her drink from the floor. 'Eveline, are you alright?'

She nodded, pushing a swell of nausea down. 'I'm fine. It's just a little painful, that's all.'

'May I see?'

She held her arm out to him. 'There's nothing really to see. Honestly, it's okay.'

Henry was frowning as he stared at her skin. 'It looks really red. Have you been to the doctor?'

'She won't go,' Estelle grumbled.

'I'll go if it's not better on Monday,' Eveline replied. 'But these things always take time to heal.'

'What did you do?' Henry asked.

'A mild cut, a graze really, when I was fixing the pen the other day.'

'Hello,' a velvety voice said behind them.

'Speaking of pigs...' Estelle muttered as the three of them turned as one to face James Hunter-Savage.

Eveline nudged Estelle's foot with her own and extended her hand.

'Hello!' she said brightly, trying to ignore the pain still shooting from her arm to her stomach. 'I'm Eveline Shaw, the vicar at Saint Saviour's.'

James shook her hand, almost masking the flicker of surprise in his eyes when she said the word 'vicar'.

'Lovely to meet you. I'm James. I've just moved to the area with my family.'

'How many children do you have?' Eveline asked, trying to blind him with sunshine, whilst Estelle and Henry silently thundered on either side of her.

James chuckled, his eyes briefly flitting to Estelle before

replying. 'No children. My parents have bought the property on the other side of the river.'

'Well, it's delightful to meet you. You and your parents are welcome to visit the church or the rectory at any time.'

'Eveline!' hissed Estelle. 'No!'

'James, have you met Estelle yet?' Eveline continued. 'She's my best friend and really is utterly charming.' She turned to Estelle, who looked like she was trying to summon lightning bolts from her eyes.

'Yes, she is...' James extended his hand to her.

Estelle's remained at her sides, clenched into fists.

'This is the second time I've had the pleasure,' James continued, dropping his arm. 'And it would appear she still doesn't want to touch me.'

'Not even if you were the last man on earth!' Estelle spat.

'Estelle! James, I must apologise—'

He shook his head. 'No need. I'll move on. Lovely to meet you, Eveline.' He nodded at Henry. 'Foxy...' then turned to Estelle, a dark and devilish sparkle in his eyes. 'Foxy *lady*...'

James stepped back and turned away as Eveline grabbed Estelle to hold her back.

'See what I mean?' Estelle said as they watched him move away through the crowds.

Eveline gazed at her friend. She had a look of fury about her, but it was wavering, as if she wasn't sure exactly how to define why James was riling her so much.

'Well, I thought he was friendly and polite.'

'He called me "Foxy lady"!'

'After you called him a pig, refused to shake his hand, then said you wouldn't touch him even if he was the last man on earth.'

'Humph.'

'Eveline,' Henry began. 'James can be extremely charismatic, but trust me, he's a bad sort. I would hate for you to have your head turned by him.'

'Well, thank fuck Eveline's head's been turned by someone far better,' Estelle replied.

'Huh? Who?'

Estelle grinned and pointed across the room as Jack weaved his way towards them, a huge smile on his face. 'Him.'

30

The stress of organising such a big event and Simon's fuckwittery receded from Jack's mind as his eyes locked on Eveline's.

His heart and mind always seemed to stutter whenever he saw her, as if recalibrating to hold bigger and bigger feelings. Now he wasn't sure if there was any room left in his chest to breathe.

It was like being back in London, just over a year ago, and yet so utterly different. Eveline was at a bar, in the same red dress, and still as achingly beautiful as before. But back then he'd been Jasper, hiding his true self behind layers of lies and artifice. Now he was just Jack and loved her down to his bones.

Love?

The realisation made his feet falter. *Did* he love her? He knew the answer was self-evident, but it was a truth he'd avoided and ignored. The emotion was limitless and utterly destabilising—like standing at the edge of a black hole, with no knowing if he would live or die should he dive in. And even more terrifying was the fear he would let her down, that his past would come back to haunt her, or that he wouldn't be enough.

Shut up! Just fucking shut up!

Eveline looked happy, excited, and nervous as he approached. This was the moment when they would acknowledge publicly how their relationship had changed. This was when he truly left his old life behind and started a new one, here in Foxbrooke, with her.

His mind may have been in turmoil, but his body was drawn to hers with a force more inescapable than gravity. He reached for her and she arched into his arms. Lowering his head, he kissed her, his lips assured and possessive. Her hand gripped the back of his neck and he deepened the kiss, his tongue flicking into her mouth to meet hers, and sending a shock of pleasure through him.

'Ahem,' said Henry.

Jack slowly disengaged, watching the realisation that they were in a crowded room redden Eveline's cheeks.

'You're so beautiful,' he murmured, smiling as her blush deepened.

'So, there we have it,' said Estelle to her brother. 'Eveline's won the "jack-pot", and James Hunter-Savage goes home empty-handed.'

Jack straightened, still holding Eveline to him. 'Who's James Hunter-Savage?'

'Some arsehole from Henry's past,' Estelle replied. 'Mom invited him.'

'Sorry about that. I didn't get to see her guest list.'

'It's not your fault. Anyway, all Mom's cronies are in the other dining room so we can avoid him.'

'So, erm...' Henry began, still appearing shell-shocked at the sight of his oldest friend snogging the vicar.

'Jack's my boyfriend,' Eveline said proudly.

'Congratulations, Eveline. He's a wonderful man,' said Henry. 'Is this your first official outing as a couple?'

She nodded.

'Well then, I think that calls for champagne, don't you think?'

Jack felt her stiffen.

'Actually, Henry, I'll just have a soda water,' he said quickly. This was his first proper test of a life without alcohol and, to his horror, he was craving a drink.

Henry frowned. 'You sure?'

'Yes, definitely. I, er, want to keep a clear head.'

'Fair enough. Eveline?'

'Could I possibly have another elderflower pressé with soda please?'

'Estelle?'

'Champagne all the way,' she replied cheerfully. 'And I'm drinking their share.'

THE BALL WAS FLOWING ACCORDING TO PLAN. EVERYONE seemed to be enjoying themselves, and Jan Perry, Foxbrooke Manor's cook, had the catering in hand. As the gong sounded for the meal, Jack left Eveline's side to do a walkthrough of the ground floor, checking there were no last-minute hiccups before it began.

In the doorway to the second dining room, he paused as people took their seats. On the largest table were Henry's three parents—his biological mom and dad, Vivienne and Arthur, and his second mum, Dervla. Their marriage and the sex parties they ran at the Manor made his own career as an escort seem relatively tame.

On the same table was another stunning Black woman who bore a striking resemblance to Vivienne. This must be her elder sister, Simone. Next to her was—*No. No way. No fucking, fucking way. It couldn't be.*

A woman in her fifties had her back to him, her blonde hair tied in a chignon to show off her slender neck.

Less than a month ago, Jack had kissed that neck, untied that chignon, and fucked that woman six ways to Sunday. A cold sweat broke out across his skin. *Please God, let it not be her.*

As if hearing his thoughts, the woman turned to the side, laughing at something Simone said. Jack clutched the doorframe for support. It *was* her. It was Antoinette Lavigne.

But how the *fuck* was she in Foxbrooke when she lived in Nice?

Drawing back from the doorway, he breathed deeply, trying to order his thoughts. Antoinette's husband owned an exclusive luggage company, and they split their time between Paris and the south of France.

It made perfect sense for Antoinette to know Simone. And if Simone was coming to the Duke and Duchess of Somerset's famous Winter Ball, it wasn't too much of a stretch to imagine her inviting a friend.

He couldn't let her see him. She knew him as Jasper, not Jack. As an escort, not a friend of her friend's niece and nephew. And what if Eveline saw her?

Calm the fuck down. Think. Antoinette is married. She would never make a scene. And Eveline doesn't know who she is.

He just needed to get through the meal. After that, could he persuade Eveline to leave? She hadn't seemed completely well earlier. Maybe it was better for her to go home and rest? But what if she wanted to stay? What then? Could he feign illness?

On the way back to his table, Jack slipped the Jasper mask back on. He was calm. He was confident. He needed a drink... Fuck! Was this how he managed it for so long? When was the last time he'd had sex with a client when completely sober? Three years ago? *Five* years ago? He couldn't remember.

Eveline was waving him over from across the larger dining room. He stared blankly at her, then raised his hand. *Smile!* With heavy feet, he crossed the room towards her and took his seat.

'Everything tickety-boo?' she asked.

Jack nodded as his heart cracked. Who even *said* 'tickety-boo' or 'fiddlesticks'? People like Eveline did. People who didn't have a bad bone in their body. People who talked to god and never swore.

'Have you seen the menu? It all sounds so yummy.'

He stared at her, as if trying to commit every perfect feature to memory.

'Jack, are you alright?'

'Yes, yes, fine. How are you feeling?'

A flicker of distress crossed her features, and he noticed a faint sheen of sweat on her forehead.

'Super-duper,' she said with enthusiasm.

'No, she's not,' Estelle butted in, leaning over. 'She nearly fainted earlier, and asked if the rectory was hot, which means she's either got a fever or is in advanced stages of hypothermia.'

Jack reached to touch Eveline's forehead. 'Angel, you're burning up.'

She huffed. 'I'm not ill, I promise. It must be just the start of a cold or something.'

He pushed back his chair. 'Let me take you home.'

'No! Absolutely not! I'm staying to support you.'

'It's all in hand. It doesn't need me. I want to be there for you.'

'And I want to stay!'

In the pause that followed Eveline's shout, she clapped her hand to her mouth, looking as shocked as he felt.

Her eyes filled with tears. 'I'm so sorry, Jack. I didn't mean to yell.'

'Hey, hey, it's all good. We can stay. Whatever you want.'

She dabbed at the corners of her eyes. 'I don't know why I'm so emotional right now.'

Jack reached into the centre of the table. 'Let me get you some water.'

'Are you *sure* you're not pregnant?' Estelle asked her.

The bottle slipped out of his hand, falling to the table and knocking over several glasses with a crash.

'Fuck!' He grabbed the bottle and tried to mop up the spill with his napkin.

Estelle helped him out. 'Steady on, butterfingers. If you're going to be a daddy, you need steadier hands than that.'

Panic and fear sliced through him. 'Not fucking funny, Stelle,' he growled.

She raised her hands. 'Jesus, Jack, it's only a joke. She's already assured me she's not up the duff.'

His gaze shot to Eveline.

'Don't worry,' she whispered. 'I'm not pregnant.'

Despite her attempt at a smile, he could see how upset she was. *See that? You did that. You made her unhappy.* He glanced at the bottles of wine on the table and her eyes followed his. *Fuck!*

The waiting staff appeared with their first course and diffused some of the tension. Jack tried to relax, but everything inside kept coiling back up, tighter and tighter.

I need a drink.

He felt Eveline's hand on his.

'It's okay,' she said quietly. 'You've got me. You've always got me.'

Taking a deep breath, he poured himself a glass of water,

then downed it. Tonight was meant to be the start of something new, but right now it felt like he'd dug his own grave and was standing at the edge, waiting for the inevitable.

Estelle knew something was amiss, so, like the true friend she was to both him and Eveline, became the life and soul of the party. Libby was sitting across the table from her, and the two of them traded jokes and banter until the table was in stitches.

But Jack couldn't relax. Eveline may have been smiling and laughing, but she kept pressing her napkin to her forehead, and hadn't eaten much. And underneath his concern was the gut-churning knowledge that he wasn't good enough for her and could never give her what she needed.

'Are you sure you're okay?' he asked as the desserts were brought out.

'Please stop asking me that. Really, I'm fine.'

'Sorry.'

Eveline pushed back her chair, and he went to stand. She put her hand on his arm and shook her head. 'I'm just going to the ladies. I'll be back in a bit.'

She dashed off, and Jack reached for his glass of water again.

'What's up?' Estelle asked. 'You've had a face like a dog's dinner since we sat down.'

'I'm worried about Eveline.'

'She'll be okay. You'll be going back with her tonight?'

Am I? He nodded.

'Well then, she's not going to be on her own. Hopefully she'll feel better after a good night's shag.'

Jack gave her a look.

'Sleep! I meant sleep!'

He stood. 'I'm just going to check on her.'

'Want me to come?'

Jack shook his head. 'If we don't come back, it means I've taken her home. I know it's a dick move, but can I leave the rest of the night to you and the staff?'

'Yeah, no worries. There's fuck all to do now, anyway. You go.'

He moved, and Estelle grabbed his arm. 'There is one thing...'

'Yes?'

She eyed his untouched dessert. 'In case you don't come back, can I have your pudding?'

He managed a smile. 'Of course.'

'Excellent.' She reached for his plate.

'Er, I haven't even left yet and I might come back?'

Estelle grinned. 'I'm banking on the fact that you won't.'

OUTSIDE, JACK STRODE DOWN THE CORRIDOR TOWARDS THE nearest toilets.

'Jasper!'

He froze.

'Sacré bleu! C'est toi! It *is* you!'

Panic rushed through his veins, pushed by the frantic thud of his heart. *Breathe! Breathe!* He turned slowly, a smile on his face.

'Antoinette, what an unexpected pleasure.'

Jack glanced around the corridor as she approached. They were alone. Antoinette was unsteady on her feet—a fact he might not have noticed if he'd been drinking. She reached for him and he kissed her cheeks.

'Jasper, my darling, what are you doing here? Are you alone?'

'I'm with a client.'

'In England? Mon Dieu! Is she as grey as the weather and as dull as the food?'

His jaw clenched. He'd been so desperate to get to Eveline, but now he was praying she took her time.

'Or is she *wild* like the Duchess of Somerset?' Antoinette continued, running the tip of a manicured finger down the front of his dress shirt. 'Or me?'

Words were lost under memories of the last time he'd been with Antoinette—her nails raking his back as he pounded into her. Then images came to him of Eveline—her writhing with pleasure beneath him. His sick, twisted mind kept throwing him snapshots of the two women, until his head was light and he couldn't breathe.

'You're thinking about me, non?' Antoinette purred. She came closer and leaned in, her lips right by his ear. 'I've missed you, Jasper. When are you coming—' She broke off, looking behind him.

He stiffened.

'Alors, this must be her.' Antoinette pulled away, a smirk on her lips.

Jack turned, his head pounding.

Eveline.

Despite the heat in her face, she looked as though she'd seen a ghost. Her lips were parted, her eyes wide as they flicked between him and Antoinette.

This was his fate. This was the destiny his life choices had led to. No matter how understanding Eveline could be about his work in the abstract sense, the reality was a different matter. Eveline was staring at Antoinette's designer dress, the jewels around her neck, her tanned and toned body, as if comparing the two of them and finding herself lacking. Self-loathing and disgust turned Jack's stomach.

'Eveline,' he said, keeping his hands by his sides in case she recoiled if he reached for her. 'This is Antoinette Lavigne... Antoinette, Eveline Shaw.'

He may have been rooted to the spot, but Antoinette was not. She crossed to Eveline, kissing her on both cheeks.

'Enchanté, chéri.'

'H-hello,' she stammered.

'Aren't you a beauty?' Antoinette murmured. 'And so young and fresh. What a treat for Jasper.'

Eveline flinched at the sound of his fake name.

'Antoinette,' he began, his voice rough as he forced it through his constricted throat. 'Eveline is my—' He cleared his throat.

'Girlfriend,' said Eveline. 'I'm his girlfriend.'

Antoinette arched an eyebrow. 'Aren't we all, chéri. At least for a night or two.' She turned her attention back to him. 'I was your girlfriend, what... Three weeks ago?' Her gaze travelled lasciviously down his chest to his crotch. 'C'était incroyable, as it always is.' She smiled at Eveline and lowered her voice. 'His cock... Magnifique, n'est-ce pas?'

Eveline was trembling, sweat breaking out across her brow.

'Antoinette—' he began.

'Chéri, are you well?' she asked Eveline, her perfectly shaped eyebrows drawing together with concern. 'Please, don't feel threatened. I'm not going to steal Jasper away. He's yours for tonight. Unless...'

His heart was pounding so fast in his head he almost didn't hear Eveline's reply.

'Unless what?' she whispered.

Antoinette ran her finger down the outside of Eveline's arm. 'I have a room upstairs.'

Eveline shivered.

'I haven't eaten pussy for a while,' she continued. 'But yours, chéri... I'm sure is as délicieux as Jasper's cock. What do you say, pretty one? A ménage à trois? Will you share him tonight?'

No! No! No! NO!

Eveline took a stumbling step back, shaking her head, then turned and ran.

'Oof!' Antoinette said, raising her hands. 'Even more English than I thought. You'd better go after her, or she'll ask for her money back.'

JACK DASHED THROUGH THE CORRIDORS OF THE MANOR towards the front door. He was trapped in a nightmare and every one of his demons was at his heels.

In the entrance hall, he found Eveline fumbling to find her coat on the rack.

'Eveline!'

Her whole body was shaking. 'I n-need to go home.'

'Let me go with you, please.'

'No, Jack. I'm n-not well. I need to go to b-bed.'

He followed her out of the front doors into the cold night air.

'Eveline, I'm sorry, please—'

'There's no n-need to apologise. You've done n-nothing wrong.' She was shaking so violently that her teeth were chattering. 'A s-situation like this was always p-possible. I just n-need some space to p-process it. Everything will be b-back to normal in the m-morning.'

The weight of responsibility for her happiness sank into his stomach, taking his heart with it. He couldn't ruin her life anymore. First the shitshow with Simon, and now this? Maybe he couldn't save himself, but he could save her. He followed her down the drive.

'No. No, it won't.'

'Yes, it w-will. It's been a sh-shock, that's all, but I will pray to G-God and he will help m-me.'

And there it was. Once again, proof that Jack had no right to crawl up to heaven and drag Eveline back down to his own personal hell.

'It's not going to work.'

'It w-will. God is always there for m-me.'

'No, Eveline. *We're* not going to work.'

She stopped and faced him, the colour draining from her face. 'What are you t-talking about?'

'Us. It can't happen.'

'Why n-not? I told you, I'll d-deal with what happened t-tonight. I will!'

Her eyes filled with tears, and the sight cracked him open.

'Eveline. I'm not the right man for you. I'm a fucked-up sex worker and an alcoholic. I don't have any qualifications, career, or any transferable skills. I don't even have any fucking A-levels! I've got nothing to offer you.'

'That's not t-true! You've got everything to offer m-me!'

'I don't. You need someone like Isaac, Connor, or Finn. Someone who can give you what you need. What you want and deserve. Fuck's sake, Eveline, can you imagine me as a father?'

She nodded, her tears flowing freely. 'Yes, yes, I c-can!'

He shook his head. 'I'm sorry.'

'Jack...'

Fuck, don't say it. Please don't say it.

'I love y-you.'

He couldn't breathe. Inside his chest, his demons were gleefully ripping everything they could find to shreds.

'And I know you l-love me.'

He stared at the ground. If he saw the pain on her face, it would annihilate him.

'I'm not capable of love,' he whispered.

She stepped towards him. 'Jack!'

He stepped away. 'Please, Eveline. Just go.'

There was a soul-searing pause, then she turned and walked away. Jack followed from a distance, making sure she reached the rectory, then watched as she entered and closed the door with a thud behind her.

31

Jack stared at the darkness of the rectory, everything inside him numb.

What now?

Turning to the brightly lit façade of the Manor, the urge to drink himself into oblivion sucker-punched him. Hands shaking, he took out his phone and dialled. It connected almost immediately.

'Jack?'

'Hi Kieran, I know it's late but—'

'No, it's fine. If you're struggling, you must ring. Any time, day or night. Where are you now? At the Winter Ball?'

'Outside.'

'Have you had a drink?'

'No.'

'How are you feeling? What's going on?'

Jack leaned against a pillar flanking the entrance to Foxbrooke Manor, his gaze still on the rectory.

'Everything's gone to shit.'

'In particular? Has something triggered your need for a drink?'

Jack paused. At his first AA meeting, he'd talked about his upbringing but hadn't shared with anyone that he'd been an escort. Afterwards he'd reminded Kieran, the group leader, that they'd met before at Saint Saviour's with Eveline, then asked him to be his sponsor.

'I've been a sex worker for the past ten years.'

'Go on.'

'I've fallen in—begun a relationship with Eveline and decided to leave that life behind.'

Jack hunched over, bracing one hand on his thighs as the true horror of the night flooded through him.

'And?'

'One of my clients is at the party. She... she met Eveline.'

'Does Eveline know your profession?'

'Yes.'

'But meeting your client was a shock?'

He nodded.

Even though Kieran couldn't hear his response, he continued. 'Have you talked to Eveline about it?'

'Yes. I... I broke off our relationship.'

'Why?'

'Because I don't want to ruin her life. She's just so...' He ran his hands through his hair in frustration. 'And I'm...'

'Did Eveline want to finish your relationship?'

Grief strangled his heart. 'No.'

'If you hadn't been a sex worker, or if you hadn't met your client tonight, would you want to be with Eveline?'

'Yes.'

In the pause that followed, he heard Kieran taking breaths, as if working out the best way to phrase his response.

'Just say it,' Jack told him. 'No sugar-coating. I can take it.'

'By ending your relationship with Eveline, not only did you go against what both of you want, you also made that decision *for* her.'

Jack didn't know how to reply.

'By doing this,' Kieran continued. 'You told her she can't make decisions for herself, even though she was clear about what she wanted.'

He squeezed his eyes tightly shut as pain lanced through him.

'Growing up, your father made decisions for you that went against what *you* loved and wanted. How did that make you feel?'

His legs gave way, and he slumped to the ground, his knees bent, his back pressed against the cold stone of the pillar.

'There's a lot to unpack here, Jack, but I want you to consider the possibility that you broke up with Eveline tonight, not to save her, but to save *yourself*.'

'What?' he croaked.

'You grew up in a household where love was conditional. That's extremely damaging and destabilising for a child. It teaches you that it can be taken away at any moment. It's logical to believe that it's safer to live without love than risk opening your heart fully.'

Jack thought back over his adult life. He'd never had a relationship before. His clients may have controlled the money, but he always controlled the sex. Being with Eveline was the first time he'd ever let his guard down, and it was terrifying.

'Eveline's been sober for a long time now. I think you should trust her judgement when it comes to what's right for her. And you should stop punishing yourself for your father's behaviour and your career choices. Allow yourself to be happy.'

His phone beeped with another call coming in.

Eveline Shaw.

'Jack?'

'Kieran, it's Eveline, she's ringing me. Can I call you back?'

'Yes, of course, but only if you need to. Go be with her if you can.'

'Thanks.' He switched calls. 'Eveline?'

'Jack... Not well,' she slurred.

He leapt to his feet, sprinting towards the rectory. 'I'm here. Talk to me.'

Her breathing was ragged. 'Ja—'

Then the phone went dead.

Reaching the front door, he pounded on it, then tried the handle. Locked.

He ran to the side of the house, trying the back door. Also locked.

Where did Finn say he left the spare key?

In the darkness, Jack felt for a series of clay plant pots stacked against the side of the house.

One, two, three... He lifted the fourth, grabbed the key, and fumbled to unlock the door.

'I'm coming!' he shouted, barrelling through and slamming it behind him.

The kitchen was empty, so he ran up the stairs. 'Eveline! Are you up there?'

Entering her room, the lights were out, but the curtains were open. The moonlight illuminated her, sprawled on the bed in her pyjama bottoms and a vest top, shivering as if she was lying in snow.

'Fuck!' Jack rushed to her side, moving her hair off her forehead. 'I'm here.'

She was boiling hot and dripping with sweat, her eyes open but unfocused.

'Eveline?'

She seemed lost in a nightmare, mumbling incoherently.

'Angel, I'm just going to turn the light on, okay?'

She didn't respond.

He flicked on the main light and she howled as if it was burning her, rolling onto her front, her arms wrapped around her head.

'Jesus!' He turned it off and came back to her side. 'It's okay, love, it's off.'

Her shivers were turning into shudders. The bedding beneath her was completely soaked through. This didn't look like any ordinary fever.

He took her hand. 'I'm going to call a doctor. I'm getting you some proper help.'

'No!'

'Eveline, can you hear me?'

'God... Need you...'

Was she talking to *him* or God?

The seeming clarity of her thoughts disintegrated once more into confusion. Jack heard his own name, but Eveline also cried out for her mother and God again, as if she was lost in hell with no way out. *Fuck!* He dialled 111 and got through to a nurse after explaining Eveline's symptoms.

'What's her current temperature?' the woman asked.

'I don't know.' He went to the chest of drawers, pulling out clothes for her to change into.

'Is there a thermometer in the house?'

'Er... Probably? Hang on.' He rushed to the bathroom, the sudden light almost blinding him, and opened the cupboard door. Eveline was crying louder from her room. *Fuck!* He rummaged around but couldn't see anything. She had to have a first aid kit somewhere as she'd bandaged her own arm. Was the injury causing the fever?

White hot panic flared through him. 'Look, can you just send an ambulance?'

'I need to get a little more information first so we can make an assessment.'

'I'll ring you back.' Jack cut the call and rang Estelle. *Please pick up. Please pick up.*

'If you want your pudding, I'm afraid it's long gone,' Estelle said as she answered.

'Stelle, Eveline's super fucking ill and I need a thermometer. Do you know where it is?'

'Oh, shit. Yeah, it's in the kitchen. Has she got a fever?'

He ignored Eveline's cries and ran down the stairs, his phone clamped to his head.

'She's fucking delirious. I need to take her temperature and call the nurse back, then try to get her into dry clothes.'

The background noise behind Estelle quietened. 'I'm on my way.'

Thank fuck. 'Back door's unlocked.'

'I'll be two minutes, tops.'

The phone went dead. Jack put it in his pocket and started systematically going through every cupboard. *Come on! Where the fuck are you?*

His heart was pounding in his chest, his brain a cacophony of screams. He had to help her.

The back door slammed, and Estelle rushed in.

'I can't fucking find it!' he shouted.

'It's okay, I know where it is.' She opened the cupboard under the sink and took out a plastic box. 'Here we go.'

'Who keeps a fucking first aid kit next to the fucking bleach!' he yelled.

She touched his arm. 'Hey, it's okay, Jack. She's going to be fine.'

He shook his head, struggling to breathe. 'She's fucking ill and I'm freaking out.'

'Come on, show me where she is.'

Jack led the way, turning the lights off as Estelle followed him.

'Don't turn on any lights,' he said. 'She screamed when I did, as if she was on fire.'

'But how are we meant to see?'

'There's enough light coming in from outside, and we can use our phones.'

Entering the room, he took Eveline's hand.

'Jack! Don't leave... Don't go!'

'I'm not, love. I'm right here. And Stelle's here, too.'

'God... Help...' Any coherence was lost again in fragments of disjointed sentences.

'Fucking hell,' Estelle said.

'Pass me the thermometer.'

She did, and he shook the mercury down, then tried to place it in Eveline's mouth. She bucked and writhed to get away, screaming through gritted teeth.

He clutched his head, trying to stop it from splitting in two. 'We need to get her to the hospital.'

'Do you have a car?'

He shook his head. 'I can use Mum's but it's at hers. Do you have yours?'

'At the livery. I rode over on Duke this afternoon.'

'Fuck! I'm ringing 999.'

'Hang on. Let's try her armpit. See if you can calm her down.'

Jack passed Estelle the thermometer and went to Eveline's head, stroking her hair. 'Angel, it's me. I don't know if you can hear me, but I'm here.'

She grabbed his hand. She was still shivering and mumbling, but no longer fighting to get away. Estelle carefully put the thermometer under Eveline's arm.

'We need to get her dry,' she whispered.

'I know,' he whispered back. 'As soon as we've got a temperature, we can do that.'

Every minute that ticked by was painfully slow.

'Have you looked under the bandage on her arm yet?' Estelle asked.

He shook his head. 'I wasn't able to. After we've done this, put the torch on your phone and I'll see.'

'It must have become infected. When did she do it?'

'Few days ago? She kept telling me it was fine.'

'Fuck's sake.' Estelle let out a huff and slid the thermometer out. 'I'll go into the corridor and take a look.'

Jack reached for the bandage and tried to peel it off, but stopped when Eveline cried out in distress.

Estelle re-entered the room. 'It's nearly forty degrees. That's super fucking high.'

'Can you take the bandage off? I don't want to hurt her.'

Eveline jerked away as Estelle touched it. 'I don't know if you can hear me, but we need to look underneath, okay?' She tried again, but Eveline flailed her arms. 'Fuck this.' With one hand, Estelle held Eveline's arm down. The other ripped the bandage off.

Eveline screamed, curling towards him.

'It's okay, it's okay, love,' he soothed, as Estelle turned on her phone's torch. 'We're just going to take a quick look, then turn it off, okay?'

Jack took Eveline's hand, pulling her arm away from her body as Estelle leaned forward with her phone.

'Jesus fucking Christ,' Estelle whispered.

The wound was puffy and inflamed, pus oozing from the livid cut. Streaks of red stretched down Eveline's pale arm.

'Can you call 111 back?' he asked. 'I don't want to leave her.'

Estelle nodded and went into the corridor.

'Angel,' he whispered to Eveline. 'I need to get you out of your wet clothes. I'll try and be gentle and I'm sorry if it hurts.'

Carefully peeling them off, he grabbed a t-shirt to absorb the sweat from her body. Eveline's skin was on fire, but her teeth were chattering. He hauled her to the edge of the bed, where the sheet was still dry.

Estelle came back in and closed the door quietly behind her. 'They're sending an ambulance, but it might take half an hour or so as it's apparently not life and death and—'

'What the fuck?' he hissed. 'This seems pretty life and fucking death to me!'

She nodded. 'But it's Saturday night so they've got to deal with drunk idiots as well.'

'Can you help me change the sheets?'

'Yes. Let me get some fresh ones from the airing cupboard.'

Holding Eveline's hand, Jack reached across her to untuck as much of the covers as he could. When Estelle returned, she helped him remake the bed, then they moved Eveline into the centre.

'Do you know where her phone is?' Estelle asked.

'She rang me from here, so it must be somewhere. Can you shine your torch on the floor?'

He found it by the bed and passed it to Estelle.

'I'm going to ring her parents,' she said.

'Do you know her passcode?'

'Yeah. I wanted her to set it to six-six-six, but she used her birthday instead.'

Estelle left the room, and Jack sunk his head, his hand holding Eveline's as if it were a lifeline. He should have known when her birthday was.

She was still shivering, but had stopped mumbling. Was she asleep?

Estelle crept back into the room. 'Her dad's driving up

from Kent now. I'm going to ring her mum back once we've got her to hospital. She might fly out first thing tomorrow.' She inclined her head to Eveline. 'How's she doing?'

'Still burning up and shivering, but she isn't shouting.'

Estelle sat on the other side of the bed and stroked Eveline's hair. 'You're going to be okay,' she whispered.

They sat in silence, Jack's ears attuned to Eveline's breathing as well as listening for any sound that might indicate the ambulance was on its way.

'Should we get a bag ready for her? For the hospital,' he murmured.

Estelle lifted her head. 'Yes—'

She broke off, her eyes widening at a sound from downstairs.

Prickles of adrenaline shot across his skin. He glanced at Estelle, his muscles tensing.

There was a creak from a footstep on the stairs.

Jack glanced around for a weapon. No-one crept into someone else's house in the dead of night with good things on their mind. But unless he started throwing Polly Hart books with the velocity of a bullet, there was nothing to hand.

Estelle had her phone out, finger poised over the screen.

Jack eased off the bed, stepping quietly to the door. He didn't know who was on the other side, but he could bet they weren't expecting to find him.

The sound of a footstep near the top of the stairs ramped up his breathing and heart rate. He knew without a second thought that he would lay down his life to protect Eveline's.

He glanced back at Estelle. She'd placed herself between him and the bed, another layer of protection between whoever was out there and Eveline. She turned the screen of her phone to face him. The numbers nine-nine-nine illuminated, just waiting for her to press the call button.

His nervous system whined in his ears as he fought to make sense of the tiniest sounds. His left hand reached for the door handle as his right formed into a fist.

The door began to move, pushed in from the other side.

Jack yanked it open.

There, on the other side, his mouth open in shock, stood Simon.

Jack punched him in the face.

Simon fell down, landing with a crash on the wooden floor, immobile.

Estelle ran forward. 'Fucking hell!'

Had he killed him? Jack flicked on the light in the hall and crouched. Simon was still breathing, but out cold.

'Motherfucker,' Estelle spat. 'Couldn't accept that she turned him down.'

'Turned him down?'

'His marriage proposal.'

'His *what?*'

'You said Eveline told you what he did!'

'His complaints to the Bishop, yes, but not that! When did it happen?'

'I dunno? Week, ten days ago? What the fuck does it matter? We need to get you out of here. Now.'

'What? Why?'

'Because I need to ring the police to get this fucker arrested before the ambulance arrives. It's going to look a hell of a lot better if they find him here with two women, one of whom is practically unconscious, rather than a fit bloke half his age.' Estelle dashed back into Eveline's room, returning with a handful of her scarves. 'Quick, help me hogtie him.'

Jack turned Simon on his side and helped her knot the scarves around his wrists and ankles, then tied them together behind his back.

'Now go!' Estelle cried.

He didn't want to leave Eveline. 'But—'

'Think, Jack. The best thing you can do for Eveline now is to leave. I'll ring you the moment I can. Okay?'

He nodded, cast a quick glance at the bedroom door, then ran down the stairs.

STANDING IN THE SHADOWS JUST INSIDE THE MANOR'S gates, Jack's heartbeats marked time as he stared at the rectory. His limbs ached as adrenaline continued to fire through his muscles. Should he call Kieran back? *No.* Despite the most acute stress of his life, Jack didn't want alcohol. All he needed was to be with Eveline and make sure she was okay. And he didn't want to drag Kieran into the situation with Simon.

Kieran's words circled his mind on an endless loop, wearing down deeper and deeper grooves until he had no choice but to acknowledge their truth. Just as he'd buried his father, he also needed to bury the beliefs beaten into him by his dad. By denying himself happiness, he was only perpetuating his father's abuse from beyond the grave.

Blue lights flashed on the Bath Stone of the cottages leading to the high street just before a squad car screeched to a halt outside the rectory. Two officers exited and dashed to the front door. Estelle opened it for them.

Shortly after their arrival, an ambulance arrived.

Jack crept to the churchyard to get a better view, his heart in his mouth as a stretcher was taken into the house, then wheeled out shortly afterwards with Eveline strapped to it.

What now? He couldn't follow her. He wasn't family, so wouldn't be allowed to see her, or know how she was.

A paramedic's car arrived. *For Simon?* Jack rubbed his bruised knuckles. He should be pleased Simon was okay, but a large part of him wanted the man keeping his dad company in hell. A police officer opened the door and ushered the paramedic inside.

Should he wait? Jack looked at the Manor. He needed to start being honest with those closest to him as well as himself, and that might as well start now. Taking out his phone, he dialled.

❧ 32 ❧

Jack met Henry and Finn outside the office Henry shared with Estelle.

'Thank you,' he said. 'I really appreciate this and it won't take long.'

Henry unlocked the door. 'Take as long as you like. You're doing us a favour.'

He followed Henry into the room. 'A favour? Don't you want to get back?'

'Fuck no,' Finn grumbled, scratching his beard. 'That James bloke fucked off half an hour ago and Summer and Libby are now dancing and screaming in the "I don't need a man room".'

'The what?'

Henry passed his hand over his face. 'Another one of your bright ideas,' he said. 'It's absolute genius just as long as I don't have to go anywhere near it. The women love it, and men like us can safely run away without being missed.'

The penny was starting to drop. 'The *party* room?'

'If that's what you want to call it,' Finn replied. 'So far it's been wall-to-wall Destiny's Child, Aretha Franklin, Beyoncé, Donna Summer and Kelly Clarkson. We just left them with their hands in the air yelling "I will survive" louder than fucking football supporters.'

The first smile of the last few hours tugged at the corners of Jack's mouth. Both his friends looked absolutely frazzled.

There was a knock at the door and Henry opened it to let Connor in, dressed in his nurse's uniform.

'Everything alright?' Connor asked, his forehead furrowed.

Jack embraced him. 'Thanks for coming. I won't be long, then you can go to bed.'

'No hurry. I might stay on for a bit and have a dance. They've got some crackers playing in the drawing room.'

Finn and Henry looked at each other.

Connor broke into a dance. 'Cause if you like it, then you shoulda put a ring on it,' he sang.

Henry sunk his head and groaned.

'...If you like it, then you shoulda put a ring on it.'

Finn grabbed Estelle's Moody Cow stress ball and threw it at him.

Connor caught it and laughed. 'I should have known it wasn't your cup of tea.' Henry passed him a chair and he sat down. 'So, what's this all about? Is Estelle joining us?'

'Not yet,' Jack said. 'She's...' *Not with Eveline anymore. She's with the police.* He rubbed his face. 'She's going to ring me when she's done.'

Henry frowned. 'What's going on? Is Eveline okay?'

Jack shook his head, his jaw tightening to hold the emotion back.

'Mate?' Finn asked, leaning forward. 'Please tell me this isn't anything to do with me changing the locks earlier?'

Images of Simon flashed before him. He shook his head.

'Eveline's on her way to hospital now with an out-of-control fever. I think she's got sepsis.'

'Fuck!' Finn growled.

'From the cut on her arm?' Henry asked.

'Yes, we think so. Stelle and I took the bandage off and it was inflamed, with red lines coming from it.'

'Hospital's the right place for her,' Connor said, his expression grave. 'That sounds bad. Was she conscious when you left her?'

'Barely. She was delirious. Sweating and shivering and couldn't cope with any light.'

'When did the ambulance leave?'

'Ten minutes ago?'

'Okay. She'll get there in the next fifteen and will be seen immediately. I'll ring the hospital in an hour and see if I can find anything out.'

Jack's shoulders slumped with relief. 'Thank you.'

'So, where's Estelle?' Henry asked.

'With the police. She's okay!' Jack said, holding his hands up as Henry, Finn and Connor leapt to their feet. 'She's not in trouble.'

'Then what the fuck is going on?' Finn asked as they retook their seats.

Jack took a big breath. 'I'll give you the short version. Simon Little asked Eveline to marry him about ten days ago. She said no. He didn't take it very well. As well as stabbing her in the back about the pews, he's made a series of formal complaints against her to the Bishop, trying to get her sacked.'

'Cocksucker,' Finn spat.

'He also tried to get me kicked off the mural project at Foxbrooke Haven.'

'Why?' asked Connor.

Jack glanced at his friend, feeling his cheeks heating. 'I've begun a relationship with Eveline.'

Connor's eyes widened. 'But... France?'

'I'm not going back.'

'That's great news!'

'What about Estelle?' Henry demanded.

'When Eveline got worse, I rang Stelle to find out where the thermometer was at the rectory. She came over, helped me with Eveline, and rang the ambulance. We were waiting for it in Eveline's room with all the lights off when we heard someone creeping up the stairs.'

The three men leaned forward, faces grim.

'As whoever it was came to the door, I yanked it open to see Simon. I punched him and he went out cold. Stelle and I tied him up, and she called the police. She said it was best for me to do a runner and for her to claim she lamped him.'

Finn nodded. 'Sensible.'

'The police arrived just before the ambulance for Eveline. They're still there now. Stelle said she'd ring me when she could.'

Henry's knee was bouncing, and a muscle twitched in his jaw. 'I want to—I want...'

'Don't,' said Finn. 'Going over there or ringing Stelle is the last thing you should do right now.'

'I know,' Henry replied, jumping to his feet and pacing. 'I just want to make sure she's—'

'It's okay to be worried,' Connor began. 'But Finn's right.'

Henry sat, splaying his fingers over his knee to keep it still. 'That man,' he spat.

'Has been arrested,' Connor said. 'Oh, and punched. Once this all plays out, I think our sister is going to be most pissed off about the fact she wasn't the one to slug him.'

Henry huffed. 'True.' He rubbed his hand across his short

hair. 'Fucking hell. And here was me thinking Hunter-Savage showing up was the worst thing that could happen.'

'If it makes you feel any better,' said Finn. 'He didn't go anywhere near Summer.'

'Willow?' Henry asked.

'No.'

'Thank god.'

'He chatted to your mom and mammy for a while, but they had him under control.'

'In what way?'

'Your mammy pinched his cheeks like he was a cute little baby, then left with your mom to go and dance.'

Henry gave a stern smile. 'Good.'

'Jack,' Connor asked. 'How are *you* doing?'

How *was* he doing? His emotions were flayed and raw.

'I... I want to tell you all a couple of things.' He swallowed. 'You know I've hardly been back to Foxbrooke since we left school because of Dad...'

His friends nodded.

'But Dad's dead now and I've met Eveline, and...' *It doesn't matter if she doesn't take me back*. 'I'm staying here.'

'What about your work?' Henry asked.

Jack stared at his hands, his heart rate rising. 'I...' He took a breath. 'I don't want this to be common knowledge, but you're my closest friends and I don't want to keep lying to you.'

At the edges of his vision, he could see them leaning closer.

'What about Stelle?' Finn asked.

'Eveline knows and I expect she'll tell Stelle at some point,' he replied. 'I'd rather it came from her than me, to be honest.'

'Tell her what?' Henry asked.

'About my real job. I'm not a party-planner. The Winter Ball was the first event I've ever had anything to do with setting up.' He raised his head to look at Henry. 'I'm sorry for lying to you.'

Henry shrugged. 'Don't be. You did an amazing job and more than doubled our profits. If you're staying in Foxbrooke, then I want you to do it again next year.'

'So, what *is* your job in France?' Connor asked. 'And why the secrecy?'

The back of Jack's neck pricked with sweat.

'You don't have to tell us,' Connor continued.

Jack cleared his throat. 'I want to. I think it'll help me draw a line under it and move on. I don't want it to be a part of my life anymore, or define who I am.'

The silence roared as his friends waited.

'For over a decade now,' he continued. 'I've been earning money on the edges of the law. I'm very successful, but—'

'Holy shit,' Finn interrupted. 'You're a contract killer... Like John Wick.'

'No!' *Fuck's sake*. 'Why is that everyone's first thought?'

Finn shrugged. 'Because it's cool?'

'Was that Eveline's first guess?' Henry asked.

Jack nodded, then turned to Finn. 'And killing people is not cool.'

'What about Simon?' Finn replied.

Jack hesitated, the knuckles on his right hand tingling, as if itching to connect with Simon's face again.

'See?' Finn said. 'Suddenly, being an assassin makes perfect sense.'

'I've never killed anyone.'

'So, not a serial killer then?'

Jack raised his hands in frustration. 'No!'

Finn grinned. 'Was that Eveline's second guess?'

He nodded.

His friend laughed. 'Epic. Great minds and all that. Jewel thief? Like the Pink Panther?'

Jack let out an exasperated sigh. This was almost as bad as when he'd told Eveline.

'Austin Powers? Doctor Evil? Drug lord? Mafia—'

'Finn,' Connor interrupted. 'Not helping.' He turned to Jack. 'This is obviously difficult for you, but we're not going to judge.'

'But—' Finn began.

'Mate,' Henry said. 'Shut it.'

'Sorry, Jack,' Finn said. 'I'm a bit pissed. Crack on.'

Jack rubbed the back of his neck. *Come on, just rip the plaster off.* 'For the last ten years I've...' He took a big breath and held his friends' gazes. 'I've been sleeping with women for money. I'm—I *was* an escort.'

Silence. Henry and Connor looked shocked, but a shit-eating grin spread across Finn's face.

'Mate, you've outdone yourself. That trumps builder, nurse and—what are you now, Henry? Estate Manager?'

'Finn...' Connor began.

Finn waved his hand as if brushing off Connor's warning. 'That's fucking cool, Jack. You were *paid* to get women off.' He leaned back, shaking his head. 'Jesus, you must have—how many women *have* you slept with?'

'Finn—' Connor warned.

'I haven't kept count,' Jack replied.

'Bloody hell.' Finn whistled. 'And you're giving it all up for a vicar...'

Yes, he was. But even if Eveline didn't want him, he was done with being an escort. He wanted a different life, and he *did* want a relationship. However, the only woman he wanted one with might not take him back.

Henry cleared his throat. 'Well, er... That is an *unusual* line of work. But if our parents have taught us anything, it's to be open-minded when it comes to, er, *sexual* matters.'

Finn snorted. 'Mate, you crack me up.'

'Have you looked after your mental and physical health?' Connor asked.

'Physical, yes,' Jack replied. 'I've always used condoms and have never caught an STD. My mental health, however...'

'Have you ever been in a dangerous situation?' Connor continued.

Jack shook his head. 'Not really. I vet—*vetted* my clients well. But I've realised over the last year, and in particular since Dad died, that my job has been taking a toll.'

'I can imagine. It must be extremely stressful—'

'Stressful?' Finn interjected.

'Shut up!' Henry shouted.

Finn slumped in his chair. 'Sorry, Jack. I just can't get my head around it.'

'It's okay.' Jack rubbed his hands over his face. 'This part is actually the hardest to talk about because I've only just admitted it to myself.' He took a breath. 'And I really need your help.'

'Anything,' Henry said. 'Anything at all.'

Jack took a deep breath. 'I'm an alcoholic and need your support to stay sober. This isn't a "dry January" time-out kind of deal. It's a commitment for the rest of my life. Before the funeral, I can't remember the last day I went without a drink. In France, it's easy not to think about it because wine is part of the culture. But since coming back... I know I need to stop for good.'

'We're here for you, Jack,' said Connor.

'One hundred per cent,' Henry added.

'Yeah, of course, mate,' said Finn. 'Fuck... Does this mean I'm an alcoholic too?'

Jack smiled. 'No idea. I think only you can answer that.'

Finn scratched his beard. 'Fuck me. What a night. Anything else you want to hit us with?'

'Actually, yes.' Jack squared his shoulders. 'There is something else I wanted to talk to you about...'

❀ 33 ❀

Eveline blinked. 'Dad?'

'You're awake! How are you feeling?'

Her father's eyes were red and puffy. Despite the exhaustion weighing her body to the bed, this didn't feel like a dream. 'Where am I?'

'In hospital, love.'

'Where? What happened?'

'You're in Bath. Your friend rang me last night to tell me you had a fever.'

Friend? Eveline's mind ran back through her memories. The ball, then Jack's client... Her heart jolted with pain as she remembered his words outside the Manor. She couldn't remember anything else from that point on.

'Was it Jack that rang you?'

Her father frowned. 'Who's Jack? No, a lady called Estelle. She was at the rectory with you. The cut on your arm got infected.'

She looked down to see a fresh bandage and a cannula in the back of her hand attached to a drip.

'You were very poorly, love.'

'The pigs. They—'

'Estelle said she'd look after them.'

'Thank goodness.'

'Your mother is on her way.'

'Mum?'

'I'm leaving to pick her up from Bristol airport in a moment.'

Tears pricked Eveline's eyes. 'What day is it?'

'Sunday, love.' He pulled a tissue from a box and passed it to her. 'The doctors say you'll be very tired and emotional for a while.'

Jack. She needed him. It didn't matter that he didn't want her.

'Is my phone here?'

Her father reached into a locker by the bed and pulled it out. 'Estelle packed a bag for you and I charged it up when I got here.'

'When *did* you get here?'

'Three a.m. They wouldn't let me see you until you were... You were in this ward.'

'Oh Dad, you must be exhausted.'

'Not as much as you. I can sleep later.'

'When can I go home? I've already missed morning service.'

'Eveline...' Her father's voice was stern. 'You almost—' He cleared his throat. 'Your flock can wait. Nothing is more important than your health.'

She closed her eyes, sending a tear tracking down her cheek. *Jack...*

'I've got to go and pick up your mum. Won't be longer than a few hours, okay, love?'

She nodded.

'I'll tell the nurses you're awake.' He leaned over and kissed her forehead. 'Please rest.'

WHEN HER FATHER LEFT THE WARD, EVELINE TURNED ON her phone. There were messages from Estelle, Finn, Henry, Connor, her mum, her sisters, and several parishioners. She ignored them all, instead opening the ones from Jack.

> Jack: I don't know when you'll get this, but I need you to know that I'm sorry and want to take back everything I said to you last night outside the Manor XXX

> Jack: When you're well enough, please can I see you? XXX

Her thumbs couldn't move fast enough.

> Eveline: I'm in Forrester Brown ward. Please visit whenever you can xxx

Hit with a wave of tiredness, Eveline put her phone on the table next to her and closed her eyes. She didn't even have the energy to look at the messages from Estelle.

God, thank you for saving me and I'm sorry I didn't take better care of myself. I promise I'll do better. It must have been bad for my parents to come all this way. Please look after Jack. He's been through so much and needs to know that he is loved by you as much as he is by me.

'Eveline?'

Her eyes shot open. 'Jack?'

'Hey don't get up!'

'But—'

He sat on the edge of the bed. 'I've been in the café for a few hours, hoping you might text me back.'

She reached for his hand. 'Did Estelle tell you?'

'Tell me what?'

'That I was ill.'

His face tightened. 'I was there. You called me about five minutes after we...'

'Dad said Estelle called him.'

He looked completely wrung out. 'She did. I didn't have the passcode for your phone.'

'Jack, I'm so sorry.'

'What—'

She squeezed his hand. 'For not taking better care of myself and not accepting help more readily. For ignoring your concerns, and for making you and everyone else worry so much.'

Jack briefly closed his eyes, then fixed her with a look that stopped her heart.

'Eveline. I'm the one who's sorry. For everything I said to you last night. I've been in a really bad place, and when... When you met Antoinette, something inside me snapped. I spoke without thinking where my words were coming from... After you left, I spoke to Kieran, and—'

'Kieran *Mitchell*?'

He nodded.

'I don't understand... You only met him, what... once?'

Jack's thumb moved over the back of her hand. 'I did a "you"...'

'A "me"?'

'I was walking back from Foxbrooke Haven after Si—after a certain *someone* tried to get me kicked out, and asked God to give me a sign. Two seconds later, a woman dropped her car keys as she entered the Baptist Chapel and didn't notice. I picked them up and followed her inside to find Kieran about to start an AA meeting.'

Eveline's eyes filled with tears. *Thank you, God, thank you.*

'Please don't cry, angel!' He passed her the box of tissues.

'I'm happy, not sad.'

'I wasn't ready to tell you. It just felt like another way I'd failed.'

'No! That's the opposite of failure! It takes bravery and humility to take that step. I'm so proud of you.'

He shrugged, as if to brush off her compliment. 'Kieran said that it wasn't my place to make decisions about what you wanted.'

Her heart beat faster.

'And the reason I said we... we couldn't be together, was because it was safer to live without love than to open myself up to it.'

She nodded.

'Kieran said I should stop punishing myself for the way my dad treated me, and what I did for a job. And allow myself to be happy.'

'Would you be happy with me?' she whispered.

He lifted her hand and brushed his lips over her knuckles. A shiver ran down her arm.

'So much it terrifies me,' he said, his voice tentative. 'The moment your eyes met mine in that bar, it was like a lightning bolt tore through me, cracking my world apart. I fell in love with you then, but didn't want to name the feelings. From that night, you just became this constant presence in my life, behind all my thoughts and dreams. But I never thought I would ever see you again.'

He swallowed, his thumb moving in circles across the back of her hand.

'I've told you I don't want children, but it's not true. I'm just scared of fucking it up.'

'Jack, you wouldn't. You're the kindest, sweetest soul with the biggest heart.'

He let out a sigh. 'I'm shit-scared of being a dad, and terrified of how much I love you. But you know what?'

She shook her head.

'I'm even more afraid of being without you.'

She held her breath, not wanting to move a muscle in case she broke the spell.

'I want to go to bed next to you every night and wake up by your side in the morning. I want to support your dreams and always have your back. To be for you what you are for everyone else. I love you, Eveline. And I'm all in... If you'll have me back?'

'I never let you go,' she choked out, tears spilling down her cheeks.

He leaned forward, his own eyes liquid, and kissed away her tears. 'I love you with everything I have to give.'

'I love you, too. I'm so happy right now I think I might burst.'

He smiled. 'I need to ask you something.'

'Anything.'

'Will you marry me?'

Her heart stopped as she stared at him.

'I know marriage is important to you, so it's important to me. Nothing would make me prouder than being your husband.'

'Are you sure?' she whispered.

'One hundred per cent. I should have married you a year ago, so by that logic we've already been engaged for over a year. Do you know the hospital chaplain? Want to get hitched today?'

Eveline laughed, her heart overflowing. 'I look an absolute mess!'

Jack cupped her jaw and brushed her lips with his. 'You're the most beautiful woman in the world.'

She sighed into the kiss. It felt like coming home.

'So, was that a yes?' he murmured. 'Will you marry me?'

'As you wish.'

She felt his smile against her lips. 'My Princess Bride. You never gave up on me.'

'Never give up...' she whispered.

'Never surrender,' he replied, deepening the kiss and sending tingles down to the tips of her toes.

He pulled away, and she whimpered.

'We need to get you well, and that starts with...' He pulled a foil-wrapped packet out of his jacket pocket and passed it to her. 'It'll be cold by now, but it's homemade.'

She unwrapped it. 'A bacon sandwich!'

'Foxbrooke Jewellers is shut today, otherwise I would have brought you a ring. The sandwich will have to do until you're better and can choose one.'

Thank you, God. Thank you.

Jack nudged the edge of the sandwich. 'Come on, use that beautiful mouth for eating, not smiling.'

'You pick the ring. I know I'll love whatever you choose,' she said.

'You sure?'

She nodded.

His smile was as light as her heart. 'I'll be outside the shop when it opens tomorrow. Can we get married next week? You must know a vicar who would do the honours at short notice?'

She giggled. 'I know a few.'

'DARLING!'

Jack stood in the corridor as a woman in her late fifties entered the ward and rushed to Eveline's side. A man in his sixties followed a few feet behind her. *So, these are her mum and dad...*

Her mother reminded him of his, with her trim figure and immaculate presentation. He knew that some people wore their Sunday best when flying, but he was sure Diana Barclay dressed like this all the time. Eveline's father, Peter, was extremely handsome, with a shock of thick white hair, but was clothed in crumpled jeans and a hoodie.

Her mum kissed Eveline's cheek, tucked a strand of hair behind her ear, patted the pillows behind her head, then touched the full glass of water on the bedside table. She fussed in a way that was completely ineffectual but designed to reassure both of them that she was actually there. Peter stood at the foot of the bed, his hands in his pockets, staring with deep affection at his ex-wife and daughter.

Jack flexed his fingers as if to offload some of the adrenaline in his body. He'd never been in a relationship before, so had no experience in how to handle 'meeting the parents' for the first time. On top of that, her mum and dad had no idea he even existed.

'Jack!' Eveline called out. 'Come in!'

Here we go... He lifted his shoulders, hid his nerves behind a smile and entered the ward.

Eveline beamed at him, whilst her parents frowned in confusion.

'Mum, Dad, I'd like you to meet Jack Newton. My fiancé.'

'Your fi—what?' her mother gasped.

'My husband-to-be,' Eveline replied, her eyes sparkling with happiness. 'We're getting married next week.'

Jack grinned at her excitement and the way she delivered the news with no preamble, as if nothing could stop it from bursting out. In the exquisite moment of silence that followed her words, he dedicated his life to keeping that look of pure joy on her face.

He extended his arm. 'Mrs Barclay, Mr Shaw, it's a pleasure to meet you.'

'Er... Hello?' her mother said, taking his hand and glancing between him and Eveline as if waiting for the punchline of a joke.

Her father looked even more flummoxed, but shook Jack's hand firmly. 'Call me Peter,' he said, gruffly, his chest puffing as if to assert dominance in the face of a new male entering his pack.

Her mother cleared her throat. 'I'm afraid you've caught us rather on the back foot.' She levelled a look at her daughter and raised her eyebrows.

'I first met Eveline over a year ago,' Jack replied, deflecting her attention. 'My family is from Foxbrooke and we reconnected recently after the death of my father.'

'Oh,' said Diana. 'I'm so sorry.'

Jack nodded. 'I've been living in France for the last few years, working in the hospitality industry, but now I'm moving my life back to Somerset to be with Eveline.'

Diana's eyes flicked back to her daughter. 'But, er, *married*? Next *week*?'

'With Eveline's job, it's preferable that we marry before living together,' Jack began. 'And we both want children, so it didn't make sense to wait any longer than necessary.'

That was the moment her mother started to soften. 'Grandchildren,' she breathed. 'How...' She gazed at Eveline, emotion tightening her jaw. 'Lovely, darling.'

Jack: Eveline's awake and on the mend. She
had cellulitis in the tissues around the wound,
but the antibiotics are taking care of it,
thank god.

Jack: I also wanted to let you know before
anyone else that Eveline and I are getting
married next week, or as soon as we can get
it arranged. Eveline's already bagged Stelle to
be best woman/ bridesmaid, so will you three
be my best men?

Jack: Btw, she doesn't know about Simon
yet. Stelle's coming later to the hospital so we
can talk to her about what happened.

Connor: CONGRATULATIONS! I'm so happy
for you both, and glad you took my advice
last night.

Finn: Congrats. That's the best news, mate.
Connor, what advice?

Connor: If you like it then you shoulda put a
ring on it. Woah oh, oh…

Jack: Lol. Not till tomorrow morning when
Foxbrooke Jewellers opens.

Finn: And there was me thinking that Henry
would be the first to fall…

Henry: All in good time. Congratulations,
Jack. Need a reception venue?

Estelle: OMGGGGGGG!!!! This is so exciting!!!
If you want it, Henry and my gift will be the
reception at the Manor. We owe you big time
for the Winter Ball and it can serve as a dry
run for if we do any weddings in the future.

Jack: Wow, thank you! To be honest, I hadn't thought any further than the church bit. Henry, can I borrow a suit?

Henry: Of course.

Finn: Can I borrow one too?

Connor: Me three please…

Henry: Estelle?

Estelle: Fuck off. I'm going to see if Aunt Simone can get Eveline and me anything. She doesn't go back to France till Tuesday, so she can take measurements.

Estelle: Jack, give Eveline a hug from me and I'll see you at the hospital in a couple of hours xxx

JACK SAT ON ONE SIDE OF THE HOSPITAL BED, ESTELLE ON the other. Eveline's parents had returned to the rectory where they would be staying, and her mother was making plans to fly her husband and other daughters over for the wedding.

He held one of Eveline's hands in his. 'We won't stay long, angel. You need to rest.'

She opened her mouth as if to argue, then yawned and nodded.

With her free hand, Eveline reached for Estelle. 'Thank you for taking care of the pigs and for helping me last night.'

A flash of pain crossed Estelle's face, and she blinked, her eyes liquid. 'It's nothing. I'm just so fucking glad you're okay.'

She smiled. 'Never felt better.'

Jack's stomach twisted with what was coming next, but he couldn't lie to her.

'Eveline,' he began. 'Stelle and I need to tell you something about last night.'

'You do?' She glanced between them. 'What happened?'

He caught Estelle's eye, and she nodded as if to encourage him to continue.

'When we were waiting for the ambulance, Simon Little broke into your house.'

Eveline frowned. 'I don't understand. Broke in? Why?'

'You were reacting badly to any light, so the house was completely dark, and we weren't making any noise,' he continued. 'We heard the back door open, then someone creeping up the stairs.'

She gripped his hand, her eyes wide.

'He... He was being careful to be quiet. And—' Jack swallowed a swell of nausea. 'Simon came straight to your room.'

'What happened then?' she whispered.

'I pulled the door open and punched him. Stelle and I then tied him up, and she called the police.'

Eveline stared at him—white as a sheet.

'Sweetheart,' Estelle began. 'I made the decision that it was best for Jack to leave, and for me to say I hit Simon.'

'Why?'

'We need to make sure he can't touch you ever again.' She sighed. 'Charges are more likely to stick if it's seen as him against two women, one of whom was incapacitated.'

'Oh.' Tears filled Eveline's eyes. 'Poor Simon.'

Jack stiffened. Surely, she wouldn't try to excuse him?

'He must be desperately unhappy to have done such a terrible thing...'

'When the police arrived, they could see how ill you were and so won't be questioning you,' Estelle continued. 'I told them about Simon's recent behaviour and accusations and they arrested him on the spot.'

'And... They believed you punched him?'

Estelle turned her hand over, showing Eveline the bruised and swollen knuckles.

'Oh, my goodness! You *did* hit him?'

'I... I thought it best if he was only hit once, so I punched the wall instead.'

'Oh, Estelle... That must have hurt so much.'

Estelle's eyes welled up. 'I would cut off my fucking arm for you, Eveline,' she muttered. Tears spilled down her cheeks. 'I'm sorry,' she said, angrily wiping them away as if furious to be showing emotion. She gulped another ragged breath. 'I'm s-sorry...'

Jack moved to the other side of the bed and put his arm around Estelle.

Her shoulders were heaving. 'It's just delayed sh-shock, that's all,' she sobbed. 'And, and I'm so grateful that—that you're okay...' she said to Eveline. 'I was so fucking w-worried.'

'My sweet friend,' Eveline said, her own voice cracking. 'I love you so very, very much.'

Jack held Estelle tighter as she cried, a lump in his throat. She always came across so strong, but this was a reminder that she was a sensitive soul underneath the front.

God, if you're actually there. Please give Estelle love. Jack caught Eveline's eye and suddenly it was as if they were one mind and one soul again. *I know Eveline's asking you the same thing right now, so if you don't want to listen to me, please listen to her.*

❄ 34 ❄

'Jack! It's so big!' Eveline cried.

'Do you like it?'

They were sitting in the living room of the rectory, with Eveline confined to the sofa to rest. Her mother was in the kitchen and her father was tending to the pigs. Eveline had been out of hospital for a day and another vicar had been called in to cover her work at Saint Saviour's until she was better.

She stared at the huge ruby, surrounded by diamonds. 'I, I love it! But...'

'Ye-es?'

'It looks, er...' She bit her lower lip. 'Terribly expensive...'

It was, but he wasn't going to tell her how much. If she loved it, then it was worth every penny. 'I can afford it.'

Her eyes kept drifting to the ring, moving her hand to watch as the stones caught the light.

'It's so beautiful. I feel... very fancy.'

He leaned in and kissed her cheek. 'It's almost as beautiful as you.'

She moved her head, her lips finding his. 'And I love it almost as much as I love you,' she murmured. 'Thank you.'

Her words and touch sent a pulse of desire down his spine, straight to his cock. They hadn't had sex since before the Winter Ball, and it was killing him.

She placed her hand on the front of his trousers. 'Please, can we make love?' she pleaded.

'Minx,' he growled. 'Not until you're better, we're married, and your mum isn't in the next room.'

'But on our wedding night, my dad, stepdad and sisters will be here as well,' she grumbled.

'Stelle and Henry are giving us the use of a holiday rental on the estate.' He smiled. 'It's in the middle of nowhere, so you can make as much noise as you like.'

Eveline squealed with excitement. 'Can we check it out beforehand? Today maybe? Now?'

He grinned. 'Your wiles will not work on me. I'm made of hard stuff.'

She stroked his length through his jeans. 'I can tell...'

Groaning, Jack pulled her head to his, losing himself in the hot sweetness of her mouth, his need for her running like molten gold through his veins.

There was a knock at the door.

He pulled away and chucked a cushion onto his lap.

'Come in!' Eveline called out, fanning her cheeks.

Her mother entered. 'I've brought you a cup of tea, darling.'

'Look at my engagement ring!' Eveline said, holding out her hand.

'Good grief!' Diana put the mug of tea down in front of her daughter. 'That's quite the rock! I don't even need my glasses to see it.' She looked in astonishment from the ring to Jack. 'That must have cos—er... Gosh, it's quite lovely...'

Jack schooled his features. He chose the ring because it was the most beautiful and he thought Eveline would like it. But he also knew that spending that amount of money would send a clear message to her concerned parents that he had the means to look after their daughter.

'Is it terrible, Mum? How much I want to show it off?'

Her mother kissed the top of her head. 'Not at all, darling. You can start this afternoon at the old folk's home.'

Eveline checked her watch. 'Shouldn't we be setting off soon?' she asked him.

He raised an eyebrow. 'Did you intend to walk?'

She glanced away. 'Maybe?'

'And what did the doctor say?'

She gave him a cheeky grin. 'I can't remember the specifics...'

'Well, luckily, I can. I'm driving you.'

'Did you borrow your mum's car?'

'Nope. She needs it back now that her eye's been given the all-clear. I'm going to need a car anyway, so I picked one up this morning.'

'Really? Where is it?'

'Outside. Drink your tea and I'll drive us over.'

'Jack...' Eveline clutched his arm.

'Yes, love?'

'It's a Range Rover... And it looks brand new.'

He shook his head. 'I couldn't get a new one quickly enough. But this one's less than a year old and a hybrid, so it should do us for a while.' He opened the front passenger door. 'Your chariot awaits, milady.'

Eveline climbed in, smoothing her hands over the leather seats, her eyes wide.

Easing away from the rectory towards the high street, he could feel her gaze on him.

'Jack...'

'Yes, fiancée?'

She smiled. 'I really don't mean to pry, and I don't want—' She broke off and shook her head. 'Sorry. Please ignore me.'

'I would never ignore you. It's actually difficult to drive with you there because you're far more interesting to look at than the road.'

'Eyes ahead...'

'Yes, ma'am.'

She laughed and his heart got a little bigger.

'Eveline...'

'Hmm?'

'I know we haven't talked about money, but I thought I'd tell you how I'd like things to be, and then you can choose what you want to do.'

'Okay...' she replied, fiddling with her engagement ring.

He cleared his throat. 'When I said I was "all in", I meant it in every way. You can keep your bank account separate if you want, but I want you to have joint access to mine. I know I don't have a job yet, but if we're not too extravagant, I have enough saved up to last us a couple of years—'

'*Years?*' she squeaked.

'Er, yes... And if that runs out, then I can always sell my flats in London or Monaco.'

'You *own* a flat in London *and* Monaco?'

He pulled the collar of his shirt away from his neck, suddenly too hot.

'Jack?'

He nodded. 'And a car.'

Eveline shifted in her seat to face him. 'I presume it isn't a beat-up Fiat 500?'

He shook his head. Compared to her, he was a flash git with more money than sense.

'Go on, what do you own? And does my dad know? He's going to be beside himself with excitement.'

'I haven't told him yet, but he approves of the Evoque. I... I've got an Aston Martin.'

She sunk her head into her hands and snorted with laughter. 'And now you're with someone who earns less per year than the cost of this car, and drives a second-hand Škoda...'

THE MAIN LOUNGE AT FOXBROOKE HAVEN WAS FILLING UP when Jack and Eveline arrived.

'Congratulations!' Erica cried, pulling them both in for a hug.

'How did you know?' Eveline asked.

Erica turned to Jack. 'Your mum told me just now.'

He looked across the room to see his mother chatting with one of the staff.

'I didn't think she would come,' he murmured to himself.

'Have you got a ring?' Erica asked, grabbing Eveline's hand. 'Bloody hell! Would you look at that! Pardon my French, but that's a big one.' She cackled with laughter. 'Hey, Doris! Ada! Shirley! Enid! Come and look at Eveline's rock!'

Jack stayed close to Eveline's side as white-haired well-wishers surrounded them. Their unconditional happiness for the two of them was almost painful to receive, and he wondered if he'd ever been the recipient of so much love before. His childhood had been harsh, and his adult life swathed in secrets. He may have received validation in private from his clients, but never anything in public like this.

Jack had believed himself happy in the south of France. He had the clothes, car, and he attended the fanciest parties. But it was a superficial veneer that never touched his heart. Here, now, as Jack rather than Jasper, he felt truly seen, appreciated, and loved for the person underneath the façade. This was happiness beyond anything he could have imagined.

'Congratulations,' Robert called over to him from a position of safety, outside the scrum of excited women.

Jack checked Eveline wasn't being jostled, then went to join him, clasping his outstretched hand.

'Thank you, Robert. I couldn't be any luckier.'

Robert gazed over at Shirley, a huge smile on his face. 'I know what you mean. I never thought I'd find love at this stage of my life, but look at me! I feel fifty years younger.'

'I'm so happy for you both,' Jack replied.

'Well, I don't think I could have done it without you. You gave me the push I needed.'

There was a pause as they both gazed at the women they were in love with. Eveline was so breathtaking, Jack couldn't drag his eyes from her.

'Jack?'

'Hmm?'

'May I ask you something?'

He turned back to Robert. 'Yes, of course. Go for it.'

Robert lowered his voice. 'I'm planning on popping the question to Shirley soon, and, if she accepts me, I wanted to ask if you would consider being my best man?'

A lump rose in Jack's throat, but it couldn't block the smile spreading across his face.

'I don't have any family,' Robert continued. 'And my close friends have unfortunately passed on. You've been such a wonderful friend to me, and if I'd ever been fortunate enough to have had a son, I hope he would have been just like you.'

Utterly overwhelmed, his eyes stinging, Jack held his breath and tensed his jaw, fighting to keep the feelings down. Whatever demons drove his father to treat him and his sister the way he did was not their fault. And now, with Robert, he'd been given the gift of his friendship, and a father figure to put his childhood into perspective.

'I'd be honoured,' he finally managed. 'Thank you.'

Robert clapped an arm around his shoulder and squeezed. 'You're a good man, Jack. A good man.'

'Okay everyone, can I have your attention, please?' Erica clapped loudly to silence the chatter, then went to the end of the room where the mural was hidden behind a temporary curtain of dust sheets. 'Can I please have the photographer from the *Journal*, and our Lady Mayoress?' Erica caught Jack's eye. 'You too, sunshine, come on up here,' she beckoned. 'And you, Eveline.'

Jack took Eveline's hand and squeezed it, moving in front of the mural but positioning himself furthest away from the centre. Butterflies fluttered inside his stomach. *Come on, it's not exactly a tough crowd.* His mother had made her way to the front, her phone held up to take pictures. This made the butterflies thrum their wings faster.

Erica corralled all the residents who'd helped paint the mural into a group to one side of her, then turned to face the throng, a huge smile on her face.

'Ladies and gentleman, boys and girls, I'm absolutely delighted to welcome you to Foxbrooke Haven this afternoon for the official unveiling of our mural...'

Jack gazed from Eveline's happy face to the sea of smiling ones in front of them. *So this is what it feels like to be part of a community.*

'... First proposed by Saint Saviour's vicar, Eveline Shaw—'

An unprompted round of applause started amongst the residents who'd painted the mural and rippled around the room. Eveline's cheeks flushed, and Jack grinned, clapping harder.

'... Her idea was to paint our community at Foxbrooke Haven, and some of the events in the past that have shaped the town and our residents' lives.' Erica paused. 'But we had a problem... Despite us all excelling at most tasks—' Laughter murmured through the crowd. 'None of us could paint... However, luckily for us, Eveline found us Jack Newton—a Foxbrooke local and gifted artist who has spearheaded the project. Jack's been an absolute joy to have around. He's a fabulous teacher, as well as occasional dance partner, wonderful company and extremely easy on the eye...'

Doris wolf-whistled, setting off whoops, cheers and claps. Jack tried to shrink back, but a beaming Eveline dragged him forward to show him off.

'Thanks to Jack,' Erica continued. 'The mural has been completed *ahead* of schedule, and today we're delighted to have the Mayoress of Bath, councillor Karen Hartley here to unveil it to you all...'

As the Mayoress began speaking, Jack gazed at Eveline, his heart full. She looked so happy, so fulfilled. He understood now how rewarding it was to have a life purpose. Hers was making the world a better place. And right now, his was to support her in that mission.

'... And so, without further ado,' the Mayoress said. 'I am delighted to unveil the Foxbrooke Haven mural and see it myself for the very first time. Erica, if you'd like to give me a hand?'

Jack moved with Eveline out of the way, as the two women pulled each section of the makeshift curtain aside to deafening applause as the painting was revealed.

Everyone's eyes were on the mural, but Jack's were on

Eveline, watching her expression as she took it in. Her mouth was open, her free hand pressed to her chest.

'Oh, Jack...'

She hadn't seen it for a while, and definitely didn't know about the last touch he'd made—a portrait of the two of them standing outside Saint Saviour's church.

'It's...' She gazed up at him, her eyes shining. 'You're incredible.'

'Come on, you two lovebirds,' Erica said, bustling up to them. 'Photo time!'

The next few minutes were spent with the photographer from the local newspaper as he snapped pictures of the mural and everyone who'd been involved in it, as well as individual pictures of each resident next to their portraits.

When the hubbub died down, Jack went to find his mother.

'Thanks for coming, Mum.'

She nodded at the mural. 'It's much bigger than I thought.'

'Yes. It did take a while.'

'It's, er... You've done a good job.'

Jack smiled. *I'll take that.* 'Thanks, Mum.'

She indicated her phone. 'I've taken lots of pictures to show Betsy.' She paused. 'You know, it must run in the family.'

'What?'

His mother waved her hand at the painting. 'A gift for art. Betsy's *extremely* artistic. Very advanced for her age. I'm sure she'll be doing things like this in no time at all.'

‭❧ 35 ❧

‘**W**ow... Just... Wow,’ said Estelle.

Eveline glanced from her friend to the full-length mirror in front of her. Estelle’s aunt, Simone, had arranged for five wedding dresses from her fashion house in Paris to be sent to Foxbrooke. Simone had also stayed on a week after the Winter Ball to take care of any alterations needed.

Eveline blinked as she stared at her reflection, hardly recognising herself. The dress was a couture masterpiece in ivory silk satin, with ornate crystal beading adorning the bodice and swirling in patterns over the full skirts.

‘It’s so beautiful,’ she whispered.

‘*You’re* so beautiful,’ Estelle said firmly. ‘Jack’s going to pass out or explode when he sees you.’

Eveline smiled. She was so excited, she expected to run up the aisle towards him. ‘I feel like a princess.’

‘You’re a queen, Eveline. And a goddess. You’re just perfec—oh! I almost forgot.’

Estelle turned to the bed and pulled a slim black box out of her bag.

'What's that?'

'Peace offering from Gram-Gram,' Estelle replied, opening the lid and showing Eveline what was inside.

She gasped. 'Oh, my...'

Estelle lifted out the diamond and pearl necklace and undid the clasp. 'It first belonged to my great-grandmother, then Gram-Gram wore it when she married my grandfather. No bride has worn it since, as Mom and Dad eloped to Paris, and when they married Mammy, it was flower garlands and antlers all the way.'

She fastened it around Eveline's neck. 'This is Gram-Gram's way of saying sorry for being such a grotty cowbag over the last couple of years.'

'She hasn't been *that* bad...'

Estelle looked over Eveline's shoulder at her in the mirror and pulled a face. 'She's my grandmother and I love her, but come on, she's been an absolute bi—'

'Estelle!'

Her best friend grinned. 'Anyway, after "he-who-shall-not-be-named" was arrested, and Gram-Gram found out he'd tried to get you sacked, she changed her tune and has even—' Estelle broke off and went to the bed to pick up a long tulle veil.

'Has what?'

'You'll find out later. It's part of Jack's wedding present to you.'

'But he's already given them to me.'

'Huh? What are you talking about?'

'He bought me a new boiler, new washing machine, and vacuum cleaner, as well as a tumble dryer and dishwasher.'

Estelle howled with laughter. 'Who said romance was

dead?' She clutched her sides as she guffawed. 'Fuck me. What is this? The nineteen-fifties?'

Eveline's mouth twitched as she tried not to smile. 'He actually said that they weren't presents for me, they were essentials he needed for his day-to-day life as a house-husband, and buying them was a condition of him moving in.'

'Oh my god,' Estelle snorted. 'Did he order himself a pinny as well?'

Eveline blushed, remembering that in their one-sided nego-tiation on white goods, Jack had offered to do housework only wearing her apron. She bit the inside of her cheek to stop a sigh from escaping. Her body ached for him. It had been nearly ten days since they'd been intimate, and she'd never been this frustrated in her life.

Estelle narrowed her eyes. 'I do *not* want to know what you're thinking about right now, missy...'

The sigh escaped. 'I'm so happy.'

'And so you should be. Have you heard from the Bishop yet?'

She nodded. 'Yesterday afternoon, I got the formal corre-spondence saying no further action would be taken. Jonathan also rang me to say that Simon is being stripped of his post within Saint Saviour's.'

'Do you have anyone who can take on his role as treasurer?'

'Your father's offered to do it for the time being.'

'Dad?' Estelle spluttered.

'Well, he attends most services, can do basic arithmetic, and is extremely trustworthy.'

Estelle paused, her brow furrowing. 'All true...' Her face brightened. 'And the more he does with the church, the less he can fuck about with the Manor.'

'Your dad did say that since Henry returned, there was less and less for him to do.'

'And that's how it needs to be if we're going to make the estate profitable. Plus, he has fun doing the living history tours with Libby.'

Eveline smiled. 'Yes, he says he loves them.'

'Although he's still talking about doing a medical-themed one and using leeches and arsenic.'

'Oh, no!'

'Don't worry, Connor gave him a stern talking to, so it's not going to happen.'

There was a knock at the door.

'Come in,' Eveline called. 'We're nearly ready.'

Her mother entered and clutched her hands to her chest. 'Oh, darling!'

Eveline twirled. 'You like?'

Diana dabbed at the corners of her perfectly made-up eyes. 'You're an absolute picture.'

'Speaking of which,' Estelle said, smoothing her hands down her long lilac dress. 'Has the photographer arrived yet?'

'Yes,' Diana replied. 'Just now.' She lowered her voice. 'There's a whole *team* of them down there!'

'A team?' Eveline asked.

Estelle grinned. 'That's what you get when your mom's one of the world's most famous models. She's hired Davide de Lisa for you.'

'The... The *famous* one?'

'How many Davide de Lisa's do you know?' Estelle replied with a smirk. 'He bloody leapt at the chance, probably because he thinks he can persuade Henry to pose for him again. He was the photographer on the shoot Henry did for Aunt Simone's fashion house.' Estelle took her bag from the bed and cast her eyes around the room. 'I think I've got everything.' She squared her shoulders. 'Right then, let's get you downstairs so we can immortalise your beauty with the help of a sexy Italian.'

EVELINE STROLLED THE SHORT DISTANCE TO SAINT SAVIOUR'S from the rectory, her father on one side and Estelle on the other, as the sound of ringing bells filled the air.

God, thank you for this day and for bringing Jack back to me. You've found me my perfect person and I couldn't be happier. Please bless this day and all the wonderful people who've worked so hard to make our wedding happen in such a short amount of time.

'Oh, Eveline! Just look at you!'

They were met outside the front doors by Janice, a vicar Eveline had trained with many years ago.

Janice embraced her. 'You're absolutely gorgeous! Your mum and sisters are all settled at the front, so we're good to go whenever you are.'

Eveline's heart raced with excitement. 'I'm ready now.'

'Fabulous. Give me thirty seconds to stop the bell-ringers. When you hear the music, make your way in.' Janice dashed into the church.

Estelle cast an appraising eye over Eveline's dress. 'Perfect,' she murmured, before giving her a sly grin. 'Any second thoughts?'

'About you being my bridesmaid? Never.'

Her friend snorted. 'Cheeky bug—*beautiful bride*... Shall I help you with the veil?'

Eveline paused. She knew it was tradition to have it over her face, so her husband-to-be could uncover her when she reached him. But she didn't want anything to detract from her view of Jack.

'I want to leave it as is,' she replied.

'Fair enough.' Estelle stepped back as the bells stopped. 'Go knock 'em dead. I'll be right behind you.'

Her father's eyes glistened as he smiled. 'Ready, love?'

Eveline nodded and linked her arm with his. 'Absolutely.'

Organ music spilled joyously through the air as they walked into the packed church. Everyone was smiling, but no matter how much Eveline wanted to acknowledge each person in turn, she wanted to look at Jack more.

Standing at the altar, next to Henry, Finn and Connor, he was so handsome, she thought her heart might burst. He stared at her, his gaze full of love.

I love you. I love you. I love you.

Eveline tugged on her father's arm to hurry him up. He was stepping as if he'd been in the military all his life and was now heading up the funeral procession for a head of state. His left foot went forward, then his right joined it and both feet paused. A beat later, his right foot went forward, then his left snapped smartly together next to it, followed by another pause. If they were racing a glacier and a snail, they were definitely going to come last.

A metre in, and already out of step, Eveline decided enough was enough. Dragging her father by the arm like a little boy who didn't want to go to school, she marched up the aisle at a speed she hoped was merely brisk. However, judging by the look on Jack's face, the laughter around them, and the fact her dad now appeared to be running, she had to concede it was more of a jog.

Even though Eveline wasn't meant to hold Jack's hand until her father formally 'gave her away', the moment she got to his side, they reached for each other.

Jack's eyes were shining. 'I love you. You're so beautiful you take my breath away.'

'I love you too,' she replied, her own eyes tingling.

Everything around them faded into the background as she held his gaze, his perfect face blurring as her happiness overflowed.

Janice loudly cleared her throat, and Eveline remembered where she was.

Estelle held a handkerchief out to her, and Henry held one out to Jack, whilst some of the laughs from the congregation changed to happy sniffs.

'Well,' said Janice loudly. 'What a wonderful expression of love. Although it does feel like we've skipped straight to the *I-now-declare-them-man-and-wife* part!'

'Fine by me,' said Jack, wiping the corners of his eyes. 'That's the best bit.'

Eveline giggled, then thought about what would happen at the end of the night when they were finally alone.

As if reading her mind, his gaze darkened, sending a shiver of anticipation through her.

'Shall we begin?' Janice asked.

Still looking at Jack, Eveline nodded. 'Yes, please...'

ON THE RETURN JOURNEY DOWN THE AISLE, EVELINE walked slowly, revelling in the feel of her hand in Jack's, the pride she felt at being his wife, and happiness that so many people she knew were there to witness it. They paused in the doorway for photos, then Jack led her in the direction of the Manor where everyone who'd attended the service was invited for tea and cake.

But instead of heading by the most direct route, he took her via the church hall.

'Jack?'

'Yes, wife?'

Eveline squealed inside. She was his wife! *'Husband,'* she

said, trying the word on for size and deciding it fitted perfectly. 'Why are we here?'

'Your wedding present,' he replied.

'But you've already given me so much!'

'Fiddlesticks. All those appliances were for me.'

'*Fiddlesticks?*' She grinned. 'Who even *says* that?'

He flashed her a devastating smile. '*We* do.'

Eveline held his gaze. *Thank you, God. Thank you.*

'So, my darling wife,' Jack continued, leading her to the door of the hall. 'You will need to use your imagination, and apply quantum physics, but here is your wedding gift.'

'Quantum physics?'

'Yes, you need to appreciate that this moment contains the past, present and future in perfect synchronicity.'

'O-kay...'

'This may *look* like a run-down building with a knackered roof. But actually, it's a completely refurbished church hall, hosting everything from AA meetings to yoga.'

'But—'

'I can't take all the credit,' he said quickly. 'As well as some of my—*our* money, I'm going to put Dad's bequest into the pot. We also did a whip-round in the church whilst we were waiting for you to arrive, and your new treasurer is currently counting the haul ready to take to the bank next week.'

'Oh my goodness!'

'And that's not all,' Jack continued, clearly delighted with her response. 'Estelle's gran has spoken to the Bishop about the plans and told him that, as well as approving the upgrade, he's also expected to rubber-stamp the extension.'

'What extension?'

'Think of it as "the Gram-Gram wing". She's going to pay for it and Finn's going to help with submitting the proposal to the planners. At the very least, you should get a bigger and upgraded kitchen, but hopefully you'll also get another meeting room as well.'

Possibilities rushed through Eveline's mind. With the pews staying for the foreseeable future, finally having enough money to bring the hall back into service *and* make the space bigger, would be a lifeline for the church and community.

'This is incredible,' she murmured. 'Thank you.'

'It's not the most exciting present, or the most romantic—'

'Oh, Jack, it *is*! It's the most thoughtful gift in the world!'

'For the most thoughtful *person* in the world.' He smiled at her. 'How did I get so lucky?'

She leaned closer. 'You're going to get even luckier tonight,' she whispered.

He brushed his lips over hers. 'Minx,' he murmured. 'I can't wait.'

 ❧ 36 ❧

It was nearly midnight by the time Jack pulled the Range Rover off the narrow road and down a track, the headlights illuminating a fairytale cottage surrounded by trees.

'I'll take our bags in, then come back for you,' he said, turning off the engine.

Eveline unfastened her seatbelt. 'I can help.'

Jack leaned across the centre console and kissed her. 'I want to carry you over the threshold.'

She smiled, happily. 'You really are my hero.'

'Your Wolf Redwood?'

'A million times better.'

He gave her another kiss, then pulled away. 'If I don't go now, I'll never be able to.'

Leaping out of his seat, he collected their bags from the boot.

Eveline watched him, happily exhausted from the day but definitely not yet ready for bed. Lights went on inside the cottage. Then he was back and lifting her into his arms.

After the heat and noise of the day, the wood was cold and quiet. All Eveline could hear was the rustling of her dress, their breathing, and the sound of Jack's feet as he walked.

The cottage may have appeared ancient on the outside, but inside, the decor was Scandi chic.

'Oh Jack! This is so lovely.'

He smiled. 'Happy Wedding, wife,' He rested his forehead on hers. 'We did it.'

She ran her fingers up his neck into his hair. 'I don't think we have...'

'Huh?'

'Done it,' she whispered in his ear.

She felt his smile against her cheek. 'An omission that shall be rectified immediately.'

Jack strode to the foot of the tiny staircase and paused, frowning. Holding her in his arms, there was no way it was wide enough for him to walk up with her.

'Shall I get down?' she asked.

'Absolutely not,' he retorted. 'Never give up—'

She shrieked as he threw her over his shoulder.

'—Never surrender!' he continued, striding up the stairs as she laughed.

'Which door is it...' he muttered to himself. 'Aha!'

Entering a room, he transferred her gently to the middle of a large bed covered in rose petals, and lay above her.

'If I were ever to be stuck reliving one day over and over for the rest of my life,' he murmured. 'I would want this one to be my Groundhog Day.'

She nodded, her heart stuck in her throat.

'You're my everything,' he said, kissing her softly.

'And you're mine,' she replied, her fingers trailing down the front of his chest. 'Every... Single... Inch...'

As her hand closed around the hardness of his cock, he growled. 'Minx,' he muttered. 'You'll be the death of me.'

Giddy laughs burst out of her. 'If you are planning on expiring, could you possibly wait twenty minutes?'

'Twenty minutes?' he exclaimed. 'Is that all? Give me some credit.' Eveline squeezed his length through his trousers and he groaned. 'Actually, after this last week of abstinence, I doubt I'll last two.'

Turning her over, he ran his fingers down the back of her dress. 'Please let there be a zip...'

She giggled. 'It's couture. There are no shortcuts.'

'Scissors?'

'Jack Newton! Don't you dare!'

He huffed as he started on the countless buttons. 'I don't think you understand the urgency of the situation,' he grumbled. 'I need you naked right now.'

Eveline reached behind her to undo the ones from the bottom. As soon as she met him in the middle, he cheered with triumph and grabbed the silk and voluminous net to pull it over her head.

'It's like a bloody tent!' he cried in exasperation as she was lost inside the skirts. 'Where *are* you?'

The more irate Jack became, the more Eveline laughed. He finally freed her, threw the dress to the floor, and stared at her.

'Jes—Go—Eveline...'

'Do you like?'

As well as a designer dress, Estelle's aunt had also gifted Eveline designer underwear. Jack's gaze raked over her as if melting the lace with the white-hot heat of his desire.

'You're...' He blinked, as if to convince himself she was real.

Time stopped in a delicious moment of calm.

Then Jack unleashed the storm.

He clutched Eveline to him, raining down kisses, as if needing to mark every inch of her.

She pulled his shirt up, desperate, fizzing need prickling across her skin. Her body was one frustrated itch, and only the feeling of his naked body on her, in her, could relieve her suffering.

He knelt, tugging the shirt over his head.

'Hurry, hurry,' she muttered, ripping off her underwear.

Throwing his trousers to the floor with his boxers, he lay his hot and hard body over hers with a groan.

She spread her legs, holding him to her, her lips crushing to his, her tongue slicking into the fire of his mouth. This was not the time for leisurely lovemaking. Having him inside her was the only way to satisfy the burning, aching space in her core.

He ripped his mouth from hers, his breath ragged, and moved lower.

'No!' She clutched his back, her nails digging in.

'But—'

'I need you in me. Please, Jack.'

He squeezed his eyes tightly shut. 'Eveline. I won't last—'

'We've got all night.' She soothed away the lines on his forehead. 'And the rest of our lives.'

Opening his eyes, he stared at her. 'I've never had se—done this without a condom before.'

'Never?'

He shook his head.

Giddy excitement sparkled in her tummy. 'So, I'm your first?'

'My one and only.'

She wiggled her hips. 'That makes me very happy.'

'Not as much as it makes me,' he replied, his gaze darkening.

Running a hand beneath her, he cupped her bottom, the head of his cock at her entrance. He pushed in an inch, and pleasure flared at the sweet stretch, goosebumps shivering across her skin.

More, more, more…

She bucked her hips to take him deeper, her tissues tingling as he eased inside.

'God, god, fuck, Eveline,' he muttered, burying his face in her neck, shuddering as he breathed.

She wrapped her legs around the backs of his. 'More, Jack.'

He paused, his body tensed, then, as if he could no longer deny his own urges, he thrust.

Sparks of electricity shocked through her core. 'Yes!'

He withdrew slightly, and she dug her nails into his back, clawing to keep him close.

'Ja—'

He thrust again.

Eveline could feel him holding back, his muscles trembling. She wanted to surrender herself completely, for him to take control and lose control.

'Let go, Jack…'

He raised his head, his eyes pinning hers, the tendons in his neck strained.

Lifting her arms over her head, she arched her chest, laying herself open to him. 'I need you to let go.'

Under the fog of lust, a light of understanding flickered in his eyes. Holding her gaze, he pushed up onto his hands, his arms locked.

Eveline's heart skittered faster, energy crackling across her skin. Jack pulled his hips back, and she held her breath.

He snapped them forward and her breath rushed out with a cry.

He did it again. And again. And again, his cock pinning her to the bed with deep, pulsing pleasure.

She forced her eyes to stay open, the sight of him above her amplifying every sensation. The threads of her orgasm were drawing together, but the feelings were everywhere. They shimmered through every cell, shining out from her skin, binding her to him.

They were joined completely and perfectly—transcending the physical plane to create something beyond all understanding. Eveline saw and felt Jack as if she was inside him as much as he was inside her, feeling the shift in his energy, the moment when he could no longer control the onrushing tide of his own climax.

Bringing her hands to her breasts, she pinched her nipples.

Her orgasm cracked through her like a whip, a snap of pleasure that bent her in two, lifting her chest off the bed to meet his. She held onto his neck, her pussy convulsing around his cock as he roared with his own release.

Clinging to him, she gasped and shuddered in the pounding surf of sensation, the waves of her orgasm rolling through her, over and over.

His hips were still moving, pushing the feelings on, until she went boneless, collapsing back to the bed.

'I love you, I love you, I love you,' he murmured, his body covering hers completely as he kissed her. She clutched the hard planes of his back as she returned his kisses, pouring her love into him.

His cock was still hard inside her and she shivered, squeezing around him.

He lifted his head. 'Minx,' he rumbled.

'You're still hard.'

Jack's smile was sinfully sexy. 'I haven't come since I was

last with you, and that was far too long ago. At this rate, I'll be hard for a week.'

Eveline grinned. 'Well, I did say we had all night.'

He kissed her, his eyes shining with love. 'And the rest of our lives...'

EPILOGUE

'**G**o on, lick it...' Jack said.

Eveline leaned forward, her tongue flicking out for a taste, then sucking it deep with a low hum of appreciation.

'Greedy little minx.'

She raised her head. 'But it's so good...'

Jack's eyes were sparkling. 'You've got it all around your mouth now.'

She poked out her tongue to clean it up.

'Other side... Hang on, let me...' He bent down, kissing and sucking at her lips.

Her breath quickened, and she moaned, pushing herself closer.

There was a clatter as he dropped the spoon. Then his hands were on her hips, lifting her to the countertop. She spread her legs, tangling her fingers in his hair to pull him closer.

Jack bunched up the skirts of her dress, his fingers trailing sparks up her thighs, then stopped and lifted his head.

His face was flushed with desire, but he still managed a look of consternation. 'You're wearing *underwear?*'

'Well, we *are* expecting guests.'

'Not for—' he glanced at the clock '—half an hour yet.' He pushed the bulge of his cock against her aching clit and rubbed her hardened nipples through the fabric of her dress.

Desire arced between the points of his touch. 'You're right. You're so right.' She undid the button of his jeans and pulled down the zip. His cock sprang free.

'See,' he murmured. 'No boxers. If it was summer, I wouldn't bother with clothes at all.'

She giggled and stroked his shaft, spreading the precum over the head. 'I can't wait...'

'Neither can I,' he growled, hooking his fingers into the sides of her pants. 'Lift up.' She did, and he pulled them down her legs and off, jamming them in his trouser pocket.

Eveline spread her legs wider and beckoned to him. 'Come here, husband. I'm ready for you.'

Jack raised an eyebrow. 'No foreplay?'

She shook her head, her muscles clenching with impatient need. 'Watching you make a cake is all the foreplay I need.'

'Well, Mrs Newton...' He brought his body flush with hers, his cock pushing at her entrance. 'Later tonight, I'm going to take my time...' He eased into her tightness and she shivered with pleasure. 'I'm going to bury my face between your legs and lick you till you lose count of how many times you've come.'

'Yessss,' she exhaled. 'Oh, that feels so good.'

He clasped her bottom, pulling her onto his cock with a growl.

The doorbell sounded.

She froze.

He turned his head. 'Fuck off!' he yelled, the sound echoing around the kitchen and out the door.

'Jack!' she hissed, trying not to giggle. 'It could be anyone!'

In the silence that followed, Eveline heard the faint sound of the letterbox on the front door banging open.

'I heard that!' Estelle's voice called through it. '*You* fuck off. I'm here early for Eveline.'

Jack dropped his head and huffed.

Eveline kissed his forehead. 'Later isn't that long away?' Gently pushing him from her, she hopped off the counter.

His cock bobbed as if lost and disorientated. He tucked it back inside his jeans with a sigh. 'Can we give them takeout instead?'

'Not on your nelly.' She smiled at his forlorn expression. 'I'll let her in.'

Running her fingers through her hair, and smoothing her dress back into place, Eveline made her way to the front door, suddenly conscious that her pants were still in Jack's pocket. Could she nip back for them?

'Thank god it's you,' Estelle said through the letterbox.

Eveline opened the door and drew Estelle in for a hug. 'It's fine. We were just about to get the cake in the oven.'

Her friend drew back and raised an eyebrow. 'Are you sure it wasn't a bun?' She glanced at Eveline's stomach. 'In *that* oven?'

Heat tore up Eveline's neck into her cheeks. 'I am *quite* sure,' she said firmly, then lowered her voice. 'Although, since the wedding we have been putting a lot of, er, *effort* into that particular endeavour.'

Estelle snorted. 'I can tell. I don't think I've ever seen anyone so happy, or so well fuc—'

'Estelle!' Eveline dragged her friend into the house and

propelled her into the front lounge, shutting the door behind them. 'Behave!'

'I can't help it.' Estelle giggled. 'And I promise this will be the last time I ever mention it, however...' She shook her head. 'I still can't get my head around what Jack used to do as a *job*.'

'Well, after he told Henry, Finn and Connor, he said it was only right that you also knew. But...'

'Yeah, yeah, I know. Circle of trust and all that.' Estelle sat on the sofa and let out a sigh. 'To be honest, it's going to be easy to forget, as it's so surreal.'

Eveline sat next to her. 'I know it might seem strange, but I don't think about it at all anymore. It's in the past and has no bearing on the present or our future.'

Estelle gave her the side eye. 'Yeah, but...'

'But what?'

'He must have mad sex skills.'

Heat flushed through her face again, and she clenched her thighs as lurid thoughts tumbled through her mind.

'Fuck me,' Estelle murmured. 'I'll take that as a "yes" then...'

Eveline cleared her throat. 'Anyway. Why are you early? Is everything alright?'

Her friend's face fell, and she stood, turning towards the fireplace, her hands flexing in and out of fists.

'Estelle?'

'I went to Bath to meet the guy I'm going to be working with next year.' Her voice was cold and brittle.

'Oh yes! The new owner of the event management company. I'm so sorry, I totally forgot. How did it go?'

Estelle turned, her body vibrating with rage. 'It was...' She raised her head to the ceiling. 'Fuck!'

Eveline stood, her heart thumping. 'What's happened? Who *is* he?'

Estelle fixed her with a look, spitting out each word in turn. 'James... Hunter... Savage...'

'W—what? How? I don't understand.'

'That fucking cocksucking-bastard's father bought the company and installed his obnoxious gobshite of a son as the CEO.'

'But... How come you didn't know?'

'Because all our dealings were with the original company, then some minion emailed us to confirm the new owners were honouring the contract, just with a few "minor alterations". How the fuck were we to know that "BDE Entertainment" was a front for that wanker?'

'Oh. What does the "BDE" stand for?'

Estelle let out a bitter laugh. 'You're not going to believe it. I thought it was some kind of fucking joke, but it's what they're registered at Companies House under.'

Eveline's mind boggled. *Bastard Dickhead... Entertainment?* No, that wouldn't work. 'What is it?'

Estelle shook her head as if she still couldn't believe it. 'It stands for "Big Dick Energy Entertainment".'

'What does it mean? That Mr Hunter-Savage has a... erm... big...'

'No. Anyone who calls their company that is guaranteed to have a cock so fucking small, they need a magnifying glass to find it. He doesn't *have* a big dick, he *is* one.'

'But why the "energy" part? I don't understand.'

Estelle sighed. 'My sweet friend. Anyone who has "Big Dick Energy" is so magnetic, they have the gravitational pull of a small moon. They exude confidence and don't feel the need to justify anything they say or do because they're so fucking self-assured.'

Eveline cleared her throat. 'I've only met Ja— Mr Hunter-Savage the once, but he does appear quite confid—'

'Don't. He's not confident, he's *arrogant*. There's a big difference.'

Eveline paused, trying to think of what to say. 'Well, out of the two of you, I think you've got more, er, *BDE* than he could ever have.'

Estelle slumped onto the sofa, her head in her hands. 'Thank you, love, but it doesn't solve anything.'

Eveline sat next to her friend, putting her arm around her shoulder. 'Is there any way you can get out of it? Have someone else represent the Foxbrooke estate?'

'I don't think so. Henry's looking over the contract now. I wanted to ask Jack if he would take my place if he has the time.'

'That sounds like a possibility. Why don't we chat about it over dinner?'

HENRY PASSED HIS HAND OVER HIS FROWNING FACE. 'I'M sorry, Estelle.'

Libby took Henry's hand and gave it a squeeze.

The mood around the dinner table was sombre as Henry outlined exactly how the estate—and Estelle—couldn't get out of the contract without incurring huge penalties.

'We've already invested significant time and money into the project and if we pull out, we won't be able to cover the cancellation fees.' Henry sighed. 'And don't forget you also managed to secure *UberGraft* as a headline act...'

'But can't Jack take my place? And I work behind the scenes?'

'Me?' Jack asked.

'Yeah, sorry,' Estelle said. 'You did such an amazing job with the Winter Ball. I wanted to ask if you were interested in helping out with the music and arts festival?'

Jack shrugged. 'Maybe? Does this mean I have to work with this dude you all hate?'

Henry cleared his throat. 'Unfortunately, the new amendments to the contract specify that Estelle has to work directly with... In the same office.'

'The contract *says* that?' Connor asked.

'Yes,' Henry replied. 'He's fuck—messing with me.' He turned to his sister. 'Estelle, I'm so sorry. He's only doing this to get to me.'

'Henry...' Eveline began.

'Yes?'

'Are you *sure* about that?'

He looked blankly at her. 'Why else would he be doing it?'

Eveline swallowed. Was this a moment when it was better to keep her mouth shut? *God, any thoughts on what I should do?*

Estelle leaned forward. 'Do you know something we don't?'

Eveline shook her head. 'It's nothing.'

Jack leaned in and whispered in her ear. 'Let your light shine, angel.'

She blushed.

'What did he say?' Estelle asked, 'Actually, I don't want to know. Go on, Eveline, if you've got an insight into what game this cretin is playing, then I need to know.'

Eveline sat up straighter. 'Okay, but it's just a thought, that's all.'

Everyone leaned closer, apart from Jack, who lazily stroked up and down her back.

'Henry,' she began. 'In your most recent dealings with Mr —*James*. Did you behave badly, or unkindly?'

Henry visibly bristled. 'He stole my biggest client.'

'You *did* punch him,' Libby said quietly.

'And after that incident, would you say you were even?'

Eveline asked. 'Or perhaps that *he* had done more wrong to *you* than the other way around?'

Henry shrugged. 'Yes, I suppose so.'

'So, you don't think there is any other reason for James to go out of his way to make your life difficult?'

'Apart from just being an inherent prick,' Estelle huffed. 'That "man" has been an arsehole to Henry since they were at school. Come on, Eveline, what's your theory? Please tell me you think he's got a terminal illness and will be dead by the spring.'

'Estelle!'

Finn snorted with laughter. 'Honestly, Stelle, I don't know what you're worried about. By the end of the first day, you'll have served him his bollocks on a plate.'

'Only if I know what he's up to,' Estelle replied.

All eyes returned to Eveline.

'I don't think his behaviour has anything to do with Henry,' she began.

'Shit,' said Henry. 'You think he's still after Summer? Is that what this is all about?'

Next to Eveline, Jack started to chuckle. She caught his eye and smiled. *He knows what I'm thinking...*

'What?' Estelle demanded.

'I only met him that once,' Eveline continued. 'But I had a very strong sense of what is motivating this behaviour.'

'You do?' Henry and Estelle asked in unison.

Eveline nodded, looking at her friend. 'He's specified that you have to work closely with him, because...' She took a fortifying breath. 'He really likes you.'

'Me?' Estelle cried. 'Are you mad? He can't stand me! And I can't stand him!'

'How do you know that?' she asked.

Estelle's mouth flapped open and closed a few times before she spoke. 'He called me "Foxy lady"!'

'He *did*?' Connor asked.

'Twice!' Estelle continued.

Finn started laughing. 'Sorry Stelle, but this is hilarious.' He shook his head. 'That poor fucker doesn't know what he's let himself in for.'

'And what is *that* supposed to mean?'

Finn patted her shoulder. 'Only that you've got bigger balls than he'll ever have.'

'That's what I told you,' Eveline added. 'You've got more big dick energy than he does.'

Heads swivelled to stare at her.

'Er...' Jack began. 'Angel?'

'I learnt the term from Estelle earlier,' Eveline said to him. 'Apparently, women can have big, er... *BDE* as well as men. It's about confidence and attitude, not genitalia.'

Finn leaned back in his chair and howled with laughter. Libby was giggling, and even Connor was failing to hide a smirk.

Estelle sat back and crossed her arms. 'Well, come my first official day of work next year, that fucker's not going to know what's hit him.'

Standing at the front door of the rectory at the end of the night, Eveline hugged Estelle goodbye.

'I know you're not a believer,' she said to her friend. 'But I promise you it's going to be okay. God loves you and has a plan.'

'Does it involve a good smiting? A plague of lice, fleas and midges? Boils?'

'Fortunately not.'

'Humph. You need to have a word.'

Eveline smiled. 'You're always in my prayers.'

'Not totally irredeemable, then?'

'Never.'

'Come on,' Henry called from further up the street with Libby. 'It's cold. You can chat tomorrow at Sausage Saturday.'

'Two secs,' Estelle shouted at him before turning back to Eveline. 'Honestly, he just wants to get back to the Manor for a shag.'

For a moment, the light in Estelle's eyes dimmed, then she turned it up again. 'Well, even though we've got a couple of weeks to go before New Year, I'm making my resolutions now. Number one, James Hunter-Savage is going down. And number two, I'm going to get laid.'

Eveline channelled her inner vicar to keep a straight face. 'In that order?'

'Yep. I'll text Isaac and see if I can book a private yoga class.'

'Er... Haven't you tried that already?'

'This time I'm going to give a fake name.'

'Estelle! You can't do that!'

She stuck out her tongue. 'You're no fun.'

'Come on!' Henry yelled.

Estelle rolled her eyes and hugged Eveline again. 'I love you. Thanks for tonight.'

'Our pleasure.'

'Good god, listen to you all coupley!' Estelle sighed. 'Right, go inside and have fun with your husband. I'll see you tomorrow.'

EVELINE FOUND JACK IN THE KITCHEN, WIPING DOWN THE surfaces, and humming along with the new dishwasher.

'All good?' he asked.

She nodded. 'Estelle will be fine.'

He frowned. 'You sure? Henry's convinced James is the devil incarnate.'

'Libby doesn't think so. She told me she thinks he's actually just insecure.'

Jack rinsed the cloth out, hung it over the edge of the sink, and washed his hands. 'Well, I hope Stelle will be okay.'

'She will. I have faith.'

Jack wrapped his arms around her. 'That you do.'

'Husband…'

'Yes, wife?'

'I do believe you have something of mine.'

He leaned down and brushed a kiss across her lips. 'Your heart?'

'That's a given. I was actually thinking of something else.'

He grinned. 'Your undying love and devotion?'

Eveline slid her hands inside the front pockets of Jack's jeans. They were empty. Through the thin cotton lining the inside, she stroked the solid length of his cock.

'Ah, yes,' he said. 'That is most *definitely* yours.'

They turned off the lights, and Jack led her upstairs. Within an hour, he'd made good on his earlier promises, and Eveline had not only forgotten how many orgasms she'd had, but also her own name.

Then, when she was drowsy with pleasure, his hard weight covered her, and he pushed inside. As Jack filled her body, he saturated her soul—whispering how much he loved her, how beautiful she was—until every fibre of her being drew together once more, only to shatter again in another breathtaking release.

Then he held her tightly as sleep settled on her like a soft blanket, stripping away everything, until only one word and one feeling remained—love.

THE END

❧

Thank you so much for reading An Unholy Affair! Want more of Eveline and Jack? Read their swoony French extended epilogue by joining my newsletter list at **www.eviealexanderauthor.com/subscribe**

❧

Estelle and James's story is up next in The Upper Crush...

James Hunter-Savage is a cocky city boy who isn't used to anyone else taking the reins. Lady Estelle Foxbrooke is a fiery country girl who's about to show him who's boss.

Can Estelle and James learn to fight for love rather than with each other, or will their love hate relationship destroy everything they're working for?

Get The Upper Crush in print, audio, or eBook format now from www.eviealexanderbooks.com

REVIEW AN UNHOLY AFFAIR
WRITE A REVIEW & MAKE MY DAY!

Thank you so much for reading An Unholy Affair! I hope you enjoyed reading it as much as I enjoyed writing it!

Even if just a few lines (or star rating), writing a review is the most amazing thing you can do! It helps people find my books, and lets them know what you loved about them.

You can review An Unholy Affair at:
Apple
Amazon
Bookbub
Goodreads
Kobo
Barnes & Noble
Google Play

And any other storefront or platform you use!

And, if you want to share more about An Unholy Affair on social media or your blog, please **help yourself to our library of graphics, elements and more by going to**

www.eviealexanderauthor.com/an-unholy-affair/

Thank you!

READ THE UPPER CRUSH

Next up is Estelle and James's story!

Lady Estelle Foxbrooke is done cleaning up the mess left by her wild parents. Her goal? Save the family estate, *her* way. The problem? James Hunter-Savage. Her twin brother's nemesis and her very unwanted new business partner.

James was living the dream in London until his career crashed and burned. Now he's back in the countryside, licking his wounds and stuck working with Estelle – the sharp-witted, maddeningly gorgeous woman who seems to enjoy making his life hell.

But when their fiery clashes spark something steamier, suddenly the estate isn't the only thing on the line. With tempers flaring, passions blazing, and the biggest event of the year teetering on the brink of disaster, can James and Estelle put their differences aside long enough to save the day?

NEWSLETTER SIGN-UP

Ooh la la! Want to read Jack and Eveline's swoony French extended epilogue? Sign up to my newsletter to get it today, plus so much more...

In my newsletter you get Evie news before anyone else, as well as exclusive content and goodies.

Newsletter subscribers are my extra special friends, and get everything from bonus epilogues, 19,000 words of deleted sex scenes, free stories, free audiobooks, extracts from my current work-in-progress, and exclusive offers and giveaways.

Sign up now!

www.eviealexanderauthor.com/subscribe/

SEX INDEX

(AKA THE GOOD BITS)

There have been many great contributions to the world of literature. Gutenberg invented the printing press, Shakespeare invented romantic comedy, and J K Rowling invented Harry Potter. However, all of these achievements pale into insignificance compared to my contribution – the sex index.

Using this sex index, you can easily find the steamier moments from An Unholy Affair. Enjoy...

Page 48 – Taking care of business in the shower
Page 165 – Well, that's one way to cure hypothermia
Page 198 – It's oh! Oh! OH! ORGASM TIME!!!
Page 250 – Kitchen sink fantasies
Page 282 – Time to blow Jack's...
Page 392 – You may now consummate this marriage
Page 399 – Kitchen coitus-interruptus

And if that wasn't enough, don't forget I've got nineteen thousand words of super-hot deleted sex scenes from Highland

and Hollywood Games as well as Jack and Eveline's extended epilogue available exclusively for newsletter subscribers.

If you want some extra action, then sign up to my newsletter today!

www.eviealexanderauthor.com/subscribe/

ACKNOWLEDGMENTS

Whoop whoop! It's the acknowledgements! Here's the place I get to thank all the amazing people who have helped me get this book to publication.

This book is dedicated to YOU the reader! You inspire me to keep writing, and make my books the very best they can be. Chatting to you via email and social media gave me the injury and sick-bed storylines in An Unholy Affair, as well as the scene involving a discussion about pegging... Even silly conversations about names gave rise to Polly Hart characters and story scenarios.

Even if you never reach out to me directly, just by reading and reviewing my books you help me keep the faith in what can often be a solitary and challenging career. An Unholy Affair is all about faith, whether it's faith in a higher power, faith in the paths we choose to take, or simply faith that we're doing the right thing in our day-to-day lives.

I hope that you always have faith, even if just in yourself.

Speaking of faith, I could not have written this book without a wonderful vicar who helped with my research. She found her calling before women were allowed to be ordained as priests in the Church of England, and was one of the early pioneers, dedicating her life to God and the community. She gave me so much of her time and knowledge, and it was her experiences that gave me the pew plot line (although, thank goodness, there was no Simon Little for her to contend with). She is a truly warm and wonderful human being and embodies the best parts of Christianity. I could not have written this story without her inspiration.

Next up, a huge thanks goes to Dr Beth (@smuttybookreviews), who advised me on all the medical details in An Unholy Affair and checked my work. She has a deep love for sick-bed scenes in romance novels, and this particular kink of hers was inspirational in so much of this book.

Thank you to my dear friend, Hannah K, who lost both parents in a short period of time and was so helpful in explaining to me what she had to do to organise their funerals.

Thanks as ever go to my alpha reader, Pash Baker, Tori Ross for reading an early draft (and educating me about pegging and more), and my epic editing team - Margaret Amatt and Mike AF. Thank you to Matt Wellsted for designing this wonderful cover and Mark Karasick for taking such fabulous photos of me.

My team at Emlin Press: Victoria, Mandy, and Liezl. Thank you for doing everything I can't, won't, or don't have time for. Thank you for tolerating my foul mouth, laughing at my unfunny jokes and sticking around.

Thank you to my husband—the best decision I've ever made, and to my daughter—the best luck I've ever had. I love you both to the ends of the multiverse and back.

And last, but by no means least, I want to thank my fabulous ARC team, the incredible online community of book lovers and, once again, YOU, the reader! Thank you for your continued support and for reading the second book in the Foxbrooke series! Each time you read my books, write me a review and recommend me in countless different ways, my heart gets a little fuller. Thank you!

Evie ♡

Ps - I love love LOVE hearing from my readers so please get in touch via email or social media to ask me anything or just tell me about your day!

ALSO BY EVIE ALEXANDER

Get all of Evie's books in print, audio, or eBook format, as well as special offers, early releases, and exclusive deals at www.eviealexanderbooks.com

THE KINLOCH SERIES

HIGHLAND GAMES

Zoe's given up everything for a ramshackle cabin in Scotland. She wants a new life, but her scorching hot neighbour wants her out. As their worlds collide, will Rory succeed in destroying her dream? Or has he finally met his match? Let the games begin...

Tropes

Small Town, Enemies-to-Lovers, Grumpy/Sunshine, Fish-out-of-Water, Opposites Attract, Forced Proximity

HOLLYWOOD GAMES

In a last-ditch attempt to save Kinloch castle, new lovers Rory and Zoe throw open the doors to a Hollywood superstar. But when it all goes south, it's up to them to rewrite the script, save the castle's future, and find their own happy ending.

Tropes

Small Town, Soulmates, Grumpy/Sunshine, Fish-out-of-Water

KISSING GAMES

Bodyguard Charlie has a new mission: teach workaholic Hollywood actress Valentina how to play, one wild adventure at a time. But when no-strings fun turns into something more, they have to face some hard truths. Can they find a future together, or will their love remain a Highland fling?

Tropes

Small Town, Dark Secrets, Bodyguard/Actress, Forced Proximity, Alpha-roll hero, Dating Game

MUSICAL GAMES

After lying to a Hollywood megastar, Sam needs Jamie to write an album with her in just ten days He's got the voice of an angel and the body of a god, but fame is the last thing on his mind. Will he help make her dreams come true?

Tropes

Small Town, Grumpy/Sunshine, Male Virgin, Cinnamon Roll Hero, Opposites Attract, Fish-out-of-Water, Forced Proximity

WEDDING GAMES

Rory and Zoe want to get married. Not easy when their mothers are mortal enemies and Rory's step-father is a Hollywood star with a death wish. Can they unravel the tangles in time to tie the knot, or is eloping the only answer? Get ready for Scotland's wedding of the year!

Tropes

Small Town, Grumpy/Sunshine, Opposites Attract, Soulmates, Fish-out-of-Water

CHRISTMAS GAMES

Having a baby's easy, right? Until wayward in-laws, an out-of-control cow and mad Santa get in the way. All Rory and Zoe want is a relaxing Christmas before their baby arrives, but straightforward is not their style...

Tropes

Small Town, Grumpy/Sunshine, Opposites Attract, Soulmates, Fish-

❧

THE FOXBROOKE SERIES

ONE NIGHT IN FOXBROOKE

When chef Ben 'Kenobi' Walker gets the call to help save a VIP dinner at Foxbrooke Manor, he doesn't expect to run into old flame Leia Perry. She's all grown up and even more attractive than when they were teenagers – but she hasn't forgotten what happened ten years ago, and she *definitely* hasn't forgiven him. Will one night give Ben the second chance he needs to prove himself and win back Leia's heart?

<u>Tropes</u>

Small Town, Second Chance, Return to Hometown, Enemies-to-Lovers, Bet, Brother's Best Friend, Work Colleagues, Forced Proximity, First Love, Reverse Grumpy-Sunshine, Opposites Attract

LOVE AD LIB

Shy and reserved Lord Henry Foxbrooke needs a fake girlfriend. Free-spirited actress Libby Fletcher needs a job. But when they arrive in Somerset for Henry's birthday celebrations, neither are prepared for their reception. As friendship blurs and faking it starts to feel a little too real, disaster strikes. Can Libby and Henry stick to the script, or has their entire act just bombed?

<u>Tropes</u>

Small Town, Fake Dating, Grumpy/Sunshine, Opposites Attract, One Bed, Different Worlds, Fish-out-of-Water

AN UNHOLY AFFAIR

Gorgeous Jack Newton has fallen in love with Eveline Shaw. But she's a female vicar dreaming of marriage and kids, and he's a male escort heading out of town. Can Jack show Eveline heaven and keep his secret safe, or are they both headed straight for hell?

Tropes

Small Town, Forbidden Love, Love at First Sight, Sworn off a Relationship, Priest, Different Worlds, Opposites Attract, Dark Secret

THE UPPER CRUSH

James Hunter-Savage is a cocky city boy who isn't used to anyone else taking the reins. Lady Estelle Foxbrooke is a fiery country girl who's about to show him who's boss. Can they learn to fight for love rather than with each other, or will their love hate relationship destroy everything they're working for?

Tropes

Small Town, Enemies-to-Lovers, Alpha Hero, Love/Hate, Playboy in Love, Different Worlds, Workplace Romance, Fake Dating

THE LOVE POSITION

Beautiful academic, Sophia Hunter-Savage, has run away to an ashram to reinvent herself. Hot yoga teacher, Isaac Hayward, has left town to avoid the only woman able to tempt him off the spiritual path.

But karma sucks.

Now Isaac's teaching Sophia and they're finding themselves in all kinds of unexpected positions. Will their forbidden love bring inner peace and happiness, or end in a tangled mess?

Tropes

Forbidden Love, Opposites Attract, Teacher/Student, Sworn off a Relationship, Forced Proximity, Love at First Sight, Different Worlds, Fish-out-of-Water

CHRISTMAS OFF SCRIPT

Best friends, Leo Foxbrooke and Ella Chamberlain, have never been single at the same time. Until now... Playing Cinderella and Prince Charming in the Christmas pantomime, their on-stage chemistry kindles an unexpected spark behind the scenes. Can they rewrite their friendship this festive season and finally unwrap true love?

Tropes

Small Town, Friends-to-Lovers, Best Friend's Ex, Oblivious to Love, Unrequited Love, Fake Relationship

ONE NIGHT ONLY

Pop star Avery Taylor craves a break from her public life, and a one-night stand with a stranger feels like the perfect escape. A year later, while recovering from an injury, she's stunned to find her nurse is Connor Foxbrooke, the man who touched her soul that night. Avery is ready to break the rules for love, but Connor, who values his quiet life, fears heartbreak. With Avery set to return to the spotlight as soon as she's recovered, can they bridge their worlds and turn their one night into forever?

Tropes

Second-Chance, Mistaken Identity, One Night Stand, Different Worlds, Opposites Attract, Injury, Forced Proximity, Fish-out-of-Water, Celebrity, Pop Star, Small Town

RIGHTING MR WRONG

Mooning a party of nuns is bad for anyone, but for TV star Aiden Wilder, it's catastrophic. Enter Willow Foxbrooke, a quiet PR worker who's tasked with saving his reputation through a fake relationship. As Willow teaches him how to recover his image, they start to fall for each other. But how can true love grow from something that was never real to begin with?

Tropes

Small Town, Fake Dating, Grumpy/Sunshine, Celebrity, Opposites Attract, Different Worlds, Fish-out-of-Water

UNDER THE INFLUENCER

Sunny Summer Foxbrooke's career as an Influencer is over. Now she's forced to work with grumpy Finn Oakley, the man who's avoided her for years. Will Finn finally return her love, or will she always just be his best friend's little sister?

Tropes

Brother's best friend, Grumpy/Sunshine, Beauty and the Beast, Age Gap, Unrequited Love, Rivals, Different Worlds, All Grown Up, Small Town

Get Evie's books in all formats as well as special offers, early releases, and exclusive deals direct from her website:

www.eviealexanderbooks.com

EMLIN PRESS

ABOUT THE AUTHOR

Evie Alexander is a multi-award-winning author of sexy romantic comedies, blending snort-laugh humour and panty-melting chemistry into unputdownable stories that will steal your heart.

When she's not dreaming up swoony heroes and relatable heroines, Evie can be found in the beautiful West Country of the UK, where she lives with her ridiculously patient husband, miracle daughter, and two dogs who think they run the show.

eviealexanderbooks.com

www.eviealexanderauthor.com

instagram.com/eviealexanderauthor
facebook.com/eviealexanderauthor
x.com/Evie_author
bookbub.com/authors/evie-alexander
amazon.com/Evie-Alexander/e/B08ZJGLP29?ref=sr_ntt_s-rch_lnk_1&qid=1630667484&sr=8-1
pinterest.com/eviealexanderauthor